# THE PUCKING WRONG SERIES

*The Pucking Wrong Number*

*The Pucking Wrong Guy*

*The Pucking Wrong Date*

*The Pucking Wrong Man*

*The Pucking Wrong Rookie*

*A Pucking Wrong Christmas*

# THE 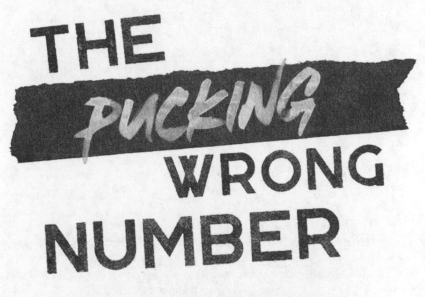 PUCKING WRONG NUMBER

## THE PUCKING WRONG BOOK #1

DALLAS KNIGHTS

# C.R. JANE

Copyright © 2023 by C.R. Jane

Cover design by Cassie Chapman/Opulent Designs
Photography by Cadwallader Photography
Editing by Jasmine J.

ISBN: 978-1-0394-8645-4

Published in 2024 by Podium Publishing
www.podiumentertainment.com

**Podium**

*To S—*

*The only person I ever needed to love me . . . was you.*

My Dear Red Flag Renegades,

I call you this because entering the world of the Dallas Knights means embracing the fact that the best book boyfriends often come with a few red flags—or a lot of red flags if we're talking about Lincoln Daniels.

After listening to T-Swift's *Mastermind* a few dozen—okay, a few hundred—times, I started to daydream about a character who would do anything to get his girl . . . and I do mean *anything*. A character who had the ability to manipulate everything behind the scenes to achieve what he wanted. A character who was the villain and the hero all at once.

While we're used to these types of characters in enemies-to-lovers type stories, I wanted Lincoln to be the opposite of that. All the couples in this series are soulmates of the highest order, but the heroines' tragic pasts sometimes make them a bit stubborn when it comes to accepting all the love that their hockey player dreamboats want to give them. Good thing Lincoln and the rest of the boys are willing to step in and make sure they get their happily-ever-afters, no matter what.

I've found over the years that the greatest love stories are often found in the shadows. Those love stories are often messy and complicated. And that makes them perfect.

Welcome to the world of the Dallas Knights, and while I call you red flag renegades right now, by the end of the book you might find that those red flags, well . . . they look a little green.

XO
CR
Jane

# DALLAS
# KNIGHTS

## TEAM ROSTER

| | |
|---|---|
| LINCOLN DANIELS, CAPTAIN, | #13, CENTER |
| ARI LANCASTER, CAPTAIN, | #24, DEFENSEMAN |
| NICK DALTON, CAPTAIN, | #33, RIGHT WING |
| CAS PETERS, | #42, DEFENSEMAN |
| KY JONES, | #18, LEFT WING |
| ED FREDERICKS, | #22, DEFENSEMAN |
| TYSON BENDER, | #1, GOALIE |
| SAM HARKNESS, | #2, GOALIE |
| NICK ANGELO, | #12, DEFENSEMAN |
| ALEXEI IVANOV, | #10, CENTER |
| MATTY CLIFTON, | #5, DEFENSEMAN |
| CAM LARSSON, | #25, LEFT WING |
| KEL MARSTEN, | #26, DEFENSEMAN |
| DEX MARSDEN, | #8, CENTER |
| ALEXANDER PORTIERE, | #11, RIGHT WING |
| DALTON JACOBS, | #42, GOALIE |
| COLT JOHNS, | #18, WING |
| DANIEL STUBBS, | #60, WING |
| ALEX TURNER, | #53, CENTER |
| PORTERS MAST, | #6, DEFENSEMAN |
| LOGAN EDWARDS, | #9, DEFENSEMAN |
| CLARK DOBBINS, | #16, WING |
| KYLE NETHERLAND, | #20, DEFENSEMAN |

## COACHES

TIM PORTER, HEAD COACH
COLLIER WATTS, ASSISTANT COACH
VANCE CONNOLLY, ASSISTANT COACH
CHARLEY HAMMOND, ASSISTANT COACH

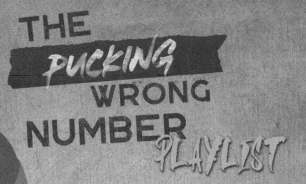

# THE PUCKING WRONG NUMBER PLAYLIST

**MASTERMIND**
Taylor Swift

**HURT**
Johnny Cash

**CHASING CARS**
Ryan Waters Band

**BLOODY VALENTINE-ACOUSTIC**
Machine Gun Kelly, Travis Barker

**YOUNG & BEAUTIFUL**
Lana Del Rey

**EYES CLOSED**
Ed Sheeran

**PRETTY HEART**
Parker McCollum

**THE MOST BEAUTIFUL THINGS**
Tenille Townes

**ALL EYES ON ME**
Bo Burnham

**NEVER ON THE DAY YOU LEAVE**
John Mayer

**VULNERABLE**
Selena Gomez

**TURNING TABLES**
Adele

**SOMEDAY**
OneRepublic

**ANTI-HERO**
Taylor Swift

LISTEN TO THE FULL PLAYLIST HERE:
HTTPS://OPEN.SPOTIFY.COM/PLAYLIST/3OVARKOESAUB3KVTJLA7NV

# TRIGGER WARNING

Dear readers,

Please be aware that this is a dark romance, and as such, contains content that could be triggering. Elements of this story are purely fantasy and should not be taken as acceptable behavior in real life.

Our love interest is possessive, obsessive, and the perfect shade of red for all you red flag renegades out there. There is absolutely no shade of pink involved when it comes to what Lincoln Daniels will do to get his girl.

Trigger warnings for this book include stalking, some scenes of dubious consent (but Monroe is always a very willing participant by the end) manipulation, somnophilia, dark obsession, and sex. There are no harems, cheating, or sharing involved. Lincoln Daniels only has eyes for her.

Prepare to enter the world of the Dallas Knights . . . you've been warned.

# THE PUCKING WRONG NUMBER

# WHY IS A PUCK CALLED A PUCK? BECAUSE DIRTY LITTLE BASTARD WAS TAKEN.

—Martin Brodeur

**Hockey Boyfriends Anonymous** ✔
@hockeyboyfriends_anonymous

Bunnies, do we have some news for you. Knights star forward, and our personal dream bb @lincoln_daniels is taken. #fml In last night's game Daniels declared his everlasting love to his new girl by throwing up a heart sign after every goal he scored #swoon And ladies...he scored four times. #gasp To drive the knife in deeper, Daniels was spotted wearing a jersey with her last name after the game! We can't find any social on this girl, but apparently her name is Monroe...Bardot. I guess time will tell if our playboy has finally been tamed. I know what I'll be wishing for.

9:17 PM. April 12, 2023 · Twitter for iPhone

**18k** Retweets   **101,325** Likes

# PROLOGUE
## MONROE

**M**onroe. My pretty little girl," Mama slurs from the couch. She's staring up at the ceiling, and even though she's saying my name, I know she's not talking to me. Or at least the me that's standing right here, scrubbing at the vomit stain she left on the floor. She's talking to the me from the past, or wherever it is her brain takes her when she's high as a kite.

There's a knock on the door, and I glance at it fearfully, dread churning through my insides. Because I know who it is. One of her "customers" as Mama calls them.

The door opens without either of us saying anything. I'm not sure Mama even heard the knock. In steps a sweaty, pale-faced man that I've seen once or twice before. He has rosy cheeks and a belly that protrudes over his jeans. Like a perverse Santa Claus. Not that I believe in that guy anymore. He's certainly never come to our place on Christmas Eve.

The man's eyes gleam as he stares at me, but then Mama groans in a weird way, and his attention goes to her.

"Roxanne," he says in a sing-song voice as he makes his way over there.

I want to say something. Anything. Tell him that Mama's in no shape for company, but I know it's no use. Besides, Mama would be furious with me later on if she missed out on the money she needs to get her fix.

I leave the room and lock myself in the one bedroom we have in this place. Mama and I share the room, but more often than not, she can't make it any further than the couch.

The disgusting noises I've learned to hate start, so I turn on the radio, trying to drown them out. I fall into a fitful sleep, and my dreams are haunted by the image of a healthy mother that cares more about me than she does about escaping the life she created.

I wake with a start, panic blurring the edges of the room until I can convince my brain that everything's fine.

Except everything doesn't feel fine. It's so quiet. Way too quiet.

I creep towards the door, pressing my ear against it to see if I can hear anything.

But there's nothing.

I slowly open the door and peek out into the room. There's no sign of the man, or my mother. Thinking the coast is clear, I make my way out of my room, only to come to a screeching halt when I see my mother on the ground by the front door, a pile of green liquid by her face.

I sigh, thinking of the cleanup ahead. Again. I hate these men. Every time they come here, they take a piece of her, while leaving her with nothing. It's always like this after they're done with her.

When I walk over with a rag and bucket, I see Mama is shaking, tears streaming down her face. She's a scary gray color I don't think I've ever seen before.

"Mama," I whisper, reaching down to touch her face, only to flinch at how icy cold her skin is. Her eyes suddenly shoot open, causing me to jump. They're even more bloodshot than normal.

Her bony hand claws at my shirt, and she frantically pulls me closer to her. Her lip is bruised and bloody. The bastard must've gotten rough.

"Don't let 'em taze your heart," she slurs, incomprehensibly.

"Mama?" I ask, worry thick in my voice.

"Don't . . . let a man . . . take your heart," she spits out. "Don't let him . . . " Her words fade away and her chest rises with one big inhale . . . before she goes perfectly still.

"Mama!" I whimper, shaking her over and over again.

But she never says another word. She's just gone, like a flame extinguished in a dark room.

And I'm all alone, with her last words forever ringing in my ears.

# CHAPTER 1

## MONROE

I sat on the edge of my bed, staring out the window into the dark, seemingly starless sky. Freedom was so close I could taste it.

Eighteen.

It felt like I'd been waiting my whole life for this moment. For this specific birthday. The thought of finally being able to leave this place, to start my life, on my own terms . . . it helped get me through each day.

I knew it would be difficult when I left. I only had my scrimpy savings from my after-school job at the grocery store to start my life. But I'd do whatever it took to make something of myself.

Something more than the empty shell my mother had left me that day.

I'd been in the foster system since I was ten years old, the day after that fateful night where I'd lost her. Everyone wanted to adopt a baby, and a baby I had not been. I'd gone through what seemed like a hundred different homes at this point, but my current home was where I'd managed to stay the longest.

Unfortunately.

My foster parents, Mr. and Mrs. Detweiler, and their son Ripley, seemed like nice people at first, but over time, things had changed. They were different now.

Mrs. Detweiler, Marie, had come to think of me as her live-in maid. I was all for helping out around the house, but when they got up as a collective group after every meal and left everything to me to clean up—as well as every other chore around the house —it was too much.

Someday, hopefully in the near future, I would never clean someone else's toilet again.

While I could deal with manual labor for another month, it was Mr. Detweiler, Todd, who had become a major problem. His actions had grown increasingly creepy, his longing stares and lingering glances making me sick. Everything he said to me had an underlying meaning . . . was an innuendo. He'd started talking about my birthday more, like he wanted to remind me of it for reasons far different than the promise of freedom it represented to me. I'm not sure it had even occurred to any of them yet that I was actually allowed to leave after that day. Both my birthday and high school graduation were the same week. Perfect timing. I just hoped he could control himself and keep his hands off me long enough to get to that point. Some people might not think a high school graduation was anything special, but to me, it represented *everything*.

Ripley was fine, I guess. He was more like a potato than a person, which was better than other things he could be. His eyes skipped over me when we were in the same room, like I didn't actually exist. And maybe I didn't exist to him. As long as his bed was made every day, and he had food on the table, and toilet paper stocked to wipe his ass, he couldn't care less. He was much too involved in his video games to care about the world around him.

I glanced at the clock. It was 4:55 p.m., time to get dinner started before Mr. Detweiler got home from work. Sighing, I absentmindedly smoothed my faded quilt that Mrs. Detweiler had brought home from who knows where, and headed out to the hallway and down to the kitchen. The house was a three-bedroom rambler in an okay part of town. It was nicer than other places I'd stayed, but I'd found that didn't matter all that much. The hearts beating inside the home held a much greater significance than how nice, or not nice, the house actually was.

I'm sure I could have been perfectly happy in the hovel I'd started life in with my mother . . . if only she'd been different.

I came to a screeching halt, and panic laced my insides, when I walked into the kitchen and saw Mr. Detweiler leaning against the laminate counter. How had I missed him coming into the house? I couldn't recall hearing the garage door opening.

He was nursing his favorite bottle of beer, which was actually the fanciest thing in the kitchen, costing far more than any of the other food they bought. Todd Detweiler was still dressed in the baggy suit he wore to the accounting office he worked at. He had a receding hairline that rivaled any I'd seen, so he brushed all the hair forward, carefully styling it to a point on his forehead right above his watery blue eyes.

He raised an eyebrow at the fact I was still frozen in place. But he usually didn't get home until six thirty, long enough for me to get dinner on the table and hide away until they were done.

"Well, hello there, Monroe," he drawled, my name sounding dirty coming from his lips.

I schooled my face and steeled my insides, taking methodical steps towards the fridge like his presence hadn't disarmed me.

"Hello," I answered pleasantly, hating the way I could feel his gaze stroking across my skin. Like I was an object to be coveted rather than a person.

I knew I was pretty. The spitting image of my mother when she was young. But just like with her, my looks had only been a curse, forever designed to attract assholes whose only goal was to use and abuse me.

I reached into the fridge to grab the bowl of chicken I'd put in there earlier to defrost . . . when suddenly he was behind me. Close enough that if I moved, he'd be pressed against me.

"Is there something you need?" I asked, trying to keep the edge of hysteria out of my voice. His hand settled on my hip and I squeezed my eyes shut, cursing the universe.

He leaned close, his breath a whisper against my skin. "You've been thinking about it, haven't you?" Todd's breath stunk of beer, a smell that would prevent me from ever trying it, no matter how expensive and nice it was supposed to be.

"I—I'm not sure what you're talking about, sir." I grabbed the chicken and tried to stand, hoping he would back away. But the only thing he did was straighten up, so our bodies were against each other. I tried to move away, but his hand squeezed against my hip. Hard.

"I need to get this chicken on the stove," I said pleasantly, like I wasn't dying inside at the feel of his touch.

"Such a tease," he murmured with a small chuckle. "I love how you like to play games. Just going to make it so much better when we stop." There was a bulge growing harder against my lower back, and I bit down on my lip hard enough that the salty tang of blood flooded my taste buds.

My hands were shaking, the water sloshing around in the bowl. An idiot could figure out what he was talking about.

"Have you noticed how much I love to collect things?" he asked randomly, finally releasing my hip and stepping back.

I moved quickly towards the sink, setting the bowl inside and going to grab the breadcrumbs I needed to coat the chicken breasts with for dinner.

"I have noticed that," I finally responded, after he'd taken a step towards me when I didn't answer fast enough.

How could anyone miss it? Todd collected . . . beer bottles. Both walls of the garage had various cans and bottles lined up neatly on shelves. There were so many of them that you could barely see the wall—not sure how social services never seemed concerned he might have a drinking problem with that amount of empties. But Todd was never worried about that. He added at least five to the wall every day.

"Virgins happen to be my favorite thing to collect."

I'd been holding a carton of eggs, and I dropped them, shocked that he'd outright said that, shells and yolk ricocheting everywhere.

Just then, Mrs. Detweiler ambled in, her gaze flicking between her husband and me suspiciously. "What's going on in here?" she asked, her eyes stopping on the ruined eggs all over the floor.

Marie had once been a pretty woman, but like her husband, her attempt to hold onto youth was a miserable failure. Right now, she was wearing a too tight flowered dress that resembled a couch from the eighties. It accentuated every roll, and there was a fine sheen of sweat across her heavily made-up face, probably from the effort she'd had to make to get out of her armchair and storm in here. Her hair was a harsh, bottle-black color, and though she attempted to curl and keep it nice, it was thin and limp and I'm sure disappointing for her.

I usually didn't pay attention to looks; I knew better than most they could be deceiving, but Todd and Marie Detweiler's appearances were too in your face to ignore.

"Just an accident, honey," he drawled, walking towards her and pulling her into a soul-sickening kiss that made me want to puke, considering Marie most likely had no idea where else that mouth had been.

They walked out of the kitchen without a backward glance, leaving me a shaking, miserable mess as I cleaned up the eggs and tried to make dinner.

If that interaction hadn't sealed the deal that waiting for my birthday to leave wasn't an option . . . the next night would.

I was in bed, tossing and turning as I did every night. When your mind was as haunted as mine was, sleep was elusive, a fervent goal I would never successfully master. I'd never had a night where I could relax, where the memories of the past didn't creep in and plague my thoughts.

It was 3 a.m., and I was on the verge of giving up if I couldn't fall back asleep soon.

Light footsteps sounded down the hallway by my door. I frowned, as everyone had gone to bed long ago. I knew their habits like they were my own at this point.

Was someone in the house? Someone who didn't belong?

The footsteps stopped outside my door, and shivers crept up my spine.

"Hello?" I whisper squeaked, feeling like a fool for speaking at all when the doorknob tried to turn, getting caught on the lock I was lucky enough to have.

I felt like the would-be victim in a horror movie as I slid out of bed and yanked my lamp from the nightstand, prepared to use it as a weapon if need be.

The person outside fiddled with the lock and it clicked, signaling it had been disengaged.

There was a long pause as I stared breathlessly at the door, waiting for the inevitable.

The door creaked open and a hairy hand—that I recognized —appeared.

It was Mr. Detweiler's.

I didn't think, I just started screaming, knowing I had one chance to get him away from my room.

I needed to wake up his wife. With their bedroom right down the hall, I just needed to be loud enough.

Sure enough, a second after I started screaming, the door banged shut, and footsteps dashed away. A moment later, I heard the Detweilers' bedroom door fly open, and then a moment after that, my door cracked against the wall and Marie's harried form was there. Her chest was heaving, pushing against the two-sizes-too-small negligee she was wearing—that made me want to burn my eyes—and her gaze was crazed as her eyes dashed around the room, finally falling to me standing there in the middle of it, a lamp clutched to my chest.

A red mottled rash spread across her chest and up to her cheeks as anger flooded her features.

"What the fuck is wrong with you?"

"Someone was trying to get into my room. Someone unlocked the door."

I didn't say it was her husband, because that would give me even more problems.

A moment later, Todd was there, faking a yawn with a glass of water in his hand. "What's going on?" he asked casually. Our eyes locked, and in that moment, he knew I knew it was him. His features were taunting, daring me to say something, like his wife would ever believe anything that came out of my mouth when it came to him.

"The girl's saying someone was breaking into her room," Marie scoffed before pausing for a second and examining her husband. "Why were you up?"

The way her lips were pursed, the way her flush deepened—it told me a lot. Apparently, Marie wasn't so unaware of her husband's true nature after all.

Not that she would ever do anything about it.

"I was getting some water when I heard Monroe scream. But I didn't hear anyone else in the house." His gaze feigned concern. "Are you sure you didn't just have a nightmare?"

I stared at him for a long, tense moment before I took a breath. "Maybe that's all it was," I finally whispered, eliciting a loud huff from Marie.

"Get yourself under control, you brat. The rest of us need our sleep!" she snapped, whirling away and leaving, curses streaming from her mouth as she walked back to her room.

Todd lingered, a smug grin curling across his pathetic lips.

"Sleep well, Monroe," he purred, a firm promise in his eyes that he would be back.

And that he would finish what he started.

I fell to my knees as soon as the door closed, sobs racking through my body.

I'd never felt so alone.

He had ruined everything. A month away from a high school diploma, and he'd just torn it from my grasp.

If Todd got his hands on me, he would break me. And I wasn't talking about my body—I was talking about my soul.

The image of my mother's desolate, destroyed features flashed through my mind.

That couldn't be my story. It couldn't.

I had to leave. Tomorrow. I had no other option.

———

The Detweilers lived in a small town right outside Houston. I decided Dallas would be my destination, about four hours away. I'd never been there before, but the ticket price wasn't too bad, and it was big. Just what I needed to hopefully disappear. Surely the Detweilers wouldn't try and go that far, not with only a month left of state support on the line. I bet they wouldn't even tell anyone I was gone. They'd want that last check.

I didn't let myself think about what my virginity would be worth to Todd. Hopefully, "easy" was one of his requisites, and he would forget me as soon as I disappeared.

I went to school, my heart hurting the whole day. I'd never been one to make close friends—when you never knew when you'd be moving on, it was best not to make any close connections—but I found myself wishing I had longer with the acquaintances I did have. I walked the familiar hallways, wondering if it would have been hard to say goodbye at graduation, or if I was simply feeling the loss of my dream.

Mama had never graduated from high school. In her lucid moments, though, even when I was little, she would sometimes talk about her dreams for me. Dreams of walking across that stage.

*I'd just have to walk across a college stage*, I told myself firmly, promising myself I'd get a GED and make that possible.

After school, I went to the H-E-B grocery store where I worked, putting even more hustle in than usual since I'd be pulling a disappearing act after this shift. The timing worked out, because it was payday, and I was able to get one more check to take with me. Every penny would count.

After my shift, I bought a prepaid phone, since I didn't want to take my Detweiler phone with me. Knowing them, they'd probably try and get the police to bring me back by saying I'd stolen their property. A part of me was a little afraid they could track me with it, too. I knew I wasn't living in a spy thriller . . . but still, better to be safe than sorry.

Once I got home, I packed a small bag with some clothes, my new phone, and the cash I'd saved up. And then I sat on my bed, hands squeezing together with anxiety.

I didn't have a good plan. For as much as I'd been dreaming of getting away, my plans were more fluid than concrete. And all of them had depended on me having a high school diploma so I could get a better job, as well as not having to look over my shoulder every second for fear the Detweilers were after me. The state also had a support system for kids coming out of foster care, and I'd been hopeful I'd have that to lean on.

But I could do this.

I cleaned up after dinner. Marie had ordered pizza, so it didn't take as much effort as usual. And then I sat in the corner of the living room, biding my time until I could say goodnight. It was a tricky thing. I had to escape tonight—late enough that they'd gone to bed, but not so late that Todd decided to give me another late-night visit.

My departure was the definition of anticlimactic. My mind had conjured this image of the Detweilers running after me as I escaped with my bag out the window, the sound of a siren haunting the air as I ducked in and out of the bushes, trying to avoid the police.

But what really happened was that I slipped out the window, and everyone stayed asleep. I walked for an hour until I got to the Greyhound station, and no one came after me. The exhausted-looking attendant didn't even blink when I bought a ticket to Dallas.

It was nice for something to go my way every once in a blue moon.

The bus ride took twice as long as a car would have. And although I tried to catch a few hours of rest, I kept worrying I'd somehow miss my stop, so I never could slip into a deep sleep. My mind also couldn't help but race with thoughts of what my future held. Would I be able to make it on my own?

Despite my worries, a sense of relief flickered in my chest as the distance between Todd and me grew with each mile that passed.

At least I could cross keeping my virginity safe off my list of to-dos.

When we finally arrived in Dallas, the morning sun was just peeking over the horizon. Even with the dilapidated buildings that surrounded the Greyhound station, I couldn't help but feel excitement. I was here. I'd made it. I may have never been to Dallas before, and I may not have known a single soul here, but I was determined to make a new life for myself.

This was my new beginning.

———

It took about twelve hours for the afterglow of my arrival to fade and for me to find myself on a park bench, debating whether I could actually fall asleep if I were to try. Or if it was even safe to attempt such a thing.

I'd gotten off the bus and was in the process of calling for a cab to take me to the teen shelter I'd found online. And then I'd been fucking pickpocketed while I looked the address up. They'd taken all the cash in my pocket that I'd pulled out for the cab, and swiped my phone right out of my hand.

You can bet I ran after them like a madwoman. But with a backpack containing all my earthly possessions weighing me down, the group of boys easily outran me.

I hadn't dared to spend any of the rest of the cash I had left, except to get a bag of chips from a gas station that had seen better days.

I'd walked all over for the rest of the day, trying to find the shelter, scared to ask for directions in case anyone got suspicious and reported to the authorities that I looked like a runaway teen.

Obviously, I never found the place, because there I was, on the park bench. Cold, hungry, and pissed off.

And exhausted.

Apparently, when you hadn't slept for close to forty-eight hours, you could fall asleep anywhere, because eventually . . . that's exactly what I did.

———

I woke with a start, the feeling of someone watching me thick in my throat. Night had fallen, and a deep blue hue had settled over the park. The trees and bushes were indistinct shadows against the darkened sky. The street lamps had flickered to life, casting a warm glow on the path and the nearby benches. The light danced and swayed with the gentle breeze, casting long shadows on the ground. You could hear the rustling of leaves and the chirping of crickets.

I yelped when I saw a grizzled old man sitting next to me on the bench, a wildness in his gaze that matched the tattered clothing on his body. There was the scent of dirt and body odor wafting off him, and when he smiled at me, it was only with a few teeth.

"Oy. I've been a watchin'. Making sure you could sleep, my lady," he said in what was clearly an affected British accent.

I flinched at his words, even though they were perfectly friendly and kind, and scooted away from him.

"Oh, don't be afraid of Ole Bill. I'll watch out for ye."

I moved to jump off the bench and run away . . . but I also had a moment of hesitation. There was something so . . . wholesome about him. Once you got past his looks and his smell, obviously.

"This park's mine, but I can share. You go back to sleep, and I'll keep watch. Make sure the ruffians stay away," he continued. Even though I had yet to say anything to him.

I opened my mouth to reject his offer, but then he pulled a clean, brand new blanket with tags out of his grocery sack. When he offered it to me . . . instead of talking . . . I found myself crying.

I sobbed and sobbed while he watched me, frantically throwing the blanket at me like it had the power to quell hysterical women's tears. When I still didn't stop crying, overwhelmed by the events of the past few days . . . and his kindness, he finally started to sing what I think was the worst rendition of "Eleanor Rigby" that I'd ever heard. Actually, it was the worst rendition of *any* song I'd ever heard.

But it worked, and I stopped crying.

"There, there, little duck. Go to sleep. Ole Bill will watch out for ya," he said soothingly after he'd finished the song—the last few lyrics definitely made up.

I was a smarter girl than that, I really was. But I was so freaking tired. And everything inside of me really wanted to trust him. After all, he had called me "little duck." Serial killers didn't have cute pet names for their victims, right?

"Just a couple of minutes," I murmured, and he nodded, smiling softly again with his crooked grin that I was quite fond of at that moment.

I drifted off into a fitful sleep, shivering from stress and exhaustion, and dreaming of better days.

When I woke up, it was far later than ten minutes. It was the rest of the night, actually.

Bill was still there, watching over me, and whistling softly to himself, like he hadn't just stayed up all night. My backpack was still under my head, the cash still in it, and at least I didn't *feel* like anyone had touched me.

Fuck, I'd gotten desperate, hadn't I?

"Do you have a place to stay, lassie?" he asked softly. I shook my head, biting down on my lip as I thought about spending another night on this bench.

"Ole Bill will take you to a good place. It's not as nice as my castle, but it will do," he said, gesturing to the park proudly as if it was in fact an English castle complete with a moat, and he was its ruler.

Despite the fact that he'd at least proven trustworthy enough not to do anything to me after a few hours, it was still pure desperation that had me following him to what I was hoping wasn't a trafficking ring, or something else equally heinous.

I relaxed a little as he took me to a slightly better part of town than where I'd been walking the day before. He chattered my ear off, all in that fake British accent, regaling me with stories about places I was sure he'd never visited.

Before I knew it, we were standing in front of the entrance to what appeared to be a fairly new shelter. The sign read that it was a women's shelter, and the sight made me want to cry once again.

"When you get in there, tell 'em Ole Bill sent you . . . they'll give you the royal treatment," he chortled, and tears filled my eyes for what seemed like the hundredth time, causing him to take a step away—probably fearing I would burst into hysterics again.

I hesitated for another moment before I finally ascended the steps that led to the shelter doors. Stopping halfway, I glanced back at Bill, who gave me another charmingly snaggletoothed grin. "I see great things for you, little duck," he called after me when I continued to walk.

I knew I'd never forget him. He may have been homeless and slightly crazy, but he was also one of the kindest people I had ever met. He'd watched over me, a stranger, and helped me when I needed it the most.

As I walked inside, exhaustion still stretched across my shoulders, I strangely felt at peace right then that everything was going to work out.

"Welcome to Haven," a kind woman murmured as I approached the front desk.

Haven indeed.

I could only hope.

# CHAPTER 2
## LINCOLN

**DALLAS KNIGHTS**

I stepped onto the ice, the cold biting at my exposed skin as I made my way to the rest of my team. It may have just been practice, but I lived for this game. It was the only thing that made me feel . . . well, anything.

The rink was alive with the sound of blades slicing through the ice, the occasional clank of a stick hitting the puck, and the laughter and banter of my teammates. I joined them, a small smile tugging at the corner of my lips as I exchanged playful jabs with the guys, a buzz of energy zipping through my veins at the thought of what was to come.

Our coach appeared in front of us, his gray eyes scanning us with a critical gaze. He was a jerk, but he was also the best coach I'd ever had, so I didn't mind it so much. "All right, listen up, assholes," he said, his voice firm and commanding. "Today we're working on passing drills, since you all seemed to forget that particular skill in Tuesday's game."

We all chuckled, but he wasn't lying. We were fucking awful on Tuesday, barely scraping past the last place RedHawks. We needed to get our shit together because Toronto wouldn't lie down for us this weekend.

We started with a simple drill, passing the puck back and forth in a tight circle. It was a drill we'd done countless times before, but likc the last game, we fucking sucked.

"Tight fucking passes!" Coach screamed.

"Sounds a little close to something else," Ari, my best friend, grinned next to me. "Something I happen to have."

I rolled my eyes, but still chuckled. Because we were idiots like that.

We moved on to more complex drills, and we pushed harder, the intensity ramping up. Not enough to stop our normal shit-talking though.

Bender leaned forward, one hand gripping the goal, and the other holding his back.

"What the fuck's wrong with you, old man?" Ari called out as he skatcd a loop around the goal.

"Rough night," Bender sighed, before leaping up and thrusting his hips, "With your mama riding me so hard she broke my back."

The team roared, and Ari shook his head in disgust. "That wasn't even a good one. Fuck, you're thirty-four years old and now I gotta picture my mama riding you like a fucking horse."

"Are you shitheads done fucking around?" Coach roared, and we dispersed to get ready for the scrimmage on the docket for the next hour.

My adrenaline coursed through me as I skated forward, making a quick pass to Dalton, then watching as he took the puck down the ice and scored a goal.

The players on the bench erupted in cheers like we were in a real game. Dalton accepted their high fives and fist bumped each one. Would be nice if he could do that in the fucking game once in a while. I was the starting forward on the team, but Coach had me playing wing for the scrimmage so Dalton could try and get out of whatever rut he was in. I obviously wanted him to get his head straight, too . . . but I also loved being the one to fucking score.

Ari turned to me and said, "We going out tonight?" This was asked right as he shoved me into the glass.

"Fuck," I groaned as I pushed him off me. "You're fucking weak, Lancaster. Soto hits me harder than that." Ari gritted his teeth at me and growled. Soto played for L.A. and Ari *hated* him. It was one of my favorite things to throw his name around anytime Ari did . . . well, fucking anything.

"Better watch out," he shot back. "Dalton's going to steal your spot." The second the words passed his lips, he was laughing though, because we both fucking knew that was never going to happen.

I was the best scorer on the team.

And the league.

No one would replace me anytime soon. When my rookie contract expired at the end of the season, it was already a done deal. I'd be landing the largest contract in NHL history. Ownership had been breathing down my neck, trying to get me to sign before other teams could start their offers.

If it were up to me, I would have signed it already . . .

"Fuuuck," I growled as Peters almost laid me out. That was what I got for letting my fucking father fill my thoughts again.

"Daniels, where's your fucking head?"

"Probably with some choice pussy," Lancaster called out.

Coach growled and threw a puck at him. "Line up again!"

Shaking my head, as if that could undo all my issues, I gritted my teeth and refocused. Skating hard, I kept my eyes on the puck, listening as Coach ran through the play.

The whistle blew, and I skated forward, positioning myself in front of the net, ready to pounce. The puck came towards me, and I didn't fucking hesitate. I snatched it out of the air with my stick, spun around, and fired off a wrist shot. The puck sailed through the air, a blur of speed and accuracy.

"Don't blink, motherfucker!" I yelled as the puck whizzed past Bender's glove and found the back of the net. I pumped my fist in the air, a surge of adrenaline coursing through my veins.

Bender cursed and threw one of his gloves.

"Got to be faster than that against Toronto, old man," I crowed as I did another lap around him . . . just for fun.

"Yeah, yeah," he growled.

Coach's face was wide with a grin, and he was nodding so hard he resembled a fucking bobblehead. "That's what I'm fucking talkin' about!" he shouted, pumping a fist in the air. "Nice fucking shot, Daniels!"

We continued the scrimmage for another thirty minutes, but once I scored four more times, Coach sent me to the bench.

"You're a fucking animal today," Ari laughed, tossing me a water bottle as I wiped my sweaty face with a towel.

"It's fucking fun, right?" I grinned, spraying water on my face to cool off.

"Yeah, Golden Boy," Ari purred.

I rolled my eyes at the nickname the media had given me.

"Har, har. Douchebag."

Ari snorted, and we watched as a new line faced off against each other.

"I think Dalton gets worse every play," Bender commented, trying to catch his breath as he hoisted himself over the boards and plopped himself down on the bench.

"Hmm, how many did I score on you?" I retorted back.

Bender huffed and shook his head. "I stopped counting."

Ari and I both laughed, and we finished watching the rest of practice.

Back in the locker room, after showers, Ari snapped me with his towel before going back to drying his wild black hair. "You never answered about tonight. I need to get laid."

I raised an eyebrow. "I don't think I can help you with that, Lancaster. You haven't even bought me a drink yet."

"Funny," he sighed, before shooting me a wink. "Are you in? We can try that new bar on Emory Street."

I brushed my hair out of my face and banged my head on the locker behind me with a groan. "I would, but I've got that fucking gala thing with Kara."

"You're going on a date with her fucking highness? Did you hit your head too hard in practice yesterday? What the fuck, Daniels?" Ari shook his head in disgust. He'd been my best friend ever since our prep school days. He was well versed in how much I decidedly did not like Kara Lindstrom.

I held up my hands. "I know, I know. But *he's* breathing down my fucking neck. He's in talks with her dad for some merger . . . and he—"

"Fuck your father, Linc. If you try and screw her tonight, your balls are going to fall off. Come get trashed with me."

I opened my mouth to say something—not sure what—then closed it, because he was right.

Just then, my phone buzzed. Speak of the devil. A text had come in from dear old Dad himself.

F: Don't fuck tonight up, boy.

His words thrashed around in my gut. The usual dread mixed with a heavy dose of guilt lying in wait.

I shook it off, forcing a grin to my lips. Fuck him.

"I know that grin. It's going to be a good night, isn't it?" Ari whooped.

I glanced up at him, my smile widening. "It's going to be a great fucking night."

# CHAPTER 3
## MONROE

As I walked down the sterile white halls of the medical office, I could feel the fatigue weighing me down. Another double shift here and at the catering company yesterday, followed by a late-night class, and I was beyond drained—physically and mentally.

But I had no other choice.

I'd had to wait a month after getting to Haven to take my GED test, wanting to make sure I was eighteen and the Detweilers had no legal claim over me before I did anything that left a paper trail. The shelter had been crowded. But it was clean . . . and safe. So I'd been okay. I'd gotten a job at another grocery store, but I hadn't been able to save up enough to actually move out of the shelter until one of the staff members had heard about a job as a receptionist in a medical office.

It had been a year since I'd moved into my new place. Between Tres Medical and the catering company, I did okay. But add in attending community college, and it was exhausting.

I greeted my coworker, Katie, with a forced smile as I fidgeted in my scrubs that everyone had to wear, trying to keep up the facade of being cheerful despite my exhaustion. She was one of the popular ones at the office, always eager to socialize and make plans. Living a carefree lifestyle that I could only dream of, a life I could never afford.

As the day went on, my workload piled up, and my energy levels dwindled. I was barely keeping my eyes open as I went through the motions, taking patient histories, scheduling appointments, and doing whatever the doctors needed. I also had a paper to write tonight before class started. Classes at the local community college weren't glamorous, but every credit got me closer to my dreams.

I sat in the cramped break room of the office, exhaustion seeping through my bones. Only a few hours left. I could do anything for a few hours, right?

It seemed to be what I told myself every day. And kind of like when someone said, "just one step at a time," thinking they were being helpful . . . the words rang hollow.

I was nineteen, and yet, I felt like I was a hundred-year-old bag of bones.

Because the day just had to get harder, Kevin, one of the doctors in the practice, walked in then. He had an annoying smirk on his face that he thought was sexy and cool, but actually had him resembling a demented clown. The side part comb-over and the smirk together had that effect. A pang of annoyance flashed through me as I braced myself for what was to come. He was always trying to flirt with me, despite my obvious disinterest.

"Hey there, gorgeous," he said, leaning against the counter with a cocky grin. "You look tired. Why don't you let me take you out and help you relax?"

I forced a polite smile, while my mind continued to race with irritation. Didn't he understand that I was juggling two jobs and night classes just to make ends meet? I'd mentioned it every single time he'd asked me out. I didn't have time for his shit.

"Thanks, but I'm really tired," I replied, trying to keep my tone civil. "I have a long evening ahead of me at the catering company after this, and then I've got night classes."

Kevin's grin faded, replaced by a look of disappointment. "Come on, babe, don't be like that. We could have some fun together," he persisted, moving closer. "Why don't you just take the rest of the day off?"

Of course he would say that. He was a trust-fund baby, and I was still shocked he'd somehow made it through medical school. I had a sneaking suspicion his family had padded quite a few pockets in order for him to do it. If not for the other doctors here stepping in, this place would've closed long ago because of malpractice claims.

I felt my patience wearing thin. "I appreciate the offer, but I'm really not interested. As you know," I said firmly, hoping he would take the hint and back off.

Kevin's expression turned sour, and he crossed his arms over his chest. "You're always so serious," he muttered, frustration laced through his voice. "Maybe if you had a better attitude, you wouldn't walk around like you have a stick up your ass all the time."

I clenched my jaw, my fatigue momentarily forgotten as my annoyance flared. Who the fuck did he think he was? I was working my ass off; I didn't have time for distractions, especially not from someone like Kevin.

"I know how to have fun just fine," I retorted, my voice tinged with irritation. "But right now, my priority is taking care of my responsibilities, and I would need it to be worth it for me to ignore them."

His jaw dropped. My point, that he wasn't someone worth hanging out with, hitting home.

With that, I stood, grabbed my bag, and headed towards the door, leaving Dr. Kevin behind in the break room, his smug expression replaced by a scowl.

If I wasn't sure that the other doctors would side with Dr. Kevin, I would have reported him ages ago.

I stepped out of the office and into the fresh air, taking a deep breath and closing my eyes for a moment, trying to center myself.

I could do anything for a . . .

Fuck.

———

I was feeling slightly better after the walk to my apartment. I lived in a studio shithole, but it was *my* studio shithole, and there was something to be said about that. I'd done my best to make it livable . . . I'd painted the walls a bright cream color and scrubbed it from top to bottom when I'd moved in.

But there was no central air, just a window unit that only operated if the temperature was below seventy-five . . . rendering it pretty useless. The carpet was old and threadbare . . . and so dirty when I'd moved in that I had to spend money I didn't have to get it professionally cleaned. Cleaners I'd hired had done what they could, but it was still this questionable gray color, and there were stains all over whose origin I never wanted to know. The kitchen sink dripped, and there was no oven.

And those were just some of the things wrong with the place.

But I made it work.

I sighed in annoyance as I walked through the very unlocked front gate and up the steps to my apartment. Every month, when I paid my rent, I'd ask my greasy landlord, Jared, to fix the gate. And every time, he'd ignore me. It would have been nice to have an extra barrier between my apartment and our sketchy street considering all I had on my door was one flimsy lock . . .

Speak of the devil. I'd been in my apartment for less than five minutes when there was a knock on my door. When I peered through my peephole, there was my landlord, Jared Thomason, himself. As I opened the door to greet him, I was met with the unmistakable sight of a man who had let himself go. His sweat-stained shirt clung to his massive belly, and his pants were unbuttoned and barely hanging on. His thinning hair was slicked back, and his beady eyes scanned me up and down, leaving me feeling exposed and uncomfortable.

His leering gaze lingered on me for a moment too long, and I could feel his hot breath on my face as he leaned in. The sour stench of his breath filled my nostrils, and I had to suppress a gag.

I tried to keep my eyes from wandering to his flabby arms and the thick layer of hair that covered his knuckles, but it was impossible to ignore. He was like Jabba the Hutt in human form —grotesque and repulsive.

"Hey, Monroe," he wheezed, his eyes roving over me in a way that left my skin crawling. I was on the third floor, so I'm sure the trip up had been a journey for him. "I just wanted to see if everything was okay with your apartment."

I forced a smile. Of course, he was just checking . . . he was always checking. But any time I told him about all the things that were, in fact, not alright with my apartment . . . he had decidedly not been interested.

"Yes, everything's fine. Thanks for asking." I moved to close the door, and he stepped closer to me, sticking his foot in the door. "You know, Monroe, I've been thinking about you a lot lately. A beautiful woman like you . . . all alone."

That wasn't creepy at all . . .

"How about we go out for a drink tonight?"

I resisted the urge to roll my eyes. As if I would ever want to go anywhere with this creepy old man. "No thanks," I said, trying to push the door closed once more.

But he wasn't finished. He reached out and grabbed my arm, his grip tight and insistent. "Come on, honey, don't be shy. I know you barely make rent. I could help you out . . . if you know what I mean."

My stomach churned. This was the last thing I needed, the last thing *anyone* needed.

"I could waive your rent for a few months if you spend some time with me."

My heart raced, and I worked to control my breathing. I didn't want him to know how terrified I was. I tried to yank away, but his grip only tightened. "Let go of me," I hissed, my voice shaking with anger.

He chuckled, as if I'd actually complimented him. "What's the matter, sweetheart? You're not into older men?"

My stomach turned as I continued to try and pull away from him. Obviously, this was wrong, but I also knew I couldn't afford to lose my apartment. I took a deep breath, pushing down the anger choking me, and stammered out a reply, "Not really. I— I've got to get to work."

Jared squeezed my arm, his voice growing angry. "You ungrateful little brat. I'm doing you a favor, and you won't even consider it? You're lucky I haven't kicked you out on the street already."

"Jared, I just want to be left alone. I can't accept your offer. I'm sorry."

But he didn't budge. Instead, his grip tightened even more, turning painful. "Don't be like that, sweetheart," he sneered. "You know you want it."

Bile rose in my throat. How could anyone be so disgusting, so vile?

"Let go of me," I snarled again, my voice turning low and menacing.

He only chuckled. "Why so hostile, little bird? I can give you everything you want. All you have to do is play nice."

I was going to get a complex at this rate. All the men around me seemed to think I resembled a bird.

Nausea churned in my stomach. The thought of giving in to him, of letting him touch me, made me want to scream. But I knew I had to be careful. This man held all the power, and if I wasn't cautious, he could destroy me.

So I did the only thing I could. I balled my fist and lunged forward, punching him as hard as I could in the face. He stumbled backwards, clutching his nose as blood poured down his chin.

His skin turned mottled red with anger, matching the blood on his face as he leveled a heated glare at me. "Fine," he choked out as he backed away. "Suit yourself. But don't come crying to me when you're homeless and penniless."

The threat was implicit—things were about to get much harder for me.

Worth it, though.

I watched as he stormed away, dread coiling in my gut. I couldn't afford to move. But I had to find a way out of this, and fast.

Why were men such fucking douchebags?

# CHAPTER 4

## MONROE

I slammed the door behind Jared and sank against it, my heart racing with fear and disgust. Was I cursed? Because it certainly felt that way at the moment. Between Jared and Kevin, I'd won the award for most asshole interactions in a day.

Rubbing my face, I took some deep breaths, feeling violated and powerless.

*Think, think, think . . .*

At that moment, my phone buzzed. No one ever called or texted me unless it was about work, so I quickly pulled it out to look at it. It was from an unknown number.

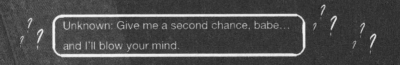

Unknown: Give me a second chance, babe... and I'll blow your mind.

I stared at the text for a moment in disbelief. Was today national douchebag day, when everyone came out of the wood-work? Which creep was texting me? Kevin? Sleazy Jared? Someone else I didn't know?

I moved to put down my phone and ignore it . . . but then I changed my mind.

*Not in a million years could you blow my mind*, I typed back angrily. Setting the phone down, I felt strangely better.

The phone buzzed. *We both know that's not true*, the text read.

What a conceited asshole. Of course, he would think he was God's gift to women. I could just picture both Kevin and my landlord sending these texts to some poor girl.

> We both know your penis is barely visible in the light, let alone enough for a vagina.

There was a longer silence after this response, and I moved to set my phone down again, satisfied I had successfully embarrassed him.

*If this was your attempt to get a dick pic, it actually almost worked*, the text read when it came in.

I sat down on my bed in a huff, snorting to myself. The last thing any girl wanted was some guy's wrinkled old balls on their phone.

*I'll pass*, I wrote back. *Old wrinkled balls are not my thing.*

> Unknown: See, now I feel like you've been stalking me. How did you know being insulted turns me on?

A grin snuck onto my face. This guy may resemble my landlord, but at least he was funny.

*If I'd known you were actually interesting, I would've shown up last night*, the next text read, and my grin quickly faded. Who the fuck was this guy?

*Well, I* knew *you were uninteresting. So I didn't bother showing up either*, I quickly typed out.

My homework started calling for me then. As much as I'd

enjoyed the brief reprieve, I knew it was time to get back to work. Especially if I was going to have to find another place to live. I didn't make enough to come up with a first and last months' deposit right now—and I knew I wouldn't get my deposit back from Jared obviously—so finding somewhere that didn't require that was going to cut into my already nonexistent time.

My phone buzzed again.

*Let's be uninteresting together*, it read.

I scoffed. *You have the wrong number. Hopefully whatever girl you ditched doesn't ever text you back*, I typed before pulling out my calculus book, knowing that it wouldn't make any sense today, just as it hadn't yesterday.

*Kara?* the next text read.

I ignored it.

*It's B.S. to pretend this is the wrong number and ignore me, Kara. It's like putting blood in the water*, he texted.

I don't know what I was thinking—maybe I wasn't—because I quickly snapped a selfie with my middle finger up and shot it to him.

A second later, *Please, please don't be Kara*, the text read.

I put my math book down. *I believe I already told you I wasn't her. Now, good day, sir.*

*What's your name?* came the immediate text.

> I said, good day, sir.

> Unknown: Please. 🙏

> I'm not giving you my name, you creep. Ever heard of stranger danger?

> Unknown: You literally just gave me your picture, but you're afraid to give me your name? Maybe you are Kara.

I wrinkled my nose. *My name is Monroe.*

I threw my phone down, furious with myself. I wasn't sure why I was answering. Maybe it was my desperation to have any sort of human contact. That was the only thing that could account for me losing my mind at the moment.

> Unknown: So . . . has anyone told you that you're fucking hot?

> Keep dreaming, big boy. I'm way out of your league, and I'm sure Kara's out of your league as well. But good on you for shooting your shot.

*So you do know who I am . . .* his next text read.

I sent him a confused emoji, followed by, *What part of that sentence said I knew who you were?*

There was a long silence, and when he hadn't answered back after five minutes, I forced myself to pick my math textbook up and start working on my homework.

———

### *Lincoln*

I stepped off the ice and headed straight to the locker room, eager to take off my gear and get in the shower. I smelled like sweaty balls after the sprints Coach had us doing for the last thirty minutes. At least we looked better today. I was feeling pretty good about our chances in tomorrow's game.

As I walked past the mirror in the locker room, I caught a glimpse of my reflection and regret immediately flooded my insides. The world thought I was *everything*, with my golden hair and piercing amber eyes—their words, not mine—but all I could see was my brother's reflection staring back at me. We'd had the same eyes, the same hair, and yet, it was only me still standing there.

I took a deep breath and tried to push the memories away, but they were always there, lurking just beneath the surface.

I had everything. And I would give it all back. Just for one more day . . .

Every time I caught my reflection in the mirror, I was reminded of what I'd lost. What I'd done to the only person who'd ever loved me.

The guilt that gnawed at me, the sense of responsibility that weighed me down like a heavy burden. Every time I looked in the mirror, all I saw was his reflection gazing back.

"Staring at yourself again, beauty queen?" Lancaster teased, stripping off his practice jersey.

I forced my lips to curl into a smug smile as I sidled over and opened my locker before sitting on the bench and taking off my skates.

My phone buzzed, and I pulled it out.

> Father: The fuck you doing, boy?

Fuck.

Ari's little boys' night had turned into both of us getting completely shit-faced. Some girl had sucked my dick in the club hallway . . . and I'd forgotten all about Kara.

And now my father was going to make me pay for it.

You wouldn't think I'd be at his mercy at twenty-four, but when you were responsible for killing his only other son, his heir to the Daniels empire . . . it was complicated.

*Fix this now*, he sent, before I could even respond.

*Got it*, I messaged before pulling up my contacts and scrolling to Kara's number, something I thought I'd never use.

> Give me a second chance, babe . . . and I'll blow your mind.

I huffed and set the phone down, dreading eventually meeting up with Kara. She had the personality of drying paint, and her body wasn't good enough to make up for it. She was so stuck up that I was sure she had the vagina of a frozen fish. My dick would freeze if it ever made contact.

My phone buzzed, and I glanced over, eyes widening when I read Kara's response.

> K: Not in a million years could you blow my mind.

Well, that was unusual. I had expected Kara to offer to meet me anywhere . . . for anything. She was desperate like that.

I was . . . a little intrigued by this new side of her.

*We both know that's not true*, I sent back.

> K: We both know your penis is barely visible in the light, let alone enough for a vagina.

My jaw literally dropped. Had some alien come down and taken over Kara's body? Had she been hit in the head and sustained a personality change? Every interaction I'd had with her had been a slow death . . .

*If this was your attempt to get a dick pic, it actually almost worked*, I typed.

> K: I'll pass. Old wrinkled balls are not my thing.

I mean, she would know that my balls were, in fact, perfect, considering I'd fucked some of her friends, and I know those chicks talked about *everything* . . .

> See, now I feel like you've been stalking me.
> How did you know being insulted turns me on?

> If I'd known you were actually interesting, I would've shown up last night.

Lancaster's breath hit my head, and I turned and glared at him.

"Is there a reason you're trying to make out with me?"

He grinned and winked. "Just wondering what has the golden boy so entranced."

*Well, I* knew *you were uninteresting. So I didn't bother showing up either*, came the next text.

I scrolled through the messages so he could read them. He lifted an eyebrow. "Why is this turning me on?"

I snorted. "Probably because we love a game," I mused.

*Let's be uninteresting together*, I typed out.

"That's what you came up with? How do you get anyone to suck your dick?" Ari mused.

I lifted an eyebrow. "I don't need game with a face like this," I shot back, ignoring the pang of guilt that sliced through my insides.

> K: You have the wrong number. Hopefully whatever girl you ditched doesn't ever text you back.

"No way," I muttered, quickly responding. *Kara?*

I tapped my fingers on the bench, my earlier amusement gone, replaced by annoyance. Waiting for her response, I watched the bubbles showing she was typing . . . but then they disappeared. The minutes passed and I realized she wasn't planning on answering.

> It's B.S. to pretend this is the wrong number and ignore me, Kara. It's like putting blood in the water.

The picture that came in then, it was life changing. Like my

DNA had been rewritten. Like my stars had rearranged themselves.

I didn't believe in love at first sight.

I didn't believe in love at all.

But if I could have, I would have fallen in love with the girl in that picture.

Her face left me breathless, with sharp, delicate features that seemed almost too perfect to be real. Long black hair cascaded down her shoulders in soft waves, framing her face in a way that had my heart racing. Her verdant eyes hit me in the gut, pools of emeralds I wanted to dive into. They were eyes I could get lost in for days on end, drawing me in with their hypnotic gaze.

The girl's face was like a lightning strike of beauty and rebellion, with full lips that begged to be kissed . . . or wrapped around my cock.

She was flipping me off in the picture, a firecracker for sure —the kind of girl who could make my blood boil with desire.

I stared at her picture, obsession stirring in my veins.

"Dude. Where's that picture from? That's girl's fucking fiiiine."

I jolted. I'd forgotten Ari was there. Quickly swiping from the picture, irrational anger threaded through me that he'd seen her.

Ari gave me a knowing look. "Sharing is caring. Especially when she looks like that."

"Get fucked," I huffed, ignoring his existence when it hit me . . . it was still probably Kara sending me these texts. Which meant the perfect goddess in this photo could be anywhere in the world, impossible to find.

> Please, please don't be Kara.

> > K: I believe I already told you I wasn't her. Now, good day, sir.

I felt a tinge of relief. I mean, I had thought that there was no way Kara could be sending these messages. So there was a chance . . .

> What's your name?

> K: I said, good day, sir.

> Please. 🙏

> K: I'm not giving you my name, you creep. Ever heard of stranger danger?

I laughed, and Ari shot me a look as he finished getting dressed.

> You literally just gave me your picture, but you're afraid to give me your name? Maybe you are Kara.

> K: My name is Monroe.

Monroe. I mouthed the words, my obsession threading through every letter. What the fuck was wrong with me?

> So . . . has anyone told you that you're fucking hot?

> K: Keep dreaming, big boy. I'm way out of your league, and I'm sure Kara's out of your league as well. But good on you for shooting your shot.

I frowned. Shoot your shot. This was fucking Kara, or at least one of her friends.

> So you do know who I am . . .

> K: 🙄 What part of that sentence said that I knew who you were?

I felt possessed as I stood up, flipping back to the picture of the girl . . . Monroe . . . and saving it to my phone. Tossing my bag over my shoulder, I walked away. I had to get to a computer. I had to figure out if this girl existed.

I wouldn't be able to think about anything else . . . wouldn't be able to eat or sleep, or fucking breathe, until I knew what I was dealing with.

"Lincoln, what the fuck? Where are you going?" Ari called after me.

"See you later," I responded, not bothering to look back as I shot him a middle finger over my shoulder.

*Please be real.*

# CHAPTER 5
## MONROE

I was organizing files at the doctor's office the next day when my phone buzzed again.

*Monroe Bardot,* the text read from the same number as last night.

I stiffened.

> Please don't be creepy and make me regret all my life choices. How did you find out my name?

He sent a meme of a guy holding up his hands in front of him, placatingly.

> Unknown: Not trying to be a creep. Promise. I thought we could be . . . friends.

> That's a lot of dot, dot, dot for friends. Have you found Kara's real number and apologized yet?

> Unknown: Nope. I've decided that I was meant to accidentally text you. Don't want to mess with the good vibes I've got going for me.

I rolled my eyes at his attempt at charm and glanced around the room.

I was alone in the front office, and it was a slow morning; only one patient sat in the waiting room, and they'd already checked in.

I inwardly shrugged. I guess I could play along for a little longer in the name of socialization and distraction.

*You must be pretty desperate if you think texting a random stranger is the universe giving you good vibes*, I typed out.

He sent back the picture I'd sent him last night.

> Unknown: Have you seen yourself? You're fucking gorgeous. As long as you're not some dude in his mom's basement trying to catfish me, I say that I'm definitely in the universe's good graces right now.

For some reason, a blush spread across my cheeks. I'd been called "hot" in my life quite a few times. But, his "fucking gorgeous" hit me a little harder.

> Well, I showed you mine, now show me yours.

*I thought you said you didn't want to see wrinkled old balls*, he quickly typed back.

A giggle escaped my lips. I glanced around again to make sure no one had come in and heard me. Although anyone who did would probably faint if they saw me doing anything other than work.

> Your face. I meant your face. You can keep your wrinkly balls to yourself, thank you.

He sent me a picture of a forehead, golden hair cut in a sexy hot guy style falling in gentle waves against tan skin. The golden strands glimmered even in the picture, like he had a spotlight shining on him. I'd never imagined being attracted to a forehead and a little hair . . . but here I was.

> Nice dye job to cover your grays, but a little lower might be nice.

To my surprise, I got a picture of his leg next, showcasing powerful thighs that were, in fact, drool-worthy. They were sculpted and toned, every muscle visible beneath his skin.

*I can do that too*, I wrote, sending a picture of my big toe.

*LOL,* he typed back. *I just spit my protein drink all over my best friend.*

*So how long are we going back and forth before you send me what you look like?* I asked.

> Unknown: Has anyone told you that your big toe is hot? I mean, I'm not a foot guy, but I can admit it.

I giggled again, shaking my head and quickly sending him a gif of a gross-looking blonde guy.

> This is what I'm envisioning you look like.

> Unknown: So you're really turned on right now, is that what you're saying?

This was definitely more than I'd smiled in a year. I really was desperate.

Just then, my coworker Angel came in.

*I gotta get back to work*, I quickly typed out before throwing my phone in my purse.

I stayed busy for the rest of the day, pushing all thoughts of the charming stranger out of my head.

It was finally time to leave. I opened the door only to realize it was pouring rain. Normally, I walked to the bus stop, but I had my rented laptop with me today so I could finish the homework I didn't get to last night . . . and I couldn't afford to ruin it.

Deciding I had to wait it out since I couldn't afford a cab, I sat on a chair by the door and stared at my phone.

The stranger had sent a few texts since I'd last looked. Random tidbits about his day . . . like we really were friends.

*It's raining*, I inanely texted.

*That it is*, he immediately answered back, as if he'd been waiting for my text since the moment I'd stopped working. Did that mean he also lived in Dallas? Oh, I guess his area code was 817, I hadn't noticed that last night . . . which meant that he could be somewhere in the city right now. Something that faintly resembled butterflies stirred around in my chest at that thought.

I read through more of the texts he'd sent since I'd been working. There were a couple of pretty funny memes. But still, no picture. I decided to let it go for now.

I usually walk to the bus, so I'm waiting it out.

Unknown: What for?

My bank account's not a fan of cabs. LOL.

There was a long silence.

Unknown: Want me to get you one?

I scoffed.

I'm good. Also, you shouldn't offer money to strangers.

Unknown: We're not strangers, Monroe. We're practically best friends.

Okay, best friend . . . tell me my favorite color.

*Dark pink*, he quickly responded. I frowned. That was my favorite color.

Okay, I guess a girl liking dark pink isn't too hard to guess . . . but that doesn't mean anything. Because I don't know what your favorite color is, and I would definitely know that about my best friend.

Unknown: My new favorite color is green.

New favorite color?

Unknown: The color of your eyes inspired me, what can I say . . .

You should see the eye roll I have going on right now.

*I bet it's really hot*, he said with a wink face.

 Unknown: So how about that cab? Because my weather app says it's supposed to rain the rest of the day.

I groaned and pulled up the Weather Channel. Sure enough, it was forecasted to rain until tomorrow morning.

> Unknown: How about this . . . give me the address of some random corner near you, and then it can drop you off blocks from your house so then you can be assured I'm not some creep just trying to find out where you live.

I snorted.

> I'm pretty sure that negates the purpose for the cab in the first place since I would be soaking wet with that plan, I tell him. But seriously, I don't take things from strangers.

> Unknown: You really don't know who I am, do you?

I frowned at his comment. Was this some famous person that had accidentally texted me? Once again, I reminded myself that I shouldn't be talking to a stranger anyway.

*I really don't know who you are,* I texted. *And unless you're a thigh or forehead supermodel, I'm not sure that I'm going to recognize you by what you've sent.*

*So you follow thigh and forehead models?* he asked with a laughing face.

Another one of those new weird snorts came out of my nose.

> You're right, even if you were an international thigh model, I would have no idea who you are. I'm a big fan of shoulders though. I bet I could tell who you were from that.

> Unknown: I can't tell if you're serious or not, so just to be safe, better not send the shoulder pic. How about this instead?

What followed was the hottest thing I'd ever seen.

Now I knew that eight packs weren't real; at least, not according to my science textbook in high school that weirdly outlined that sort of thing. They were a myth. But I felt like writing the publisher at that moment, because what I was seeing could only be categorized as that. In the picture, he'd lifted his shirt, showcasing a pair of tan, perfect abs that made Michelangelo's sculptures look like he'd gotten it all wrong. Even the arm in the picture was hot, chiseled and strong, tattoos all over. There was the bottom of what looked like butterfly wings poking out from under his lifted shirt. I never would've thought of a butterfly tattoo as hot, but here was living proof that on the right guy, it could be everything.

*Please tell me that picture's really you,* I quickly typed back.

*You liked it,* he said with a wink emoji.

> Why are you texting me again? Because I'm pretty sure that Kara would be returning your text with abs like that.

> Unknown: Maybe I kind of like talking to someone who doesn't know who I am.

If you could read emotion in that innocuous text, and I wasn't sure you could, there was almost something vulnerable to that.

> Well, I'm going to start walking.

> Unknown: I thought you didn't want to ruin your stuff?

> There's gotta be a plastic bag around here somewhere. I have my classes tonight.

> Unknown: You're taking classes, too??

> Two jobs and school . . . It's my life.

> Unknown: How old are you?

*How old are* you? I texted back, since I seemed to be the only one offering information at that point.

*24,* he quickly typed.

> So probably no wrinkly balls then, huh?

> Unknown: Monroe, if I didn't know better, I'd think you were obsessed with my wrinkly old balls.

I snorted and rooted around for a plastic bag in the supply closet, doing a fist pump when I found one from a bag of drugs a medical salesman had dropped off that day.

*Today's my lucky day. I found a bag,* I texted, wondering why I felt so comfortable with this guy. I was freaking texting him about a plastic bag, like he would care.

*Be careful out there,* he immediately responded.

> I always am.

*Good girl,* he texted.

Heat rushed through me. I told myself it was the abs picture he'd probably gotten off the Internet somewhere. It was the only reasonable explanation for why two words could hit me like that.

Pushing those thoughts far away, I forced myself not to go any further down that path. We'd probably stop talking to each other by tomorrow, no need to get attached to the phone stranger now.

I set off down the street, decidedly not thinking about the fact that a perfect stranger had turned me on more than I'd ever been in my entire life.

Just with two words . . .

# CHAPTER 6

## LINCOLN

I t's amazing what you can find out by padding a few pockets. The PI I'd used a few times in the past to suss out some stalkers had now allowed *me* to become the stalker.

Monroe Destiny Bardot. My fingers traced the letters like a man possessed, my eyes gobbling up the folder like it held the keys to eternal happiness.

With how I'd felt since I'd seen her picture, maybe it did.

Destiny was an apt middle name for her, since that's what I felt like she'd become.

"Need anything else from me?" David, the PI, asked. He was an extremely innocuous looking dude, the kind that your eyes would immediately brush over if you saw him in the streets, never thinking twice about him. Maybe that was why he was so fucking good at his job.

"Nope, I'm good. Thanks for this," I told him, holding up my phone to show him I'd wired his money, and trying to keep the impatience out of my voice. I used him because he was one of the few PIs in the city that didn't do work for my father, but you never knew where allegiances lay, and the last thing I wanted was for him to hear about my new obsession.

David nodded and strode out of the room, and the second the door clicked shut behind him, I was flipping open the folder, staring at the pictures he'd managed to dredge up.

Holy fuck.

This girl.

I'd been obsessing over the picture she'd sent me for the last two days, but having new ones was almost more than I could handle.

She was gorgeous.

More than gorgeous. Golden and perfect. Her beauty hit me like a train wreck, knocking me into some sort of crazy trance. She was the kinda girl where you had to actually blink a couple times to make sure you weren't hallucinating. My fingers traced one of the pictures. She was seated on the grass, her head tipped up into the sunlight, a soft smile on her face. She was blowing my fucking mind.

I dragged my eyes away from her perfection and read through the information he'd gathered.

She was an orphan. The death dates of both parents were listed, and it looked like she'd been in the foster system since she was ten.

I knew I should feel bad about this angel being alone for so long, but I also knew she probably felt like an outcast. Abandoned. Rejected.

Maybe she'd been waiting for me like I'd been waiting for her.

Maybe I could get her to want me as much as I was wanting her.

*You're an asshole*, my inner voice seethed, but as my eyes roved over her picture, reminding me that she was the most beautiful thing I'd ever seen, I couldn't find it in myself to fucking care.

I was fucking hooked, like there was something magical about her.

I continued reading, noting the address he'd provided. It was in a really shitty part of town, and I immediately began obsessing over if she'd be safe getting to her place, especially since her preferred method of transportation was walking.

He'd found the companies she worked for—one sounded like a doctor's office and the other, Great Food Kitchen, sounded like some kind of restaurant. I scanned the rest of the list . . . which was short. She was taking classes at the local community college, and she had straight As.

There were two other pictures of her. One was the one I'd just been dying over, and the other was of her as a little girl that must've been in her state file. In the picture, she was staring at the person taking it with those big golden eyes, heaviness and sorrow there that you never wanted to see in a ten-year-old. I could feel the aching sadness that lived within her.

And that was what got me. That was what threw me over the edge, spiraling me forward where I wouldn't be able to control myself anymore. Because the look in her eyes, the pain reflected there . . . it was the same pain that I felt every fucking day. This was a girl that could understand.

Without thinking, I got up from the couch a moment later, grabbing my keys and clutching the paper with her address tightly.

A second later, I was racing my Corvette down the street, breaking every traffic law as I rushed to get to her place to do . . . I don't know what.

To see her in person? Even though I wasn't sure that was a good idea. I already felt like I'd chase her to the fucking ends of the earth.

But a part of me was still worried she wasn't real, that something inside of me had imagined all of this. Because a person as broken and worthless as me, he didn't deserve the stars to align like this. He didn't deserve a goddess like her.

But there was no part of me that cared.

Deserving or not . . . she was going to be mine.

———

I was two blocks away, in the shittiest neighborhood I'd ever seen, when I realized how much my lime green Corvette would stand out. She was sure to notice a vehicle like this if it was parked nearby.

I maneuvered the car into a tight parallel parking stall and climbed out. There was a group of kids playing on the sidewalk across the street, an abandoned basketball at their feet as they stared with wide eyes and mouths at my ride. I locked the doors and strode over to them.

"If my car's still here, and still has all of its parts when I return, I'll give each of you a hundred bucks," I told them.

The five little boys' eyes widened even further, and they all nodded eagerly. I shot them a chin lift, and I set off down the street, annoyed that two blocks still separated me from her.

I growled when I turned the corner and saw the complex that matched the address on the paper. She lived in a shithole. More than a shithole. This place should have been condemned years ago. The front gate hung askew, and with the peeling paint and the decaying wood, the whole place looked seconds away from collapsing.

There was a homeless man camped out in front of the building, for Christ's sake.

The street was pretty quiet though, and it gave me some time to plot how I would convince my girl to leave and move in with me.

Burn the place down?

I'd just had that thought when, like a mirage, she turned the corner. Her backpack was held tightly against her chest, and her face was pointing down, like she was trying to make sure she didn't make eye contact with anyone.

The pictures hadn't done her justice. I was thirty feet away, and I was getting hard from the combined effect of that face . . . that hair . . . and that body . . .

It was ludicrous how beautiful she was.

I wanted to kidnap her and lock her away so no one else could see her perfection.

I tensed when she passed the homeless man and he sat up from the pile of ratty blankets he'd been under, the color of them no longer recognizable under their filth. I could hear the low murmur of voices as she talked to him, the tension in her body fading.

And then she smiled.

And it felt like I'd been cursed, like my cock would never relax again. That smile undid me. My heart was thumping violently against my ribcage.

I'd always considered myself a pretty reasonable guy. Ever since my brother's death, I'd done my best not to be a shithead. If I saw an old lady walking across the street, I helped her. I never gave a girl any expectations. I followed the law—except on the road.

Part of my appeal was supposedly the wholesome "golden boy" persona I had going.

But here I was, contemplating things I never would've considered before I saw that picture.

All I could think about was devouring her. Keeping her forever. Dirtying her with my cum, spreading it across her skin every day.

I wanted her.

It took every ounce of willpower I possessed to watch her wave goodbye to the homeless man and then start up the stairs, disappearing from sight.

My phone buzzed in my pocket, and I cursed when I pulled it out and looked at the reminder that practice was starting in thirty minutes and I was at least forty-five minutes away.

I reluctantly dragged my gaze away and started back to my car, feeling more rabid and savage than I'd ever experienced in my life. The boys were gathered around the car, none of them touching it, but all of them practically frothing at the mouth as they stared. I did a quick check and saw that all the wheels still appeared to be there, which was better than you could expect in this neighborhood.

I quickly pulled out five hundred-dollar bills and passed them out, giving them a casual wave as they squealed in joy and ran away.

I didn't remember the drive to the stadium, and it barely entered my consciousness when Coach screamed at me for my tardiness.

I was thinking about my angel. My obsession. Mine.

# CHAPTER 7

## MONROE

I headed down the street to the restaurant where my study group was supposed to be meeting. I didn't plan on getting anything; heavens knew I couldn't afford to eat out right now, but the rest of the group had insisted we get together at this place.

And frankly . . . I was too exhausted to argue about it.

Last night's job with the catering company hadn't wrapped up until 1 a.m. Tuesdays were usually when I was able to catch up on a little bit of sleep, since I didn't have class, but that had all gone out the window when I hadn't gotten into bed until after two, only to be up at six thirty to drag myself to Tres Medical.

I'd stay for a couple of hours, keep my head down and work hard, and whatever we got done, we got done.

I walked into the trendy restaurant, suddenly very aware of the simple jeans and T-shirt I was wearing. This was the kind of place that you dressed up for, and I wondered why the group thought it would be a good place to get anything done.

I glanced around, trying to spot anyone from the group.

"Monroe!" a familiar voice called out from my left.

I glanced over to see Connor, one of the guys in the group, getting up from a table and striding towards me.

"Hey," I said cautiously, peering around him to see if I could see anyone else. "Is anyone here yet?"

"Nope, you're the first to arrive," he responded with a charming smile, gesturing towards the table. I followed him and slid onto the bench seating. Connor sat across from me, and a second later, the waitress was at our table, dressed in a skintight, blood red, dominatrix-type outfit. "Can I get you anything to drink?"

"A Guinness for me," Connor said, and I shifted in my seat. The project we were working on was complex, and it didn't seem like a great idea to drink while we tried to put it together . . . but being here in general didn't seem like a great idea, so I guess who gave a fuck.

The waitress glanced at me expectantly. "And you?"

"Just a water, please," I answered quietly. Her fake grin dropped, and she strode away, obviously annoyed I hadn't ordered anything that would reflect on her tip money.

"Sure you don't want a glass of wine or something like that?" Connor asked, his gaze sitting heavily on my face.

I brushed away the flicker of unease curling across my chest. Connor had never given me anything to worry about. He was a pretty good-looking guy, with his caramel-colored hair and dark brown eyes, but I'd never been interested, and he'd never attempted to flirt with me.

I glanced away, staring out at the dimly lit bar like I was actually interested in it. "I'm good. Work starts early tomorrow."

His eyes flashed in disappointment, but he nodded. "It's been a ridiculous semester, hasn't it? I swear I get anxiety just entering the classroom."

I smiled and nodded, relaxing a little. I could talk about school and be normal for a little while.

The waitress sat our drinks down. "Have you decided what you want to eat, or do you need a little more time?"

I opened my mouth to tell her we weren't actually ordering anything, but Connor spoke before I could. "A few more minutes, please," he said, casting her a smug grin.

As she walked away, I checked the group text on my phone to see if anyone else had said they were here. The chat was completely silent, unfortunately.

"I heard this place is really great. You should look over the menu. You gotta be hungry. It'll be my treat."

Oh.

"Do you think we should wait for the others, at least?"

It was terrible of me, but I was probably going to take up his offer of a free meal. I was starving, and sick of Ramen packets. And everything on the menu looked amazing.

Guilt slid over me, a memory of my mother floating through my mind. Of what she'd done to get things from men.

Of how they'd left her.

I pushed the memories out of my head. It wasn't like that. This was just my friend offering to pay for a meal. It didn't mean anything.

It didn't mean I was like her.

The waitress came back, and I asked for the burger.

"Do you like steak? You should get it."

A blush hit my cheeks. The steak was the most expensive thing on the menu.

"You really should get the steak. It's the best thing here," the waitress offered unhelpfully.

I closed the menu and slid it forward. "All right, I'll have that."

She walked away, satisfied with the upsell, and Connor and I engaged in a little bit of small talk about other classes we were taking. The conversation was probably the longest I'd ever had with him, and through it all, he stared at me so interestedly.

It was weirding me out.

"Should we call the others?" I asked. I glanced down at my phone and realized that the two other girls in the group were forty-five minutes late.

Connor pulled his phone out. "Oh, they both texted. I guess they were driving together but they couldn't make it. Bummer," he said, not actually sounding bummed at all as he slid the phone back into his pocket. "But that's okay. We can still work on the project." He slid his hand forward and grabbed mine. "And I've been wanting to get to know you better."

Fuck, this was a date. He'd conned me into a fucking date.

My stomach chose that moment to rumble. And fuck, I was going to stay here because I really wanted that steak.

"Excuse me for a minute, I need to use the restroom," I told him, sliding out of the bench seat and heading towards them before he could say anything else.

My phone buzzed just then, and I pulled it out, blindly hoping that maybe it was one of the girls in the study group saying she was making it after all.

A small smile hit my lips when I saw that it was Lincoln. He'd finally given me his first name two days ago, excluding his last name, of course. And although I thought this would fizzle out, here we were, six days after that first text, still messaging throughout the day.

*I think I broke my back lifting today*, the text read.

> Poor baby. Well, I got tricked into going on a date, so I might win.

His text was instantaneous. *You're on a date?*

I used the restroom and washed my hands before answering him.

*I was* tricked *into a date*, I corrected him. *Doesn't count. We were supposed to meet here for a study group, and weirdly, the other two didn't show up . . .* Lincoln: Why don't you leave?

> Because I'm hungry and he convinced me to order a steak . . . and that sounds much better than the Top Ramen I've got waiting for me at home. Plus, I can maybe get some of the project done.

*I can send you a steak,* Lincoln texted back.

Again, a lot of times I found text messages to be unhelpful when reading people's emotions, but Lincoln sounded almost . . . jealous.

I rolled my eyes and texted back what I always texted when he said something ridiculous.

> You shouldn't offer money to strangers. I think I've told you this before.

> Lincoln: We're not strangers, remember? I'm your best friend.

I chuckled and slid my phone back into my pocket as I returned to the table.

"I don't think I've ever seen you smile like that before," Connor commented.

I blushed, my smile slipping away. "I think I'm too tired for that most of the time . . . should we start working on the project while we wait for the food?"

"No, the project can wait. I'd love to get to know you better," he said.

I nodded, trying not to look like I hated everything about this night, and decided I'd give it a few minutes before forcing us to work on the project.

"Are you from Texas originally?" he asked.

"The Houston area, but yes."

Before he could ask what brought me to Dallas, I began to pepper him with questions. It was a skill I'd learned. People usually enjoyed talking about themselves, and if you asked them the right questions, you could avoid talking almost entirely.

As he told me a story about playing for his high school baseball team, I pulled my phone out from my purse, keeping it under the table as I read the text that had come in from Lincoln.

> Lincoln: I think you should just leave. Fuck this guy.

"Everything okay?" Connor asked, annoyance etched on his face.

I forced out a smile. "Yes, sorry. I'm expecting a text about work and wanted to check if it came through yet. I could use the night off tomorrow."

He seemed to buy what I said and continued talking about himself. I learned about his major in accounting and his love for golf, both equally boring topics.

The waitress arrived with the meal, and I stared at my plate excitedly as she walked away.

I'd taken my first bite, however, when the waitress returned to the table, her ruby red lips curled into a frown.

"I'm so sorry, but the restaurant is closing for the night."

Connor stared around the room at the patrons, who had suddenly started leaving, his face completely bewildered.

"What do you mean it's closing? Isn't this place open until three in the morning? It's barely seven."

The waitress gave him a tight, annoyed smile. "I'm sorry, sir, but we're asking everyone to leave. Here are some boxes for your food, and then if you could please follow everyone else out, dinner's on the house tonight." She walked away without a glance back, and my insides were doing excited cartwheels. Whatever had happened, I'd gotten a meal for free that

I didn't need to feel guilty about. I could now end the night without feeling like I needed to undergo more awkward conversation.

The situation called for a fist pump.

I boxed up my steak while Connor sulked across from me, finally throwing his food in his container when we were almost the last ones left in the place. Fed up with how slow he was going, I slid out from the table and he reluctantly followed me. I gritted my teeth as his hand went to the small of my back as he led me towards the exit.

"How about we go back to my place and we can work on the project?" he suggested, an undertone in his voice I wanted nothing to do with.

Right. "The project." I was sure we were going to work on it, just like I was sure the two others in our group were actually planning on showing up tonight. It was all I could do to keep in my eye roll.

"Sorry, I need to get back . . . so I don't fall asleep on the way home," I said, my tone apologetic.

Connor's disappointment was palpable, and he opened his mouth to argue with me, but I was already backing away.

"But we'll have to set up another meeting to talk about the project," I offered.

He took a step forward, his hand settling on my waist. "That sounds great," he murmured, before shockingly brushing a kiss across my cheek.

What the fuck?

"Okay," I stammered, turning around and practically running down the sidewalk. I could feel his gaze boring into my back, and I couldn't shake the feeling that he didn't want the night to be over and he was planning on following me.

I didn't have anyone to call for help, but my anxiety spiked as I heard footsteps behind me.

On a whim, I took out my phone and called Lincoln. We'd

only exchanged text messages, but I was desperate. It rang and rang, and I'd almost given up when a sexy voice answered.

"Monroe?" he said, sounding breathless.

"I'm so sorry to call. I'm just afraid that this creeper's going to follow me home, and I wanted to talk to someone so maybe he won't."

"Of course, sweetheart. I'm glad you called," he soothed, his voice sliding over me with a graveled husk that sent strange shockwaves across my skin, even under the circumstances. His voice was deep, with a hint of a southern accent.

"Go ahead and glance behind you, and see if anyone's there," he ordered gently, the rasp in his voice running like silk through my insides.

"Okay," I squeaked, shooting a glance behind me and breathing a sigh of relief when I didn't see anyone there.

"I don't see him. And why would I? I'm probably being crazy," I murmured.

"I'm really glad you called. I don't like the thought of you being scared."

It's amazing how much he seemed to . . . mean it. I got a little lost in his voice, the fear sliding away as I listened.

"Hi, by the way," he said, his chuckle laced with an edgy heat. "We've officially popped our phone call cherry."

I snorted at that, and his chuckle deepened.

Just then, footsteps sounded nearby, and my breath hitched as I glanced behind me and saw the shadow of someone coming from around the corner. I took off down the street in a light jog.

"Monroe, are you okay?" he asked, the levity in his voice gone. I glanced back again, only to see that it was an old woman with a bag of groceries.

"I don't know why I'm so spooked. I'm being ridiculous."

"No, it's better to be safe than sorry. Especially after he tricked you into a *date*." There was a slight bite of anger to his voice when he said the word "date."

I huffed out an exasperated laugh. "Right? I mean, who does that?"

"Desperate men do desperate things, I guess," he murmured, darkness threaded in his words, or maybe that was my imagination based on the weird turn the night had taken.

"Tell me a funny story to take my mind off the walk," I asked, once again not recognizing myself with this man. It somehow made it easier, to talk to this person I couldn't see, someone who didn't know me, who couldn't be disappointed with me.

"Hmmm, a funny story . . . "

My heartbeat had finally calmed as I got within three blocks of home. A little longer and I'd be there.

"Well, one time I got knocked out. They took me to the hospital and they put me in one of those hospital gowns that tie in the back. I guess when I woke up, I got out of the hospital bed, still loopy as hell, and decided that the gown was scratching me. So I stripped it off and proceeded to drag my IV out into the hallway, showcasing my goods to everyone in the wing before they finally got me back into my room."

I giggled, imagining some guy streaking through the hospital wing. "I'm sure it was quite a hit with the nurses," I teased.

"Oh, no doubt. I think they made up excuses to keep me at the hospital the whole week after seeing the family jewels."

"For sure. Especially if you had those abs back then."

"Nope. It was the wrinkly old balls that definitely had them going," he teased.

My fingertips went up to my lips, tracing the smile plastered on my mouth. In my nineteen years on this earth, my most prevalent emotion had been sadness. Even as a little girl, I hadn't been the type to laugh with friends. I'd always had something serious to think about. And just in the brief amount of time I'd been talking to this guy—whose voice did not sound like he was a scary old man creeping on me, by the way—I was smiling constantly.

Fuck.

I got to my building, walking through the gate and breathing a sigh of relief that I was almost safe behind my door.

"Well, I made it to my place," I murmured.

"Good girl," he whispered back with a husky growl. And fuck. If I thought that reading those words did something to me, it was nothing compared to hearing his voice say it. It hit my insides, sending tingles between my legs, having a physical effect on me.

"I'm going to bed," I told him, my voice sounding shaky and unsure.

"Lock your door behind you," he ordered. I nodded my head up and down, taking a second to remember he couldn't see me, that's how much I felt his presence surrounding me.

"Okay."

I heard some voices in the background and wondered what he was doing.

"I gotta take care of something, but you get some rest. I'm so glad you called."

"Thanks for picking up," I whispered.

"Always," he answered, and even though he couldn't have meant it, I felt like there was a promise in his words. Like he, unlike every single person who had always disappointed me in my life, was promising he wouldn't.

"Good night," I said, forcing myself to end the call because I could feel myself getting fucking attached, which was the last thing I needed to be doing.

"Good night, dream girl," he said in a thickened accent.

And then the phone clicked off.

I walked into my apartment and then locked it behind me . . . before sliding down the wall, my hands clutching my cell phone like a lifeline.

Dream girl . . .

# CHAPTER 8
## LINCOLN

So, have you met the mystery girl yet?" Ari asked, throwing a puck at me as I slid on my skates.

I caught it and grinned. "Soon."

He raised an eyebrow. "So you're still talking to her? Dude. Don't be surprised when you find out your mystery girl is actually a sixty-year-old nudist named Frank."

I rolled my eyes, a small smirk on my lips. "Don't worry, she's real . . . "

"So, you have met her?"

I forced my grin to fade away. Ari had known me for a long time, but the fact that I was basically stalking the girl at this point would come as a definite surprise to him.

I mean, fuck, it was still a surprise to me.

I had to put my gloves in front of me to try to hide the hard on I had just from thinking about our conversation last night.

I'd been catching glimpses of her every day since I'd gotten her address, but hearing her voice, the kind of voice that broke your heart and body, had me losing my mind even fucking more. It was like an angel's, one that was dirty, with a light smoke to it that gave her innocence the lust-filled undertone that would make any man desperate.

I could understand her classmate tricking her into a date.

Like I told her, desperate men do desperate things.

I could understand it, but it didn't mean I was going to let it happen.

Once I'd allowed myself to fall over the cliff of insanity, it wasn't a big deal to get to the step of tracking her whereabouts so I always knew where she was. When she'd texted me at the restaurant, I'd used my special app to figure out exactly what restaurant she was at . . . and then it was a simple phone call to buy it out for the night . . . starting immediately.

When I'd called the owner, he'd almost choked to death at the number I'd offered him to close for the evening, but of course he wouldn't understand; there wasn't a number too high when it came to my girl.

I should've stopped there, but hearing the fear in her voice when she'd called me . . . that's how her douchebag classmate ended up in the alleyway afterwards, my fists destroying his face. I'd been wearing a ski mask, and I'd never spoken, so I wasn't in any danger there . . . But I'm sure she might have questions when she saw him in class next time sporting two black eyes.

I skated onto the ice, the sound of blades against the cold surface echoing through the arena.

My mind was supposed to be focused on practice, but all I could think about was her. The girl with the wavy black hair and green eyes that had captured my soul.

"Yo, earth to Linc, you playing?" Ari chided, breaking me out of the daze I'd fallen into thinking about her . . . my dream girl.

It slipped out last night, but it was an apt description for this girl who had embedded herself under my skin.

And to think she had no clue the effect she had on me.

"So I was talking to Bender about going out on Friday when we're in New York. You in?" he asked as we skated around the ice.

A week ago, I would've been salivating at the thought. Once upon a time I thought it was delicious to mess with East Coast girls. They were always wildcats in bed, sexual creatures just waiting to be unleashed under their buttoned-up cardigans and pearl earrings.

But now . . . the thought of any other girl was as palatable as a dick punch.

"Let's just go to a bar, man, and watch a game."

Ari threw his glove at me.

"Boys, are you hearing this? Golden Boy's got it bad for Frank," he tossed out as he skated a circle around me.

"Frank?" Bender asked, lifting an eyebrow.

"He's only into older men now. You might have a chance, buddy," Ari called to him, never missing an opportunity to razz Bender about his age. I sighed and waited until he was skating by me again before I tripped him with my stick, sending him sprawling.

Peters chuckled next to me.

"You being paid to gossip like you're at a slumber party, cunt worms?" Coach called as he skated on to the ice.

He blew his whistle a couple times for good measure, and we were off, starting with some warm-up drills, skating around the ring in laps, gradually picking up speed as we went. I was usually at the front of the pack, but I was distracted today, my mind consumed with thoughts of her. Obsessed with retracing every word that she'd said last night, and I'd started plotting when I could hear her voice again.

"Daniels, get your motherfucking ass in gear. Unless you want New York to fuck you tomorrow night," he screamed. I gritted my teeth, trying to concentrate as we moved on to puck handling drills.

"Oh, he doesn't want that," whispered Ari slyly.

"Dude, what's wrong with you?" Peters hissed as he slammed me into the glass.

I shook my head at him, going through the motions of team drills as we practiced power plays and penalty kills.

What was she doing at that moment? Was some guy talking to her? My fingers itched to grab my phone and check where she was. She was usually at the doctor's office at this time of day, but I was desperate to make sure.

Practice finally ended, and I was the first off the ice, ignoring the grumblings of the coaches as I practically sprinted back to the locker room to check my phone. She'd sent me a text thanking me for last night, and I quickly responded, asking how her day was going. What I really wanted to ask was where she was, who she was talking to, if she was ready for me to sweep her off her feet.

It was everything I could do to try to play the fucking long game.

I groaned when my agent texted me, reminding me that I had a photo shoot tonight. That was the last thing I wanted.

Ari slid onto the bench next to me.

"Fuck, Linc, I think that was the worst I've ever seen you play," he said dryly.

"It's still better than your ass," I quipped back.

He rolled his eyes. "So are you going to meet her? Fuck her out of your system? Because I need your ass in the game. Half the team was still sucking balls out there."

I reached over and punched him in the shoulder, grimacing at how sweaty he was.

"I got this. You know that," I scoffed, while grabbing my stuff out of my locker and heading towards the shower.

Now, I just needed to set the plan in motion.

———

I was in a fucking bad mood when I got to the magazine shoot. I'd worked with this photographer before, so I tried to paste on a smile, but I already knew it would be a long night.

One of the things that my stardom brought with it was modeling gigs like this one. People loved to see me in a tight pair of underwear. Understandable, but still fucking weird that this was my life.

I was shown to my dressing room and took a minute to shoot a text to Monroe. I already knew she was in class, and that it wasn't the class she shared with Mr. Douchebag. But she'd barely talked to me today except for her thank you text, and I was like a junkie needing my next fix. I was already furious that I was at this shoot and that I'd had to miss waiting outside her apartment and seeing her as she came home from work and headed to class.

> What are you doing?

Only a few seconds passed, but I was pacing impatiently, desperate for the time when I could talk to her constantly without coming off as clingy.

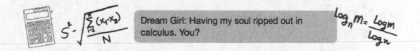

> Dream Girl: Having my soul ripped out in calculus. You?

How should I answer her? I couldn't exactly explain that I was about to have oil rubbed all over my chest, and people were about to take pictures of me in my skivvies. But it was a good chance for a photo op. I stood and strolled to the mirror, angling my phone so it caught my chest and the top of my bulge.

I sent it to her.

There were dots on the phone for at least two minutes, and I could picture her typing and erasing something over and over.

Finally, one word came through, right as the makeup artist and hair team arrived.

Dream Girl: Wow.

I was a pretty confident bastard, but the *wow* had me wondering. Was it a good wow? Was it a *holy shit, that's the hottest fucking thing I've ever seen* kind of wow?

This girl had me tied up in knots.

They started to pull and tug at my hair, and I kept my gaze averted from the mirror. It was one thing to snap a shot of myself for my girl, but another thing to have to stare at my face and be reminded of my brother for an hour straight.

She would've liked him better than me. He was always the one doing the right thing, sacrificing his hopes and dreams to make the family happy.

And I was always the one doing everything to disappoint them.

The makeup artist applied powder to my face. Something that was fucking annoying, but apparently necessary for the camera. Between that and the grease they'd lathered in my hair, I already needed a shower. I wondered what Monroe would think of all of this? Because there was no end game where she wasn't a part of this world right along with me.

They were finally done with me, and I headed out to start the shoot. When I got out there, Carmen, the photographer, directed some girl to oil my chest.

She was one of those girls who walked around like they thought everyone should bow at their feet. It was more than obvious. She had bleached blonde hair and a nose that a surgeon gave her, along with tits they'd given her too. With the fuck-me eyes she was flashing me, I could've had her bent over in the dressing room in a hot minute. Hell, I could've had her right there if I wanted to.

I waited to see if I'd imagined this new obsession, if my dick would stand at attention as she rubbed my chest.

But there was nothing, not even a spark of interest in the girl in front of me.

*Good boy.*

The only woman I was interested in was only available to me on the other end of my phone.

The girl tried to flirt with me, her touch lingering, and then her palm grazed my dick . . . not accidentally.

Suddenly, I found myself with my hand around her neck, pushing her away.

"Don't ever touch me again," I hissed, causing a shocked silence to descend on the crew.

Carmen hustled towards me, wringing her hands, a nervous laugh slipping from her lips. "Natalie, why don't you take the rest of the night off?" she suggested. The girl, Natalie evidently, had tears gathering in her eyes. Her face, the picture of devastation.

And I couldn't fucking care less.

"Your staff needs to be fucking professional," I snapped at Carmen. She nodded frantically, not wanting to sour our relationship. I'd made her a lot of money, after all. The staff walked back to their places, because that's what sheep fucking do, and then I was instructed to pose a million different ways.

I wondered if Monroe would see this magazine. If she knew who Lincoln Daniels even was? I imagined her getting herself off to my photos.

I was deep in thought, picturing Monroe coming, when all of a sudden, a voice cleared. "Um, Lincoln . . . Is there something you can do about that? This publication piece isn't X-rated." I glanced over at Carmen and saw she was keeping her eyes averted. It took me a second to realize I was fully aroused, the tip of my dick peeking out from the briefs I was wearing.

I quickly turned around with a curse, trying to think of

puppies getting hit by cars and other dreadful things. After a few minutes, I managed to get it down. That had certainly never happened before.

"Sorry about that," I said, unashamed, when I finally turned around. "I've got a new girl, and thinking about her causes problems."

Everyone's interest was immediately piqued, but I just flashed a false grin and posed a few more times before I was finally finished. Carmen met me at the door as I was walking to the parking lot to head home.

She handed me a photograph. "For your girl. I'm sure she'll enjoy it," she said with a wink before walking away.

"I know I will," she threw over her shoulder.

I glanced down at the picture and saw it was one of me fully aroused, a dark, lusty, almost feral look in my eyes that made it obvious I was thinking of fucking.

I grinned and threw the photo in my car, confident that some-time, very soon, Monroe would get to see that look in real life.

———

I climbed into the shower as soon as I made it home, washing off the oil coating my skin . . . but my mind got away from me. I couldn't get the image of her out of my head. Picturing her in the shower with me, naked and wet, was the most beautiful fucking thing I'd ever seen. Her small, slippery hands gripped me tightly, exploring me like she was as addicted and as desperate for me as I was for her. Her hair was plastered to her smooth, perfect skin. Her rosy nipples peeked out. She was a goddess, my every wet dream come to life as she slowly slid her hands up and down the length of me. I was in agony, ecstasy stretched tightly across my skin as I watched her . . . as I felt her. I was on fire, desperate to experience her touch like that . . . forever. So desperate I'd die if she left.

"Lincoln," she whispered, my name a prayer across her lips. I couldn't even answer; I was destroyed, pleasure erupting inside me, so intense, I was sure I'd never recover from it. As her pace increased, I moaned her name and then . . . hot cum exploded everywhere, coating her hands, and her breasts, in ropy strands. I rubbed it into her skin . . .

Fuck, I was coming in real life from my little dream, emptying myself into the drain, when I should've been doing it with her.

The scary part . . .

I'd never come so hard in my life.

And she hadn't even touched me yet.

# CHAPTER 9

## MONROE

"Oy, little bird," Bill's voice called out. My head snapped up. I'd been lost in thought . . . Lost in lust actually, ever since Lincoln had sent me that picture. I'd never seen someone so outrageously . . . *everything* in my entire life. His chest was a perfect, sun-kissed bronze color, with tattoos everywhere, including that huge butterfly inked towards the bottom. Everything about that picture was over the top, so gorgeous it was dangerous.

"Everything okay?" Bill asked again. Over the past year, Bill and I had become extremely close friends. He was still homeless —and still crazy, for the most part—but still the only good man I'd ever met. He'd appointed himself as something of my protector, and on nights when I had class, he was usually hovering on my block, watching for me to come home and make it to my place safely.

I had offered many times for him to come stay on the futon in my room, but he wanted nothing to do with it. He preferred his "castle," as he called the park where I'd met him that first fateful night. I made sure to give him meals, and I tried to slip him some money when I could, but he usually refused that.

"Sorry, I've got a lot on my mind," I told him, rolling my shoulders back as I reached him. Bill always smelled pretty awful, but there was something about his toothless smile that made him a prince in my mind.

"How's class?" he asked as we walked the rest of the block to my place.

I yawned, weariness stretching tight across my skin. "Exhausting," I admitted.

"Calculus giving you trouble, lass?"

"I think it would be easier if I wasn't so tired when I got to class," I admitted to him. I knew it didn't do any good to wish things were different. This was my life, and it was all necessary, but what I wouldn't give for a full eight hours of sleep. Just one night.

"Have I told you I'm proud of you, little bird?" Bill asked suddenly.

I stopped, emotion clawing at my insides at his words.

I'd never had someone tell me they were *proud* of me, not in my entire life. Growing up, no matter what I'd done, it either wasn't seen by my foster parents, or they just didn't care. And Mama had never been around enough to know one way or the other what I was doing.

I took a deep breath, trying to get it together. "Thank you," I finally murmured. He patted my arm, a tender smile on his face, like he could see right into my head and knew what I was thinking.

We got to my front gate. "Oh, I almost forgot, I saved this for you." I pulled out a big Styrofoam box of pizza. They'd ordered some for lunch today at the office and I'd asked if I could take the leftovers.

Bill's eyes lit up, even though it was cold pizza that had been out for at least a couple hours. We were both the same that way; we weren't going to say no to a meal, no matter what it was.

Thunder groaned across the sky, and I winced as a drop of

rain fell and hit my cheek, knowing that Bill would be out in the elements all night.

"Why don't you come upstairs for a while?" I suggested, wanting to get him out of the rain.

Like always, though, he patted me on the shoulder and gave a little whistle. "Ole Bill will be just fine in my castle, little bird. You get in your room now, and lock that door," he ordered, reminding me of a similar statement that Lincoln had made a few nights before.

I nodded and waved to him, watching for a moment as he walked away, an edge of melancholy laced through my veins. It was amazing where you could find good in the world. Bill had been unexpected, but he was one of the biggest blessings I'd found in this new life of mine.

I trotted upstairs, coming to a screeching halt at the top when I saw my landlord leaning against the wall opposite my door.

He didn't say anything. He just watched me with bloodshot eyes, smoke curling in the dim lighting from the cigarette shoved between his lips.

I jammed my key into the door and shot inside, slamming it behind me and engaging the two locks, even though I knew he obviously had a key to get in whenever he wanted. I wasn't sure if it was my imagination or not, but I could hear his low chuckle through the walls. Grabbing the chair and jamming it under the doorknob, I hoped that would allow me to get some rest, since I would hear the door opening if he tried to get inside.

My forehead hit the door, and I leaned against it, trying to push the fear down. That was what men like him wanted, after all. My fear.

I compared the two, Bill and him. One could've had all the advantages in life if he wasn't such a complete tool. The other one had nothing, but he was a million times over a better man.

I shook my head, realizing I would have to bite the bullet and take an afternoon off next week to continue my search for a new, cheap place. I'd tried a couple of days ago, but hadn't found anything even close to the price range I needed.

Right then, my phone rang. I glanced at it, my heart skipping when I saw it was Lincoln.

"Hi," I murmured, the words coming out shy and awkward.

"I told you I couldn't just go back to texting," he murmured in that gravelly, deep voice of his. He sounded sleepy, like he was calling me from bed, and my mind couldn't help but conjure up an image of that perfect, tattooed wonderland lounged underneath silken sheets, his hand reaching down and . . .

"Monroe, you with me?" he asked, this time sounding amused, like he knew exactly how dirty my thoughts were.

Maybe he and Bill were similar like that, able to see inside of me.

"Yes. Sorry. Got a lot on my mind," I squeaked out. He chuckled, the sound reverberating through me, right to my core.

"You wouldn't happen to be thinking of that picture, would you?" he asked knowingly.

"Calculus. I was definitely thinking of calculus."

He chuckled again. "Okay, dream girl."

"Why do you keep calling me that?" I asked, trying to ignore just how much I loved it.

"That should be obvious. That's what you are. A girl almost too good to be true."

There was a blush across my cheeks, even though he couldn't see me.

"You wouldn't think that if you really knew me," I said, the words escaping me before I even realized them.

There was a heavy silence, and I cursed myself, wondering why I'd said something so stupid. So vulnerable.

"I can 100 percent promise you that I'll still think you're my dream girl when we meet," he finally promised.

# CHAPTER 10
## LINCOLN

DALLAS
KNIGHTS

I took a deep breath as I walked through the lobby of Daniels International, preparing myself for the inevitable confrontation that lay ahead. The sleek, modern decor felt cold and sterile, a reflection of the man who owned it. Anstad Daniels, my father, the billionaire mogul who ran the largest hedge fund in the country.

After a week of ignoring his calls and texts, I'd finally given in and agreed to meet with him. As much as I hated the idea of seeing him, I knew I couldn't keep avoiding him forever.

I walked into my father's office without knocking, and a gasp sounded in the room. Turning towards it, I saw his secretary, a woman my age, quickly getting up from the floor, adjusting her skirt. The woman's face was a mess, her red lipstick smeared all over her lips—and even beyond—like garish artwork, just like how I was sure it was smeared all over my father's cock.

My stomach rolled, but I was used to this scene. I was pretty sure out of the thirty years my parents had been married, they'd been faithful to each other for three of them. Disgusted with the scene nevertheless, I looked away and tried to focus on the matter at hand.

"Lincoln, you're late," my father barked, not sounding at all bothered by what I'd walked in on. "Sit down."

The secretary quickly scurried out of the room, her face flushed with embarrassment and shame. Not that it would stop her from doing it again. Fucking my father was probably in the job description they posted when hiring his secretaries.

I took a deep breath and sat in front of him on the stiff, black leather couch, bracing myself for the usual lecture.

I could feel his eyes boring into me, and I tried to seem calm, staring around the room, taking in the sight of papers stacked precisely on his desk and empty liquor bottles in a cart nearby. The stench of stale alcohol and sex was suffocating, a testament to the life my father led on a daily basis.

I could already sense the tension in the air, like a thunderstorm waiting to break.

When I finally glanced at my father, he was glaring at me from behind his desk, his hands clasped tightly in front of him. I cocked an eyebrow, daring him to get on with it.

"About time you showed up," he snapped. "What's your excuse this time? Break your phone?"

I rolled my eyes, already tired of it all. "I had things to take care of," I replied coolly, examining my father's features. I knew everyone still found his appearance quite striking, the only real sign of age his graying temples mixing in with his dark hair. He had a chiseled jawline and prominent cheekbones that gave him a distinguished persona. But his piercing brown eyes seemed to radiate an aura of malice and cruelty that should've made even the bravest of souls shudder. He was only an inch or two shorter than me, and he took care of his physical appearance, dressing impeccably in a tailored suit every fucking day, making sure he projected an air of sophistication. Part of his success, though, was that there was something unsettling about him that left a sour taste in your mouth . . . that made you want to keep your distance. One glance at my father, and you knew he was the type of man who would stop at nothing to get what he wanted, regardless of the cost.

My father snorted in disbelief, breaking me from my thoughts. "Things to take care of? Like what, drinking yourself into a stupor?"

I gritted my teeth, trying to keep my temper in check. "Look, I'm sorry I missed the date," I tossed at him sarcastically. "But I won't fuck some girl just because you want me to."

My father's face turned an ugly, blotchy, red color. "You ungrateful little shit," he spat. "I give you everything you could ever want, and you can't even do this one thing for me?"

I clenched my fists, a surge of anger and frustration racing through me. "It's never just one thing with you. It's never-ending, actually. But I had to draw a line somewhere . . . might as well stop at prostitution."

He leaned forward, his eyes blazing. "You fucking asshole . . . "

"I'm not a little schoolboy who's waiting around to fulfill all your *fucking* demands at the *fucking* snap of your fingers. I have a life."

"A life?" he laughed cruelly. "What life is that, exactly? Playing a stupid game on ice? That's not a life, Lincoln. That's called a waste of time."

I bristled at his words, feeling a surge of defensiveness. "Not that this should be news to you—since we've had this conversation before—but hockey isn't a waste of time. It's my passion, my career. I make millions, without you involved in any way."

My father snorted in disdain. "Passion? Career? You're nothing but a glorified monkey, dancing around for the entertainment of the masses."

My blood boiled at his insults. "You have no idea what you're talking about," I growled.

"Your brother was *everything*. He was born to lead this company. And because of you, he's gone now. The future I built has disappeared. And if you think I'll let my sniveling spare ruin my plans even more than you already fucking have, you're out of your fucking mind. You will go on a date with that girl. You *will* fuck her. And then her father *will* agree to the terms of the contract I want. And that is how it's going to be."

I leaned forward, trying to ignore the way his words sliced into my fucking soul. I made sure to keep my gaze locked on his. "You're the one out of your *fucking* mind."

He leaned back in his chair, his eyes gleaming with malice. "Boy. I own you, and I can destroy you just as easily."

I jumped from the couch, a cold shiver running down my spine at his words. It was true that my father held all the power in our relationship. Hell, he held most of the power in this fucking country. A day didn't pass where I didn't feel like I was walking on eggshells around him.

But not today. Today, I'd had enough. "I'm done with this," I said firmly. "I'm leaving."

My father's eyes bulged out in surprise. "What? You're not fucking walking out of here."

My eyes blazed. "Watch me."

I sauntered out of the room, my head held high, but as soon as I made it down the forty fucking floors, through the pretentious lobby, and out into the street . . . I found a trash can and puked.

Every time he brought up Tyler like that, he rocked me.

I stood there, taking huge gulping breaths, my insides quaking.

My phone buzzed, and I fumbled to get it out of my pocket.

*Hope you're having a good day,* Monroe's text read.

Immediately, the nausea and dread dissipated. She was such a fucking sweetheart.

I had to go to her street, I needed to catch a glimpse of her.

With one glimpse of her, I knew everything would be okay.

# CHAPTER 11

## MONROE

**M**y cell rang, and I winced when I saw who it was. "Monroe, darling," my boss purred. Crap, I already knew what she was calling about. Clarice was the head of the catering company I worked at, and the only time she deigned to speak to me was when she needed employees.

And I'd already worked every night this week.

"Hey Clarice, what do you need?" I asked, assuming my professional voice.

"I just need one little itsy-bitsy favor from you, dear . . . "

"Okay?"

"We got called in last minute to cover some fancy party downtown. Apparently, the other company didn't have suitable vegan options, so you know it's one of *those* parties. It'll take twice as much staff as usual to cover it, and I'm short. Can you help out?" She was presenting it like a question, but I knew Clarice well enough to hear the warning in her voice. If I didn't say yes, I wouldn't be working for her anymore.

"Of course. I can be downtown in an hour," I responded.

feeling like I was going to burst into tears because I was so fucking tired.

"Make that forty minutes, please," she snapped, before rattling off the address like she was doing me a favor.

Clarice hung up without a goodbye. I sighed and hopped off my bed, the weight of the day heavy on my shoulders.

Here we go again . . .

———

Forty minutes later, I'd made it downtown, having to use precious funds to catch a cab, since there were no buses that could get me there on time.

I walked up the stairs of the back entrance of the hotel, into the familiar scene of a kitchen filled with a whirlwind of activity, with cooks yelling and pans clattering. It was a different kitchen with every gig, but there was always the scent of searing meat mixed with the tang of fresh herbs and spices, creating a mouth-watering aroma that lingered in the air. Despite the chaos, there was a method to the madness, with each of the company's chefs working in perfect synchronization to create culinary masterpieces that drove guests crazy. It was a symphony of culinary talent, a well-choreographed dance of pots and pans that was nothing short of mesmerizing.

At least it would be if I hadn't seen it a million freaking times.

I smiled when I saw that Caleb had also been called in. He was my favorite person to work with on the team. Caleb was a huge flirt who somehow succeeded in never making you uncomfortable. He was one of those people I could've seen myself actually being friends with, or even dating, if I ever allowed myself anything like that.

Staring at him now, though, he didn't seem quite as handsome as usual.

I blamed Lincoln's stupid abs.

"She dragged you here tonight, too?" he asked, eyeing me appreciatively.

"I don't want to talk about it," I moaned in exasperation.

He nodded. "I can't say I'm mad about it," he murmured with a wink. We tied the violet colored catering aprons on over our goofy white button-ups and organized the trays.

"Man, this must be a nice party. They made the garlic-crusted crab cakes," Caleb said appreciatively. I nodded, not caring one way or another how fancy the party was. I just hoped there'd be some leftovers we'd be able to take home with us so I could hold off on grocery shopping, aka ramen shopping, for a couple more days.

A buzz in my back pocket had me reaching for my phone. It was Lincoln.

My cheeks flushed with heat as I read those four words, and I couldn't help but smile to myself. It was like a bolt of electricity running through me, giving me a warmth I couldn't deny. It was a feeling of excitement, of anticipation, of hope. And just like that, my smile dimmed. Because I knew I was falling for him.

And I knew I'd regret it.

I should meet him in person. Get it over with. Find out once and for all if he was some complete weirdo, and if I needed to lose something that had become so weirdly important to me.

Clarice came hustling into the kitchen, dressed in a glamorous black, floor-length gown, stress thick on her brow. "What are you all doing standing around?" she screeched. "The guests are arriving. Get out there."

I picked up the crab cakes and Caleb lifted a pair of pear-stuffed gorgonzola pastries—weird sounding, but delicious tasting.

"Here we go," he tossed at me with a wink before we headed into a glamorous ballroom.

I wasn't usually impressed by fancy things—my mother's "fancy visitors" had cured me of that when I was young—but my throat caught as I stared around at the glittery surroundings. The marble floors shone like glass, reflecting the sparkling chandeliers above. The room was alive with the sounds of music and chatter, and the air was heavy with the scent of expensive perfumes and colognes.

As I walked through the crowd carrying my tray of food, I was surrounded by a sea of designer gowns and tuxedos. I wasn't very up on celebrities, but I could tell the attendees were big time, up there on the list of wealthy elite. The atmosphere was electric with excitement, and I couldn't help but feel . . . completely out of place.

The tables were draped in crisp white linen, adorned with towering floral arrangements and glittering centerpieces. Other members of the staff floated through the room, offering trays of elaborate hors d'oeuvres and drinks. The champagne flowed freely, and the guests were all smiles and laughter.

As I made my way further into the ballroom, I caught sight of the stage where a band was setting up. When a woman laughed hysterically nearby, already drunk despite the event just starting . . . I wondered. What was it like to not worry about keeping a roof over your head? Or going to the grocery store and getting whatever you wanted—not that any of these people would be shopping for themselves.

I was being a bit judgy, but I couldn't help but think about it.

"Ooh, are those crab cakes?" a deep voice called from behind me. I turned around, a blush hitting my cheeks at the gorgeous man in front of me. He was tall, at least six foot three, with wild black hair and piercing green eyes that lazily glanced down my body. He was wearing a very fitted tuxedo that showcased the fact he was seriously built. A tattoo peeked out from his stiff collar.

There was a spark in his eyes, almost like he recognized me, but it disappeared.

"Okay, now I'm wishing I had made the mistake," he muttered, his gaze catching on my face.

"Pardon?"

He shook his head, like he was shaking himself from a reverie, and he reached out to grab a crab cake. "Delicious," he purred after he took a bite . . . but I got the distinct impression that he was talking about something other than crab cakes.

"Enjoying the party?" he asked, cocking his head, still studying me in that unnerving way of his.

"This feels like a trick question."

He threw his head back and chuckled, the sound of it garnering admiring stares. I couldn't blame them; it was a good laugh.

"Touché." He held out his hand. "Ari," he said, introducing himself.

I tentatively reached out, furtively looking around because this felt like some kind of setup. I'd had men hit on me at these parties from time to time, but I definitely hadn't had an introduction like this before.

"Monroe," I murmured.

He nodded, like he'd expected me to say that. That was weird.

"Well, enjoy the night, *Monroe*. I have a feeling it'll be one to remember." There was that smirk again, like he knew a secret I didn't. He leaned in, his lips brushing my cheek, making my stomach flip a million times, and then he strolled off without another word.

I stood there, my mouth gaping as I stared after him.

"I'm about to have an orgasm," Caleb whispered as he appeared at my side. I snorted and raised an eyebrow.

"What? Your cheese wontons just doing it for you?"

"Do you even know who you were talking to?"

"Umm, I think he said his name was Ari?"

"Ari Lancaster. Star defenseman for Dallas. He's won best defenseman every year since he started. He's the one who puts on this event. Raising money for poor kids is his thing."

"Oh," I murmured, my gaze darting to where he was flirting with a woman whose breasts were each bigger than her head. She resembled a shrew.

Caleb sighed in fake exasperation, used to the fact that I lived under a rock and had no idea who most celebrities were. "I bet we'll get a big tip at the end of tonight. This is like the event of the year in this city. I think I just saw Ryan Reynolds."

My eyes widened, because I did know who he was. I had a major crush on his wife.

"You said this was for an underprivileged youth charity?" I asked, staring at the tables set with what I believed were actual gold plates. The money would have gone a lot further if everyone had just donated straight to the charity rather than wasting it on all of this, but I guess that was how these things always went. Or, at least all the events our company seemed to help out with.

Before Caleb could answer, he was called away by a vaguely familiar-looking woman wrapped in a gorgeous bright yellow gown, gesturing for the tray that Caleb had in his hand.

Thirty more minutes passed, and I was already dragging. The women were being snooty and my ass had been grabbed more times than I could count. Considering the clientele that was here, I felt more like I was serving at a saloon and not some fancy charity event. I was going to have a bruise from how hard the last guy had pinched me. People thought it was weak that women let these things happen, but they must not have ever been desperate. I had no intention of going back to sleeping on a park bench, so as long as nothing went too far . . . I could handle it.

There were screams and shouts outside suddenly, far more than any other guest had garnered. I glanced towards the front entrance, and a million flashes assaulted my vision, like the paparazzi stationed outside had decided to go with fireworks rather than their cameras.

I was about to turn to head back to the kitchen to get another tray, not particularly caring who was coming in, just wanting the night to be over . . . when *he* walked in.

*Holy fuck.*

The man standing in the entry, I couldn't look away.

Tall. Commanding.

Beautiful.

A golden god that the rest of us were destined to worship.

My eyes didn't know where to focus.

His fitted tuxedo hugged his broad shoulders and lean frame in all the right places.

But it was his golden hair and eyes that truly captured my attention, shining like rays of sunlight in a sea of darkness. Every step he took was like a symphony, commanding the attention of everyone in the room. My cheeks flushed with heat just staring at him.

He was dangerous, reckless, and untamed, his presence so magnetic people flocked to him like moths to a flame. And it wasn't only his striking good looks and the undeniable charm you could spot fifty feet away that caught you; there was something deeper there, something raw and intangible, lurking right beneath the surface.

I couldn't help but wonder what lay behind that perfect face, what secrets he might be hiding, what scars he might carry.

He was the kind of man who could change your life in an instant, who could make you feel alive in ways you never thought possible. But he was also the kind of man who would break your heart without even trying, leaving you shattered and alone. And as I watched him walk through the crowd, for the first time since Mama had given me that warning . . . so long ago . . . I wished for the chance to have that heartbreak and head down whatever path a man like that would lead me.

His golden hair fell in soft waves around his face, framing his handsome features and making his golden eyes even more striking. Every time a strand fell in his face, he would sweep it away with a casual gesture, his fingers brushing against his forehead in a way that made my heart skip a beat. The way his hair caught the light made it seem like liquid gold, cascading down his features in a way that was both mesmerizing and hypnotic. I found myself wanting to reach out and run my fingers through his hair, to feel the silky texture against my skin. That was obviously impossible, so I contented myself with watching as he moved, his hair shifting and dancing with each step he took.

"Fuckkk mee," a voice slurred behind me, and then I was fucking spanked on the ass.

My empty tray clattered to the ground, the sound somehow making its way above the music and the din of the crowd.

I stood there shocked, with what felt like a million eyes staring at me, judging me.

"Pick that up, you idiot," Clarice's voice snapped, and I turned to see that she was standing there, the face of fury.

I was going to get fired, all because of some asshole . . . who was currently snickering behind me, totally unaware of the carnage he'd created.

I bent down to pick up the tray.

And suddenly there he was.

The golden god.

My heart nearly jumped out of my chest. He was watching me, his gaze filled with something that resembled shock—over what, I hadn't the slightest clue.

Up close, his beauty was even more overwhelming. I'd never

seen anyone so outrageously . . . masculine in my life. It was filling the air around me.

Was it hot in here? I quickly averted my gaze back to the tray we were both hovering over. I could be in danger of a heart attack with how fast my heart was suddenly beating at his proximity.

"Let me get that for you," he murmured . . . in a very familiar voice.

I was dazed as I stood up without the tray, my gaze focused on the gorgeous man in front of me, taking in his confidence, his charisma, his . . . everything.

Lincoln.

My stranger.

"Oh, Mr. Daniels. You don't need to get that. My employee was about to grab it—I'm so sorry for the inconvenience—I promise she'll be dealt with." Clarice's voice floated around us, flustered and annoyed, but it was like we were trapped in our own little bubble, just the two of us.

His gaze slowly danced around my face, like he was memorizing every feature. I hurriedly brushed down my hair, my cheeks flaming even more as I thought about what I looked like right then. My uniform was about the most unflattering thing ever. Clarice didn't bother with exact sizes, so the white button up was too tight, the buttons stretched across my chest, and the black trousers were at least a size too big, held up by a bulky black belt.

I was sure my hair was a mess. I'd been running around since I'd gotten here.

And there he was. Looking like more than a dream. Because he was so perfect, no one could have dreamed him up.

Disappointment. That's what I was feeling. Because apparently I'd fallen harder than I thought. If he'd been a normal guy . . . albeit a guy with hot hair and abs . . . maybe there would've been a chance . . . for something.

Instead, he had to be a golden god NHL player . . . probably a star, because a guy like that would be.

I'd told him about my two jobs and attending a community college . . . and all along he'd been . . . this. A celebrity. My cheeks burned with embarrassment. We didn't exist on the same planet. We didn't even exist in the same universe.

And after today, now that he'd met me face to face, he wouldn't want anything to do with me.

And once again . . . I'd be all alone.

"Monroe!" Clarice snapped, jerking me from the stupor I'd fallen into. It was torture to drag my gaze from his, like he was some kind of drug that had already gotten under my skin. "Let go of Mr. Daniels, right now!"

Shocked, I stared at my hand, which had somehow ended up on his forearm, indeed clutching it like I was desperate to keep him next to me.

Seriously . . . could this day get any worse? I released my grip, but before I could fully move away, he took my hand, the warm callouses of his palm feeling like an anchor for the storm raging inside me.

"I need to talk to Monroe for a few minutes," Lincoln said, that sexy rasp sounding even better in person than it had through the phone. He was still staring at me, and I don't think he'd looked away since he'd walked over here, his hot, searing gaze heating my insides beneath thick lashes.

"Well—" Clarice began to object.

He dug in his pocket for a second and practically threw what appeared to be a few hundred dollar bills her way. She grabbed them with her bony hands and stormed away. I was sure I'd hear about this later on. I'd probably be fired over it, actually.

But I couldn't find it in myself to care.

"Come with me," he ordered, and like I was a puppet; I followed him eagerly towards an exit. I was vaguely aware of all the stares crashing into my back, but I was lost in the lavender haze of whatever was happening at that moment.

------

### *Lincoln*

I sent Monroe another text as the limo took me to Ari's fundraising event. She hadn't answered the three I'd already sent, but I was hoping I'd hear from her soon.

When this one went unread as well, I tossed the phone onto the leather seat and sat back with a sigh, running my hands through my hair anxiously. My app was down, some kind of bug the company was trying to fix. So I had no way to track where she was tonight . . . figure out why she wasn't answering me.

I wished I'd already moved to the next step with her. She was like a scared rabbit, ready to bolt at any second. I'd never taken a date to this event, not wanting to be distracted by a vapid puck bunny on Ari's big night, but I felt sick at the idea of her not being by my side. Every time I'd attempted to broach the subject of meeting by text and in a call . . . she'd quickly pushed the conversation off course, clearly avoiding it.

The limo turned the corner, and I groaned at all the paparazzi gathered outside the entrance. I guess I'd be blind for the first part of the night, since there were enough photographers gathered there to light up all of Dallas.

At least it was for a good cause.

I'd known Ari for a long time, and he'd still never opened up to me about his childhood. Based on how passionate he was about this charity, and a few other things he'd said over the years, I'd gleaned it wasn't good.

I didn't press him too much about it, though. I knew all too well some secrets were best kept in the grave.

Frustrated with the dark direction my thoughts had taken— again—I checked my phone once more and then slid out of the limo, pasting on a plastic smile as I walked the red carpet that had been set up in front of the entrance. There were fans gathered behind the photographers, and they were screaming my name so loudly I was sure I'd have hearing loss because of it. I waved at them, grateful for the security lined up. I loved my fans, but I wasn't in the mood for the craziness tonight.

The air felt different when I stepped inside—electric—full of promise somehow. I scanned the crowd of celebrities, trying to make out what was different.

"Fashionably late, as usual," Ari snarked as he came up and clapped me on the shoulder.

"I'm like fifteen minutes late," I drawled.

He just smirked at me.

"Why are you looking at me like that?"

"I'm not looking at you in any way," he answered.

"Okay . . . " I stared around the room. "Quite the crowd you've got here. Any new additions to the list?"

His smirk widened. Creepily, if I was being honest.

"Oh, there's a couple of unexpected additions."

"Party crashers? How'd they make it past security?" This event had more security than Fort Knox. Ari had made sure of that after the first year when a group of female streakers had invaded the event, apparently trying to impress the crowd with their . . . assets.

"Not exactly party crashers," he hummed, that same weird smile on his face. Before I could say anything else, he strolled away. "Got to go mingle. See you at the table in a bit," he threw over his shoulder before disappearing into the crowd.

A crash sounded nearby, and I turned towards it, only to see . . .

Her.

Monroe.

I stood there in total shock for a moment, panicking a little, like I needed to run away. But no—this was it—a chance to force a surprise meeting.

I pushed my way toward where she was bending to grab a fallen tray, desperate to get to her before anyone else.

I knelt down to grab the tray . . . and then she looked at me. And the whole world froze.

Of course, I'd been stealing glimpses of her every day, but being this close to her . . .

The effect was dizzying.

She was flawless, my every desire in one perfect package.

Up close, I could see she had a light scattering of freckles that peppered her nose and cheeks, and her stunning green eyes, like fresh wands of grass, were staring at me, wide-eyed and wondering.

Her lips were outrageously full and pink, the shape that the women in this room spent thousands on to try and achieve, never coming close to the perfect plumpness that called to me. My cock was on high alert just staring at them.

*You're mine,* something growled inside of me. The room felt like it was a hundred degrees. I was hungry and desperate, needing her with every cell in my body.

She was so damn . . . pretty.

"Let me get that for you," I told her, and I saw when it hit her . . . that she knew me. There was a myriad of complicated emotions floating through her gaze, and I wanted to know every one of them.

She straightened, seeming a bit unsteady as she did so. I grabbed the tray and followed her . . . because I had no choice. I needed her.

"Oh, Mr. Daniels. You don't need to get that. My employee was about to grab it—I'm so sorry for the inconvenience—I promise she'll be dealt with." A shrill voice assaulted my ear drums, but I ignored it for a moment. I just needed to look at her more, because I knew I'd never get my fill.

Whatever uniform she was wearing was hideous . . . and yet, she blew every polished and glittering person in this room away with it.

A pretty blush hit her cheeks, and I was desperate to know what had brought it on.

Was she attracted to me? Was she disappointed that I was her mystery guy? It was amazing how this girl could tie me up into a million knots of self-doubt when I'd never experienced such a thing before.

"Monroe!" the voice snarled again, and I glared at the offending woman, feeling a bit rabid that she would dare talk to my girl like that. "Let go of Mr. Daniels, right now!"

Glancing down, I saw that she'd grabbed onto me, and the rush of possessiveness that gripped me by the balls at that moment . . .

She tried to move, but I immediately grabbed her hand, desperate to keep her touch.

Desperate.

The word was on replay in my head; it was the only way to describe the fervor that beat like a drumroll in my soul from the second I saw her picture.

"I need to talk to Monroe for a few minutes," I said, unable to look anywhere but at her gorgeous features.

"Well—" the crone began . . .

I threw some bills at her, not caring one way or the other how much I'd just given her. I needed more. More time. More everything . . .

"Come with me," I asked, although it came out more as an order, because I wasn't sure I could deal with it if she tried to leave me right now. And that wouldn't be good for my plans if she saw how over-the-top crazy I was for her.

Already . . .

# CHAPTER 12
## MONROE

He didn't let go of me once as he all but dragged me into the back hallway, growling when he saw how many people were there. Abruptly changing directions, we made our way through a few more twists and turns until we were completely alone.

He caged me against the wall, his gaze so fucking . . . interested.

I'd never felt more seen before in my entire life.

I'd been the shadow in the corner ever since I was little, first forgotten by my mother, and then unwanted by all the foster parents that came after.

Lincoln's attention was heady. It was addicting. It was already a craving I didn't know how to get rid of.

"Lincoln," I whispered.

He closed his eyes as if he was in pain. "Love the way you say my name, dream girl."

Butterflies were free-falling in my stomach as I absorbed the tenor of his voice, the way it seemed to caress my skin.

*Dream girl.*

"I didn't know you'd be here," he murmured, one of his

hands suddenly cradling my face, his thumb brushing against my cheek. I had the urge to nuzzle into his hand, but I held myself back.

This was all moving way too fast. But he was intense and spellbinding . . . and I was hooked.

I didn't even try to move away from him.

"Neither did I. It was a last-minute call."

"I'm so fucking glad you are."

He smiled lazily, a brief flash of perfect white teeth against his tanned skin.

"Lincoln—"

He cut me off . . .

With a barely there kiss, a brush of lips, that nonetheless had me gasping. The sound seemed to spur him on, and he boldly parted my lips with his tongue, not an ounce of hesitation anywhere to be found.

The air crackled around us with electricity as if the universe knew something magical was happening.

I melted as his tongue slid over mine. There was an ache deep in my core growing with every pass of his mouth. He moved forward until we were perfectly flush. Until I could feel everything. The hardness of him. My heartbeat a roar in my ears.

His hands gripped my hips, tiny pinpricks of pain where he touched, like he was afraid I'd disappear if he let go.

My reaction to him was violent. I'd never in my fucking life done anything like this. I'd just met him in person and yet I had the urge to let him do *anything* he wanted to me. One of his hands moved from my hip to the base of my neck. His fingertips gently gripped me, massaging my throat and igniting a trail across my skin. His lips left mine and I whimpered, the sound only to be replaced by soft moans as his lips ghosted over the sensitive spot I had behind my ear.

My body was lax, melted against him. His smell enveloped me, a combination of fresh, crisp notes, mixed with something deeper and more masculine. It was a heady scent that made my knees weak and my heart race with desire.

His length felt huge nestled against my stomach.

Then his lips returned to mine, a feverish energy behind his movements. His kiss turned desperate, a combination of lips, tongue, and teeth. "Fuck," he breathed, pressing harder against me, the gravelly sexiness stoking the ache between my thighs.

Another whimper escaped my lips, building in intensity as my hips rocked against him, lost in the lust burning between us.

I gripped his shoulder with one hand, while the other wrapped around his waist, exploring the hard, powerful muscles of his back. The sensation of his strength under my hands fueled my desire even further.

"Ride my thigh, baby," he commanded, his hand on the small of my back holding me in place. Unable to resist, I rubbed against his hard thigh, shivers of pleasure spiraling through my body, my mind clouded with lust and longing.

"Make yourself come, Monroe," he growled into my ear, his voice rough and demanding. His hand on my neck squeezed, forcing me to stare up at him. He searched my gaze, for what, I wasn't sure. But I hoped he found what he was looking for.

I wanted to be special to him. I wanted to be different from the millions of girls I imagined had come before. I wanted more of him. I wanted everything.

There were gas lanterns on the walls in the hallway, the flames set to flicker, casting shadows across his features as I stared up at him. He was too gorgeous to resist. I wanted him to make me fly.

Lincoln started fucking my mouth with his tongue, deep, long licks that resonated everywhere. He dominated my mouth, his hand on my lower back pulling me closer, pushing his firm thigh against me as my breasts pressed on his chiseled chest.

I moved my hips in a frantic, driving rhythm, rubbing my core on his thigh as he breathed dirty words against my lips, promising me everything if only I would come. His lips captured every whimper and moan from my mouth.

I faintly remembered we were in public, but it seemed unimportant at that moment. I just needed release.

And then it happened—my core spasmed, waves of pleasure shooting through my body as I shook against him, my whole body throbbing. It took my breath away, leaving me feeling dazed and out of sorts.

He pressed his cheek upon mine, his tongue darting out to lick my sensitive skin before he growled, "Good girl. That's my fucking girl."

Once more, he pushed his thigh against my core, the scent of him wrapping around me, suffocating me with its heady intensity. His lips roamed along my neck, sending shivers down my spine as I surrendered myself completely to his touch, the rush of desire overwhelming me.

The door at the end of the hall suddenly slammed open and a rush of photographers poured in, their cameras all aimed at us.

"Fuck," Lincoln growled as I froze against the wall.

"Who's the girl?" was yelled by one guy in a thick black trench coat, his camera shuttering away as he took a million photos. It was finally enough to jerk me out of the lust fog I'd been temporarily paralyzed by.

I lurched to the side, removing Lincoln's hold, and then I took off down the opposite way of the photographers.

"Monroe!" he yelled after me, but I didn't look back.

I opened the first door I came across, yelping when I saw a couple fucking against a wall.

"Sorry," I squeaked, slamming the door shut and taking off again, my heart hammering in my chest.

I glanced over my shoulder and saw that Lincoln was talking to the photographers. A small part of me winced that he wasn't coming after me, but I pushed that thought away.

Why would he?

After checking two more doors, I finally found one that led back into the staff area. I ran through a doorway, and there was the kitchen.

"Monroe!" Caleb called as I dashed past him.

"Sorry, I've got to go," I tossed over my shoulder before bursting into the cool night air.

The door slammed behind me and I closed my eyes, a shudder racing across my skin.

Flashes of *him* hit me like a bullet train. His hands caressing my skin, the feel of his lips tasting mine . . . I'd just left him. And I already felt hungover. Undone.

Destroyed.

Because I wasn't sure that I would ever recover from what had just happened.

Not for the rest of my life.

# CHAPTER 13

## MONROE

**B**y the time I made it home, a stumbling wreck through the dark, cool night . . . my walls were up.

That had just been a glitch in the system.

Something to keep me warm for the rest of my life, my night with the hockey star.

It was better that way. He was a distraction, and when he left, because a girl like me could never be more than a passing amusement to a guy like him . . . I'd have probably messed up my whole life trying to keep him.

*"Everything's going to be different," Mama said excitedly as she helped me into the only dress I owned. She looked different than usual. Her eyes were happy, and she was smiling. That never happened. She was dressed up, too, in a tight black dress, and her lips were painted a dark red. I wondered if she'd let me wear some lipstick.*

*As soon as the dress was on, she was brushing my hair. I winced when she hit a mess of tangles. I tried to brush my own hair when Mama was gone, but it was hard.*

*"Now, I need you to be on your best behavior tonight. Do you understand? Everything has to be perfect."*

*"Where are we going, Mama?"*

*"To a nice dinner with one of my friends. He wants to meet you."*

*A fancy car was waiting for us outside, and I spent the car ride tracing my hand over the smooth seats, never having felt something so soft before.*

*The car dropped us off at an expensive-looking place with the best smells coming out of it. There was a handsome man waiting by the door, and he crouched down and shook my hand when Mama introduced me to him. He told me his name was Carlos, and he was so happy to meet me.*

*Carlos took us inside the restaurant and we were taken to a back room where more food than I had ever seen was laid out on the entire table. He laughed at my wide eyes and then made me a plate before he made his own. Mama was glowing, her laugh filling the whole room every time he said something.*

*It was as if I was in a dream. I never wanted the night to end.*

*A server had brought us chocolate cake, and I was munching away while Mama and Carlos talked to each other.*

*Suddenly, a woman burst through the door, her cheeks a splotched red color. She wasn't pretty like Mama, but I could tell her clothes were a lot more expensive.*

*"So this is the tramp you've been out with. My God, Tom, you would think you'd have some class."*

*I looked around, confused, because there wasn't a Tom in the room, but Carlos was standing up, his hands in front of him and his eyes squinted around the edges . . . like he was worried.*

*"Darling, this isn't what it looks like. This is nothing," he told the woman soothingly.*

*I glanced at Mama, and there were tears gathered in her eyes.*

*"Nothing? Her child is here," she said, gesturing to me with wild eyes.*

*"Nancy. It's just a little fun. It's—"*

*"'A little fun?' It's going to be 'a little fun' when I take you for all you're worth!" She stormed out of the room and Carlos darted after her.*

*"Carlos!" my mother cried, reaching out and grabbing his arm.*

*He shook her off, so hard that she fell to the ground. "Get lost," he seethed before running after the woman.*

Carlos, aka Tom, had been a small-time news anchor who had solicited my mother for her services. He'd fallen for her, and had made her all sorts of promises . . . but of course all those promises hadn't meant anything, not when his wife, and the mother of his three children, had threatened to leave him . . . and take all of his money.

Shortly after that was the first time Mama had overdosed.

I was broken out of my dark thoughts by banging on my door. My heart clenched in fear, followed by confusion when I heard Lincoln calling my name.

I tentatively opened it, staring at him in shock as he stood there. He looked all wrong in this place. A bright, shiny light amid the ruin of the complex.

"We need to talk," he said firmly, pushing his way inside. His bowtie was undone, falling haphazardly around his neck, and his hair was wild, like he'd been dragging his fingers through it over and over. There was a pinched, worried strain around his eyes . . . that hadn't been there at the gala.

"We don't have anything to talk about except why you're here," I told him, doing my best not to stare at him. I needed my wits about me for this conversation. I couldn't be pulled back into his glittering orbit.

My cheeks flushed as I stared at my worn carpet. What he must be thinking right now. I'm sure he'd never seen such a shit-hole in his whole, perfect life.

"I had to see you. I couldn't let you just disappear after . . . "

"After I embarrassed myself," I whispered, wondering if the

images of me pressed against him were going to be on the front-page news tomorrow.

"I paid them all off; no one will see those pictures," he said fiercely. "And even if they did, we wouldn't have anything to be ashamed of." He ate up the distance between us and tipped up my chin, pressing a breath of a kiss across my lips that threatened to break me because of how sweet it was.

It took me a second to remember myself, to remember the decision I'd come to.

I stepped out of his reach, trying to ignore the spark of pain in his gaze.

"I need you to leave. I don't know how you know where I live . . . but you've overstepped some major boundaries."

"Monroe . . . "

"There's nothing you can say. You need to leave."

His face was tight as he stood there, a tic in his cheek as he bit down on his plush bottom lip. I wanted those lips. And I hated myself for that.

———

*Lincoln*

I hadn't intended to show her that I knew where she lived . . . but desperate times called for desperate measures, a refrain I found myself saying all the time nowadays. When she'd run away tonight, and I'd had to stay to deal with the piranhas that would have tried to ruin her life, it literally felt like she'd taken off with a chunk of my soul.

I couldn't let her leave like that, just disappear, sure to never answer one of my calls or texts again. Watching her come like that, making those little gasps I wanted to swallow whole . . . I could only imagine what she'd sound like impaled on my cock . . .

As I stood there staring at her now, trying to hold in the

madness that just glancing at her sparked in me . . . I could tell nothing I did tonight would change her mind.

"In the position I'm in, I have to be sure about people. My team ran a background check to make sure there wasn't anything . . . that would come back to bite us."

I prepared myself for the onslaught that confession would give her—even if it wasn't a true confession. I could have found out she murdered someone and it would have done nothing to stop the need coursing through my veins. That background check was purely to find out information I could use to get her closer to me.

But Monroe surprised me, like she did constantly, actually. Instead of appearing furious at my—false—confession, her eyes widened and she took a step back, clearly taken aback by what I'd said. Her lips upturned . . . almost like she was pleased. "So you know about my mother . . . and the foster homes?" she murmured shyly.

I regarded her for a second before slowly nodding.

"And that wasn't something you thought would 'come back to bite you'?"

Ah, I understood then. She'd been sure that if I found out about her past, I wouldn't want anything to do with her.

"Only made me fall for you harder."

"Don't say that," she murmured fiercely.

"Say what? That I'm already falling for you?" I responded, the words not coming close to the depths of my obsession. But I didn't want to scare her even more than I already had by showing up at her place.

She pursed her lips and glanced away, and I sighed. Of course she wasn't going to just fall into my arms and declare her undying love to me before I whisked her away.

Baby steps and all that.

At least I'd be able to get off tonight with her scent coating my clothes, the memory of her falling apart against my thigh inked in my head . . .

"Alright, dream girl. I'll give you tonight. But you and me . . . it's fucking real. It's the realest fucking thing I've ever felt in my life. And sooner or later, you're going to realize, it too."

I strode to the door and stopped, needing one more fix of her before I was forced to go back to my empty place. She was standing in the same spot, her eyes misty and unsure, like she was as desperate for me to stay as she was for me to go.

"Goodnight, baby," I whispered before I walked out the door, knowing that it would be the longest fucking night of my life, getting to the next step.

# CHAPTER 14

## MONROE

In the light of the morning, last night felt like a dream. The best kind of dream and a shuddering nightmare all rolled in to one. His promise that we were real coated my skin, and my stupid heart was at war with itself, both wanting, and not wanting him to keep it.

I dragged myself to Tres Medical, going about my work at half speed, the world blurry and gray around me.

Right as I was getting done with my shift, my phone rang.

It was Clarice.

"Darling," she purred, and I lost my footing for a moment because she sounded so . . . happy.

I hadn't expected her to call. I'd expected a text firing me, or just never hearing about another gig at all.

I'd certainly not expected this . . . whatever this was.

"Hi Clarice," I said carefully.

"You naughty girl. You didn't tell me you were dating Lincoln Daniels. It's absolutely delightful."

"Well, we're not—" I began.

"Nonsense. You two were the talk of the party. You mustn't

deny it, dear. I told everyone how it couldn't have happened to a nicer girl."

Shit. Of course she did. And I'm so sure that's what she'd said. Insert sarcasm, of course. Clarice was a viper.

"Now, I know you're probably caught in your little love bubble this week, but next week I've got some wonderful jobs lined up. Maybe we can even talk about moving you up from waitstaff."

I felt sick to my stomach. Her words like hot oil on my skin. I wasn't even dating the guy and already people were trying to use me.

I was all for moving up in my jobs; I needed the money desperately . . . but not like this.

"We'll talk later, ta-ta," she said, before abruptly hanging up without me saying a word.

I shook my head and walked outside, staring up at the sky that, while I'd been working, had gone from a perfect blue to a canvas of deep, swirling clouds, the kind that promised a storm was coming. There was a charged electricity in the air that prickled at my skin and made the hairs on the back of my neck stand up. I walked quickly down the sidewalk, wanting to get back to my place before the storm broke. Just then, though, like the crack of a whip, the thunder rumbled overhead, making me jump.

I looked up, watching as the lightning sliced through the sky like a jagged knife, illuminating everything in stark relief. It was both beautiful and terrifying. I shivered, from the cold and the anticipation, as I walked.

I usually hated the rain, but there was something thrilling about this storm. Like it was a signal that something was coming . . .

———

It had indeed started raining on the walk back, and by the time I'd gotten home, I was a sodden, soaked mess. I'd had to walk the entire way since the bus was delayed because of the storm, so I'd gotten home with just enough time to grab my backpack. I didn't even bother changing; I would be soaked on the way to my classes anyway. Next paycheck, I really needed to invest in an umbrella.

I rushed down the sidewalk, desperate not to be late since the professor of tonight's class was a hard-ass. And the whole time, I kept thinking that Lincoln hadn't called . . . or texted.

Regardless of who he'd turned out to be, I'd come to rely on the comfort that came from my phone stranger. At least once a day, he'd send something that would make me laugh.

I missed . . . smiling.

It was for the best, though. That was why I'd pushed him away to begin with.

A smile wouldn't feed me. A smile wouldn't ensure I didn't end up like Mama.

I resembled a drowned rat as I stepped into class. Connor tried to get my attention, gesturing to the empty seat next to him, and I pretended not to see him as I went to the opposite side of the room and slunk into my seat. He'd somehow ended up with two black eyes after our disastrous dinner, which he claimed was caused by an errant football. They had healed, for the most part, but unfortunately it hadn't knocked any sense into him that I wasn't interested.

Some girls giggled as I wrung out my hair, and a literal puddle of water fell to the floor. I laughed weakly and prayed class would pass quickly.

Professor Watkins strode in, appearing much more cheerful than usual. Giddy, in fact. There was a flush to her cheeks and some of her hair had fallen from its severe bun. I exchanged a smirk with the girl next to me.

"Class—" she clapped her hands and practically jumped in

the air. "We have a surprise guest today, here to talk about his incredible career. A star in our midst for sure."

Sparks burst in my chest, caused by both anticipation and dread. I mean, surely . . . it couldn't be.

"Please give a loud round of applause . . . for Lincoln Daniels!" She practically shrieked his name like a thirteen-year-old at a boy band concert.

And then there he was.

Smoldering gold eyes and a wild mane of golden hair. His aura hit me hard, like I was seeing him for the first time all over again. Everything about him emanated raw masculinity, seeping into my skin, and making me dizzy as I sat there. He was wearing a fitted black Henley that showed off his massive and ripped physique . . . and that stupid backwards hat that succeeded in making women all over the world go . . . well, stupid.

He was staring at me, a naked, hot yearning in his gaze that hit me . . . right between my thighs. He was turning me into a monster. A few weeks ago, the idea of sex or anything related to it was a topic I literally never thought about . . . unless someone was threatening me with it.

But now . . . "Hey guys, how's everyone doing tonight?" he drawled in that sexy rasp of his.

The girl next to me was literally melting in her seat, her breath coming out in gasps like she was about to orgasm right there.

I mean, I understood what she was feeling, but it didn't stop the jealousy from licking at my insides.

"For those of you who don't know me, I'm the starting forward for the—"

"The star starting forward," a guy breathed from the front row.

"Well, I—"

"Born in a private wing of the Arlington Memorial Hospital to billionaire moguls Anstad and Shannon Daniels, you were a star prodigy from the time you stepped on the ice at twelve. Signed by the Dallas Knights when you were fourteen, you went to Dartmouth College for hockey, where you led them to four National Championships before going to the NHL. You were rookie of the year your first year, and the last two, you've led the league in scoring," the guy continued, rapt awe in his voice.

"Well, that was creepy," Lincoln quipped, and the whole class roared with laughter.

"Will you marry me?" the girl next to me suddenly shouted.

"Class," Professor Watkins admonished, actually not looking that upset. Probably because she wanted to marry him, too.

"Easy, everyone," Lincoln held up his hands in front of him to quiet the room. "I told your professor that I would talk about the business side of hockey—and I'll get to that—but I need your help with something first."

"Anything!" someone else shouted, and the whole class laughed . . . including me.

"Well, you see, there's a girl in here I'm pretty crazy about, but she's told me to get lost."

The whole class started talking at once and I slid down in my seat, my ears feeling hot with embarrassment . . . not that anyone in the class knew who he was talking about—but I was sure that was coming.

Lincoln motioned for the class to quiet down.

I gripped the edges of my desk for support. I felt like I was about to slide into a puddle on the floor.

Lincoln's warm golden gaze slid over me, and I tried to make a discreet slice across my neck—for him to stop—but he just smirked at me lazily, the sight of it playful and hot . . . and annoying.

"So, I've decided I need to play a little hardball. I'm prepared to pay for everyone in this room's tuition for the whole year—if she agrees to go to my game on Friday, followed by dinner after."

My mouth dropped open in complete shock.

A year's worth of tuition.

I couldn't even imagine that kind of help. What it would mean to me and probably most of the people in the class. There was a single mom in the back with tears streaming down her face.

Bastard.

He was such an asshole.

A generous, gorgeous . . . ASSHOLE.

The girl next to me literally started shrieking, her hands on her cheeks as she rattled her desk with her exuberance.

"Alright—who's the girl?" someone asked, and everyone started looking around the room.

I slunk down further in my desk, but some of my classmates were already staring at me, Connor included.

Lincoln was really enjoying himself. His head was tilted slightly to the side and his sexy smirk had widened.

"It's Monroe—she's the only one fucking hot enough to date you," the guy who knew far too much about Lincoln quipped after one of the longest minutes of my life.

"Language!" Professor Watkins snapped, a small gleam of amusement in her gaze.

"I'll forget how creepy you are for guessing right," Lincoln laughed.

Then everyone's eyes were on me. Heat crept up my neck, spreading like wildfire across my skin. My pulse quickened, and I knew my face had flushed beet red. My hands trembled, and I clasped them tightly together to hide the shaking. It was as if the temperature in the room had skyrocketed, and I was trapped in a suffocating heat wave.

"You've got to be shitting me," the girl next to me snapped. "Why is this even a thing? I would do anything for that man. ANYTHING. I would literally let him fu—"

"Alright, that's enough, Lanie. Thank you," the professor quickly inserted.

"Well, Monroe, what's it going to be? Free tuition for the whole class for the year, or are you going to disappoint everyone?" drawled Lincoln.

The whole class burst into loud and emphatic chatter, everyone urging and yelling at me to say yes. Everyone except for Connor—but I already knew from our contrived date he came from a wealthy family, so a year's worth of tuition wouldn't have been a big deal to him.

I was going to kill Lincoln

I would probably end up kissing him first.

But then I was definitely going to kill him.

"I'll come to the game," I finally muttered when I was afraid the class would riot.

He leaned forward, putting a hand to his ear, his bicep pulling at his shirt. "Sorry, what was that?"

"I'll come to the game!" I snapped, crossing my arms in front of me.

"And the date?" the girl next to me—Lanie—said, sounding very put out.

I squeezed my eyes shut for a moment before opening them, momentarily riveted by the burning want in his gaze.

"And the date," I whispered after a moment, only half aware of the whole class jumping out of their seats and cheering.

I was completely lost in him.

Enraptured

Caught in his spell.

I was so fucked.

# CHAPTER 15

## MONROE

I was fucking late.

I hated being late.

And he'd even sent a car to take me to the game. Which was both thoughtful and infuriating, since I wouldn't have the need for a car if he wasn't forcing me to go to the game in the first place.

I'd been asked by Dr. Kevin to stay thirty minutes longer to fix files that *he* had messed up, which had led to me being late for the bus and missing it. Because of course it had been on time today for the first time since I'd come to Dallas.

The car had already been waiting outside when I got home, and I had to hurry and take a shower and get dressed, because there was no way I was showing up to Lincoln Daniels' game looking like the swamp rat that I resembled after running all the way home.

Now here I was, in a car that was so nice I was afraid to touch anything—late.

I thought about jumping out of the car at every stoplight. Running home and forgetting this whole stupid thing.

But of course, I stayed.

And it wasn't just because of his promise to pay for everyone's tuition.

It was because I knew he was special. Magical. A once-in-a-lifetime, or five-lifetimes, kind of moment.

There was the possibility that he could be the greatest thing that had ever happened to me.

And I didn't want to be the fool that walked away.

———

The game had already started when the driver got to the arena. He drove around the side, to a deserted-looking part of the building with more shadows than lights, which gave me a bit of a stranger danger vibe. Before I could freak out ridiculously, he stopped the car, got out, and opened my door, gesturing to the illuminated entry that had just appeared in front of us.

"Thank you," I murmured, a fluttering sensation building in my stomach, as if a thousand tiny wings were beating against the walls of my gut. The sensation grew stronger with every step toward the smiling woman standing in the doorway, like a swarm of butterflies were dancing within me, twirling and pirouetting, a kaleidoscope of color and movement. I took a deep breath and tried to calm myself.

But there was no calm to be found.

"Monroe, welcome to American Airlines Center. Mr. Daniels is so thrilled you've chosen to join us. I'm Ashley."

The words sounded so unlike the Lincoln I'd been getting to know, so much more polite than the roughed up alpha personality I associated with him.

But what did I know?

"Sorry I'm late," I responded lamely, but she just continued to smile at me in a weird, overenthusiastic way.

"No worries. Let's get you to your seat. We're only about ten minutes in."

The click of her heels echoed through the bright hallway she led me down, and I fidgeted with the jeans and white tanktop I'd thrown on, wondering if I'd misjudged the proper attire for a hockey game. She was dressed to the nines, her body accentuated by a tight pencil skirt that hugged her every curve. The smart blouse she wore was the color of fresh cherries, and it was tucked into the waistband of the skirt. As she walked, the fabric swished and rustled with each step.

"You'll love these seats," she told me once we'd gotten to a metal door, through which I could hear the faint din of a crowd. She opened the door and the din became a roar, motioning for me to walk down the tunnel in front of us. Right as I moved to walk, she held up a bag in her hand.

"I almost forgot. I have a jersey for you! Mr. Daniels was very insistent about that."

"Oh, okay," I said as she reached into the bag and pulled out a Knights jersey. Except . . .

"Is it supposed to have Ari Lancaster's name on the back?" I asked, a little confused.

Ashley burst into almost hysterical laughter, having to wipe a few tears from her eyes. "That's too good. He's going to freak," she finally breathed.

"So, I'm not supposed to wear it?"

"Oh no, you're definitely supposed to wear it," she squeaked out while continuing to chuckle.

Alright. I guess this was a joke you had to be in on.

I slipped on the jersey, and I couldn't help but admire how nice it was. In fact, it was the nicest freaking thing I'd ever worn.

We headed down the tunnel, towards the ice I could see at the end.

I stepped out of the tunnel, and a rush of sound hit me like a tidal wave. The crowd was a chorus of voices, each one clamoring to be heard above the others. The ice stretched out in front of me like a vast, frozen lake, shimmering under the bright lights. There was a chill against my cheeks, the air cold and crisp. The scent of popcorn, hot dogs, and beer filled my nose, making my mouth water. Colorful dots moved across the ice, the players' skates scraped and their sticks clacked as they played. It was a sensory overload, and my heart raced with excitement.

"Pretty cool, right? I fucking love my job," she giggled, leading me to seats that were in the second row, right across from the Knights bench.

"This is my seat?" I asked, a little awe in my voice.

"You must be doing something right."

I blushed a bit at the *heavy* insinuation in her voice . . . choosing to ignore it.

She didn't leave until I was settled in my seat, promising that someone would be by to take my food order in just a few minutes. I finally allowed myself to breathe a bit as she hustled away to do whatever it was she did for the Knights.

As I sat there, the energy of the crowd washed over me like a warm blanket. The stands were absolutely packed with fans, each one wearing the colors of their team and waving signs in support—most of them having to do with Lincoln. A Jumbotron displayed player stats, replays, and the occasional message from sponsors. An announcer's voice boomed through the speakers, adding to the frenzied atmosphere.

Players moved with lightning-fast speed, gliding across the ice and slamming into each other with thunderous force. I could hear the thud of the bodies hitting the boards and the crack of the sticks as they collided. The crowd roared with every move they made. The energy was palpable, and I felt myself getting swept up in the excitement of the game.

I scanned the ice, my eyes searching for Lincoln.

And then I saw him, gliding across the ice with a fluidity that was almost otherworldly. From the Internet search I'd done on him, I knew he was considered a phenom in the hockey world, and even with my limited knowledge of hockey, it was obvious why. He wore the number thirteen on his jersey—something pundits made a big deal about—and it seemed like every time he touched the puck, something incredible happened. He moved with such grace and precision that it was almost mesmerizing. I could see the concentration on his face as he weaved in and out of the opposing players, his stick deftly handling the puck. He was like a magician, performing impossible feats with ease. My heart rate sped up as I watched him, and awe trickled through me.

———

### Lincoln

I stepped onto the ice, feeling the familiar cold seeping through my skates and into my bones. It was game day, and I should have been fucking pumped. Instead, I was worried as shit.

Would she show up?

Had I done enough?

I'd left right after her class, leaving her alone except for sending a text with directions and arranging a car to pick her up, since I knew public transportation was unreliable as shit, and it drove me crazy that she used it to begin with.

I tried to shake off the feeling of unease as I joined my team for the pregame skate. My coach was yelling out orders and the other players were joking around, but I could hardly hear any of it. My mind was consumed with thoughts of her.

Every time I glanced up at her seat . . . she wasn't there.

The buzzer sounded, signaling the end of the warm-up. I took one last look up at the stands, hoping to catch a glimpse of her. But her seat was fuckin' empty. My heart sank like a fucking rock.

I tried to focus on the game, but my mind was gone. The clearheaded coolness that I'd made famous was nowhere to be found. This girl was driving me insane, somehow rearranging my cells into a creature I no longer recognized.

I was out of control right from the get-go, laughing madly when I was checked hard against the boards.

I needed the pain, anything to help erase this ache she'd created inside me.

And then . . . when the first period was halfway done . . .

There she was.

The most gorgeous thing I'd ever seen in a hockey jersey.

It was as if someone had shot me with a rush of adrenaline. The pumping thud of my heart echoed in my ears, drowning out the screams of the crowd.

I'd never been nervous playing hockey before.

Until now.

She was so dazzlingly beautiful.

My own dream girl.

I wanted to make her first time here perfect.

I wanted to make all her first times perfect.

*Down boy,* I cursed as my dick tried to make an appearance.

This game would go down in history. I'd make sure of that.

But it wouldn't be because I'd popped an erection getting thrown into the boards.

I chased down every loose puck, made every pass with fucking perfect precision, and shot every chance I got. The other team couldn't keep the fuck up.

In the second period, I scored a goal. And then another. And then another. I got a hat trick, but that wasn't enough for me. Not with my dream girl watching me. The crowd fuckin' roared as I neared five goals.

But the only person I gave a fuck about was her. I looked up at the stands and saw her on her feet, screaming her sexy heart out.

The energy in the arena grew more and more intense. It was electric, unlike anything I'd ever experienced.

Further proof that my girl was fucking magic.

The crowd was on their collective feet, screaming my name.

And as I scored my final goal, breaking the record for the youngest player to ever score five goals in a game . . . I pointed to Monroe.

The arena exploded the sound barrier.

But all I saw was her . . .

And the fact that she was fucking wearing Ari's fucking number on her back.

# CHAPTER 16

## MONROE

It happened so fast. One second Lincoln was scoring what seemed like his millionth goal of the night . . .

And the next, he was right in front of me, banging on the glass and seemingly pointing at my jersey.

The buzzer sounded, signaling the end of the game . . . and then Lincoln was sucker punching Ari Lancaster in the face, all while pointing to me . . . continuously.

The crowd around me was giving curious glares, so I innocently glanced around, trying to pretend like the scene had nothing to do with me.

Ari didn't seem perturbed by the blood dripping down his face. He was laughing as hysterically as Ashley had—about what, I had no idea. But the surreal night had taken a turn into weird town.

Speak of the devil. Ashley appeared next to me.

"Come with me before the crowd gets too crazy. They love when he gets into fights. It's going to be even more of a mad house since that performance just clinched a playoff spot."

"Hey, was Daniels pointing at you?" one girl asked as we walked to the exit.

"Ignore her," Ashley whispered, looking a little nervous as others peppered us with the same question.

I thought sneaking out was more suspicious than just saying no, but what did I know? I didn't have any experience with anyone being interested in me.

I followed Ashley through a door and down another hallway. This place was like a maze.

"So they clinched the playoffs with that win?"

"Yes," Ashley said dreamily. "Before Mr. Daniels got here, we hadn't made it to the playoffs in twenty years. Now we're basically a shoo-in, as long as he's on the ice." She stopped so abruptly I almost ran into her. She turned towards me, her face serious.

"It's my job to make sure he's happy, and he doesn't ever want to leave. Do you understand what I'm saying?"

"Ummm . . . no?"

She sighed, her friendly demeanor slipping for a second. "I'm saying that we can't afford anything that won't make him happy. Is that going to be a problem?"

Alright, I got that he was a big star, but this was getting ridiculous. I felt sorry for any girl who lived to make a man happy just because he was a celebrity.

"That's not my goal in life, no," I said stiffly, causing her features to scrunch up. For the first time tonight, she looked ugly.

Before she could say anything else, the door in front of us flew open, and a woman with her hair held up haphazardly with a pencil, tortoise shell glasses that framed big blue eyes, and Dallas sweats burst through. I immediately liked her.

"What's taking so long?" she snapped, peering over her glasses like she knew exactly what Ashley and I had been talking about. "Daniels is asking for her." Her tone gentled as she glanced at me. "Monroe, come with me."

I didn't bother saying goodbye to Ashley. She didn't seem to be in the mood for niceties at the moment.

"Ignore her," the new girl whispered as she held her hand over a clipboard for me to shake. "I'm all about not slut shaming, but that girl has a screw loose when it comes to these hockey boys. She believes in very *personal* service, if ya know what I mean . . . "

I'd gotten that vibe from her . . .

"Anyways . . . my name's Tenley," she said as we shook hands. "And I want you to know that despite whatever she was saying out there to you, Daniels is actually a good guy. And he's never done anything like what he's set up for you tonight. Not for anyone."

Hearing that she liked him, and that I wasn't the latest in a long line of girls to get the VIP treatment, *did* make me feel better . . .

Not that this had impressed me at all. Or that I cared about other girls.

Or, at least that's what I was telling myself.

Tenley chatted away as we walked down the hall. She stopped in front of a metal door. "Are you ready for this?" she asked.

"What do you mean? Ready for what?"

"It's always a bit of a circus around Daniels. I just didn't know how prepared you were for all of it."

Not prepared at all.

"What kind of circus?"

"I mean, with how good he is, and how good he looks, and who his dad is . . . it's a pretty lethal combination."

"Yeah," I whispered, remembering everything I had Googled about him before tonight.

What the fuck was I doing?

Tenley's eyes softened as she tilted her head slightly, a small frown forming on her lips. She held my gaze for a moment before giving me a gentle smile, wordlessly conveying her sympathy, like she knew something about what lay ahead that I did not. And then she opened the door, the scent of sweat and dampness hitting me like a wave. The musky odor permeated every corner of the room, mixing with the faint scent of Icy Hot and an odd splash of male cologne. My nose wrinkled as I took a deep breath, but I was immediately distracted from the smell by the sight of the locker room full of hockey players.

Half naked hockey players.

My cheeks blushed as two guys lounging around in nothing but their hockey pants whistled as I passed by, and Tenley shot them a middle finger.

"Behave. Daniels will kill you," she snapped.

"She's Linc's?" one of the guys muttered. "Lucky fucker."

She grabbed my arm and pulled me further, around a corner, and then . . .

There was Lincoln. Wearing nothing but a pair of tight gray briefs. I tried not to stare . . . I really did. But there was nothing I could do. All that smooth, golden skin. I'd never seen anything like it. His abs were like chiseled marble, each muscle perfectly defined, his chest broad and powerful. I found myself fixated on his shoulders, the way they moved as he pulled his pads out of his jersey, the flex of the tattoo inked across his skin. And then there was the one he'd given me a sneak peek of before . . . the butterfly.

A massive butterfly tattoo that spanned the expanse of his pectoral muscles. The butterfly was larger than life, its wings outstretched and seemingly ready to take flight.

The tattoo was rendered in stark black-and-white tones, a stunning piece of art. The detail in the tattoo was incredible, each individual vein and contour of the wings expertly rendered. It seemed to almost come to life, its delicate beauty standing out in stark contrast against his rugged physique.

A flush crept up my cheeks as my gaze danced across his

features, unable to tear my eyes away from the spectacle before me. It was as if the world had faded away, leaving only him and me in the room, and for a moment, nothing else mattered but the beauty of his body.

Finally, as if he'd sensed my presence, his gaze met mine. A jolt of electricity raced through my core as I stared into the pools of molten gold, blazing with a fiery intensity that was impossible to ignore.

The way he saw me. No one had ever seen me like that.

A shiver raced down my spine. I think I hated how he seemed to peel back every layer I'd built up across the many desperately hard years.

I didn't want him to see beyond the surface, beyond the mask that I wore.

It wasn't pretty.

"Hey, dream girl," he said lazily, his gaze licking at my skin . . . and it was all I could do not to melt into a puddle of want.

"Hi," I gulped out . . . because I was burning alive inside as I stared at pure perfection. He grinned knowingly, and I was almost blinded by the smile combined with the rest of him.

His gaze suddenly hardened as it centered on my jersey.

"Take it off," he snapped, all the smooth easiness of his voice completely gone.

"What?"

"Take it off, right fucking now."

"I'm—"

In what may go down as the smoothest move in the universe, the jersey was suddenly torn off me, and I was standing there in my white tank top.

"I could have been naked underneath that," I seethed, outraged as he held the jersey in between two fingers like it was tainted. The bastard just smirked.

Before he could say anything, the jersey was snapped from

his fingers, and a large, hard body was holding it against my chest, his hands right above my heaving breasts.

Lincoln's eyes took on a red haze as Ari Lancaster invaded all of my personal space.

"Get away from her," he seethed, a darkness in his voice that I hadn't imagined him capable of. In my interactions with Lincoln, whether in text or in person, he'd always seemed sunshiny, fitting his golden looks.

Right now, he seemed capable of murder.

I glanced at Ari to see how he was taking the threat evident in Lincoln's voice, but his lips were turned up in amusement and there was a twinkle in his gaze.

"What's wrong, Lincoln?" he teased. "Why are you taking away my gift to our girl?"

A giggle escaped me and Lincoln's face softened momentarily, as if my laugh was a gift he wanted to savor.

He hardened again as his gaze shifted back to Ari. "If you want to be able to hold a stick ever again, I suggest you let her fucking go."

"Which stick are we talking about?" Ari asked casually, his eyebrows going up and down like a cartoon villain. His hard body was still against mine, and I was feeling a bit lightheaded.

In a move that again felt practiced, I was ripped away from Ari's grip and plastered against Lincoln. A soft moan fell from my lips as I felt him harden against my stomach. The world faded around me as my hands involuntarily clutched at his shoulders.

"That's better," he murmured, his lips grazing mine so softly it could have been a brush of wind, if not for the shock wave it sent spiraling through my freaking soul.

"If you ever wear another man's jersey, I *will* kill that man. So be careful, sweetheart."

I searched his face for the punch line, because of course he was joking.

I just didn't find it.

All I saw was a stark coldness, that . . . was actually terrifying.

Arms were suddenly wrapped around the both of us, and Lincoln let out a soft sigh of annoyance.

"So, we're all partying together tonight, right? We made the playoffs, baby!"

"You knew we would," Lincoln told Ari, who obviously had no idea what personal space was.

"Still feels fucking good," Ari responded, holding a fist up. "Stanley Cup. Stanley Cup."

I had to admit, I'd missed this in my vision board. That I would find myself standing in a room full of half naked, perfect specimens of men as they all started chanting along with Ari.

Lincoln's hands tightened around my waist as he stared around the room, bemused.

Ari moved into us even more, his face so close to Lincoln's it would seem like they were kissing at the right angle. "Stanley Cup! Stanley Cup!"

Lincoln rolled his eyes at Ari's antics and then glanced down at me.

Although I was still confused and overwhelmed by the situation, the urge to join in suddenly came over me. Feeling playful —not an emotion I felt often—I found myself chanting right along with everyone else in the surreal world around me.

Lincoln's eyebrows lifted and his gaze heated, like the words "Stanley Cup" just did something when they came out of my mouth—and maybe they did—who knew what got famous hockey players off?

"Stanley Cup," he finally yelled, raising one fist in the air. "Fuck yeah!" The whole room went absolutely crazy, and I was jerked around as they all started piling on us.

I gasped at the amount of hands on my body, and that was enough for Lincoln to yank me out of the pile and wrap himself around me like he was trying to smother me in his scent.

"This is a weird day," I mused as we watched his teammates form some sort of super hot doggie pile.

He brushed a kiss across my shoulder, his hands going up and down my ribcage, in that space right under your breasts that makes your breath gasp because you wonder if he'll go any higher.

"This is the best day," Lincoln murmured as he brushed a kiss against my hammering pulse.

"You move really fast," I told him, my words coming out breathy and embarrassing.

"I just know what I want," he answered, absolute surety engraved in every syllable that came out of his mouth.

He turned me around in his arms, his hands never straying from the skin that had peeked through the band between my leggings and tank.

"I want to take you home, learn everything about you, but I probably need to make an appearance at the afterparty. Forgive me?"

A rush of disappointment hit me that the night was over. I felt a bit like Cinderella when the carriage turned back into a pumpkin. "Oh, yeah, of course. I can get an Uber . . . "

"What?" he asked quickly, his fingers pressing into my skin like he was trying to hold me here. "I meant *we* had to make an appearance . . . not that I would go by myself."

I blushed as his hands slipped from my waist to my hair. Suddenly, he was cradling my head tenderly. "I would put you in my pocket if I could, baby. Keep you with me always."

The force of his emotions were overwhelming, threatening to choke me, drown me, because I'd never felt anything like this before.

I yanked my gaze away. Everything was too much, but it ended up with him cradling my cheek.

I had the strange urge to cry, because no one had ever held me like that before.

Like I was priceless. Wanted.

Worthy.

"I'm going to throw some clothes on," Lincoln finally murmured gently, and I started because I realized we were standing there, me pressed against his body, lost in our own world. Half of the locker room had somehow cleared out in the moments we'd lost.

"Right." I cleared my throat, remembering just how little clothes he had on. His length was its own presence in the room, the top of it visible when I glanced down, peeking out from the band of his briefs.

Holy fuck, I think I had a mini orgasm staring down at the monster.

I tried to push away, but he held me there for a moment, his eyebrows furrowed, his lips pressed together, a mix of emotions playing across his face like he was torn about letting me go.

Finally, his hands left my face.

And I immediately missed them.

"Don't move," he ordered, turning away and grabbing a bag sitting at the bottom of the large locker. He set it down on the bench nearby and took out a pair of jeans and a plain white V-neck. A thin gold chain followed, and he'd somehow unlocked a new level of hotness I'd never seen before.

I had no idea that watching a man get dressed could be as delicious as watching them get undressed.

Or, maybe it was because he was staring at me, his gaze hot and lust-filled, like it was doing as much to him having my eyes on him as it was doing to me watching him.

"I can't take it," he finally groaned.

"What?" I whispered.

Before I could blink, I was backed against the wall and the

golden-haired god was on his knees. I pushed at his head, panicked as I stared around the room.

Except it was now completely empty. Like he had some kind of magic that bent the universe to do his will.

Everything inside of me screamed this was too fast. But my head fell back as his fingers rubbed over the seam of my leggings, somehow finding the sensitive, swollen flesh there that had been throbbing since I first saw him on the ice. His eyes tracked mine, a kind of madness there that perversely caused my mouth to water.

Pleasure built as I continued to let him touch me, and suddenly I was flying, soaring above a million shooting stars as he brought me to orgasm.

Again. Just like at the gala.

I was half drunk with love when I heard him roughly mutter, "Fuck this," and then my leggings were ripped and he was pushing my legs wider with a brutal strength that was impossible to resist.

Cool air brushed against my folds, and then his tongue was licking deep inside me. An insatiable invasion that was soaked with darkness and desire. He worshiped me, his tongue touching everywhere, pushing in and out as his rough fingers slid all over. I was soaking his face, the gleam of my slick all over his gorgeousness. His gaze stayed on me, his tongue and fingers swirling and pressing, and playing me like he knew my body better than I did.

My hips moved on their own, and he groaned, the sensual sound decadent and delicious . . . and I wanted more. My inner muscles squeezed as his tongue pushed deeply inside.

A rush that felt like it might kill me hit me all at once. I wanted him to stop staring at me like that, stop making me feel that way. Like I wouldn't recover if I never tasted this again.

I once read an article about heroin that said the reason it was so addictive and dangerous was all tied to that first hit. It made the body feel better than it ever could again. It took more and more each time to get even close to how you felt that first time, until finally you went so high you overdosed . . . still not touching that initial high.

A high you spent your whole life chasing, it said.

This felt like that.

My breath was coming out in gasps as I stared at the wide grin that spread across his face, his eyes crinkling in pleasure, like he'd been the one to come instead of me.

He slowly stood, his fingers gliding up my neck, into the roots of my hair as he gripped me, his lips crushing against mine. I'd never thought of how intimate it would feel to taste yourself on someone else's lips . . .

He pulled away from me, decadently licking his lips like he could read my mind and he was trying to keep every trace of me inside him.

We just stood there, our breaths intertwined.

And I was scared.

I closed my eyes because it was too much. It was squeezing my chest because I knew he was going to disappoint me.

He was going to break my heart.

I went along with it when he pulled my hands up over my head and slid another jersey down my body.

This time, of course, with his name.

The jersey was long enough to hide the fact that there was a fucking hole ripped in my leggings . . . but at least my underwear was still intact, since he'd pushed that to the side. Still, it felt awkward.

He finished getting dressed and then took my hand, like we'd been doing this our whole lives and my hand was never meant to be without his. He led me out of the locker room and into an elevator that took us to an underground parking garage. There were only a few cars left, but even if it was packed, there'd be no missing his pretty car parked in a prime spot just a few feet away from the elevator.

Once we got to it, he opened the door for me, a warm, gentle smile on his face that felt like too much, especially since I knew it was still coated with my wetness. "Get in, baby," he murmured as he brushed his lips against mine.

"Lincoln—" I started, not knowing what to say . . . but knowing I needed to say something.

"Just get in the car, baby," he repeated patiently, like he knew the words I didn't. "When something feels this fucking good, you don't fight it. You just follow it to the ends of the earth, no matter where it takes you."

"I'm scared," I admitted, and he nodded.

"I'll show you how good it can be. Until you're not scared anymore. Until trusting me is as easy as breathing."

I got in the car, but I didn't tell him, with what I'd been through in my life . . . sometimes breathing was the hardest part.

# CHAPTER 17

## MONROE

The party was at one of the rookie's places, a player named Angelo. It was apparently a rite of passage that the rookies got to have their homes trashed for the playoff party.

It was completely packed when the elevator door opened and we stepped into the apartment, the raucous sound of the party hitting me like a wall. My heart sank as I took in the wild scene around me, immediately feeling like a fish out of water in an unfamiliar world.

The air was thick with the smell of alcohol and sweat, the noise level so loud I'd have to shout to be heard. Everywhere I looked, people were drinking and dancing, lost in a frenzy of wild abandon that left me feeling more and more out of place with each passing moment. Everyone seemed like they'd stepped out of a magazine, beautiful and polished in ways I could only dream. Other than a few guys who were wearing jerseys, I was the only girl I could see with one on. All of the other girls were dolled up in dresses fit for a club. And here I was, with my crotch ripped out.

"I'm going to find the bathroom," I told Lincoln, stopping suddenly in the front entry.

"I'll come with you," he said immediately, his hand warm on my lower back, but I shook my head. I could see a line of women down the hallway, obviously waiting their turn for the bathroom. I only needed a minute. Just to get myself ready for this night, without his overwhelming energy fogging my brain.

"I'll be right in there. Don't try to leave," he warned, like he'd stop me if I tried.

"Alright," I said with a laugh at his joke, even though there was no sign he was joking.

I got in line as he moved further into the apartment. A loud cheer went up as people noticed who had arrived. The other girls stared past me as they looked eagerly down the hallway.

"Daniels is here," they whispered excitedly to each other, before then going into explicit detail about everything they wanted to do to his body. The fact that I was wearing a jersey with his name on it didn't seem to garner any attention.

It sounded like some of them had already had the pleasure of a night with him.

"I'll never have anything like it again," a girl further up the line sighed. "I'm literally ruined, and now he wants nothing to do with me. I would do anything for a repeat. Anything," she emphasized.

Another girl asked for details, and I tried to block my ears, because I didn't want to imagine him doing anything with anyone else. Not when his mouth was still covered in me, and there was an ache between my legs that missed his tongue.

It was finally my turn, and I hurried into the bathroom, surprised at how clean it was despite the massive amounts of people using it for this party. The whole time I was in there, I tried to bolster my defenses. This was fine. Everything was fine. I could do this. This was the part of life that I'd missed out on. Actually having a social life.

I stepped out of the bathroom and headed down the hall. The throng of people had grown, and it seemed like an almost impossible task to make it to the back where I could see Lincoln and Ari talking. The music was so loud that I couldn't think, couldn't breathe, and I felt myself becoming more and more uncomfortable with each passing second.

I waded through the masses, a blur of faces and bodies surrounding me, the chaotic energy of the party all encompassing. A few people gave me appraising stares as I pushed past, like this was an exclusive club and they knew I didn't belong. For the most part, though, everyone was doing their own thing.

I finally made it through the last row of people separating me from where Lincoln was holding court, and I stopped and watched him for a moment.

He was surrounded.

By a crowd of worshippers. Beautiful, barely dressed girls whose obvious only goal was to bag him or Ari.

My chest hurt to watch them.

They practically clawed at him, grabbing onto his shirt, brushing a piece of hair out of his face if he turned his head at all. Their eyes were glued to his mouth, like they were tempted to lunge and steal a kiss.

It was almost as if he was unaware they existed, though. He was lost in a conversation with Ari, his gaze flicking to the entrance every couple of seconds like he was watching for me to appear. But they didn't seem to care that he wasn't giving them a speck of his attention. They were fine just to bask in his golden glow, desperately hoping he would turn their way.

Is this what it would be like if I gave in? Would I simply be another one of these worshippers, waiting for him to give me the time of day? Would I always hover right outside his orbit, the muted moon to his shining sun?

I stood there watching as the girls clamored for his attention, the ultimate prize. The heat of their envy seeped into my skin, and a jealous rage twisted inside me. The depth of what I was feeling surprised me. It was as if every fiber of my being was screaming at me to stake my claim on him, even if I was just the girl that happened to be caught in his orbit right now.

*"Mama needs you to stay in this room, Monroe, okay? Don't come out under any circumstance. Mama's got to work," she said sharply, glancing anxiously behind her to where the noises of people laughing and talking and making weird sounds were coming from.*

*"Okay, Mama," I answered, staring at the opulent room around me. Mama usually didn't take me with her, but the next door neighbor that sometimes watched me had moved, and Mama had said this was too good of an opportunity to pass up—whatever that meant.*

*She closed the door behind me with one more warning, and I sat in front of the large television that Mama had turned on. It was a show I'd never seen before, and I sat there for hours, completely caught up with Minnie Mouse.*

*But a lot of hours passed, and my stomach was hurting. Mama had said she would bring me something to eat; we hadn't had any food since the day before, but she hadn't been back, not even once. And I was really, really hungry.*

*Maybe I could quietly sneak out and grab a snack in the kitchen before anyone saw me. That should be okay. This place was so fancy, they wouldn't even really miss it.*

*I slowly opened the door, peeking out into the muted light of the hallway. It wasn't as loud as it was before. But there was slower music playing, the kind that made me sort of sleepy.*

*I crept carefully down the hall until I got to the entry way that led to another hallway, where the music was louder. I made it halfway down before I came to an open door, and when I peeked inside . . .*

*There were women everywhere, their eyes funny and glazed looking, like after Mama took her medicine. They were all gathered around a few men dressed in suits. The men were lounging in fancy leather seats, but the women were kneeling on the floor around them. They were stroking the men's legs, their chests, pressing kisses to their necks. Some of the girls were even kissing each other. And the whole time the men ignored them, like they weren't even there, cigars in their hands as they chatted to each other like nothing was happening.*

*And then I saw Mama. She was leaning over one of the men, her head moving up and down over his lap, her hair covering her face. I was scared, a funny feeling in my stomach that had nothing to do with my hunger. I wanted to call out for her, beg her to take me home. But something told me I couldn't do that. And so I crept back to the room where she'd left me and cried until I fell asleep.*

*Mama didn't come to get me until the next day.*

A woman's loud laughter stirs me from my dark trip down memory lane.

Disgust suddenly clawed at my insides. I was walking down the same path as my mother. I'd end up exactly like her. A pawn for a man who'd throw me away.

I moved to leave, and then a firm hand grabbed hold of my arm.

"Get off me," I snapped, panic threaded through my voice as I tried to pull away.

"Monroe, hey, it's just me," said Lincoln, and I froze and glanced at his drawn features, concern thick in his gaze. His tone was low and gentle over the pounding bass, like he could read that I was on the cusp of running. "Are you okay, baby? Did someone do something?"

I shook my head, fighting the urge to cry. Something was wrong with me. This hurt inside me, this fear, it felt like too much. My skin felt stretched too tight. The room spun, the music and chatter turning into a deafening roar. My heart raced in my chest, my breaths coming in short, panicked gasps. I felt like I was drowning, suffocating in the sea of people around me.

I stumbled backward, as far as his grip would let me go, my head churning as I struggled to keep my balance. My legs felt like jelly, and my body trembled with fear and anxiety.

"Come on, sweetheart," Lincoln soothed, his voice gentle and reassuring as he scooped me into his arms.

I couldn't talk. My mouth felt dry, my throat thick and broken. I tried to take a deep breath, but it was like I was choking on air.

He led me away from the crowd, out onto a balcony, the cool night air washing over me like a balm.

"It's okay," he said, his voice soft and comforting. "Focus on your breaths. In and out, in and out."

I closed my eyes and tried to do what he'd said, but the panic refused to subside.

He started singing a song softly then, but it took me a few seconds to recognize the tune. It was "Creep" by Radiohead, a different choice of song for the moment to be sure.

At first, I was surprised, but as he continued to sing, I felt the panic that had been gripping me slowly dissipate. His voice was deep and soothing, and it seemed to wrap around me like a warm blanket.

He sang the lyrics softly, with feeling, a slight catch to his words like the song meant something to him that extended far beyond this moment. I felt a lump forming in my throat.

The sound of his voice washed over me, calming my nerves and easing my demons. For a moment, I forgot about all the reasons this would never work, why I couldn't even try, and I let it feel like it was just the two of us in our own little world.

When he finished the song, I looked up at him and saw a soft smile on his face. "Feeling better, dream girl?" he asked.

I gulped and nodded, even as a wave of embarrassment washed over me. He'd seen me at my most vulnerable, my most fragile state. My panic attack had stripped away any facade I'd been putting on, leaving me raw and exposed.

I could feel the heat rising to my cheeks as I tried to gather my thoughts and emotions.

But as I looked up at him, there was no judgment in his eyes, only concern. The arm that wasn't holding me against him gently brushed a strand of hair from my face.

"Thank you," I whispered, still feeling a little shaky.

"What was that about?" he murmured, his gaze flicking across my features in that intense way of his, like he was mapping out the freckles that dotted my nose as though they were constellations in the heavens he was desperate to record.

"Sometimes . . . it becomes too much," and he nodded, like he understood perfectly what it felt like to be destroyed from the inside out.

"Why that song?" I asked, wanting to push the attention away from me.

I watched as his expression changed, pain etching itself into every line of his face. It was like a veil had dropped over his eyes, blocking out everything around him as he was lost in his own thoughts.

I didn't know what had caused the sudden shift in his demeanor, but I could feel the sadness radiating off him in waves. It was like a heavy weight had settled over the room, suffocating us both.

He set me down gently and pulled away, turning towards the Dallas skyline stretched out before us.

For a moment, we stood there in silence, the weight of his sadness everywhere.

Eventually, he took a deep breath, and his gaze flickered back to me, the pain still visible in his eyes. He tried to smile, but it was a weak attempt, and it only made the sadness more apparent.

"Sorry," he finally chuckled darkly, the sound at odds with

everything else about him. "Here I was trying to make you feel better, and I'm fucking it all up."

I placed my hand on his, where it clutched the railing. His gaze widened in surprise, I guessed because I'd never initiated anything close to it. He stared at it, as if fascinated. I was one shade lighter than him, and it reminded me of the imagery I'd thought of earlier, of the sun and the moon.

"It was my older brother's favorite song," Lincoln said suddenly, his voice coming out halting and broken. "My father would beat the shit out of me growing up, and my brother wasn't old enough to stop him, so he'd sneak into my room at night and try to comfort me. He didn't know any lullabies, so he'd sing 'Creep' to me instead. And every time, it would calm me down." He shook his head, the small smile on his lips at odds with the pain in his eyes that seemed etched deep into his soul. "It was the first thing that came to me. I, uh, don't have a lot of experience with this sort of thing." He shrugged sheepishly.

"What sort of thing?" I asked, cocking my head.

"At feeling someone's sadness like it belonged to me, too."

I bit my lip, heat flooding my cheeks at the way he was so earnestly staring at me.

It was the craziest thing, but I could almost feel the unspoken words he was thinking in his head. Words that made me want to stay, and run . . . all at once.

"There you are," a flirty voice struck through the moment. I turned to see a stunning woman standing in the entryway to the balcony, her body draped in a formfitting lace black dress that left little to the imagination. Her hair was long and perfectly curled, cascading down her back in waves of golden silk. She smiled at Lincoln like they were old friends, and I could feel the heat of her gaze searing into my skin.

Her attention flicked away from me after only a moment, clearly not seeing me as a threat. As she stared at Lincoln like she was undressing him with her eyes, jealousy and insecurity raised their heads within me once again. Lincoln greeted her with a disinterested smile, and it was clear he knew her.

For a brief moment, I felt like an outsider in my own skin. I tried to push down the rising tide of emotion, but it was no use.

She took a step closer to Lincoln, her body language oozing with flirtatiousness. I could feel my walls going up, brick by brick, as I tried to protect myself from the pain that was sure to come. It was a familiar feeling, this fear of being replaced or forgotten. I took a deep breath, trying to center myself, but it was hard when the air was thick with the scent of sex and alcohol.

"I'm going to go," I murmured, pushing away from the railing and heading inside without another glance back.

# CHAPTER 18

## LINCOLN

**I** watched in a stupor for a moment as Monroe walked away. Again. I only had so much patience, and there would come a time—very soon—when I'd make sure she never tried to leave again. When she wouldn't even think about doing it.

Carolyn reached out her hand to touch me, but I jerked away and stalked Monroe, who was pushing through the crowd like her life depended on it.

"Lincoln," Carolyn breathed desperately behind me. Whoever invited that bitch to this party was going to be black-listed. I'd hooked up with her a few times over the years, until I learned how sharp her claws were when I overheard her destroying a young fan about her weight who'd been waiting to meet me outside the locker room—all because it was interfering with me taking Carolyn to dinner.

I forgot all about Carolyn when I saw someone spill their beer all over Monroe as she passed by. She stumbled, clearly frustrated and on the verge of tears. The crowd was thick and slow-moving, but I bulldozed my way through it, fueled by the need to reach her. They parted much easier for me than they did for her, and in just a few seconds, she was within reach. I grabbed her hand, pulling her close to me. She froze in my grip, her body tensing as I pulled her closer. Relief rushed through me when she didn't try to move away, at least not until we were in the elevator, and the doors hid the sight of the party raging out of control.

The second we were alone, she recoiled from me, retreating to the far corner. Her arms were folded tightly across her chest, and she was trembling. I hit the emergency button to stop the elevator and closed the distance between us, pressing her against the wall. She struggled against my hold, but I pinned her wrists above her head with one hand, the other one coming to rest lightly around her throat, my thumb tracing the rhythm of her fluttering pulse, the beat of it somehow soothing to me.

"What's wrong, dream girl?" I murmured as she glared at me with red-rimmed eyes that I wanted to drown in.

"What's wrong, Lincoln? Are you serious?" she spat, her voice thick with sarcasm . . . and a hint of despair. "I don't even know what we're doing right now. Why am I with you? Why did you bring me to this party? A room full of women desperate to have you, and you let them touch you. You let them have pieces of you, all while my cum was dried all over your face!"

A sob escaped her, and a sense of satisfaction washed over me. A small smirk pulled at my lips as she struggled against my grasp, but I couldn't help it. Her jealousy eased something inside me, a glimmer of hope that this consuming, relentless hunger I felt was reciprocated. It was a monster that had grown stronger with every passing moment, but maybe, just maybe, she could feel its claws digging into her skin as well.

I felt her stop struggling, and a tear trailed down her face. "I just met you and I already feel like I'm losing my mind," she whispered.

I tilted my head, studying her intently. "Well, at least I'm not alone then," I responded, before sliding my tongue up her cheek, capturing the salty droplet. I ached to claim every part of her, to make her mine in every way possible.

But for now, a tear would do.

She was absolutely silent on the drive back to her shithole apartment, if it could even be called that. I could feel her walls building up, a fortress she thought would protect her heart as I waged war on it. Somehow she hadn't realized yet that she was in a losing battle. I was already at the gates.

She'd already lost.

My dream girl got jealous tonight. And while it was hot as fuck . . . it also wouldn't do. All I wanted to do for Monroe was to make her happy, to claim her as mine.

With what I'd read about her past in the background check, it wasn't hard to guess that Monroe wasn't used to being wanted, wasn't used to someone putting her first.

I'd make sure she never had to worry about that again.

We pulled in front of her run-down building and she immediately tried to escape, sighing in frustration when she realized she couldn't figure out how to unlock the door—not noticing, of course, that I'd engaged the child lock for this exact situation with her. I suppressed a smirk, turned off the ignition, and stepped out of the car, taking my sweet time walking over to her. I hated the thought of being away from her for even a second.

Once I reached her side, I grabbed her hand and led her to her door, grimacing and scowling at the sight of her dilapidated apartment building. But her days at this place were numbered. A few more steps in my plan, and she'd be out of this dump permanently. At least I wouldn't have to worry about her tonight. I'd copied her key, and after she fell asleep . . . we'd be having a sleepover party.

Other people might call that scary stalker behavior.

I called it true love.

"Bye, Lincoln," she said between gritted teeth, her emerald eyes flashing with fury.

I chuckled and leaned down, my lips crushing hers, knowing there was nothing I could do to quash this ache inside of me that was desperate to own her body and soul. I was so addicted to this girl, it was impossible to think straight.

Which must be why I'd absolutely lost my mind.

"Bye, dream girl," I purred with a wink, my eyes trailing over her blushing cheeks, a reaction she couldn't hide even while pretending to hate me.

*I'll be back soon.*

----

An hour and a half passed before I found myself standing in front of her shithole apartment, key in hand. With a soft click, the lock gave way, and I stepped inside, the darkness enveloping me as I closed the door behind me. Her steady breathing filled the space, and I couldn't help but hover in the doorway for a moment, taking in the sight of her sleeping form.

I bet that bed fucking sucked, and I also bet I would get better sleep being next to her than I would anywhere else.

She had mentioned in one of our texts that she slept like the dead, and I was eager to put that to the test tonight.

I knew what I was doing was wrong, that I should resist the temptation, but I couldn't help myself. Once I succumbed, that was it. I could see myself doing it every night. Unable to stop. Hence why she needed to move in pronto. We'd both be better off in my bed.

It only took me a few steps to cross the room, and I was standing next to her. The moonlight streaming in from the window illuminated her sleeping form, casting her in a soft, ethereal glow. Her chest rose and fell in a steady rhythm, her breaths coming deep and even. Strands of her dark hair were splayed across the pillow, fanned out like a halo around her head. Her lips were slightly parted, a small sigh escaping them every now and then.

In the pale light, her skin looked like it was made of ivory, smooth and unblemished. She was a study in contrasts, with the darkness of her lashes against the paleness of her skin, and the wildness of her hair against the serenity of her expression. It was hard to look away from her, to resist the urge to reach out and touch her, to run a finger over the curve of her cheek.

Dark possessiveness crashed over me like a wave, wrapping around my insides and squeezing tight . . . choking me.

Mine. It was all I could think.

My cock was instantly rock hard, pressing against my fly so painfully, I was a little afraid I would pass out. It felt like if I didn't fuck her . . . or something . . . I would literally lose my mind.

I unbuttoned my jeans and quietly pulled the zipper down, breathing a little easier when there wasn't so much fucking pressure.

I stared down at my sleeping angel. I'd never experienced this kind of lust. The kind that barreled its way deep inside of you, haunting you every second. I gripped my cock with my hand, squeezing at the base because I was on the edge of coming just by fucking watching her. She sighed, and I could picture those plump, perfect lips wrapped around my throbbing length. I gave my cock one slow stroke, precum beading at the head. I thrust forward into my fist, imagining fucking her mouth, her eyes watering, her cheeks hollowing out as she sucked, my cum spilling down her chin.

Fuck.

I was coming, as hard as I had in the shower. I had to bite down on my lip to hold in my groan. The metallic tang of blood coated my tongue. I lapped it up, the pain helping to center me for at least a moment. I'd probably be hard again in a minute. It had been a problem since the first time I'd seen her picture.

I stared down at the mess I'd made of my fist. And then I glanced over to Monroe. A primal need to mark her overtook me, a force beyond my control. It crashed over me like a wave, a fierce and all-consuming hunger. Suddenly, I was someone else entirely, a stranger in my own skin, driven by a desperate craving to make her mine. With a slow, deliberate movement, I reached out and brushed my thumb along her full bottom lip, softly spreading my cum.

She didn't even stir.

It was a satisfying sight, watching her full lips glistening with my cum, knowing that when she woke in the morning, she'd taste nothing but me.

I watched her for another hour, resisting getting into bed with her. Finally I slid to the ground and leaned against the door. I'd doze for a couple of hours and then slip out before she woke up at six.

———

I stepped into the weight room, my mind already heavy with thoughts of her . . . and I'd just left her apartment. I needed this workout to focus on something else, even if only for a little while. Ari was already there, doing some bicep curls in front of the mirror. He shot me a cheeky grin when he saw me in the glass.

"Well, look who it is," he said, smirking.

"Shut the fuck up, asshole," I snorted, heading straight for the bench press. I added more weight than usual, needing the burn to distract me from her. I lifted it with ease, the metal groaning under the weight. Ari watched with amusement as I continued to push myself harder.

"So, I'm assuming you didn't get laid last night," he commented, but I ignored him.

I tried to get in the zone, focusing on the burn as I lifted the weights over and over again. Sweat dripped down my forehead and onto the mat beneath me as I pushed myself harder.

I thought the burn would be enough to distract me, but it wasn't working, either. All I could think about was her. Was she having a good day at work? Would she need anything?

Finally, I finished my set, letting the weight clatter back onto the rack. I sat up, panting and covered in sweat, not feeling better in the least.

I looked over at Ari, who was leaning against the wall with his arms crossed, a smirk on his face.

"What's with that look?" I drawled, setting the weight down and taking a swig of water. "Jealous of my form?"

Ari chuckled. "It's just a weird thing to see Lincoln Daniels gone for a girl."

I rolled my eyes, but of course he was right. He'd find it even weirder if he knew about everything else I'd been up to lately. "She's perfect. She's everything," I admitted.

Ari snorted. "This is going to be good. I hope she's giving you a hard time."

I sighed and wiped my face with a towel. "She's trying. It's not going very well for her," I shot back with a smirk.

Ari chuckled, shaking his head for a second before his tone softened. "Are you sure about this? She doesn't seem like the others, Linc. You might wreck this one when you're done. And that's saying something considering the pile of crazy, obsessed girls you've left all over."

"It won't be like the others. She's the one," I said firmly, lifting the dumbbell again for a second set, not wanting to think about puck bunnies and the problem she'd had with them last night.

His eyes widened. "Well, I'll be damned, boys. Lincoln Daniels is in love!" he shouted to the rest of the team scattered around the weight room.

I held up a middle finger as their taunts and cheers exploded in the air.

I finished my last set, sweat dripping down my face, and I caught Ari's eye again. He was grinning wider now, clearly enjoying my torment. He was waiting for me to object. Because that was something we both didn't do. We didn't catch feelings. Ever.

But I didn't try to deny it. Because he wasn't wrong.

I was in love.

# CHAPTER 19

## MONROE

I was sitting behind the reception desk at the doctor's office, trying to focus on my work, but my mind kept wandering back to the bouquet of two dozen black roses on the counter in front of me. They were from Lincoln, delivered thirty minutes after I started for the day, and I couldn't help but feel a little giddy at the sight of them. Black was an interesting choice, but somehow, it fit. This thing between us. It felt far darker and more intense than a plain red rose.

Also, I really wanted a look at the background check he had on me, because he seemed to know everything about me at this point. I definitely had not given him the name and address of the office I worked at.

My thoughts were interrupted when Dr. Kevin walked in. He took one glance at the flowers and then at me, a knowing smirk on his face. I could practically feel the heat rising in my cheeks.

"Those are pretty," he said, his eyes lingering on me for a beat too long.

"Yeah, they are," I responded, trying to keep my voice steady. "They're from a friend."

"A friend, huh?" He leaned against the counter, his gaze still fixed on me. "Seems like more than a friend to me."

I tried to ignore the knot in my stomach as I shifted in my seat, desperate for some space between us. "Hmm," I finally said, hoping to put an end to the conversation.

But, of course he wasn't deterred. "You know, Monroe, I didn't take you for a flower kind of girl, but I'll try anything once."

My skin crawled at the implication behind his words. What was it about him that made me feel so gross?

"Not going to happen," I finally said, my voice barely above a whisper.

He snorted, like I'd told a funny joke, and then he lingered for a moment longer before finally turning to head back down the hall, leaving me slightly shaken and out of sorts.

The flowers from Lincoln suddenly didn't seem quite as magical as they did before. I picked up the heavy vase they'd been delivered in and put them around the corner, so no one would associate them with me if they walked in.

———

Darkness was creeping over campus, the light of day slowly fading. We'd just been given a new assignment that was due by next class period, and I was trying to plot out how I would fit it in when I realized someone was walking way too close.

The last thing I needed was Connor sidling up like he was trying to glue himself to me. But there he was, invading my personal space without a care in the world.

"Hey Monroe," he chirped, as if I hadn't shut him down countless times since our disastrous "study session."

I let out a weary sigh. "What do you want, Connor?"

His grin faltered for a moment, but then he rallied. "I was

thinking we could try that place again. Actually eat the steak *together* this time."

"I'm busy," I said flatly, trying to edge away from him.

But he wasn't deterred. He caught up to me in a few quick strides, his hand landing on my lower back. I flinched away from the unwanted touch, my nerves on edge.

"Connor—" I began, until a familiar form appeared out of the shadows.

Lincoln.

He stood tall, his broad shoulders taking up space, and his jaw clenched as he stared the guy down.

"Hey, dream girl," he rasped, a faint growl in his voice that sent shivers down my spine.

I quickly pulled away from Connor, wondering how this golden boy in front of me felt more like home every time I saw him.

"Ready to go?" Lincoln asked, eating up the remaining distance between us and gathering me into his arms.

We didn't have plans. I'd shot him a thank you text during my lunch break for the roses and he hadn't said anything about picking me up.

But here we were, and I had no desire to say no.

"Yep," I said in a too bright voice, and his gaze heated.

"Good girl," he muttered, instantly drenching my panties. What was it about those words that universally ruined panties?

His gaze lifted, and he stared at something—or should I say someone—behind me. "Why don't you introduce me to your friend before we leave?"

The comment seemed innocent enough, but there was an underlying tendril of madness that told me maybe that wasn't such a good idea.

But hell, if having a superstar NHL hockey player as my date wouldn't finally clue Connor in that I wasn't interested, I wasn't sure that anything else would.

"This is Connor," I said as Lincoln released me, turning me around to face Connor and wrapping his arm tightly around my waist so I was pulled in close to his side.

Connor stood a few feet away from Lincoln and me, his eyes dark and angry as he stared at us. I felt Lincoln's breath on my neck as he planted a soft kiss there, my insides sparking at the touch like the Fourth of July.

Connor's jaw was tight, and his hands were balled into fists at his sides.

Lincoln, seemingly oblivious to Connor's discomfort, continued to kiss my neck, his hold on me tightening.

"Nice to meet you, Connor," Lincoln finally grinned, a clear taunt in his voice. "I remember you from my . . . presentation the other day."

Connor didn't respond, but I could see the tension in his body, his jealousy and anger radiating off him in waves. He opened his mouth, but then snapped it closed and shook his head. Without another word, Connor turned and stormed away, leaving us alone on the sidewalk.

Lincoln stared after him, something in his gaze that I couldn't read. After a long moment, he finally glanced down at me and smiled, scattering away any thoughts that weren't about him.

As I looked up at him, my breath hitched in my throat. He was dressed casually in a simple light blue T-shirt and black jeans, but somehow, he made them look better than any designer suit. His golden locks were artfully tousled, and his honey-colored eyes were glowing under the light. Even his tan skin looked like it was lit from within, as if the sun couldn't resist kissing him.

I couldn't shake off the feeling of being overwhelmed by his beauty. It was almost unfair how effortlessly attractive he was. His tattooed hand came up and brushed some hair out of my face, and I softened against him.

"Thanks," I said finally, scrunching my nose at him and wishing I was dressed better, or at least had bothered to wear my hair down today.

Lincoln's voice was low and smooth as he asked, "Does he bother you often?"

I shook my head in response. "Not really. He's just persistent, and he gets a little too close for comfort sometimes."

Lincoln's grip on me tightened at my words, like he was tempted to steal me away at that admission. His hand slid into my hair and grasped my head possessively. "Tell me if he does it again. I don't want anyone bothering my girl," he growled, his fingers massaging my scalp as I relaxed into his touch. It was hard to remember that I barely knew him as his words skittered across my insides.

"Let me feed you," he murmured, brushing his lips against my skin.

"I really need to do some homework," I objected half-heartedly as his fingers continued to persuade me.

The thought of dinner that wasn't packaged ramen sounded so good, though.

"You can work on your homework after dinner. I've got to review some tape before the game tomorrow anyway," he cajoled. My eyes flew open, and I bit my lip. His gaze tracked the movement, his tongue licking along his bottom lip seductively.

I thought for a second, before hesitantly nodding.

That golden grin of his lit up the air as his lips pressed against mine in response, soft and warm as he angled my head right where he wanted it. His kiss was gentle, but with a hint of something more, something that licked at my insides. I melted into him, my fingers tangling in his hair, as I kissed him back with everything I had. The world around us faded away, leaving the two of us lost in the moment, lost in the feeling of our lips moving together.

"Is that Lincoln Daniels?" a girl suddenly squealed in disbelief nearby. Lincoln's kiss hardened before he reluctantly moved away. My chest was heaving as I stared up at him.

"Let's get going before more people notice us. I don't want to share you with anyone," he said, leading me down the sidewalk to the parking lot.

I scoffed. "They'd be part of *your* fan club," I reminded him. "It would be more like me sharing you."

"Mmmh, you haven't realized quite yet just how perfect you are, dream girl."

My cheeks flushed, and I didn't respond, spotting his car up ahead. Of course he would find a prime parking spot on the crowded campus. He was clearly gold touched in more ways than one.

My thoughts drifted to his brother then, though, remembering the defeat etched across his features when he'd talked about him. The things he'd said about his father beating him.

Maybe his gold touch had been well-earned.

Lincoln opened my door, helping me in and then actually buckling my seat belt for me.

I giggled and grinned at him, until he realized what he'd done. His cheeks flushed adorably.

"Love the sound of that, sweetheart."

I stared up at him. "When's the part where you turn into a monster?" I quipped. "Because you seem too perfect to be real at the moment."

Something flashed in his gaze, but he just winked and closed my door.

I thought about the fact that he hadn't answered me for the entire drive.

---

It didn't occur to me until we were pulling into one of the fancy new skyscrapers downtown . . . that we'd be having dinner at Lincoln's place.

As we descended into the underground garage, my eyes widened at the sight of the gleaming, expensive vehicles parked in the stalls. There were sleek sports cars, luxurious sedans, and even a few motorcycles lined up along the walls. Lincoln expertly maneuvered his own car into a spot, the engine purring softly as he turned it off.

"That's a lot of pretty things," I commented, my eyes scanning the rows of vehicles.

"I have a problem when it comes to cars," Lincoln responded sheepishly.

My gaze widened as realization dawned on me. "Those are all yours?" I choked. For a second I'd forgotten he wasn't only a superstar athlete . . . there was also the whole hedge fund billionaire father thing going on.

"Let me know if you ever want to drive one," he offered, flashing a charming grin.

I gulped. "You can't offer to lend me your fancy car. We've talked about stranger danger before, I believe," I teased.

He leaned forward, an intense gleam in his gaze. "I've tasted your cum, baby," he said, his voice low and rough. "I've covered my face in your sweet pussy. We're way past the stranger phase."

With that, he got out of the car and came around to get me, seemingly unaware he'd left me drowning in a pool of lust, my thoughts tracing the way his tongue had pushed inside me and set my world on fire.

We stepped into the elevator, and Lincoln pressed the button for the penthouse. As we ascended, my heart suddenly raced with nerves. Was this real life? Any moment now, I would wake up, and I'd realize that all of this had been a dream, a romance novel my overactive brain had created just to torture me.

What did it say about me that I never wanted to wake up?

The doors opened, and I followed him into a stunning foyer —is that what the rich people called this type of room? The walls were a soft cream color, and the floor-to-ceiling windows overlooked the city. A plush gray couch sat against the wall in front of us, and there was a crystal chandelier hanging from the high ceiling.

I fidgeted with my worn Dallas Cowboys sweatshirt. I'd been exhausted after work and thrown it on, thinking I'd be comfortable for class, but obviously I would've tried a bit harder if I'd known Lincoln was in the plans for the night. This was the kind of place you were supposed to wear a ballgown every day.

"Want a tour?" he asked, smirking at my wide-eyed gaze.

"Yes, please," I quipped, not even bothering to hide my enthusiasm.

Grabbing my hand, we walked to our left. The kitchen in Lincoln's penthouse was a chef's dream. Its counters were made of gleaming marble, and the cabinets were sleek and modern, all in shades of white and gray. All of his appliances were top-of-the-line, including a six-burner gas stove, a massive fridge, and a built-in espresso machine. Hanging above the island was a trio of pendant lights, casting a warm glow over the space. The island itself was large enough to seat four people comfortably, with plush bar stools upholstered in soft leather.

"I think even *I* could learn to cook in a kitchen like this," I said, my tone a bit dreamy as my hand slid along the cool marble.

"I wish that was the case. I don't think I've used anything in here but the oven," he mused, his hand fiddling with my hair as he stared around the room absentmindedly.

"You have a fancy private chef, don't you?" I teased.

He stuck his tongue out at me. "I have a fancy housekeeper who happens to be the best chef in the world. So you'll never have to learn to cook if you don't want to."

He'd thrown that out so casually. Like we weren't on date

number two of this whole thing, and *just now* getting to know each other.

I wasn't going to think about the future like that. Not happening.

Although, staring around the room, I knew my little apartment would look even more sorry tonight.

My mother's face flashed in my head for a moment, the happiness she'd had when she thought she'd found a man who wanted to take care of her.

That memory was followed by her lying in a pool of her own vomit.

"Hey." Lincoln's voice broke through my thoughts. He tilted my chin up, and his honey gaze searched mine. "What were you thinking about?"

"Nothing important," I sighed, forcing a smile.

He stared at me persistently, as if the weight of his gaze could cause me to spill my dark thoughts.

And evidently, it could.

"Just the past sneaking in," I found myself admitting.

He nodded, as if once again he completely understood me, and then he grabbed my hand and led me out of the kitchen, down another hallway, and into the living room.

If I thought the kitchen was nice, Lincoln's living room was a masterpiece of sleek modern design, with polished marble floors. The furniture was all low-slung and contemporary, with plush cream-colored sofas and chairs arranged in intimate clusters around low glass coffee tables. Large, abstract paintings hung on the walls, splashes of color against the stark white backdrop.

In the center of the room stood a massive glass fireplace. Lincoln pressed a button in the wall and immediately there were flames dancing within. The room was a mecca for natural light from the floor-to-ceiling windows, offering breathtaking views of the city skyline. There were fancy art objects and sculptures here and there, each one obviously carefully curated to fit the room's aesthetic. The room even smelled good, like those high-end stores where you walked in and immediately believed they'd bottled the scent of wealth.

A space that made you feel both small and insignificant at the same time. It was a living room fit for a king. And clearly, Lincoln fit right in.

I mouthed a breathless "Wow" at him, and he chuckled, sweeping his hand through his hair, the movement causing his inked muscles to ripple seductively.

"It's a lot. I know. But I just let the designer do her thing."

"Rich people," I huffed, winking, so he knew I was kidding.

He led me through a maze of rooms, each more impressive than the last. The weight room was a sight to behold, with gleaming metal dumbbells and machines lining the walls, and a sauna nestled in one corner, steam rising from its wooden walls misting the glass door. His office was pristine, with not a single paper out of place, and the desk made of a rich, dark wood. The dining room was stunning, with a long, polished table and elegant chairs. And then, as if that wasn't enough, he ushered me into a fully equipped theater room. The walls were painted a deep navy blue, and plush leather seats were arranged in rows, facing a massive screen that took up almost the entire wall.

I was imagining myself watching "Wedding Crashers" in there when my stomach suddenly gave an extremely loud grumble. Lincoln's eyebrows shot up in amusement, and I felt my face flush with embarrassment.

"Let's finish the tour after I feed you," he said, lacing his fingers through mine and tugging me out of the room. I stared longingly behind me at the darkened screen. I was a big sucker for movies, and right now, I didn't even have a TV.

"My theater room is your theater room," he teased as we made it into the kitchen. He let me go and wandered to one of the drawers, opening it and rummaging through piles of takeout menus.

"What are you in the mood for, dream girl? Or should we order from a bunch of different places so you can figure out what you're craving?"

I gaped at him, my hunger spiking. I hadn't thought it possible, but him talking about ordering me lots of food had just upped his hotness factor even more. My mouth was watering as I stared at him.

He sauntered over to the counter nearest me, casually tossing at least six different menus on the marble surface. "Okay, multiple places it is," he drawled, his voice low and gravelly. "Do you want to look through the menus, or should I order some of my favorites for you to try?"

I watched as he sifted through the colorful menus, his eyes scanning each one with a practiced ease. "Your favorites sound good. I'm not picky," I said with a shrug. "When you live off ramen, pretty much anything tastes great."

His face darkened slightly, the shadows playing across his chiseled features. "Don't worry, baby," he murmured, his voice deep and rumbling. "We're going to fix that."

A shiver ran down my spine at the intensity in his gaze. I licked my lips nervously, suddenly aware of how close he was standing to me. "And I don't have any allergies," I added, trying to break the spell.

"I know," he replied, giving me a sly wink.

I was still on the fence about whether it was creepy that he knew so fucking much about me.

Lincoln ordered a bunch of items from various food delivery places, and then we walked out onto the balcony to wait. His view of the city was stunning, even better than the one I had seen at his teammate's party. The city lights twinkled, a constellation of glittering lights across the Texas sky, like stars that had descended to Earth.

This view could never get old.

"So how long have you known Ari?" I asked, hoping to find

out more about him. There was only so much you could learn from a Google search, after all.

He beamed, the topic obviously a good choice. "We were roommates in prep school during our freshman year, and we fucking *hated* each other. I thought he was a stupid fuckboy, and he thought I had a stick up my ass. We basically took turns torturing each other." His body shook with laughter, the mere memory of it evidently hilarious. "I once replaced his condoms with spicy joke ones I'd found on Amazon. He was balls deep in a girl when his dick started burning. He ran out of the room into the main hallway butt naked, screaming that his cock was about to fall off."

My laughter bubbled up, tears streaming down my cheeks as I wiped them away. Especially when he pulled out his phone and showed a picture of Ari from that day, standing in the hallway, his face scrunched up, a hand towel covering his bits. It was too damn funny.

"What made you guys change your mind about each other?" I finally asked, when I'd gained control of myself.

All signs of laughter were wiped away, the broken man I'd glimpsed briefly at the party standing there once again.

"My brother died, and the only one in my life who stepped up to make sure I didn't follow him . . . was Ari."

With that pronouncement, he left the balcony to get the food that had just arrived.

Lincoln was back to his normal self when I joined him in the kitchen, as though the weight of his words on the balcony had never happened.

I didn't press him on it. I knew better than most that gashes in the heart needed to be treated with care.

And I had no desire to reveal any of my own secrets—at least the ones he couldn't possibly know about.

Lincoln heaped a mountain of food onto a plate and slid it over to me.

"I love you," I breathed, my eyes locked onto the delicious feast in front of me . . . before realizing exactly what I'd just said.

I gaped at him in horror, and I shook my head frantically, trying to take my words back. But Lincoln's cocky grin only grew wider.

"I love the food, I meant! The food!"

"Knew you'd say it first, dream girl," he teased.

I groaned, wishing the ground would swallow me whole, but a second later, I was digging in . . . because, well, food. Duh.

He slipped onto the barstool beside where I was standing and patted his lap. "Come here," he murmured.

My face turned red as I brushed my hair out of my eyes, suddenly feeling self-conscious. "I can get my own seat," I protested.

He smiled slyly. "I'm aware. But *I'd* much rather be your seat."

I hesitated for a moment, but then his golden gaze drew me in again, and before I knew it, I found myself sliding onto his lap.

"Oh," I murmured, realizing he was . . . hard.

This was going to be an interesting dinner.

"Just ignore it," he said casually. "It's been an ongoing problem since meeting you."

I stuffed a bite of orange chicken into my mouth before I could say something else awkward.

———

Dinner had indeed been interesting. He'd insisted on feeding me for half the meal, and I didn't know what it said about me, but I'd fucking loved it. I bloomed under his attention, my pathetic self soaking up everything he offered like a flower under the sun.

Now, I was curled up on the comfiest couch I'd ever been on, in the fanciest room I'd ever seen, surrounded by books and notes, trying to work on my paper. But, I could feel his hot gaze on me constantly, making me squirm. It didn't help that Lincoln had changed into gray sweatpants, and I was feeling very . . . thirsty at that moment. The fabric hung low on his hips, and every time he shifted, those delicious abs of his made an appearance. Those sweatpants should be illegal, because he was making my growing addiction even worse. And my thoughts were definitely not on my English paper.

They were on the anaconda-sized dick outlined in his pants.

I sighed, grinning over at him. "You're distracting me."

He smirked, shaking his head. "You always distract me, dream girl," he replied, his eyes lingering on me a little longer than necessary.

I rolled my eyes, focusing back on my work. "What game is that from?" I asked a minute later, gesturing towards the recording playing on the TV when I realized he was *still* staring at me.

"Just some film from the last time we played Chicago," he answered. "They're the only team to beat us twice this year, and it's looking like they'll be up in the first round of the playoffs, so I'm trying to figure out everything we did wrong." He turned his attention back to the screen.

Thirty minutes passed, and I'd finally gotten in the zone of the assignment, when I felt Lincoln's gaze on me again.

I glanced over at him.

"What's your major?" he asked, sounding perturbed there was something about me he didn't know.

I bit my lip, trying to decide what to say. He watched me, his eyes soft as he waited for my answer.

I finally cleared my throat, suddenly feeling self-conscious under his scrutiny. "Umm, I don't really know yet."

His brows furrowed slightly. "What do you mean you don't know? You're a sophomore, right?"

I shrugged, feeling a little embarrassed. "I should be. But with how much I work, I haven't been able to take as many credits as I'm supposed to. I'm on the ten-year plan at this rate," I tried to joke, even though I hated that. "I'm hoping it magically comes to me about what major to choose. I've never really had the luxury of thinking about that kind of stuff before," I explained. "It was always just about getting through the day, surviving, you know?"

Lincoln nodded thoughtfully, his expression pensive. "Yeah, I can understand that. But now that you're here, with a chance to do whatever your heart desires . . . what do you want?"

I bit my lip, feeling a strange mix of emotions. I wasn't sure he really understood. As far as I knew, he'd grown up in a mansion, everything he could ever want at his beck and call. But I loved that he at least wasn't judging me for what I'd said.

I had never really allowed myself to dream or imagine a different life for myself. It was almost too scary to think about. But as I sat there, staring at the blank screen in front of me, I knew that I couldn't keep putting it off forever.

"I don't know," I admitted quietly. "I mean, I've always loved reading and writing, but I don't know if that's something I could actually do for a career. It just seems like such a far-off dream, you know? And I don't want to ever worry about having a roof over my head, or grocery shopping. I don't care about being rich, but I want to be secure."

As soon as the words came out, I was alarmed at how easily I'd said them. I'd always been guarded, but with him, it felt like the walls were crumbling down with barely any effort on his part. I found myself sharing things I'd never even admitted to myself before.

He just seemed so genuinely interested in everything that came out of my mouth. No one had ever looked at me and really wanted to see more.

He was casting a spell on me, wrapping himself around my heart. And it was both exhilarating and fucking terrifying.

Every second with him was making it harder and harder to resist.

Lincoln smiled reassuringly at me, reaching over to stroke my cheek gently. "Everything starts with a dream, baby. And now you have me to make sure it all happens."

I wanted to scream then, tell him to stop making promises that would devastate me after he decided he was done. But instead, I found myself smiling back at him, a warmth spreading through my chest that pulled on the residual cold my memories always kept around.

He was about to say something else when his phone buzzed on the couch next to me, interrupting our conversation. And when I glanced down, my heart sank at the sight of a woman's enormous breasts on the screen.

It took me a second to actually process what I was seeing, but Lincoln was already reaching for the phone, his lips pressed into a thin, tight line as his jaw clenched.

"What the hell?" he muttered under his breath, quickly deleting the picture and blocking the number it had come from, and setting his phone facedown on the couch. He peered up at me, his eyes dark with emotion. "That's not what you think. Sometimes people get ahold of my number . . . and I guess that's their play. I have to change my number all the fucking time." His voice was low and serious, his gaze pleading as he stared at me.

"So you didn't know her?" I pressed, hating how angry and jealous I sounded.

He smiled gently, once again seeming pleased by my raging emotions.

"Well, those were just her boobs, so I can't be sure, but no, I don't think those boobs belong to anyone I've ever met before."

He was trying to joke with me, but my green-eyed monster was out of control. I never would have expected this to be me.

I started gathering my stuff.

"Hey," he said, an edge of panic laced in his voice. "What are you doing?"

"It's getting late. I need to get back home. I have to work early and all that."

He sat for a second in silence, and I didn't dare look at him.

"You're really upset," he finally muttered, as if it was just sinking in.

I chewed on my lip, shame turning in my stomach with how

easily I'd let my jealousy take control. "I'm sorry. It's not like I have any claim on you or anything."

He tilted his head, his eyes searching my face. "Are you really saying that?"

I rolled my eyes, trying to cover my sudden nervousness. "Of course I am. This is our second date—if I should even be calling it that."

He leaned in, his voice dropping to a whisper. "Alright, this is going to fucking end right now."

My breath caught in my throat, and the tears were immediate. Fuck. How had this night gone so far out of control?

I stood up from the couch, but before I could go anywhere, he scooped me up, his strong arms enveloping me. I barely had time to process what was happening before we were walking down a hallway that wasn't part of the earlier tour, and into what was obviously his bedroom.

He threw me on the bed and I froze, breathless and unsure of what would happen next.

My heart was racing, my body trembling as I tried to process how we'd gotten here, with him standing before me like a dark and dangerous god.

I couldn't even look at him, my eyes darting everywhere but at his face. I was a mess of emotions, my thoughts jumbled and scattered like leaves in the wind.

But even in my confusion and fear, I couldn't ignore the way my body was responding to him. My skin was alive with electricity, my pulse racing with desire. He stood there, watching me with eyes that were more amber than honey at the moment, his intense gaze seeming to see everything. The heat of his stare was like a physical touch, and it made me want him even more.

For a moment, we just stayed like that, locked in a tense and charged silence. And then, without a word, he was on me, his lips claiming mine in a fierce and hungry kiss. All my fear and confusion melted away in an instant, replaced by a deep and aching need for him.

He suddenly ripped away from my lips, his chest heaving, his breath coming out in heavy gasps.

Lincoln took a step backwards until he was towering over me. He shook his head, his tattooed fingers raking through his tousled hair. Then his hand moved to the waistband of his sweatpants and he pulled it down, showcasing his hot, swollen, *gigantic* dick. His thick length was a dusky, silky expanse, textured by ridged veins. The gleaming head of his arousal was slick with his precum. It was a strange thought, because I'd never thought of dicks as attractive . . . but his was . . . beautiful.

What every woman was put on this earth to desperately crave.

Desire consumed me, a fierce ache that demanded to be sated. My center throbbed, slick and hungry, as I felt myself clenching in response.

I *needed* him.

"You think you don't have a claim on me?" he finally growled, breaking the sex-fueled silence. "You think it's possible for anyone else to exist now that I've found you?"

His tattooed hand slowly traveled his length, his thumb catching his arousal and bringing it to my mouth. I whimpered and parted my lips as he slid it inside, the salty taste my new favorite thing.

"Good girl," he breathed.

My tongue swirled around his thumb, making sure to get every drop, and he slowly withdrew it.

"Look at me," he ordered, and my eyes immediately snapped to his face. "No . . . look at me."

My gaze trailed down his toned body until it landed on his dick that extended all the way to his abdomen.

And it was then that I noticed the dark black cursive script etched on the pink skin, the outline of the letters an angry red color that bordered a new tattoo.

"What?" I murmured, leaning forward so I could read it.

MONROE.

His cock was tattooed with my name.

My gaze snapped up to his smug, perfect face.

"Pretty obvious you don't have anything to worry about, isn't it?"

"When did you—?" My words trailed off . . . because, really, what did you say about a dick tattoo of your name?

"The second I knew you were real," he commented casually. Like that was normal, everyday behavior.

"I—" I still couldn't find the words.

I traced the cursive letters with my gaze, emotion thick in my throat. It was like he had branded me as his own, claimed me in a way I'd never experienced before.

I was the girl who was never wanted, passed around like a burden from person to person, never feeling like I belonged anywhere. My mother hadn't even wanted me. But strangely, seeing my name permanently etched onto his skin—his cock of all things—it filled a void inside of me that had always ached, a void left by all the years of abandonment and rejection.

I was suddenly starving.

I reached out my hand tentatively.

"Fuck yes, touch me. I'm desperate for it." His voice was a pained, delicious growl, like gasoline on the fire that was already burning in my belly.

It was getting a little out of hand, the lust coursing through me. I was pretty sure I could come just from the sound of his voice at that point.

I leaned forward and worked my way down his stomach, placing light kisses and licks on every ripple of muscle. When I reached his sexy V, I lingered there, tracing his toned abs with my tongue.

He shivered under my touch, his breath coming out in sexy gasps.

I got to his impressive length, and I hesitated for a moment. I mean, the thing was massive, at least nine inches long. But the sight and scent of him had me so turned on, I couldn't resist. My fingers trailed along the length of his throbbing cock, tracing the veins that pulsed beneath his skin. I could feel the heat radiating off him, the slickness of his arousal coating my fingertips. Lincoln was watching me intently, his eyes dark with desire. I squeezed it gently, my fingers not even coming close to touching, and another rush of slickness trickled out of the slit.

I couldn't resist the urge to taste him any longer. He'd given me a sample before . . . and I wanted more. I leaned forward, letting my tongue flick out to touch the bead of moisture gathered at the tip of his cock. He groaned and thrust as I lapped at his crown. I'd always thought cum wouldn't taste good, but his . . . I had a feeling it would become a nonstop craving.

I'd also thought I would hate this kind of thing, that I would feel demeaned . . . inferior. Now that I was older, I had distinct images of walking in on my mother in the act, and it had never been good.

But this was different. Lincoln was different. I wanted to make him lose control, to take what he wanted from me. The power I felt from making him a panting mess was heady . . . addictive even. I wanted to reward him for his gift to me.

Because that's what his tattoo was . . . the best gift I'd ever been given.

He groaned, his head falling back as I explored him with my mouth. I took him deeper, my lips forming a tight seal around him as I sucked him carefully.

"Baby, just like that," he moaned.

His words gave me confidence to experiment, and I teased him with my tongue, causing him to moan and pant, begging for more. I found an angle that I could handle and took him as deep as I could.

"Fuck, yes, sweetheart," he praised as I sucked and pulled on him. "That's so good, baby. So good . . . please, don't stop."

His hands gripped the back of my head, not forcing but not gentle either, urging me to take all of him. I tried opening my throat to accommodate his thrusts, but I gagged around his length.

"Take it all, Monroe. Just a little more. Choke on my cock." His voice turned hard and demanding. I whimpered around his length, literally dripping wet between my legs from what we were doing.

"I want to fuck that perfect mouth. Will you let me, baby? Will you make me come?"

I moaned a response around his dick and he smoothed the hair back from my face.

With his guidance, I found a rhythm that had him on edge and my pussy flooding. He groaned and thrust in deeper, pushing at the back of my throat.

And with every stroke, I wanted him more.

His hand cupped my jaw, his thumb tracing the curve of my lower lip. My lips parted and I tasted him, savoring the saltiness of his skin. My tongue teased, swirling around the head of his cock. A low groan rattled from him.

Then his hand slid to the back of my head, holding me in place as he fed me even more of his cock. He continued sliding in, steady and deep, until he hit the back of my throat.

"Relax your throat, baby," he rasped softly. I took a deep breath and tried to relax as he pushed deeper, his cock sliding smoothly down. He groaned in pleasure, his head thrown back, his hands gripping my hair tightly as he held himself there.

"Fuck." I moaned, my eyes rolling back as he moved in and out of my mouth, each thrust growing more urgent. "Yes," I gasped, my tongue swirling around him. "More, please."

"You like that, don't you?" he growled, his fingers tightening in my hair. I whimpered in response, the intensity of the pleasure sending me spiraling towards the edge.

My hand moved to touch myself, needing to come.

He pulled back, his hand stopping me. "Not yet, baby," he said, a devilish gleam in his gaze.

He withdrew leisurely, then slid back in, his hand still gripping my hair. The motion of his thrusts turned into a smooth and steady rhythm, a gentle pumping that had me wanting more. I could sense his gaze locked on me as he pushed deeper, his hard length disappearing down my throat.

"That's just perfect. You're so damn good at this," he gasped.

A raw, desperate hunger took hold of me as he plunged into my mouth with a gentle ferocity. I wanted to be good at this for him. I wanted to give him everything. My fingers traveled up and down his flexing hips, firm thighs, and sculpted stomach, feeling the tremble of his muscles as he relentlessly pushed in. His pace quickened, a symphony of grunts and moans escaping his lips. The sight of him, lost in ecstasy, only fueled my desire.

"Fuck, you look so hot with my cock down your throat, dream girl," he said, his voice rough with pleasure.

My hands grasped his firm ass, feeling the muscles flexing under my fingers. I urged him to quicken his pace, moaning hungrily as I sucked on his cock, my breaths coming out in desperate gasps.

I whimpered as he tugged at my hair, his hand tightening almost painfully. I loved the way he dominated me, took over so I didn't have to think . . . I could lose myself in the feeling of him.

"Oh, fuck. Suck it. Suck my cock," he urged, his voice low and rough with pleasure.

My cries grew louder as he pulled harder at my hair, his grunts and moans filling the room as his thrusts became more forceful.

"Fuck, you are perfect, aren't you? You really love this. You love me fucking your mouth. You're such a good fucking girl." His movements faltered for a moment, his grip on my hair tightening as he lost himself in the pleasure. I didn't get a warning before his hot seed burst into my mouth, and I swallowed as much as I could, savoring the taste of him. It spilled past my lips and onto my chin and chest. He leaned down, kissing me deeply, his tongue exploring my mouth, not giving a fuck that he was tasting himself. His thumb smeared his cum all over my skin.

"Hottest fucking thing. Ever," he whispered, his breath hot against my lips.

---

### Lincoln

I chased the taste of myself on her lips, not because I liked it, but because it meant she had a part of me inside her. She *owned* a part of me I could never get back. I wanted her to have whatever she wanted from me.

I also wanted her screaming with soul-rendering pleasure. To scream my name to the heavens because I owned a part of her, too.

"You taste so good," she murmured, her eyes dreamy and unfocused.

I started to harden again . . . because she was covered in me, her lips swollen and wet.

I knew it would be like this with her. This all-encompassing madness that grew with every touch. I knew I was staring at her like a man possessed.

But I couldn't help it.

I pulled her leggings down and my fingers immediately began to play, running through her sopping wet folds.

She cried out softly, her gaze pleading and desperate.

I wanted to fuck her. I wanted to push inside her and never leave.

But I knew she wasn't there yet.

My tattoo may have helped her trust issues, but she was still on the cusp of running the moment she got spooked again. "You're such a good girl, Monroe. I'm gonna make you come now. Make you feel as good as you made me," I murmured.

"Linc," she whispered as I glided my fingers across her clit and gently pressed into her tight pussy. She whimpered, her eyes fluttering closed. My girl loved praise, needed it in fact, desperately.

"Look at me," I snapped, desperate for that emerald gaze to stay on me, for her to understand that I was the only one who could ever make her feel this good. Her gaze locked onto mine, her clear, starry eyes radiating a soft, mesmerized glow that sent electric currents down my spine.

I almost had her. She may not have loved me yet, but she was already addicted to what I could make her feel.

I felt drunk under her attention. I wanted her to obsess over me, to think about me every second. Like I did her. Her lustrous ebony locks framed her delicate features, and she looked like a dark angel, sent from below to drag me down with her. My lips crashed against hers and I sucked on her tongue, pressing two more fingers inside of her as she writhed against me.

And then she came, her tight pussy choking my fingers.

Her cheeks took on a rosy glow.

"Good girl," I murmured, watching as her whole body melted, like I'd discovered the secret password to her soul.

I cleaned up after that, because while death by blowjob sounded like a good way to go, I wasn't interested in a raging infection in my dick thanks to an infected tattoo. I was pretty sure I was supposed to have waited at least three more weeks before . . . activity.

Oh, well.

When I returned to the bed, I cradled her against me, my hands tracing the perfect lines of her body, wishing I could freeze the moment, keep her with me like this. Forever.

Eventually, her breaths evened, and she fell asleep.

And I stayed up all night, not wanting to miss a second of the first time she ever slept in my bed.

# CHAPTER 21

## MONROE

I opened my eyes slowly, taking in my surroundings. The morning light was filtering in through the windows, casting the room in a soft glow.

I'd slept over.

I was in Lincoln's bed.

And I'd slept through the night . . . peacefully.

That was a first.

I glanced around, my eyes taking in the details of the room.

The walls were painted a dark gray, giving the room a cozy, intimate feel. The bed was a massive, king-size affair, covered in soft, plush blankets and pillows, sheets white and crisp. I couldn't help but blush as I remembered the events of the night before.

The room was decorated with dark wood furniture, all of it masculine and sophisticated. A large, flat-screen TV hung on the wall opposite the bed, surrounded by various sports memorabilia. I noticed a door to the left of the bed, leading to an en suite bathroom.

I rolled over and buried my face in his pillow, breathing in the faint scent of his cologne, trying to calm down.

Suddenly, it hit me again.

I was in Lincoln's bed.

And the sun was definitely higher than it usually was when I woke up.

I was late for work.

I sprung out of bed, glancing around the room desperately for the leggings I'd had on last night. I finally found them folded neatly on a chair. After throwing them on, I ran into the bathroom to splash some water on my face.

Fuck. Everyone would know what I'd been up to last night. There were marks peppered all over my skin, my hair resembled a bird's nest, and . . . I was radiating. Like Lincoln had given me some of his golden glow.

Interesting.

I rushed into the hallway to find Lincoln and hopefully get a ride to my place to grab some different clothes. The place was enormous, and I took several wrong turns before I finally spotted him in the open kitchen, with his bare back facing me. It was ridiculous how defined and sculpted his muscles were, like God had spent way more time on him than everyone else.

Fuck, he was beautiful.

Sadly, the kitchen island was blocking my view of his lower half. But obviously, I knew it was just as delicious.

I realized then that he was flipping pancakes, and they smelled mouthwatering. Evidently, he wasn't as bad in the kitchen as he claimed.

I must have made a noise because his attention turned to me, his gaze quickly heating as his eyes roamed over my body, getting caught on the marks on my neck and the tangled mess that was my hair.

Heat crept up my neck, and I suddenly felt shy. He smiled knowingly, the kind of grin that could only come after someone sucked your dick.

"I was going to bring you breakfast in bed," he purred,

gesturing to the table piled high with enough pancakes, bacon, and eggs to feed an army.

"I thought you didn't cook," I reminded him, lifting an eyebrow.

"Mrs. Bentley prepared all this. I'm just heating up the batter," he admitted bashfully, turning back to the pan. "But I've only burned three of them so far. So you should go hop back into bed and I'll be there in a minute with your feast."

"I can't stay," I said reluctantly, feeling guilty for ruining his plan. "I'm already late for work."

He turned, his lips pursed, something that looked an awful lot like frustration flashing in his gaze.

"Come on, Monroe," he said, his voice low and persuasive. "You work so hard. Take the day off, just this once. We can spend the day together, do something fun."

I shook my head. "I can't just call in sick, Lincoln. I need the money for rent. Literally, every paycheck counts right now," I explained haltingly, feeling beyond embarrassed admitting that to someone who had never worried about money before in his life.

He seemed to realize his mistake and set the spatula down, coming over and brushing a kiss across my lips. "I'm sorry, baby. I didn't mean to pressure you. I just want to spend time with you. And I feel bad you're always working so hard."

Hysterical laughter bubbled up inside of me, and I swallowed it down. I wanted to spend time with him, too, but I couldn't afford to lose a day's pay. "I have to go," I told him firmly, freaking out more when I glanced over at the clock and saw that my shift had started twenty minutes ago. I was so fucked.

"Of course," he said easily, his eyes softening. "We'll go right now."

Lincoln pulled up in front of my apartment and walked me inside. I didn't have time to take a shower, so I just threw on some clean clothes and tamed my hair into a sleek bun.

Lincoln never took his eyes off me. His mood seemed to grow stormier with every passing second.

"Like that you'll smell like me all day, baby," he murmured, burying his face in my neck when I tried to pass by.

When we got to the doctor's office, Lincoln parked and trailed behind me.

"I'll see you later," I told him, trying to hurry inside, but Lincoln laced his fingers through mine before I could escape and followed me into the office. "You don't have to come in. I'm good."

He brushed a kiss across my forehead. "Just want to make sure you don't get in trouble for being late."

I snickered. "Going to use your celebrity status?"

"Something like that," he smirked, clearly amused.

As we walked into the doctor's office, I noticed Dr. Kevin was already there . . . which was odd, since I didn't think he'd ever rolled into work before ten since I'd started here. His eyes widened briefly when he saw Lincoln, and his gaze flicked to the black flowers I'd been sent yesterday. Someone had moved them back to my station. I shifted, slightly embarrassed. I'd always kept my personal life separate from work . . . not that I'd ever had a real personal life before. And this was throwing everything in the mixing bowl at once.

"You're late," Dr. Kevin said coolly, his gaze studying me with a critical eye. It was too warm today to get away with wearing a scarf or something else that would hide the marks on my neck . . . and he was definitely noticing them.

I opened my mouth to apologize, but before I could say anything, Lincoln stepped in.

"We lost track of time," he said smoothly, his hand possessively on my waist, his voice laced with an insinuation that made me flush, but also didn't help the situation at all. I'm sure that was what every employer loved to hear—that their employee couldn't be bothered to come into work on time because they were in the bedroom.

I glared at him, silently urging him to stop making things worse, but he just grinned and kissed me deeply, as if to prove his point. As soon as his lips touched mine, my heart started racing. His mouth was hot and electrifying, and I melted into his kiss, forgetting for a moment that we were in the middle of a doctor's office . . . in front of one of my bosses. He licked into my mouth, and I tasted the sweet hint of maple syrup on his lips, from the pancakes he must have "sampled" while he was cooking. I found myself wrapping my arms around his neck, pulling him closer . . . the heat between us intensified. The world around us disappeared, and I got lost in him.

Again.

A throat cleared and I startled, wanting to melt into the floor when I realized what I'd just done.

Lincoln's lips curled up at the corners, revealing a smug expression. His eyes danced with amusement as he stared down at me, and I could tell he was thoroughly enjoying himself . . . and very proud of the way he'd made me lose control. He brushed his lips once more against mine before winking at me and walking away without another word, whistling a tune under his breath.

Dr. Kevin's expression darkened as Lincoln disappeared from sight, and he snapped at me to get to work. "You're on thin ice," he warned before storming off.

A knot formed in my stomach as I headed to my desk. Dr. Kevin's comment was a clear threat, and I knew I couldn't afford to mess up again. I couldn't lose this job.

But as I started to organize some paperwork . . . I also couldn't help but think . . .

Last night had been worth it.

———

*Lincoln*

Her boss would be a problem. That needed to be dealt with soon. Adding it to the never-ending list in my head of things that needed to be fixed, I texted my assistant, Pete, to make sure he sent lunch to Monroe. She'd refused to eat this morning in her rush to get to her job, and I wanted to make sure she got something to eat.

> P: What should I order her?

I needed to make my assistant a list of all her favorite foods. Pronto.

> Steak tacos . . . and queso. Lots of queso. And a Diet Dr. Pepper.

> P: Got it. Two things of queso.

> Make that three.

I started the car and drove away from her building. I guess I'd go to practice after all. With playoffs right around the corner, it probably wasn't the best idea to be skipping practice, anyway. I would've done it, though, if Monroe had agreed to spend the day with me. I couldn't help but want to spend every moment convincing her she was mine.

I pulled into the practice facility parking lot, and double-checked my phone for the millionth time, making sure that Monroe was, in fact, still at the office. There was a text waiting for me.

> Dream Girl: So I guess I confirmed last night, you indeed do not have wrinkly old man balls.

I snorted and shook my head, willing myself not to get hard

thinking about what she was referring to, since last night had, in fact, been the hottest night of my life.

> I'm not sure. Should we double check again? Tonight?

The three dots by her name lasted at least a minute, and I could picture her sitting at the front desk, cheeks flushed, trying to decide what to say to that.

> Dream Girl: Can't wait.

I groaned and adjusted myself before hopping out of the car. Practice was officially going to be an uncomfortable one.

# CHAPTER 22
## LINCOLN

I was in the middle of practice, skating back and forth on the ice with my teammates. The sound of our skates scraping against the ice echoed through the rink as we worked through some drills. We'd been practicing our passes and shots for more than an hour and my muscles were starting to burn.

Coach finally whistled that it was time for a break, and I skated towards the bench to get some water. I'd just sat down when my phone buzzed next to me. I usually left it in my locker during practice, but I'd wanted to make sure I didn't miss anything from Monroe.

My insides clenched when I saw that the text was, in fact, not from Monroe. It was from my father, demanding I be at the "fucking house" by five for dinner.

I let out a frustrated sigh and slammed my phone onto the bench, causing it to vibrate and catch the attention of Ari, who'd plopped himself next to me.

"Lincoln?"

I shook my head, but, of course, the nosy bastard picked up the phone and read the message himself. His jaw clenched, and he shook his head in disgust. "Why do you put up with that?" he finally asked, looking at me with concern in his eyes.

I sighed, not wanting to talk about it. We'd had this same conversation a million times . . . and he never understood. But Ari leaned closer, his voice low. "Lincoln, when are you going to stop letting him hang—"

I cut him off with a shove, not wanting to hear my brother's name. "Shut up, Ari," I growled.

"Fine," Ari snapped, jumping off the bench and skating out onto the ice.

We continued our practice, but I was sloppy, rage and frustration muddling my movements.

"Hey, Lincoln, did you forget how to skate?" shouted Dalton, grinning when a rut in the ice almost took me down.

I rolled my eyes, trying to calm down.

I was about to take a shot when Ari's body slammed into mine. It was a hard check, and it sent me flying across the ice.

As I got back up, I saw Ari skating towards me, his fists clenched and his face contorted with anger. I knew what was coming next, and I braced myself for impact. We collided, and suddenly we were both throwing punches, trading blows as we circled each other.

I was faintly aware of shouting and lots of whistling, but my adrenaline was pumping too hard to stop as I landed a punch on Ari's jaw. He stumbled back, but quickly regained his footing and retaliated with a punch of his own. We were both breathing heavily now, our faces red with exertion and anger.

"What the fuck is wrong with you?" Ari yelled as my shoulder barreled into his stomach, taking us both down.

The coaches were on us a second later, yelling and pulling us apart as we struggled to keep fighting. Disgust with myself was coursing through my veins as I glared at Ari, still itching for a fight. But the coaches were too determined, and soon enough, we were dragged apart, our jerseys ripped and sweat dripping down our faces.

"Get to the locker room, both of you! You're done for the day!" Coach yelled at us, his voice booming across the rink.

I glanced back at Ari, still angry, but the coaches were pushing us towards the door. As we left the ice, I could hear my teammates joking and laughing about the fight.

With a huff, I stomped towards the locker room.

Ari and I entered the locker room, and he immediately exploded. "What the fuck was that?" he growled, his chest heaving with breath and a bruise already forming around his right eye.

The anger was fading quickly, replaced by guilt.

And the day had started out so promising.

I collapsed onto a nearby chair, my head drooping low in shame. A long minute passed before I glanced up, raking a hand through my hair to clear it from my face.

"Fuck. I'm sorry," I finally sighed.

"Well, I'm *not* sorry for that hit," Ari announced stubbornly, a shadow of a smile on his face though.

I shrugged. "It was a pussy hit anyway," I teased.

Comfortable silence finally settled between us . . . until Ari cleared his throat.

"Ari," I growled. "I really don't want to hear it." I pulled off my skates and slipped on some running shoes.

He stood and leaned against the wall, a stubborn tilt to his chin.

"What are you going to do if he has something to say about your girl?" he said, his eyebrows lifting in challenge. "Going to just let him walk all over you? Because I'm *so* sure he'll be cool with you falling for a girl without seven figures next to her name."

"You're a fuckhead," I snapped, grabbing my bag and stalking out of the locker room without a look back.

The whole drive to my parents', though . . . I knew Ari was right.

———

I pulled up to my parents' mansion, a towering white structure that loomed over the other houses on the street. The imposing gates creaked open, revealing the sprawling estate that I had grown up in. The mansion itself was a grand, three-story building with white columns and a wraparound front porch. It was surrounded by well-manicured lawns and towering oak trees that spanned three acres, giving the impression of a well-established family that had been living there for generations.

Appearances were everything to my parents. The mansion was just a symbol of their wealth and status in society. Every detail of their lives was meticulously planned to maintain their image, from the designer clothes they wore to the lavish parties they hosted. It was a life built on appearances, and it hid all the darkness that lived between these walls.

What the neighbors would think if they knew my mother was fucking the gardener *and* her tennis instructor . . . And that my father had probably been snorting cocaine with five hookers in his office last night.

And then, of course, there was Tyler. The ghost of him was everywhere.

I fucking hated this place.

The perfectly manicured lawn stretched out before me, the bright green grass almost glowing in the sunlight. As I climbed the steps to the grand entrance, I couldn't help but feel a sense of dread settling in my stomach. I knew what was coming.

The door was answered by Ms. Talbot, the house manager, a stiff woman who always seemed to be holding a clipboard. She was dressed in her usual black skirt suit, her hair pulled back in a severe bun. "Good evening, Mr. Daniels," she greeted me with a nod.

"Ms. Talbot," I replied, forcing a polite smile.

She'd been the house manager for at least the last ten years. And I'd never seen her smile.

As she led me into the mansion, like I hadn't grown up here, I took in the opulence surrounding me. The marble floors shone beneath my feet, and crystal chandeliers hung from the high ceilings. Everything was immaculate, without a single photograph or other personal touch, as if no one actually lived here. Everything was updated every couple of years to reflect the latest styles and trends.

The dining room was just as grand, with a long table set for ten and more crystal chandeliers hanging overhead. My mother and father were already seated at the table, dressed in their finest. attire. They barely acknowledged my presence as I took my seat.

And sitting to the right of my father . . . Kara Fucking Lindstrom.

Holy fuck.

I took in her too-tight dress, showcasing a set of fake tits that definitely weren't appropriate for this kind of dinner table. She was the typical too blonde, too-skinny socialite with fake lips and a sullen expression, like she'd smelled some shit.

Nothing like my dream girl.

But now, here I was, sitting at the dinner table with Kara, who my father had conveniently seated next to me.

"You've got to be shitting me," I muttered, earning a stern glare from my father who was daring me to fuck up the night.

"Kara," I said, ignoring her offered cheek as I shifted uncomfortably in my seat, absolutely seething. I definitely wouldn't be touching her or giving her any hope that anything was going to happen from tonight's meal. Maybe I should whip out my dick right now and show her Monroe's name?

Although, knowing Kara, that would probably turn her on— the feeling that she was hurting someone else.

"Lincoln," my mother greeted stiffly. Her eyes were slightly glazed, and I wondered what prescription painkiller she'd chosen for today.

"Mother," I replied with a head nod.

"Is there a reason you couldn't shower before dinner, dear?" she continued, her nose turning up at my basketball shorts and hoodie.

I was out of the locker room and in the parking lot before I remembered showering would have been a good idea before dinner.

And then I'd said "fuck it," and come in my workout clothes anyway, not wanting to face Ari again.

Unfortunately, Kara didn't seem to mind the fact that I was sweaty and no doubt smelled.

My mother and father were both dressed to impress, my father in a tailored black suit with a crisp white shirt and a dark navy tie. His hair was neatly combed back. My mother wore an elegant crimson gown that hugged her figure in all the right places. Her blonde hair was coiled up in an intricate updo, with a few loose tendrils framing her face.

The contrast between their getups and mine was hilarious.

"Knew you'd just be happy to see me," I replied in a mocking voice, causing Kara to shift in her seat uncomfortably.

Before my mother could say anything else, the staff filed into the dining room, balancing silver trays with various gourmet dishes. The aroma of the food filled the air, tempting my stomach to growl. But I knew I wouldn't enjoy any of it. All I could think about was last night with Monroe, eating takeout while she sat in my lap.

The thought of it made my mouth water far more than the extravagant spread in front of me.

I pulled my phone from my pocket and hid it under the table

as I checked the tracking app to make sure that Monroe was on her way to class. She'd texted me earlier to say thanks for lunch and tell me she had a catering gig after she was done.

I didn't know how I was going to survive.

Miss you.

When she didn't reply after a few seconds, I reluctantly slipped the phone back into my pocket and returned my attention to dinner.

"So, Kara, I meant to tell you that you looked absolutely gorgeous the other night at Whitney's gala. Did you have a good time?" My mother's southern accent was out in full force as she cut her salmon into small pieces, the salmon she wouldn't actually eat.

"It was such a darling event, and for such a good cause. But, Lincoln, I didn't see you there. You usually never miss it," Kara cooed, literally dragging a finger across her cleavage while she talked to try and catch my eye.

Sorry, sweetheart. Monroe's tits were a trillion times better. I tried not to envision sucking on Monroe's rosy nipples, biting down gently and getting that soft moan from her lips—Fuck. Down boy.

I did *not* want to give Kara the wrong impression.

"Lincoln was at one of his little games," my father snidely responded on my behalf.

"Dad, I'm surprised you would even know that. I didn't think you followed my schedule," I mocked, causing a red flush of anger to creep up his neck at my disrespectful tone.

"Of course we do, Son," my mother chortled, taking a big swig of her wine.

*That's it, go comatose for me, Mother.*

The three of them chatted back and forth, occasionally dragging me into the conversation to get my opinion on some inane

social event, or the new sports car their neighbor had just bought
—the only part of the conversation that was actually interesting.

My father didn't bring up anything business related, even
though Kara's presence here was solely related to the deal he
was trying to work out with her dad—he thought all women
were fools, so he wouldn't bother bringing up anything of
substance in front of them.

Dinner dragged on, because five courses were necessary for
the average family dinner.

Kara's hand went to my arm, massaging it while I tried to eat
my cheesecake. She leaned towards me, her breasts pushing
against my skin.

I froze, feeling my father's approving gaze crawling
across us.

I turned and leaned in so that my lips were brushing her ear.
Her chest was already heaving, like I was touching her clit
instead of talking.

"If you touch me again, I will stab you with this fork," I
murmured. She froze, shock and confusion in her eyes as she
stared at me fearfully. It was·clear she hadn't been expecting
that.

"Excuse me?" she whispered, her voice wavering slightly.

"You heard me," I replied with a cold smile, and then I
brought a bite of cheesecake up to my mouth—just for kicks and
giggles.

Kara's mouth hung open, and for a moment, she could only
stare at me, as if trying to comprehend what had happened. Then
she stood up abruptly and grabbed her purse.

"I . . . I'm sorry," she stammered, backing away from the
table. "I have to go."

With that, she turned and practically ran out of the room,
leaving me alone with my seething parents, in a room that
seemed to have dropped twenty degrees.

"What the fuck did you do?" my father roared, leaping up

and slamming his hands on the table so the glass plates and cups all rattled.

My mother grabbed her wine glass and stalked out of the room without a word as the staff scattered into the kitchen.

I took another bite of my cheesecake as if I was completely unbothered by the whole thing.

"Come with me, Lincoln," my father growled in a voice that brokered no argument.

I found myself standing and following him to his office, a spacious room located on the second floor of the estate. It was elegantly decorated, with dark wood paneling lining the walls and plush carpeting covering the floor. A large oak desk, an ornate leather chair, and a set of matching bookcases that were stuffed with leather-bound books and family heirlooms filled the space.

A large crystal chandelier hung from the center of the ceiling, casting a warm glow over everything in the room. My father's desk was cluttered with papers, files, and various office supplies, and there was a computer monitor on the desk with several screens open, displaying stock charts and financial data.

I stared out the large window behind the desk, studying the view of the expansive grounds. From there, I could see the lush gardens and sparkling pool below. Memories of swimming with Tyler dashed before my eyes . . . I had to look away.

The walls were adorned with several paintings and photographs, including a portrait of my father shaking hands with the current president, and a framed copy of the cover of *Forbes* magazine featuring him as the most successful businessman of the year.

Taking his time, Anstad poured himself a drink, not bothering to offer me one. When he felt the tension was sufficiently built, he placed his empty glass on the desk and turned his attention back to me. "Let's talk about Kara," he said, his voice once again taking on a menacing tone.

"It's not happening," I said with a yawn, knowing full well it would fall on deaf ears.

"I don't care if you don't want to fuck her," my father spat back. "I need you to keep her happy. Do you understand me? If this deal falls through because you can't be bothered to play nice with this girl, I'm going to—"

"What are you going to do? Kill me?" I chuckled, watching as his face turned a mottled red color.

My father sat in his office chair and typed something on his computer.

A second later . . . Monroe's picture was plastered on the screen.

My heart nearly stopped.

"Ahh, yes. Is this the girl that has you acting out?" Anstad asked, his eyes glittering. "Did you think I wouldn't find out? When I have this fucking much on the line?"

I stood there frozen, suddenly unable to move or speak. I'd always known he was ruthless, but fuck, I guess I thought there were some lines he wouldn't cross.

Apparently, I was a fucking fool.

"You will stay in line, or there will be consequences." His fingers typed something else on the screen, and a second later, a video of Monroe walking across campus, her head tucked down, filled the screen.

Anstad leaned forward. "Just in case you forgot . . . I own you."

I felt a cold sweat break out on my forehead as I watched the video of Monroe. I gritted my teeth, a surge of anger and frustration coursing through me as I worked on not lunging at him. Patricide didn't need to be on the menu tonight.

Anstad raised an eyebrow, a cruel smile tugging at the corners of his lips as he watched me.

He dismissed me with a wave of his hand, his smile only

growing wider when I flipped him off. I stumbled out of the room, my mind reeling over what just happened.

I wasn't sure what to do about Anstad, but I was desperate to protect Monroe at all costs. And that didn't include letting her go.

Apparently, it was time for the next phase of the plan.

I drove straight to her apartment complex and stormed to her landlord's door, knowing she would still be in class. I hated this fucking place. The paint on the walls was peeling, revealing layers of grime and dirt underneath. The concrete stairs leading up to the second floor were cracked and uneven, with rusted metal railings that looked like they could fall off at any moment.

I could hear the distant sound of music blaring from one of the units, and the smell of cigarette smoke lingered in the air. Most of the windows were covered in a layer of dust and grime, obscuring the view inside.

Trash littered the ground, with empty beer bottles and fast-food wrappers scattered around. The place didn't have a parking lot, so beat-up cars and trucks, some with missing windows or dented fenders, lined the streets. I compared what I was seeing to what Monroe had done to her little apartment, with the freshly painted walls, and the flowers on the welcome mat outside. She kept it perfectly clean, colorful throw pillows and knickknacks— or whatever the fuck they were called—brightening the room. Vanilla-scented candles masked the odor of mold that saturated everything else in the building.

She didn't belong here, and after today, she'd never live here again.

I pounded on the landlord's door, waiting for him to answer.

Finally, the door creaked open and Monroe's landlord appeared, leering at me with a nasty grin full of yellow-stained teeth. I was pretty sure all of his clothes were filthy at this point, because he had huge armpit stains on the shirt that barely made it over his enormous stomach. He was wearing gray sweatpants, but I was positive they wouldn't have the same effect on Monroe as mine had. Looking at his hair, I wondered if he slicked down every individual piece, or if it just laid like that. He reeked of stale smoke and sweat, the odor strong enough to bowl me over and make me want to gag.

"What do you want, fancy pants?" he sneered.

Fancy pants, that was a new one. Especially considering I was still in gym clothes.

"I want to talk about Monroe," I said, already done with the conversation.

The landlord's grin turned lecherous. "What do you want with my sweet little tenant, huh?" His voice was thick and oily, like he had swallowed a gallon of grease.

I gritted my teeth and tried to keep the disgust off my face. "I need you to evict Monroe out of her apartment," I growled. "And I need you to do it tonight."

The landlord raised an eyebrow and chuckled. "Now, why would I do that? Monroe's a good tenant. Always pays her rent on time. And she's . . . very accommodating."

Bile rose in my throat at the landlord's insinuation. I had no doubt he'd been giving her a hard time. "I don't give a shit about that. I just need her out of here."

The landlord shrugged and leaned back against the door-frame, his massive gut jiggling. "Sorry, kid. Can't help you. I happen to like having her around."

I clenched my fists and took a step forward, towering over the repulsive man. "Listen, you little shit. You're going to do what I say, or I'll make sure you're very sorry. Got it?"

The landlord's eyes widened in fear, and he stumbled back, tripping over a stack of empty pizza boxes. "O-okay, okay. J-just calm down, all right? I'll do it. Don't hurt me."

I smirked and pulled out my checkbook. "Good. You don't deserve it, but I'm going to make it worth your while." I scribbled out a number that would make him very happy.

The landlord's eyes widened in surprise and he licked his lips hungrily. "Alright," he said, taking the check from my hand. "I'll do it. But it's gonna cost you extra if you want me to make it quick."

I gritted my teeth in disgust, hating that murder was a crime. "You want to rethink that?"

He put up his hands. "Okay, okay. It'll be tonight."

"Get it done," I growled, turning on my heel and stalking back to my car.

The landlord scurried back into his apartment like the rat he was, slamming the door behind him. I sighed and rolled my shoulders back, feeling like I needed to burn my clothes and take a shower with boiling water to get his stench off me.

I needed to get back to my penthouse, though.

I was about to have a roommate.

# CHAPTER 23

## MONROE

B ill, I brought you some leftovers," I said with a tired smile as I met him at the corner where he usually waited for me on nights when I worked late.

"You're a goddess, little duck," he said, tucking my arm in his and patting my hand reassuringly. The small act after a difficult day made me want to cry. "You're working too hard, though. You're young. You should be out with friends, not pushing yourself to death," he chastised as we walked.

"Maybe someday," I murmured with a sigh. We'd had this conversation many times before. And he didn't quite seem to understand why I was so against being homeless . . .

"Somedays aren't promised," he said, right as we got to the entry to the apartment complex. I paused, hearing the ache in his voice. It was obvious there was a story there.

I didn't pry, though.

Over the last year, I'd learned that Bill only talked about some parts of his past, and whatever caused that ache in his voice . . . was not one of those parts he discussed.

I stared after him as he walked away, singing something softly to himself, before I trudged up the stairs to my apartment, my feet aching and my head pounding. Today had been one of the longest days I'd had in a while, even with the late start. All I wanted to do was kick off my shoes and crawl into bed. But as I got to my door, Jared emerged from his apartment next to mine, blocking my way. His greasy hair was slicked back, and his small, round, piercing eyes seemed to glint in the dim light of the hallway.

"Ms. Bardot," he said, his voice oily and insincere. "I'm afraid I have some bad news for you."

My heart sank. "What is it?" I asked, trying to keep the exhaustion from my voice.

"You're being evicted," he said, a sickening grin spreading across his face. My mind went blank for a moment. Evicted? But why? I'd paid my rent on time every month.

"Why?" I managed to ask, my voice trembling slightly.

He shrugged. "Business is business, Monroe. I'm sorry, but you'll have to be out by the morning." I stumbled back against the wall, my mind reeling. How was I supposed to find a new place to live by tomorrow? I hadn't found anything yet that I could afford.

"Please, I don't understand," I said, feeling confused and disoriented.

"I have someone else who wants your place, someone who can pay more. You're out, Monroe," he replied gruffly.

"But . . . maybe I *could* pay extra," I pleaded, even as I calculated in my head how I could afford to pay even a penny more.

"Sorry, girly. But we both know that's not going to happen." He gave me a sleazy grin.

I felt sick to my stomach, the world spinning around me. I didn't know where I would go. This would ruin everything.

"Please, there has to be something I can do," I said, my voice trembling.

He leaned in closer, invading my personal space. "Well, there is one thing you could do." His breath was hot and stale against my face.

I recoiled in disgust, taking a step back. "What are you talking about?" I asked, a sense of dread washing over me.

"We've had this conversation before. I'm a man with needs, Monroe. Maybe if you were a little more accommodating, I'd reconsider." His eyes roamed over my body.

I felt sick to my stomach, feeling violated and disgusted. "No, I'd rather sleep on the streets than do that," I spat. I wanted to punch him again, but I'd prefer not to. He'd kick me out tonight instead of tomorrow—although tomorrow was just a few hours away at this point.

"Suit yourself," he said with a shrug. "Just make sure you're out by tomorrow."

With that, he turned and walked away, leaving me alone in the hallway, feeling utterly hopeless and alone.

I stood there in shock for a moment, before finally willing my legs to move and walk into my apartment. The tears started then, coming out in harsh gasps as I stood in the middle of the tiny room, surrounded by the life I'd been scraping together. Jared's words echoed in my head, and I felt a sense of panic rising in my chest, like a wave in a stormy sea, threatening to drown me in an ocean of uncertainty and despair. Where was I supposed to go? What was I supposed to do?

The tears streaming down my face blinded me to everything around me as I stumbled through my tiny apartment. The feeling of hopelessness was almost suffocating. I was disappearing, with no one to save me.

The sound of my phone buzzing seemed to shake me out of my daze. I fumbled for it, wiping away the tears that were still leaking from my eyes. When I saw Lincoln's name on the screen, a small glimmer of hope sparked in my chest. It was like a tiny flame in the darkness, illuminating the way forward. I wiped away the last of my tears and took a deep breath before checking the text.

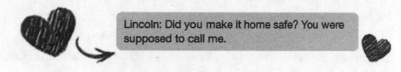

Lincoln: Did you make it home safe? You were supposed to call me.

It was like a lifeline had been thrown to me, something to hold onto amidst the chaos.

A second later, he was calling, obviously impatient with the fact I hadn't responded yet.

I fumbled to answer it, hoping to stop myself from crying again. "You're in big trouble, baby," he said. "You were supposed to tell me when you were off so I could drive you home."

The lump in my throat made it impossible to respond with anything but a sob. Lincoln's playful tone immediately disappeared as he realized something was wrong. "Sweetheart, what's going on?" he asked, concern lacing his voice.

I struggled to compose myself enough to explain what had happened, telling him about the eviction notice and how lost and scared I felt, hiccuping and sniffling as I talked.

"Oh, baby. I'm so sorry. But it's going to be okay. We'll figure this out together," he said, his voice gentle and reassuring as he spoke. "Right now, I'm going to come pick you up. We'll pack up your stuff together, bring it over to my place, and then you can stay with me as long as you need to." I heard the sound of an engine starting.

"You're coming right now?" I whispered, more tears tracking down my cheeks.

"Yep. And I'm going to stay on the phone with you the whole time, because, baby, your tears are tearing me apart. Dream girls aren't ever supposed to cry."

A hiccuped laugh escaped me and he chuckled softly, the sound like a warm caress across my skin.

"I think you're delusional," I whispered. "You see something that doesn't actually exist."

Lincoln let out a deep, throaty chuckle, the sound reverberating through the phone. "Delusional, huh?" he murmured, his voice rough and low. "You think I'm delusional for seeing how amazing you are? How special and strong and beautiful?"

He paused, taking a deep breath, like he was trying to rein in his emotions. "Monroe, I see you. I see all of you. And I'm not going anywhere. I'll be here for you, every step of the way, no matter what. Because I know that you're worth it. You're worth everything. Eventually, you'll trust me. I've been lonely all these years, too. Waiting for you."

His words were like the sun breaking through the clouds after a storm. But it wasn't just relief I felt—it was something more. Something deeper. As I watched the street through my window, waiting for his car to appear, warmth spread through my chest, like a slow-burning fire.

I realized with a start that I was falling in love with him.

It was like the petals of a flower unfolding, revealing a beauty that had been hidden away, like the universe had opened up and allowed me to finally see what I'd been missing all these years. Lincoln felt like he could be the missing piece to my puzzle, the one I didn't know I needed until he was right in front of me.

As Lincoln's car rolled to a stop outside my apartment building, a wave of relief and joy crashed over me, washing away the fear and uncertainty that had plagued me just moments before. He was still on the phone with me when I threw open my door and let him in.

Lincoln's golden gaze locked onto mine, and in a heartbeat, I was in his arms. His fingers brushed against my skin like the first drop of rain on parched earth, igniting a wildfire of sensations within me, sparking shivers down my spine and sending my heart racing. Our lips collided, igniting an inferno that left me breathless. I melted into him, feeling his strength and protection surrounding me, as if his arms were the only safe haven in the world. Every touch, every kiss, every moment with him was a fiery explosion of desire and longing that I never wanted to end.

He helped me pack up my belongings, his touch gentle yet firm as he carefully wrapped each item, which I'm sure resembled trash compared to what was in his place.

All of my belongings fit into two boxes. That was it. That was the sum of my life up to now.

It was pathetic, really.

We loaded the boxes into the car, and I couldn't help but marvel at how he seemed to effortlessly navigate the chaos of my life. With him by my side, everything felt just a little more manageable, a bit more bearable.

As we drove away from the place that had represented my new start, I felt a bittersweet sense of loss. But as I gazed at the beautiful man beside me, the one that seemed more god than mortal, his eyes flicking to me every few seconds, like he couldn't stand to look away . . .

I thought maybe it wasn't so bad.

---

*Lincoln*

I pulled the car into my parking garage. A smirk played on my lips . . . a sense of triumph surging through me. She was mine now, whether she realized it or not. Now that she was going to be living with me, I knew I could convince her to fall for me, and I wouldn't hesitate to use every trick in my playbook to do so.

I was a predator, and she was my prey.

But she was more than that.

She was my salvation, the one person who could make me feel alive again.

I was willing to do whatever it took to keep her by my side, to make her see that we were meant to be together.

And nothing, not even her, would stand in the way of that.

# CHAPTER 24

## MONROE

I woke up to the blaring of my phone's alarm clock, feeling the warmth of Lincoln's body wrapped around me. He groaned as it went off, clearly not ready to start the day. I giggled softly, feeling a mix of happiness and nerves. It was the first time I'd woken up in his arms, and it felt like a dream come true.

Last night, after I'd taken a hot shower in his bathroom that was right out of a Restoration Hardware ad, we'd gone to bed. Neither of us even thought about me sleeping anywhere but in his arms. I assumed I'd wake up feeling awful about being kicked out of my apartment, but instead, I felt good. Regenerated. Something I hadn't felt in a long time. It was as if every worry, every care, every trouble that had been weighing me down had been muted, pushed to the background, replaced with a sense of excitement. It was a feeling I couldn't quite explain, but it was all because of him.

Lincoln.

I was reborn, renewed, a phoenix rising from the ashes of my former self. Every fiber of my being was alive with a newfound vigor, and I couldn't help but feel grateful for his presence in my life. The day ahead no longer loomed over me like a dark cloud, I was actually looking forward to it.

It seemed crazy, all that could come from him sweeping in like a golden knight to save me . . . but it had. Last night was the first time anyone, besides Bill, had ever really been there for me in my life.

He pulled me closer, his hard length digging into my ass. "It's still the middle of the night," he murmured sleepily, kissing the back of my neck.

I giggled and turned off the alarm before trying to slip out of bed. He was completely wrapped around me, though; even his legs were tangled with mine. "It's six thirty."

"Five more minutes?" he groaned as his lips trailed along my neck, sending shivers down my spine as his warm breath caressed my skin. It was easy to forget about responsibilities around him, to get lost in his spell. I knew I had to get up and get ready for work, but a part of me—a huge part—wanted to stay in bed with him forever.

"Five minutes wouldn't hurt," I whispered as he moved me to my back, his lips tracing a path to my chest. I arched my back, craving more of him as he leaned over me. My legs automatically fell apart so he could press his body against mine. Everything in me ached to be closer to him, to drown in the sensations he could give me.

His lips left a trail of nips and bites down my chest, sparks of desire twisting across my skin. My insides throbbed, and I gasped, my body desperate for more.

"Do you want me to suck on your pretty tits? Make you come just like this?" Lincoln's voice was like a drug.

My body screamed out in response, begging for his touch. His teeth gently bit down on my nipple through the fabric, and my moan reverberated through the room.

"Fuck," Lincoln swore, as he tore off the T-shirt he'd insisted I "borrow" last night, exposing my naked breasts to the cool air. His mouth was on me in an instant, whispering dirty words that I never even knew existed.

"Fuck, you're gorgeous," he muttered, sending my senses into overdrive. His fingers teased and pinched my nipple, waves of pleasure radiating through my body.

"Please, Lincoln," I begged, my voice barely above a whisper. He chuckled, his tongue swirling around my nipple as he gave me what I craved. His mouth engulfed me, sucking and licking with a fierce intensity that left me reeling. His hand cupped and squeezed my other breast, driving me closer to the edge. The pleasure was almost too much to bear, but I never wanted it to end. I clung to Lincoln, my body writhing and pulsating with each sweet rush of sensation. He knew exactly what to do to make me come undone, and I surrendered to him completely as I fell over the edge.

"Fuck, you're so responsive," he murmured as he gave me an awestruck look before continuing to feast on my nipples in greedy, drawn-out pulls. His fingers slipped to my soaked thong, gliding over the sensitive, throbbing flesh as he worked magic on my breasts.

I came again, the suddenness shocking me.

He groaned and buried his face in my neck, his fingers slipping under the edge of my thong and lazily playing with my folds.

"Lincoln," I gasped. I was going to be late again. I was dying. This was . . . everything.

He lifted his head and pulled back his hand, leaving me a slippery, aching mess.

"Never going to be able to live without this," he growled, as he licked his glistening fingers. "My favorite kind of meal." His grin was smug and confident. He was so proud of himself. "I want to wake up like this every day," he murmured, staring deep into my eyes.

I stared back at him, not daring to hope that he really meant it. Part of me wondered if he was just saying it to make me happy. But then he leaned in and kissed me again, and I felt his arms tighten around me, and I let myself believe . . . just for a minute.

"I want that too," I finally said softly, my heart swelling with emotion.

"You're killing me, dream girl. I've got to get you to work, and all I want is to keep you in bed, right here, until the end of time." His arms squeezed even more, like he really was contemplating it.

"Tonight . . . I want more," I whispered shyly, closing my eyes so I couldn't see his face.

His whole body froze. He was still for so long . . . I finally had to open my eyes to check on him.

He was staring down at me, his gaze hot and hungry. "You're going to say that and then leave me all day? I won't be able to focus on anything. All I'll be doing is counting down every second until I can pick you up and have you back in this bed." His voice was thick with desire, and I whimpered.

Lincoln stared at me unfathomably, before suddenly springing up and tugging me out of bed. "We've got to get this day started, so we can get to tonight." He spanked my ass and gently pushed me towards the bathroom.

I didn't know how I'd survive until after class.

———

### Lincoln

I texted her for the thousandth time that day. I'd gotten the same answer in response, but I figured it was worth another try. I was literally counting down every fucking minute.

I'd come this morning, right in my briefs, just sucking on her magical tits. When I'd slid out of bed and she'd seen the wet spot, she'd smirked, but because she was such a fucking sweetheart, she hadn't even teased me about it.

But it wasn't like I was embarrassed. When you experience lust like this, you accept it, no questions asked.

It was my new normal.

I'd fucked my hand twice already thinking about tonight and sliding into her perfect, slick cunt. I'd always prided myself on control, but right now, I had none. And I didn't want to hurt her by being mad with raging lust when I took her fucking virginity.

I also didn't want to be a two pump chump for the first time in my life.

She needed to be addicted to what I could do to her after tonight.

She was falling for me . . . I just needed one more push.

> How many more minutes?

> > Dream Girl: Kevin will probably make me stay all the way up until it's time for class since the office now resembles a flower store. I can barely see patients when they come up. Thirteen bouquets . . . really?

> It's my lucky number. It seemed fitting.

> > Dream Girl: I love them 😍 😍 😍

I sighed, feeling like a crazed lunatic. She was so fucking perfect.

I thought about that morning. A nice guy would've asked if she was sure about what she'd said. But I'd never do that. I wanted her blood all over my dick. I wanted to mark her insides with my cum. I wanted it to be impossible for her not to think about me every fucking second.

My phone buzzed. When it was Ari, I was tempted not to pick up, but I decided he might be able to distract me.

"Dalton fucking broke his leg," were the first words out of his mouth.

"What?"

"Yeah, the shithead got wasted at some party last night and fell off a balcony . . . with some puck bunny still attached to his dick."

Hopefully, there was video . . . because that shit sounded hilarious. But it also meant we were one man down, with a home game and two road games left before the playoffs even started. Not a great time for me to be distracted out of my fucking mind.

She'd have to come to every game. I'd been thinking about it, and I didn't know how I was going to convince her to miss three days of life to come out on the road with me. But it was necessary. I wouldn't be able to do anything but think about what she was doing and worry about her if she wasn't in the stands.

"Linc?" Ari asked, his tone annoyed.

"Yep. I'm listening."

"I really want the Cup this year."

Fuck. So did I. Losing in the Finals last year had killed me.

"Dalton sucked anyway. Not a big loss."

"It means it's all on your shoulders to pick up the slack," he reminded me.

A text came in from Monroe then, reminding me just how much of a distraction she was.

"I've got it. It's our year," I promised him. But it was a weird thing . . . hockey had been my whole life since I was a kid . . . and now, it was feeling more like a side piece. My world revolved around something else now.

Fuck.

"See you tomorrow for weights," he reminded me before hanging up.

I hurriedly pulled up Monroe's text, Ari's phone call already sliding out of my mind.

Dream Girl: Class was canceled tonight. Professor's sick. See you at 5.

I glanced at the clock. It was 4:30.
Holy fuck, it was on.

# CHAPTER 25
## MONROE

I was going to die. It was official.

Lincoln had picked me up, appearing in the lobby at 4:55 like he really had been counting down the minutes. I'd thought he would rush home, throw me on the bed, and fuck my brains out.

But the hot asshole must not have been on the same wavelength, because we were at the longest dinner of my life, and Lincoln didn't seem to be in any hurry to leave. We were at some fancy place where there were seven courses. And while I'd never even dreamed of eating at a place so nice . . . I was ready for dessert.

The kind that came from Lincoln's dick.

I'd been pumping myself up all day about it. Pushing aside all the "what the fuck are you doing" comments my brain was sending me . . . and just concentrating on the good stuff. The part of me that knew losing my virginity to Lincoln would be a life-altering experience.

I fidgeted in my seat. I couldn't stop looking at his lips, imagining them on me. He was cutting into some prime rib, and every time he opened his mouth . . . I got wet.

It was a little ridiculous at this point.

But honestly, did he usually savor every bite of his food? I couldn't even taste what we'd eaten so far. I was too anxious.

I finally couldn't stand it any longer. I leaned in close and brushed my lips against his ear. "Please fuck me," I whispered.

He glanced over at me with a sly smile and leaned back in his seat. "Is my baby feeling impatient? Are you getting wet over there in your hot-as-fuck dress? Are you soaking the leather seat?"

I whimpered softly. The bastard was messing with me!

He chuckled and leaned in closer to me. "Do you need a little something to tide you over?" His voice was low and seductive, making me even wetter. "If you think this isn't all I've thought about since the moment I knew you were real. Your body against mine. Your hands on me. Your greedy pussy choking my big dick . . . you're out of your mind. I'm going to ruin you tonight. Fuck you until you pass out from orgasms." He chose that moment to slide another piece of prime rib into his mouth, and seriously . . . even his chewing was turning me on. He swallowed and leaned in closer. "So we can wait a little bit longer."

I was dead. I literally flopped back into my seat, like a sulking brat, while he laughed at me.

All the attention we got—or should I say *Lincoln* got—didn't help. Throughout the meal, women and men kept coming up to our table, interrupting our conversation, all of them trying to get Lincoln's attention. Some of them were bold enough to flirt with him shamelessly, even though I was sitting right there.

I could feel my jaw clenching every time another one approached us, but Lincoln remained unfazed. He barely took his eyes off me, even as they batted their eyelashes and left their phone numbers on our table.

I tried to make light of it. "Do they do this every time you go out?" I asked, attempting to sound casual.

He nodded, his eyes never leaving mine. "It comes with the territory."

Would I ever get used to that, everyone wanting him?

I just needed to remind myself of his cock tattoo.

None of them had that.

"I don't want them. I'll never want them. All I want is you," he murmured at one point when a pretty blonde with boobs the size of her head literally came to the table and tried to buy him a drink, despite the fact I was practically sitting on his lap.

After what seemed like twenty hours, we finished our meal and finally got up from the table. The moment we stepped out of the restaurant though, a few flashes went off, blinding us momentarily. My heart raced as I realized we'd been ambushed by paparazzi.

"Lincoln, who's the girl?" one shouted.

"Lincoln, is she your girlfriend?"

Lincoln didn't miss a beat. He pulled me closer, his arm tight around my waist. His lips brushed against that spot on my neck he couldn't seem to stay away from in public.

I shifted uncomfortably, not sure what to do. "Should you be doing that?" I whispered as we waited for the valet to bring the car around.

"Good way to make sure people know you're mine," he growled in my ear.

His possessiveness was like a drug, sending a little thrill racing through me.

But at the same time, I couldn't help feeling a little uneasy about the attention.

When the car came, I practically jumped in, eager to get away from the cameras.

As soon as we settled inside, the atmosphere transformed into a charged and electric energy that could have set the entire city ablaze. It was like a coiled spring, ready to release at any moment.

My skin prickled with nervous expectancy, my every nerve ending alight with desire. I couldn't help but steal glances at him, watching the flex of his muscles as he gripped the wheel, his gaze unwaveringly fixed on the road ahead.

The city lights were nothing but a blur as we zoomed past, the engine's low hum the only sound between us. The sexual tension built with each passing second, the anticipation almost palpable. It was like time had stopped, and nothing else existed except for us.

At a stoplight, I turned to him, capturing his lips in a fierce kiss. The heat between us was explosive, our bodies aching for release. His hand crept up my thigh, and it felt like a wild animal was clawing at my insides, desperate to break free.

As the car finally pulled into his underground garage, we were both lost in the unspoken words that floated between us. We stayed frozen in the moment, reluctant to break the spell.

But Lincoln finally spoke, his voice low and husky. "Let's go inside."

———

We stood in his shadow-strewn room, my heart beating violently in my chest, erratic beats that seemed to be pushing against my ribcage.

"Don't be scared, dream girl," Lincoln whispered as he erased the distance between us and lowered me onto his bed, his towering frame crouching over me as his muscular arms held his weight. I felt like I was fumbling around, my inexperience betraying me with every move.

"I've never—" I began, staring into his golden gaze. Not that I really needed to say that. He'd had to instruct me how to give him a blow job, for fuck's sake.

He nuzzled into my cheek, a shiver passing over his skin.

"That makes me so fucking happy, baby. Because it means you're only ever going to belong to me."

I sighed as his tongue traced the edge of my ear. "And just so you know," he whispered. "You're already the best I've ever had, and I haven't even been inside of you."

———

### Lincoln

"I want to taste you," she breathed, her mouth hovering a breath away. I waited patiently, wanting her to come to me. I'd pushed her all the way to this point.

Her lust-filled emerald eyes and swollen lips . . .

A deadly combination that could make any man lose his mind.

Break his heart.

Take his soul.

And she was all mine.

Her lips brushed against mine hesitantly, and I coaxed her to continue. "That's it, baby. Give me your mouth," I growled, my voice almost unrecognizable . . . it was so thick with lust. She obliged, and I tangled my fingers in her hair, keeping her in place. I deepened the kiss, my tongue lazily moving against hers.

She was driving me crazy.

My cock surged against her stomach, gushing precum, and I knew I was already about to explode.

She tentatively ran a finger over the head, swirling my precum over the crown. I grabbed her hand and thrust my cock into it, about to go insane without her touch.

She smirked, like she loved what she was doing to me.

"Feels so fucking good. You're so fucking beautiful," I told her as I almost died with lust.

Her smirk turned shy and she bit down on that plush bottom lip, straight out of every man's wet dream.

"There's no one else?" she suddenly whispered, her gaze darting away.

I grabbed her chin, forcing Monroe to look at me.

"How can there be anyone else when you exist in the world?" I told her. I didn't care that it was cheesy as fuck. This girl made me want to dig my heart out of my chest and give it to her on a silver platter. Beg her to love me.

She was mine. And I was hers. And before the night was over . . . she would believe it.

––––––

*Monroe*

His hold on my thighs was firm and unyielding as he pushed them apart to get closer. I gripped his broad shoulders to steady myself. My eyes were glued to his hand as he gripped his erect length, slick and glistening . . . and huge.

I'd thought that before, but when it was actually going inside of me . . . it was a whole different story.

"I'm going to take such good care of you," he soothed, as he pressed the tip against my drenched entrance, a moan escaping my lips.

"Tell me you want this. Tell me you want this more than anything," he murmured, his voice gravelly, as if he wasn't sure whether he was asking or telling me.

"Yes," I breathed, too lost in the moment to say anything else.

Slowly, he pushed his head in, the sensation of his thickness spreading me wide. I gasped, the stretch too much. I couldn't breathe. I was so full.

And he was barely in.

He paused for a second, giving me time to adjust, his teeth gritted as if he were in pain.

"You're so fucking tight. So fucking perfect," he groaned, his lips trailing down my neck. He pushed in further and I shuddered, wanting more.

"I'm going to make you feel so good, dream girl. I promise."

I squeezed my thighs around him, trying to bring him in deeper.

Slowly, he pushed in, his fingers finding my clit and rubbing until I was squirming under his touch. My walls spasmed around him, and he drove himself deeper. I cried out as he pushed through my innocence, his lips catching my cries.

"You've ruined me. Fuck—" he growled, a fierce, desperate hunger in his voice. "You're mine. You'll never want anyone else." His voice was a chant, a coaxing soundtrack . . . like he was speaking to my soul.

I clung to him, my breaths coming in short pants. He was filling me so completely, so perfectly. I was lost in the sensations, the pleasure and pain of him inside me. He shifted, pushing me into the bed, his thrusts becoming harder, more forceful.

"Come on my cock, pretty girl," he demanded, his words echoing in my ear. "Come all over me."

I couldn't resist. I didn't want to. I was on the edge, my body on fire, and as he continued to pound into me, I let myself go, the ecstasy of my release overwhelming me.

He was groaning now, too, lost chasing his own pleasure. He pulsed inside me, filling me with his heat . . . his essence. He was inside me now. A part of me that would never go away.

"Every day," he muttered, his lips pressed to my neck. "Every day I'm going to be inside this perfect pussy."

His words lingered in the air, a dirty promise I was desperate for him to keep . . . along with all the others he'd given me.

I wanted him every day, every moment, every breath.

He somehow rolled us, gripping on to me so he stayed inside me. I rested on his chest, his heartbeat my new soundtrack, his cock still hard. My cheeks were wet with tears because what just happened felt like a religious experience.

I felt a bittersweet ache in my soul, knowing that this moment would be etched into my memory forever. The sensation was like a brand, searing and unforgettable.

He'd achieved his goal.

He'd ruined me.

If he broke my heart after this, I didn't know if I'd survive.

---

*Lincoln*

"Have you ever been in love?" she murmured, those green eyes staring at me like I was fucking *everything*.

I was still inside her. It was where I wanted to live.

"Not until I saw you."

It was the most honest thing I'd ever told her.

# CHAPTER 26

## LINCOLN

**DALLAS KNIGHTS**

I stepped onto the ice, feeling the cold air hit me like a ton of bricks. The adrenaline pumped through my veins as I worked on getting my head in the game, knowing this was one of the most important games of the season. Our last home game before the playoffs to clinch home ice for the first round, and we were going to win. No matter what.

I skated towards the face-off, looking across the rink at Ari. His eyes met mine, and I gave him a nod of confidence. I knew he had my back out there.

What I didn't do . . . was look for her.

I was still coated in her scent, memories from last night on replay even though now was not the time.

The puck dropped, and we were off. The crowd roared as we started making plays, passing it back and forth. I took control of it, weaving in and out of the opposing team's players. Making a quick turn, I took the shot, scoring our first goal of the game.

The energy in the arena was electric as we continued to dominate the ice. Ari blocked a shot from the other team, causing a stir among our fans. He looked over at me, and I gave him a thumbs up. He grinned back, like the smug bastard he was.

Because yeah, he knew he was fucking good.

We kept pushing forward, with me scoring another goal, and Ari making some crucial saves. The game was going great; we had it in the bag.

I glanced up at the stands, finally unable to stop myself from searching for her face.

There she was, sitting next to—my father?

My stomach dropped. My palms prickled with sweat . . . my heart raced.

What the hell was he doing here?

He hadn't been to a game since before college, yet he decided tonight was the night? I thought for sure she'd be okay here.

What was he saying to her?

I tried to focus on the game, but I couldn't take my eyes off them. I watched as Monroe answered something he'd asked. She was trying to be confident and polite, but I could see the fear in her eyes. Her hands trembled slightly as she fidgeted with the scarf I'd given her.

I was losing my fucking mind.

I couldn't focus.

Every time I was on the ice, I was stealing glances at them.

It was like a nagging itch in the back of my mind that wouldn't go away.

And then, in a moment of distraction, I missed a shot. The puck sailed wide of the net, and the crowd groaned in disappointment.

I growled and turned to follow the puck and then . . . the impact of the hit sent shockwaves through my body before I even heard the sound of it. It was like a truck colliding with my chest, knocking the wind out of me. I was lying on my back, staring up at the ceiling of the arena, gasping for air. The pain in my ribs, like they'd been smashed into my lungs. I couldn't move, not even to sit up.

Ari's voice broke through the haze of pain, asking me if I was okay, but I couldn't respond. I was in too much agony. I attempted to get up, but my body refused to cooperate. Every movement felt like my ribs were made of glass, and they were shattering with each breath I took.

The trainers rushed out to assist me off the ice. It took all my willpower not to scream in pain as they helped me up. I was gritting my teeth so hard, it was amazing they didn't shatter.

But I refused to show any weakness.

It would be just what my father would want.

As I was being escorted off the ice, Ari skated over to me. His eyes were wide and his eyebrows furrowed in concern. I could see the worry etched in his features.

"Fuck, Lincoln," he growled.

I shook him away, and he sighed, before returning to the rest of the team.

The whole arena suddenly resembled a church, the noise of the fans extinguished by my injury.

I already knew that my rib was broken, maybe more than one. Every inhalation was torture. I didn't have to get an X-ray to figure that out.

But fuck. I needed to get Monroe away from my father and with me in the training room.

On my way there, I ordered a trainer to fetch Monroe. I was kind of an asshole about it, but he needed to know he was dealing with precious cargo. The most precious.

My heart pounded as I heard the sound of the trainer's footsteps coming back to the room, with Monroe in tow. My palms got clammy with anticipation as I waited to see her beautiful face again. The relief I felt when she appeared in the doorway was violent, and it felt like I could breathe for the first time since we'd parted ways right before the game. She was standing in front of me, dressed in the jersey I'd given her the other day.

I'd never felt so fucking proud to see my number on someone.

Her black hair cascaded down her back in soft waves. Her green eyes were captivating, with specks of gold that seemed to glimmer in the dimly lit room.

I'd never thought about eyes glimmering in my fucking life. But she was my real-life dream girl, and I was irrevocably lost. Her nose and cheeks were slightly red from the cold, and I had the urge to bundle her in a blanket, to make sure she was never uncomfortable in the least bit. All my protective urges were in overdrive when it came to her.

Monroe tried to smile at me, but there was so much worry in her gaze . . . so much uncertainty.

There was something else there, too.

Something I'd been searching for.

A transfixed, awestruck glow that told me I'd caught her.

She was so in love with me.

Relief laced through my chest.

"Lincoln, are you okay?!" she whispered, practically running to my side. She reached towards me and then hesitated, like she was afraid her touch would cause me pain.

"Touch me. You could never hurt me," I growled, pulling her forward and ignoring the ache in my ribs as I slammed my lips against hers. Desperate for any connection with her I could get.

When I finally let her come up for air, I spat out a barrage of questions.

"Did he hurt you? What the fuck was my father saying to you?"

Her eyes widened, and then her forehead scrunched up in confusion. "Your father?" she questioned slowly. "I didn't know that was your father. I thought it was just some creep." Monroe's face twisted in disgust, her nose wrinkling up like she'd caught a whiff of something gross. And then she shivered. "He kept asking if I was dating you and flirting with me."

"What the fuck?" I mumbled, lifting my arms so the trainer could lift my jersey up. I winced as he started taping strategically around my ribs to give me support for when I got back out there. "I'm so fucking sorry."

She shook her head, her eyes still holding a hint of disgust. "I'm fine," she said shortly. "It's just . . . your father. He's kind of revolting."

"There's no 'kind of' about it," I said, my voice low with anger. "I'm sorry you had to deal with that. He's fucking awful." Thinking of my father near her made me want to vomit. My insides twisted, a mixture of disgust and anger raging inside me. He was the worst kind of toxic, and something needed to be done about him before he ruined everything. The idea of him hurting her . . .

I would kill him.

Monroe's expression softened slightly at my words, and I felt a small sense of relief that she wasn't angry with me for subjecting her to that.

The trainer finished, and I took a deep breath before sliding off the table, cursing under my breath the entire time.

"Are you going back out there?" she asked with wide eyes. Worry carved across her pretty features.

I smirked, trying to lighten the mood. "Hockey players are far superior athletes to all the other pussy sports, Monroe. The only thing that keeps us out is falling off balconies."

I could tell she didn't get what I was talking about since I'd forgotten to tell her about Dalton. And my mouth had been far too busy since then to talk about anything but worshiping her fucking unreal body.

She shook her head, still looking worried. "You could get hurt worse. You should just sit out for the rest of the game."

I gathered her in my arms, trying to ignore the pain . . . and the way I immediately got hard at the sight of the tears pooling in those pretty green eyes. No one had ever cared enough about me to cry. "Nothing's going to happen to me. I promise."

She bit her lip, but then reluctantly nodded. And fuck . . . she was so fucking sweet.

I was going to give this girl everything.

I held her close to me as we headed down the tunnel towards the ice.

"You . . . move," I snapped at Jamie, a rookie, who was sitting out the game with a broken arm. He was in a prime seating location that would be perfect for Monroe. She could be seated right behind our bench, and I wouldn't have to be freaking out all game, wondering how she was doing.

He opened his mouth to give me crap, but he must've seen the crazy in my gaze because he snapped it closed and jumped out of the seat. I gave him a head nod, immediately forgetting all about him as I sat Monroe down.

"Does everyone just do what you want?" she asked with a smirk. I smiled at her and leaned forward for a kiss. She flinched back, and I frowned.

"What?"

"I don't want everyone to see," she murmured, gesturing to the crowd. "The fans will go crazy."

Okay. I fucking hated that. And I would deal with that soon.

But right then, I needed to get back out on the ice; we were down by one.

"Get used to everyone knowing you're mine," I growled, squeezing her chin gently before I hopped back into the box.

The crowd immediately went insane.

"Daniels, you good?" Coach yelled, gesturing for me to get out there before I even answered.

I skated out onto the ice, ignoring the biting pain in my ribs, my gaze automatically lifting to where my father had been sitting.

Of course, he was gone.

# CHAPTER 27

## LINCOLN

DALLAS KNIGHTS

F: I wish it had been you.

I t took me a second to realize why my father had thrown me that gem this morning.

And when it did, it was like I was dying.

It was the anniversary of Tyler's death today.

And for the first time since his death . . . I'd forgotten.

I'd forgotten the one day of the year that was supposed to be dedicated to him. And it was like I'd failed him all over again.

I could feel my carefully put together facade cracking. The weight of his death . . . the guilt, the fact that I was fucking daring to be so happy . . .

The walls were closing in on me. I couldn't breathe.

Because of me, he'd never have the chance to meet his soul-mate. He'd never smile. He'd never laugh. He'd never have another fucking day.

Because of me.

Without another thought, I walked to the cabinet and pulled out a handle of vodka.

It was better than killing myself.

———

*Monroe*

I frowned at my phone. It wasn't like Lincoln not to text me almost every second of the day when we were separated.

I was just as bad, but after the three texts I'd sent had gone unanswered, I'd stopped texting, and instead started worrying.

Was this it? Had he decided he was done with me?

It was a crazy, unreasonable thought, but it was my worry all day.

*"You think you were ever more than a good fuck, Roxanne?"*

*The man's cruel words echoed around our small apartment. I watched from a crack in the door, my mother on her knees in front of him, her body shaking with sobs. He gave her one more disgusted look before he left.*

I walked out into the muggy evening air, biting my lip as I scanned the parking lot for Lincoln. He'd picked me up every day this week and had told me he'd be here when I left this morning.

Instead, there was a black town car with a man dressed in a sharp, nicely tailored black suit, a stern expression . . . and a sign with my name on it.

Confused, I tentatively walked over.

"Good evening, Ms. Bardot. My name is Nathaniel. Mr. Daniels sent me to pick you up. He's indisposed at the moment." The man, Nathaniel, opened the back passenger door and stared at me expectantly.

I hesitated, shooting a text to Lincoln asking what was going on.

But after an awkward moment, where it never showed he'd even read the text, I got in the car.

Hoping the guy wasn't a serial killer or something.

The interior of the town car was plush and luxurious, with black leather seats and polished wood accents. I sank into the seat, nerves building in my gut, unsure of everything.

*Stupid, stupid, stupid.* My thoughts bounced around, one second telling me to stop being so crazy, and the next, cursing myself that I'd depended on Lincoln to begin with.

"Where exactly is Lincoln?" I asked Nathaniel as we set off. He gave me a small, tight-lipped smile in the rear view mirror.

"I'm not sure, ma'am."

"So, uh, how long have you been driving for Lincoln?" My voice was awkward, but silence felt like it would be too loud . . . give my thoughts too much room to roam.

"A while," Nathaniel responded curtly, eyes fixed on the road ahead.

I shifted uncomfortably in my seat. "Um, where are we going?"

"Mr. Daniels' penthouse."

"Oh, right. Of course," I stammered, feeling like an idiot for even asking.

Nathaniel remained silent for a few moments before speaking again. "Is there anything else you need, ma'am?"

"No, no. I'm good," I whispered, realizing I wouldn't get anything useful out of him.

I stared out the window, watching the city rush by in a blur of lights and colors. My mind raced with questions and worries about Lincoln.

What was going on?

We drove into Lincoln's underground garage, a good sign that I hadn't made a mistake by getting in the car in the first place, and it stopped in front of the elevator entrance. A moment later, Nathaniel opened the door for me.

"Thank you," I murmured, clutching my bag to my chest.

He nodded at me and drove off before I'd even gotten in the elevator.

As I ascended to the penthouse, my unease bubbled inside me like boiling water in a kettle, threatening to spill over at any moment. It was as if I were suspended in midair, waiting for a cruel gust of wind to knock me off balance. The ride felt never-ending, each passing second causing my heart to race faster and faster, like a train barreling towards an inevitable collision.

This shouldn't have been a big deal. Things came up in life.

I would feel like a complete idiot when I walked in and he was there . . .

But everything felt wrong.

The doors slid open and I walked into the silent foyer. A few steps in and I heard the faint din of a vacuum cleaner coming from one of the rooms.

"Lincoln?" I called out as I walked into the next room, hoping with everything in me that he'd appear, that beautiful grin on his face that I was obsessed with.

But there was no sign of him.

The sound of the vacuum subsided and the door that led to the theater room opened down the hallway. Out shuffled Mrs. Bentley, Lincoln's housekeeper, and the best cook in the world, I was pretty sure.

She was usually perfectly put together, her gray streaked brown hair in a neat bun, and her dresses she insisted on wearing perfectly pressed. Right then, she looked like she'd seen better days. Her face was red and blotchy, her warm brown eyes puffy and bloodshot. She was a short, stout English woman with a motherly air about her, perfect since Lincoln had told me she'd spent his entire life looking after him.

But right now, she looked like she could use some looking after herself.

My heart sank as I took in her appearance. "Is everything okay?" I asked tentatively. "Do you know where Lincoln is?"

Mrs. Bentley's lower lip quivered as she tried to speak. "Oh, Miss Monroe, I'm afraid it's not good news. Mr. Lincoln's not here."

"Where is he?" I asked, my voice coming out desperate.

Her eyes welled up with tears. "He's at the cemetery, love. It's—it's the anniversary of Tyler's death today."

"Tyler?"

A sob slipped from her throat. "His brother, dear."

My heart sank even further. I'd known Lincoln had a brother, and that he had passed. But Lincoln hadn't given me any other details . . . and certainly not that today was the day he'd died. It was a reminder this was all so new. We'd moved at a million miles an hour . . . but we still knew almost nothing about each other.

Correction, I knew very little about him. He seemed to know most things about me.

"Is he okay? What can I do?" I asked, my voice barely above a whisper.

Mrs. Bentley shook her head, tears spilling down her cheeks. "I don't know. He—he seemed worse than usual, love. I don't know what to do."

A deep ache tugged at my heart, and I was desperate to get to him. "Which cemetery is it?" My voice was steadying despite the knot in my stomach.

She hesitated for a moment, eyeing me carefully, but she must have seen how much I cared, because she finally gave in. "It's St. Mary's, love. But please, be careful."

I nodded, determined to do whatever it took to be there for Lincoln.

Just like he'd been there for me.

Getting to the cemetery was a hair-raising experience. I wasn't a good driver, but put me in a luxury SUV, and it was even worse. I could have called for Nathanial to come back and drive me, but I didn't know what I'd find when I got to the cemetery. And I wanted to protect Lincoln's pain.

As I approached the gates of St. Mary's cemetery, a chill swept through my body, prickling my skin. The weather was bleak and overcast, with the ominous feeling of an impending storm. St. Mary's was surrounded by a rusted iron fence that was almost as tall as me, and the gates creaked ominously as I pushed them open. Rows of headstones stretched out endlessly in all directions, and it felt like I was walking through a maze of grief and mourning.

The air was thick with the smell of freshly cut grass, and I could hear the distant sound of church bells ringing. Clouds overhead were a dark, brooding gray, and I could feel the weight of them pressing down on me. It was as if the sky was mourning with me, mourning for all the lost loved ones who were buried beneath the ground.

I walked the path that wrapped its way through the grave sites . . . until finally, I saw him.

Lincoln. Lying in front of a headstone, a handle of vodka next to him. My heart sank seeing him like that, completely consumed by his pain and grief. "Lincoln," I whispered, tears already prickling at my eyes, my voice barely above a whisper as I kneeled beside him.

He stirred slightly, muttering something unintelligible. I gently shook him, trying to bring him back to consciousness. "Lincoln, wake up," I said, my voice shaking with emotion.

He finally opened his eyes, his gaze unfocused and hazy. "Monroe?" he mumbled, his voice hoarse from crying and drinking. "I'm so sorry. I forgot."

I shook my head, unable to speak through my tears. "It's okay, Lincoln," I managed to say after a moment. "I'm here now."

He tried to sit up, but I held him down gently. "Just rest for a bit," I told him. "And then I'll get you back home, and I'll take care of you." Lincoln let himself fall, his face lying in the grass, wet from the humidity of the incoming storm.

Eventually, I helped him up, and he clung to me tightly, his body shaking with sobs. "I miss him so much," he choked out. "I'm sorry, Monroe. I don't deserve you."

I stroked his hair as we stumbled our way back to the car. He could barely walk, and it was all I could do to hold him up. He was so much bigger than me. "Shh, don't say that," I said softly. "It's going to be alright. I promise."

He just shook his head, another wave of grief clouding his golden eyes.

The car ride back to his penthouse was quiet, the only sound his ragged breathing and the occasional whimper.

Once we arrived, I led him to the couch and wrapped him in a blanket. "Stay here," I told him firmly. "I'm going to make you some tea and get you some water."

He nodded weakly, his eyes closing as he drifted off to sleep. The house was silent as I moved around the kitchen, trying to keep my hands from shaking. I knew Lincoln needed me, but I couldn't help but feel overwhelmed by the weight of his grief.

As I brought him a cup of tea and a glass of water, he stirred, opening his eyes to look at me. "Thank you, dream girl," he murmured.

But he fell back asleep before he got anything down.

I stayed there, just watching him. Thinking that some soulmates are born to find each other.

But others are ruined.

———

Lincoln's fingers twisted a lock of my hair as we laid in bed. He was still seated deep inside me in the aftermath of our lovemaking. He'd woken me up in the middle of the night, desperate for me.

I'd felt that way, too.

He was studying me now, in that intense, awestruck way of his, as if trying to read every emotion that flickered across my face. My body was sore, but it was a good kind of sore, the kind that reminded me of where he'd been. Where he still was.

I was riding the edge. If he started moving again, I would come with ease. I was so addicted to this man.

The air felt hazy around us, magical, like we were trapped in our own little world, and there was nothing that could touch us. I didn't know how I could ever feel closer to a human being than I did to him at that moment.

"Lincoln," I murmured, breathing through the sensations coursing through my body. I wanted his pain, wanted to take it from him, wrap him up in my love.

I couldn't say the words to him.

But I could show him.

_____

### Lincoln

I drank in the details of her beautiful face. I'd woken up hungry. Desperate to have her. Needing a hit of her special brand of magic to heal me.

She was riding me, her dark tresses sweeping over my stomach, her breasts bouncing with each movement. I couldn't help but obsess over her beauty as she gazed deeply into my eyes.

It was more than just a physical experience, it was spiritual.

Our minds, our souls, and our bodies were reaching out and touching each other at the same time.

I moved gently, drawing on her pleasure, and felt her tighten around me. She exhaled a soft moan as I met the gentle writhe of her body with a heavy thrust.

She was riding me, and then, suddenly, she was coming.

Those beautiful spasms gripped me tightly, and the orgasm rocketed out of me in excruciatingly intense bursts.

I owned her, and she owned me. I was addicted to the way she felt, a bittersweet pain I wasn't sure I'd survive.

She collapsed onto me, panting and dazed.

After a second, she tried to lift herself off, wincing a little. Her thighs were slick with our passion and her hair was a wild mess. She'd never looked more beautiful.

But I couldn't let her go yet. I couldn't do it. I pulled her back down, and she understood.

Of course she understood.

She was my fucking soulmate.

She was the most exquisite thing I'd ever seen in my life.

I stared at her for a long moment, my emotions swirling inside me.

"You're so damn beautiful," I said roughly.

She smiled, a small, knowing smile. "I could say the same about you."

I chuckled, and we both groaned at the sensation.

We laid there in silence for a few moments, catching our breath. I could literally feel our hearts intertwining, and it was both exhilarating and terrifying.

"I want to tell you about Tyler," I finally said, breaking the silence. She stared up at me, her green eyes soulful, understanding.

I inhaled sharply. How did I even begin to tell her about him? About the things that happened to me growing up? It all felt so heavy, so insurmountable.

Too heavy for my sweet, perfect girl.

But as I stared into those starry eyes of hers, I knew I could tell her. I could show her my scars.

"I don't know where to start," I said finally, my voice hoarse.

"It's okay," she murmured, reaching out to touch my cheek. "Take your time."

I nodded, taking a deep breath. "Tyler was my hero," I began. "He was ten years older than me. He was the only one who ever protected me from our father. The only one who ever believed in me. Tyler was everything to my parents, the perfect one, the heir to my father's throne, so to speak. But he was also my protector, my savior."

I paused, lost in the memory of my brother's kindness.

"Why did your father beat you?" she whispered in an anguished, broken voice.

I shrugged. I'd long since gotten over the fact that my parents had hated me from my birth. "They'd moved on from being active parents; they were living their lives, and then probably the one time they'd had sex since Tyler's conception . . . they ended up with me. It just pissed them off, or at least that's what I think. We've never really sat down and talked about it."

I was trying for a bit of humor, but as she bit down on her plush bottom lip, her gaze sparking with anger, she wasn't laughing.

I loved her even more for that.

"One day, after my dad had beat the shit out of me yet again, Tyler took me to the skating rink. We watched a team playing hockey, and I was . . . I was caught. It was like a whole new world had opened up to me." I smiled sadly at Monroe, remembering that moment, reliving the spark of joy, the flicker of freedom I'd gotten that day.

"He took me to all of my practices and games after that— going against my father for the first time in his life. Tyler was my biggest fan and supporter, told me he saw something in me. Thought I could really be something someday." My words caught in my throat. I tried to breathe through the pain. "He believed in me even when I didn't believe in myself."

I closed my eyes, a tear trickling down my face. Monroe's soft hand brushed it away.

"In ninth grade, there was a huge hockey exhibition in

Minnesota. Tons of scouts from colleges and the NHL were attending. I was practicing on a frozen lake near the facility, because I was fed up with how crowded the arena was, when I fell in. I was drowning when Tyler jumped in to save me."

Flashbacks of that day cycled through my mind. The icy cold darkness of the water. The realization I was going to die . . . and then the hands lifting me onto the ice.

"He got me out of the water, but . . . he didn't make it out. He drowned right in front of me."

All the pain and guilt I'd worked so hard to push down rose to the surface. It was an open wound that stabbed and twisted, refusing to close and heal. "I couldn't save him, Monroe. He hadn't even wanted to be out there. He hated the fucking cold. But he'd done it because I'd bitched so much about it." I stared at her with pleading eyes, hoping she'd understand his death felt like my own. "He was my hero, my brother, my best friend. And I killed him."

———

*Monroe*

I listened, my heart breaking for him. He was splayed open right then, his deepest pain lying before me.

I knew he didn't want to hear that he wasn't responsible for his brother's death. Those kinds of words never worked when they went against something you really believed. People said false platitudes, thinking they would make you feel better.

And it never worked.

So I just held him.

I gave him my body.

I gave him all I had.

And I hoped that it helped.

It was only later that I told him my own confession.

"I freaked out today. I thought you were done with me." I blurted it out as he ruined my body for the third time that night.

He stopped mid-thrust, staring down at me with his outrageous beauty, the kind I'd never, ever get over.

"I love you. And I'll never stop," he told me. "I'd do anything for you . . . I'd live for you."

I'd never been loved before. Not by anyone. And certainly never by someone who knew that the hardest part of a love story was when your own heart was breaking. Living for someone was the most unselfish thing you could do.

# CHAPTER 28

## MONROE

**W**e were having our first argument.

Or maybe *I* was having my first argument.

Lincoln was being frustratingly calm about the whole thing.

I stared at the black American Express card he was holding out to me, my heart racing like a wild animal. I was already living with him, eating his food, taking up his space.

This card, it was like a loaded weapon in his hand.

I backed away from him, shaking my head frantically. "I can't, Lincoln," I said, my voice cracking. "I can't take that from you."

He stared at me, his brow furrowed as he tried to understand my special brand of crazy in that moment.

I straightened up. "I don't need anything right now. I have my own money. You're already not letting me pay for rent—"

"I own the whole building. There is no rent," he interrupted gently.

I brushed my hair away from my face, the room suddenly suffocating.

"I just want you to be able to get what you need, Monroe. I just want to take care of you. I feel like it's my life's purpose."

I lifted my chin stubbornly. "I don't need to be taken care of."

"I don't like the idea of you not having it with you while you're flying to the game."

I shifted, my gaze flicking away. That was another thing we needed to talk about. He wanted me to skip school and work for the next four days. The idea of doing that was literally giving me hives.

I didn't get paid vacation time. So I'd be losing out on four full working days.

"Is this about your mom?" he asked carefully, and I stiffened. "I know your mom—"

"No, you don't actually know anything about my mom. You can read all the background checks in the world, and you will *still* not ever know what my mom was like."

He was staring down at me with so much heartfelt emotion, I wanted to cry.

"Okay, sweetheart," he murmured, putting the card back in his wallet. "We'll talk about this later."

He pulled me against his chest, and guilt flowed through my veins like a poisonous river, searing and burning me from the inside out.

"I'm sorry," he whispered, stroking my hair softly. I nodded into his shirt, still unable to look at him.

"Let's get you to work, baby."

---

### Lincoln

I'd been off all day, not liking how quiet Monroe had been this morning when I dropped her off. She'd still responded to my texts, she'd still said thank you for lunch and my daily flower delivery . . . But I could tell she was in her head. Stuck in whatever her mother had put her through.

Unlike what she thought . . . I actually *did* know a lot from her background check. She probably wasn't even aware of all the child welfare reports there were from concerned teachers, or her mother's arrest records for solicitation.

It said little for the child welfare system that she'd been allowed to stay. The reports had been . . . terrifying.

"Linc, are you ready for the road trip? It's been a minute," Peters said, yanking me from my thoughts as he stuffed an entire taco into his mouth.

I was at lunch with him and Ari, trying to distract myself from stalking Monroe at work. That fucker Kevin had literally smirked at me this morning when I'd brought her in.

He wouldn't be smirking if he knew I'd eaten her pussy out for an hour right before she'd gotten there.

*Before she got upset.*

I should've seen it coming, should've known that my Amex would be a trigger for her. I'd just been so wrapped up in how good the fucking weekend had gone.

The best fucking weekend of my existence.

I'd forgotten she wasn't in the same place as me.

"He's so fucked over his girl," Ari commented, shaking his head in mock disgust.

I threw a tortilla chip at him and he smirked before picking it off his lap, dipping it in some salsa, and eating it.

Because my best friend had taste.

"Two games, and then the playoffs. I'm ready to get this shit started," I responded, checking my phone in case she'd texted.

Peters whooped loudly, drawing the eyes of everyone in the restaurant. Luckily, we came to this hole-in-the-wall all the time, and they treated us like everyone else who came in.

"Monroe coming?" Ari asked mildly, but I could see the question in his gaze. Would I be able to concentrate if she didn't?

"Yep," I responded, taking a bite of my taco, even though Monroe still hadn't answered the question.

She had to come.

How could she stand to be away from me for four days? I could barely breathe while she was at fucking work.

Did she want me to kill my teammates? Because it would probably happen. I'd probably break a few more ribs while I was at it, too.

I shifted, sighing in annoyance at the pain still there in my side. If I could just stay inside Monroe every second, I'd probably be pain free.

My ribs never bothered me there.

Ari and Peters shit-talked each other for another thirty minutes while I stuffed chips in my mouth like an emotional eater.

Peters groaned as we left, throwing a wave at Maria, the owner of the place. "Tacos always make me want a blowjob," he commented as we walked to our cars.

Ari and I snickered. "I'm pretty sure you always want a blowjob," I drawled.

"That reminds me, Linc . . . you're looking awfully happy lately. Is dream girl as good of a fuck as you thought she'd be?" asked Ari innocently.

Once again, I found myself punching my best friend. But I aimed for his gut this time, not wanting to hurt his face for the ladies he'd be meeting up with in Boston on our road trip.

"Fuck," he groaned, "I was just kidding."

"Well, don't," I snapped.

Peters held up his hands, his eyes wide.

I knew I was acting crazy. Ari was going to die at this rate.

He straightened up. "What did I do this time? We *always* talk about girls like that."

"Not her," I muttered. "Never her."

He shook his head and stared off, his smugness melting away, replaced by something that resembled desperation.

That certainly didn't match the situation.

Not for the first time, I wondered about Ari's past. He'd gone from the streets to my fancy prep school, and although a hockey scholarship explained how he'd got in . . . I wondered if he'd ever tell me about the years that came before.

I gave them both a chin lift, and Ari slapped my shoulder, letting me know we were good. I needed to buy him a car or something. To make up for being such a raging psycho lately.

A second later . . . I'd forgotten them both as I headed to *finally* pick up Monroe.

———

I watched that fucker Kevin through the glass door as he leaned in closer to her, his eyes raking over her body. She was surrounded by the flowers I sent her every day—she wasn't hiding them anymore after I'd told her how I felt about that.

And he still hadn't gotten the hint.

My knuckles whitened as my fists clenched, the heat of jealousy consuming me.

She was mine. *Only* mine.

I couldn't take the thought of anyone else touching her.

She laughed at something he said, her long black hair swaying with the movement, but I could tell it was her fake laugh. Everything about her posture screamed that she was uncomfortable.

I tried to hold myself back. I really did. This was her place of work. It was important to her. Way more important than I could understand, apparently, judging by how this morning had gone.

But the urge to stake my claim on her was growing stronger by the second.

When he reached out to smooth her hair away from her face . . . I finally fucking snapped.

I opened the door, loudly, and their attention snapped to me.

"Hey, dream girl," I called to her, giving her my sexiest grin.

Her gaze immediately softened, into that look she only gave to *me*.

The one that always gave me hope she fucking *loved* me.

"Ready to go?"

She nodded, standing up and gathering her things.

"Want to bring some of the flowers home with us?" I asked innocently, wanting to make it clear to Kevin that she was actually living with me now.

My question hit its mark, because his face scrunched up in annoyance.

"Sure. Probably a good idea. It's getting a little . . . crowded." Monroe giggled, gathering two of the arrangements in her arms, completely unaware of my intent. She walked around the desk, giving me that brilliant, beautiful smile that caused me actual physical pain.

She turned to say goodbye to Kevin and another coworker, whose name I hadn't bothered to remember, and I stepped up behind her, my hand coming to rest possessively on the small of her back. "Missed you," I murmured, my voice purposely low and seductive.

Monroe turned to glance up at me, her green eyes brightening, a flush hitting her pretty cheeks. "Me, too." A shy smile spread across her lips.

Leaning down, I pressed my lips against hers, claiming her mouth in a possessive kiss. I could feel her melting into me, her body responding to my touch.

When we finally broke apart, I growled in her ear, gripping her ass so Kevin could see. "You're mine, Monroe. Don't ever forget that."

Her eyes glimmered in response.

The drive home was quiet. She could tell I was in a mood, but I was sure she had no idea that my mind was literally racing with anger and jealousy.

I couldn't let it go anymore. Not again. I knew what I had to do. She wouldn't quit on her own, so I had to make it happen. She wasn't going to work there another day.

I'd be put away for murder otherwise.

And we couldn't have that.

———

I waited until Monroe was sound asleep before I left the penthouse, a smile on my lips the entire drive to the asshole's house.

It was kind of fun being completely crazy.

Kevin Taylor lived in a nice neighborhood in Allen, in a modern two-story house with a sleek exterior of dark gray bricks and large glass windows.

I'm sure his wife enjoyed the place.

When she was there.

I'd found out from my PI that she was at a spa in New Braunfels with some girlfriends.

And Kevin was currently upstairs recovering from fucking her best friend, who'd just left a few minutes before.

I pounded on the heavy, dark wood door, and after a few minutes, a shirtless Kevin answered, a smirk forming on his face when he saw it was me.

"Lincoln Daniels," he drawled. "To what do I owe the pleasure?" His tone was dripping with arrogance.

This man was a fucking idiot.

Without wasting a moment, I punched him in the face, and he stumbled backward into the gray entryway, falling to the polished concrete floor. I stepped inside calmly and slammed the door shut behind me.

"I just wanted to have a friendly conversation." A smirk played on my lips as he glared at me from the ground, his face a mess of blood and bruises.

I'd definitely broken his nose with that hit.

"Fuck you."

My smile grew. I was sure I looked as demented as I felt. "I want to talk about how tomorrow is going to go."

Kevin sneered at me. "If you're worried about me stealing your girl, that's your problem. Anyone would want a piece of that."

Calling Monroe a "that" only made it worse for him.

I kicked him in the chest, grinning as I literally heard his rib crack.

He howled in pain.

I pulled out my phone and crouched down next to him, ignoring his whimpers. "Let's see what I have here."

A second later, a video of him fucking the wife of one of his Tres Medical partners started playing.

His face paled, the bright red of his blood standing out starkly against his skin.

"How did you get that?" he snarled.

"Well, it doesn't really matter *how* I got it, right? It only matters that I have it. And if you don't do exactly as I say, I'll send it to your partner, and your wife." I patted his cheek. "I don't think either of them would be too happy about this."

Kevin glared at me. "What do you want?"

"You're going to fire Monroe. Tomorrow," I said simply.

Kevin's face contorted in confusion, his brows furrowing and his lips parting in disbelief as he struggled to comprehend what I'd just said. His eyes darted back and forth, searching for the punchline, I'm sure.

But he wouldn't find it.

"Why would you want that? What kind of sick fuck are you?" Kevin finally spat.

I threw my head back and laughed. "An obsessed one."

Kevin didn't seem to find that funny. "And what brilliant reason have you come up with for why I'm firing her? She's been late one time in two years," he asked sarcastically.

"Just make up an excuse that she did some numbers wrong, or say there's a check missing. Tell her instead of going to the police, you're going to let her go." I shrugged, not really caring as long as she'd be done with her job.

He stared at me blankly before slowly shaking his head. "You're a sick fuck."

I grinned. I didn't care one bit about his opinion. My mind was already on what I'd be showing her and buying her in Boston on our trip over the next four days. My girl was about to have a lot more time on her hands. I'd already told her catering boss to stop calling, so other than a few more weeks of school before the summer, she'd be free.

I stood up and watched, detached, as he struggled to his feet, holding his ribs, drops of blood splashing to the floor from his still-bleeding nose.

I turned to go and then remembered I'd forgotten something.

"And just in case you get any ideas . . . like telling her this was my idea, I have one more thing to . . . convince you."

I pulled up another video on my phone. This one was of his wife's brother sucking on Kevin's dick like it was a popsicle. I grimaced. "The best friend's one thing, dude . . . but her brother? Ouch. That's a whole new level of messed up." A low, amused chuckle escaped my lips as I watched the utter horror that painted his face at the sight of the video.

"Tomorrow," I tossed over my shoulder as I finally strode out into the muggy night.

The sound of shattering glass and splintering wood echoed from inside the house as I made my way to my car, a wicked satisfaction curling in my gut.

It was time to get back to my girl.

I'd never let her leave, I thought as I drove.

No matter what, I'd make her happy, even if it meant locking her up and waiting for fucking Stockholm Syndrome to take hold.

My thoughts were fucked, I knew that.

But that was what she'd done to me.

This feeling. It was all-consuming. I'd never experienced anything like it before.

From the instant our eyes locked, I knew she was mine.

And she'd always be mine.

# CHAPTER 29

## MONROE

I was stirred awake by Lincoln's thick, huge length working into me. His arms were braced above me, and his half-lidded gaze was filled with desire as he slowly pushed his way in. My hips tilted instinctively as he eased out and back in, over and over again.

Finally, he sank in all the way, and his groan of pleasure sent a jolt of electricity up my spine. "I had to be inside you, baby." "I'm sorry," he murmured, pressing in deep then slowly pulling out to the tip before sliding back in leisurely. "I have to make love to you."

His words didn't register all the way in my sleep-fogged mind. All I could do was bask in the sensation of him filling me.

"I love you," he whispered, nuzzling into my hair. "You feel so good, dream girl."

A tightness coiled inside me, and my hips shifted, trying to find relief.

"Monroe," he rasped, his breathing turning labored.

But I couldn't help myself. My hips pumped of their own accord, my body responding to him without thought or hesitation. Lincoln groaned as he pushed into me, his pace picking up fractionally.

"I fucking knew it," he grunted, his breaths coming out in ragged gasps. "Every damn time I'm inside you, I go insane."

His pace continued to increase, and I felt that delicious pressure building inside me. I clenched his length as I tipped over the edge. He buried his face against my neck, his tongue coming out to lick the sensitive spot behind my ear. His movements became tender and intense as he fucked me through my orgasm.

"I'm gonna make you fall in love with me," he murmured, his breath skipping across my skin, sending starlight shooting across my soul.

With a handful of final thrusts, his body shuddered and stilled as he licked down my neck, whispering, "I'm so fucking in love with you. I'm going to make you as fucking obsessed with me as I am with you, Monroe."

My mind struggled to catch hold of his words, to comprehend the urgency that seemed to imbue them. But it slipped through my grasp like sand, and I sank back into the hazy abyss of sleep before I could make sense of any of it.

---

I woke up to the shrill sound of my phone ringing. The sky was just beginning to blush with the early colors of dawn. I groggily fumbled for it and answered.

"Monroe, it's Dr. Kevin. We need to talk," he said in a serious tone, no sign of his usually flirtatious demeanor.

I sat up in bed, suddenly wide awake. "What's going on?" I asked, heart pounding in my chest. Despite his attention at work, he'd never called me before.

"Our accounting department discovered some money missing from the office's accounts, and unfortunately, all signs point to you," he said, his voice heavy with accusation.

My mind was racing. Missing money? How could they think it was me? I would *never* do anything like that.

"That's not true! I swear, I would never steal from the company. I've always put the money exactly where I was taught," I protested, my voice shaking.

"We've already done an investigation, and the evidence is clear. We could turn you over to the police, but we've decided to terminate your employment instead. Consider it a small mercy, a chance to turn your life around."

My heart sank. I couldn't believe what was happening. I was going to lose my job, and I probably wouldn't be able to get a new one, because I wouldn't be able to use them as a referral. How would I even explain this to a potential employer?

Tears welled up in my eyes.

"Please—"

"We've made our decision. Don't push us to turn you in by making trouble."

My lips quivered as I struggled to find words.

"Have a good life, Monroe," Kevin finally said, and there seemed to be an edge of . . . sympathy in his voice.

I felt numb as he ended the call. My mind was racing, trying to make sense of what had happened. I couldn't believe I was being accused of stealing. I'd never stolen anything in my life. I was always careful to follow the rules and do things by the book. I didn't even pick money up off the street, in case it belonged to someone else and they came looking for it!

It seemed like everything I had worked so hard for was slipping away from me.

First, I'd gotten evicted from my apartment, and now this. It was like I'd been cursed. I sat on the bed, feeling lost and overwhelmed. How was I going to make it? How would I pay my bills, support myself? I was living here now . . . but how was I ever going to be able to get my own place?

*Not that I ever wanted to move out . . .*

Flashes of last night's hot dream sex filtered through my head. His whispered promises that I wasn't sure he'd even said . . .

I hadn't been totally cursed.

I stumbled out of the bedroom, barely registering the sound of Lincoln making coffee in the kitchen. As I approached him, he turned and saw the expression on my face. "What's wrong, baby?" he immediately asked, stopping what he was doing and rushing towards me.

I was fucking tired of falling apart in front of him, but it was my life at the moment.

I knew I had to tell him what happened, but I was embarrassed and humiliated. What if he didn't believe me? What if he thought I was lying? I couldn't bear the thought of losing his trust and respect.

"I was fired," I finally whispered, barely able to get the words out. "They think . . . I stole money."

Lincoln's face darkened with anger. "That's ridiculous," he snarled. "You would never do something like that."

Relief immediately flooded my insides as he came to my defense. It was like a weight had been lifted off my shoulders, and I was finally able to breathe again. A part of me, despite everything, had believed he would think the worst of me. But his unwavering support and faith in me made me feel so grateful to have him in my life. It was like he was my own personal champion, always ready to stand up for me and protect me from the world.

"We should sue those fuckers. This has to be about something else. Maybe that shithead doctor is afraid you're going to sue him for sexual harassment and he's getting the jump on it before it happens," Lincoln mused.

I frowned, thinking I hadn't gotten that vibe. "I think I should just drop it," I murmured. "He said they wouldn't press charges if I walked away quietly. I don't have the money for a long lawsuit—or any lawsuit at all."

Lincoln immediately opened his mouth to object.

"And I'm not taking any of your money to pay for a lawyer."

He frowned at me. "Come here, dream girl." Lincoln pulled me into a tight embrace, holding me as if he never wanted to let go. After a few minutes, he led me back into the kitchen, settling me down on a barstool.

"I know what this calls for," he said confidently, striding towards the massive Sub-Zero fridge and grabbing a foil-wrapped item. "One of Mrs. Bentley's famous breakfast burritos."

I wasn't sure I was in the mood to eat, but I nodded and watched him carefully heat it up and arrange it on a plate with some sliced strawberries and pineapple. The smell of chorizo and eggs filled the room, and wouldn't you know it—but my stomach actually growled. He placed it in front of me and then lifted me up before sitting down and depositing me on his lap, a small smile tugging at the corners of his lips because he knew how ridiculous our arrangement was.

I didn't give him a hard time about it, though. I needed to be close to him. I tried to take a bite, but my eyes filled with tears. It was crazy how he understood me. How he was so willing to be this steady, perfect force for me.

"You kill me when you cry," he murmured, rubbing my back.

I sniffed.

"Sorry I keep doing it. I'm not usually this much of a mess."

He tangled his hands in my hair and lifted my head up to look at him. "Hey, you're not a mess. You're just in a transition period. And I'm just lucky to be here with you."

"Fuck," I laughed, a hitched sob sneaking its way in. "You're ridiculously perfect. I can't think of anything I don't like about you."

His gaze flickered, a shadow passing over his beautiful face.

He was probably thinking of what he'd told me about his brother.

But that had made me fall harder for him. It comforted me to know that he'd experienced heartbreak. It was the only way he could understand mine.

He cut into the burrito and fed me as he told stories about the pranks they'd pulled on the rookies that year. I found myself laughing at his jokes and funny anecdotes, forgetting about everything else for a moment. The tension in my body eased, replaced by a sense of wild connectedness that made it hard to breathe.

How had he become this necessary part of my life so soon?

It was terrifying.

By the end of breakfast, the weight on my shoulders was gone.

And somehow, I'd agreed to go with him to Boston for his away games . . . that afternoon.

# CHAPTER 30

## MONROE

I wasn't sure how I'd gotten here. Waiting in the airport to board an airplane for the very first time.

The farthest I'd ever traveled was from Houston to Dallas on that fateful Greyhound trip, and now . . . here I was . . . about to fly across the country to Boston.

Growing up, I'd dreamed about what it would be like to travel the world, to have an adventure.

And here I was.

Just another way Lincoln was blowing through all my defenses and making my dreams come true.

Now that I was here, I wasn't sure why I'd been so against coming in the first place. Oh, right—it was because I used to have a job to worry about.

I pushed the thought away. It had just happened that morning, but Lincoln had bought a ticket for me a few days ago . . . just in case, he'd said.

I was ecstatic about it now.

I pulled up my ticket again in the app, checking it for the fiftieth time. Lincoln had to explain the whole process for me, because my anxiety had been through the roof thinking about traveling like this alone. Lincoln had to go on the team plane, and I felt like I'd lost my safety blanket.

I also felt like an idiot for how much I didn't know about . . . everything. Compared to Lincoln, I'd done nothing. And he didn't seem to mind at all. In fact . . . he seemed to . . . like it. He liked being the one to teach me things. He liked taking care of me. He'd texted me a million times from the team plane so far, making sure I was okay. He'd even ordered my Starbucks for me and had it waiting at pickup because I'd been nervous about stopping and possibly missing the flight because of a long line.

Lincoln seemed to revel in the fact that I'd started to depend on him for everything. It was like he was as addicted to the feeling of being needed as I was to having someone to need.

And I couldn't deny that there was a certain thrill to it all.

But it also made me feel vulnerable. Like I was at his mercy.

I should be cautious, my brain whispered . . . but my heart didn't seem to know better.

I glanced down at the ticket again, and I realized for the first time that he'd put me in first class.

I immediately texted him.

> They're going to kick me out. I don't belong in first class.

> Lincoln: Trust me, you'll class up the place.

> Lincoln: Are you happy?

> Only thing that would be better would be if you were here.

> Lincoln: I feel the same way, dream girl. I fucking miss you.

They called for first class then, and I immediately jumped from my seat, not because I was trying to beat people on the plane, but because, for some reason, I was afraid it was going to leave without me if I didn't get on as soon as I was asked.

As I waited in line on the boarding bridge, my heart thudded against my ribcage like a trapped bird. Was the plane going to feel too small . . . too confining?

Suddenly, the thought of being so high in the air was making my palms sweat. I took a deep breath, trying to steady myself before I had a panic attack without even getting on the plane.

I was greeted with a warm smile from the flight attendant, and then I was walking to my seat through the first-class cabin.

My eyes widened as I took in the luxurious surroundings. Okay, this was nice. The seats were wider and more comfortable than I'd thought they would be, with plush pillows and blankets waiting for me.

As I settled into my seat, I took in the personal TV screen, noise-canceling headphones, and the cozy pair of slippers and an eye mask . . . just in case I wanted to make use of the fact that the seats actually laid all the way down.

I was feeling very spoiled. And significantly calmer. Especially as the flight attendant came by with freaking champagne.

I sipped at it and texted Lincoln.

I miss you, too.

Lincoln: 🖤🖤🖤

Lincoln: My wrinkly old balls also miss you.

I snorted and shook my head, smiling to myself as the flight attendants made an announcement that it was a completely booked flight and cargo space would be limited.

I'd expected someone to sit in the seat next to me after the five other announcements the crew made about how full the plane was . . .

But as they shut the doors, it was still empty . . . along with the row across from me. Glancing around, it seemed like all the other seats in the plane were full.

A ridiculous thought came to my head. But surely . . . no . . .

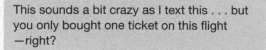

This sounds a bit crazy as I text this . . . but you only bought one ticket on this flight —right?

It was a full five minutes before he answered, even though the three little dots had been going the entire time.

Lincoln: I may have bought more.

How many did you buy?!

Lincoln: Your row and the next. They didn't put anyone in those seats, right?

Um, no . . . they're empty. But why exactly did you do that?

Lincoln: When your girlfriend is the hottest woman on the planet, you don't take chances. Meeting you on a plane—that's fucking romance book shit. Not happening.

I'm swooning. But it's also a little crazy, right?

Okay 😊😍

I settled back in my seat and turned on *Fixer Upper*. Wondering why crazy felt so good.

———

When we landed, it only got more surreal. I was picked up by a sleek limousine and driven through the winding streets of Boston. The streets were filled with an electric energy, and the city was alive with the hustle and bustle of people going about their day. The buildings towered above us, their brick and stone facades creating a stark contrast against the blue sky. The eclectic mix of old and new made me desperate to explore every corner of the city.

The car wound its way through the streets, taking us on a scenic tour of the city before finally pulling up in front of the hotel. The driver opened the door for me and I stepped out, immediately feeling . . . overwhelmed. This world that Lincoln had brought me into, it was such a far cry from the *nothing* I'd always known.

I wondered if it was possible to get used to this. To stop worrying about where your next meal would come from. Or whether you'd be able to keep a roof over your head.

I made my way through the hotel lobby, struck by the opulence and grandeur of the place. The marble floors of the lobby gleamed underfoot, and the large, modern lights overhead sparkled like diamonds, grand and opulent in every way. I was greeted by the hotel staff and treated like I was some kind of queen as they took me to the freaking *suite* Lincoln had decided to book for me.

Wandering around the rooms was a dizzying experience. The suite was massive, with three bedrooms, each containing a king-sized bed draped in soft, white linens, a plush couch, and a breathtaking view of the city skyline from the floor-to-ceiling windows.

I was staring out the window at the dazzling city below when the door clicked open behind me.

I didn't turn around. I just watched him come straight to me in the reflection of the glass.

His arms wrapped around me and he buried his face in my neck, like we'd been apart for weeks instead of a few hours.

I felt the same relief.

The same terrifying, spinning relief that you could only feel if your soul was living in another person.

It was getting harder and harder to even be away from him for a second.

*Mama's limp body on the floor, tears streaking down her face, a needle in her arm she hadn't even bothered to remove . . .*

*Stop it*, I screamed. Because my brain just wouldn't quit.

"I missed you," he murmured, an ache in his voice like he'd been suffering.

And I only nodded and thought . . .

Me, too.

---

As we got into the limo, I was instantly struck by the strong stench of perfume and the loud, high-pitched giggles of the five scantily clad women draped over Lincoln's teammates—puck bunnies, I'd learned they were called. Women that were desperate for hockey dick, no matter what it cost them.

They were all over them, stroking their arms, their shoulders, their thighs. Desperate to keep their attention.

Lincoln was unfazed by it all, not even batting an eye as the girls fawned over him and his friends. He was chatting with Ari, completely ignoring everyone else except for me. It was amazing how he could seem so involved in his conversation with Ari, and yet I knew he was aware of every movement . . . every breath I took. He had me in his lap, one arm around my waist, the other hand softly slipping up and down my leg—sending goosebumps everywhere.

The other girls' jealousy radiated off of them like heat from a raging fire. Lincoln and Ari were the trophies, after all; the two players they all desperately craved.

And they didn't even have a clue how hot Lincoln really was . . . like he'd been just an hour ago.

*His mouth closed hungrily over my nipple as he fucked my*
*core with two fingers, his thumb toying with my ass . . . my back*
*pressed against the glass . . .*

The ride to the restaurant was relatively short, but it felt like
an eternity with the inane noise of the girls giggling and actually
cooing over the guys. I was honestly surprised they hadn't
mounted them right in front of us.

When we finally arrived, I lifted off Lincoln's lap, and he
patted my ass as I ducked to get out of the limo. One of the
bunnies was already out, a wide grin on her face, like we were
long-lost best friends or something.

"This is the most expensive restaurant in the city," she whispered in my ear, linking her arm through mine. Because of
course she'd be keeping tabs on that.

I was saved by Lincoln suddenly pulling me away. Evidently,
girls were also on the list of people who weren't allowed to
touch me.

So that list basically included everyone on the planet.

We were seated at a large table in a private room, Lincoln
plastered against me in the bench seating.

An arm wrapped around my shoulders from the other side.

"So, how's my girl?" a grinning Ari asked as he pulled me
towards him and rubbed his face on my head like we were
wolves and he was scent marking me.

"I seriously think you want to die, Lancaster," drawled
Lincoln, yanking me back towards him and smoothing down my
hair like Ari had hurt it.

"You're looking stunning, but you'd look even better in a
jersey with my name on it." His eyebrows rose and fell lecher-
ously—referencing his little prank from that first game. Unlike
the scraps of clothes the other girls were wearing, Lincoln had
insisted I wear a jersey with his name on it tonight. He seemed to
be obsessed with me wearing clothes with his last name.

Lincoln sighed, grabbed his water, and then tossed the

contents right in Ari's face. My mouth dropped as Ari sputtered and the whole group roared with laughter.

Ari shook his head, wiping the water off his face, a smug grin on his lips.

"Love you too, Linc," he grinned as the waitress came by to get our orders.

The food was the best I'd ever had, and I had fun watching Lincoln interact with his teammates. It was clear they had a strong bond, and it was also clear they all thought he hung the moon. Lincoln was so relaxed, his walls down and the intense energy he usually had around me nowhere to be seen. The guys completely ignored their dates as they talked, but I guess the girls were at least getting a ridiculously expensive meal out of the night—so none of them seemed to mind.

Or, at least they were too busy giving me dirty looks to realize no one had said a word to them.

I was completely relaxed as we got up from the table to leave —at least until we stepped outside the restaurant and were accosted by flashes of cameras so blinding I'd be seeing spots for weeks.

"Fuck, which one of you called them?" Ari spat, glaring at the girls who were all primping and trying to get the attention of the cameras. My eyes darted around in confusion and anxiety. Lincoln threw his arm around me, trying to shield me from the paparazzi.

"Lincoln! Over here! Smile for the camera!" one of them yelled.

"Is that Monroe?" another yelled, and I froze at the limo door. They'd found out my name.

"Get in, baby," Lincoln murmured, and I finally slid inside.

Ari immediately started ripping into the girls as soon as the door closed, but I was lost in my head.

It was one thing for them to know my name, but what if they dug deeper? Found out about my past . . . where I came from.

My mother.

"You okay, baby?" Lincoln asked, seeming totally unfazed by what happened.

"Yeah," I whispered, staring out the window. He played with my hair for the rest of the car ride, but left me alone with my thoughts as he talked to his teammates.

It was only back in the suite that he demanded my attention.

"What's going on in that pretty head, Monroe?" he asked as he followed me into the bathroom.

"Can I have a minute?" I snapped petulantly, even though I was just going to wash my face.

"Mmh, that would be a no." He was amused as he stared down at me, like I wasn't having an inane hissy fit because some stranger took my picture. "Those assholes freaked you out."

I practically growled. "Of course they freaked me out. Who wouldn't be freaked out by that? I don't know how you ever get used to it!"

He shrugged, leaning against the doorway, his gorgeous masculinity filling the entire room.

"It's just a picture, baby. They'll never know anything about the real me." He shrugged. "And if it gets the word out about us, then I'm all for it."

I bit down on my lip, and my silence caught his attention. He stalked towards me, tipping up my chin with two fingers so I was forced to stare into his golden gaze. "Now I really want to know what you're thinking."

I jerked my chin away from him. "I just think . . . maybe we should keep things quieter. About us. We don't have to tell everyone."

His silence was a bit terrifying. Before I could say anything else though, he suddenly scooped me into his arms and stalked out into the bedroom we'd already thoroughly used that afternoon.

"Lincoln—"

"We're going to come to an understanding right now," he growled as he threw me on the bed and stripped off his clothes while I stared at him wide-eyed.

And very turned on.

"I'm going to make something very clear right now, Monroe. Teach you something you won't forget . . . "

"You *are* mine."

He ripped off my clothes, aggressively attacking my breasts, biting and sucking on my nipples until I was crying out, my moans filling the room.

"These are mine. Your pussy is mine. Your lips are mine." He made his way down my body, licking and sucking over every inch of me, eating into my core, his tongue passing lazily through my folds.

"Say it," he ordered, sucking hard on my clit while he scissored his fingers inside me until I was about to come.

It was torture, because he knew exactly how to perfectly get me off.

And he was choosing to stop, every time, right before I fell off the edge.

His tongue slipped down until it was circling my asshole, pushing the tip of it inside while he worked my other hole with his fingers. I was thrashing and screaming on the bed.

But I also was not okay with him trying to teach me a lesson.

"I'm not yours," I whispered, and he paused.

"You want to say that again?"

"I'm not yours. I don't belong to anyone."

"We'll see about that," he finally snarled as he withdrew his fingers and reached down for the belt he'd thrown on the floor while undressing. Before I could even blink, he'd tied my wrists to the headboard and laid himself down on me so I couldn't move even an inch.

"Let me go right now! Have you lost your mind?" I growled as he pressed down on me further, a glint of madness in his gaze.

I writhed underneath him, desperate for some friction to help me come. But he stayed there, perfectly still, his big body not letting me move at all.

It was amazing as I stared up at him, that he could still look like an angel hovering above me, his golden hair falling in his face, those starlight eyes glaring down at me.

"Say it," he ordered.

"Please, baby. Make me come. Fuck me with that big cock," I pleaded.

I was trying to rile him, push him over the edge so that he had no choice but to do what I wanted.

But nothing I said seemed to reach him. He slowly slid his dick through my folds, too slowly to give me what I wanted.

"Going to stay just like this, Monroe. Just like this, until you tell me you're mine." Another slow slide had tears running down my face. "Who do you belong to, dream girl? Say it."

I bucked underneath him, trying to slide his dick into me, because I couldn't stand it.

I'd never felt this reckless, so out of control. I needed him more than I needed to breathe.

"If I want to tell every fucking person on this planet about you and me, and what you mean to me, I'm going to do it. Nod your head that you understand."

I glared up at him, but I was also a very, very desperate girl. So I nodded.

His smugness only fueled my fury. "Good girl," he murmured, finally slipping the tip of his dick into my core. He still didn't press in, though, refusing to give me his long, hard length.

"Please," I whimpered.

He laughed almost evilly, before his voice turned soothing and patronizing. "Then say it, Monroe. I'll make you come harder than you ever have before. Just say it."

"I'm yours, Lincoln," I finally murmured, staring up into his gaze.

"And you're going to let me tell everyone about us? You know that I'll take care of you, keep you safe . . . Right?"

I tried to close my eyes and not answer that one, but suddenly he pushed all the way to the hilt, until I felt so full I was sure he was pushing into the entrance of my womb.

I shook my head. "Yes, I'm going to trust you," I growled through gritted teeth.

"I'm going to tell everyone," he pressed, rearing back and slamming forward again.

"Yes," I whispered, not caring about anything anymore other than him letting me orgasm.

"Such a good fucking girl," he growled as he thrust into me sharply, setting off an orgasm so intense the world blacked out for a moment.

When I came back to consciousness, he was still fucking in and out of me, his face determined, his eyes hungry and obsessed.

"I love you," he said as he pumped into me desperately. His hand came between us and pressed on my clit, and I immediately spiraled over the edge *again* as he spilled into me, filling me with so much cum, it seeped down my legs.

"I love you, I love you, I love you," he panted as he fucked me through the pleasure.

He refused to pull out when we were done, gathering me close, letting our juices drip between us. He stared into my eyes, and not for the first time, I wondered if this madness between us was okay. If it was possible for either of us to survive it. Or would it take us over and destroy us both?

I wondered these things, filled with his cock and his cum, knowing with the very marrow of my bones that I *did* indeed belong to him.

But I didn't tell him I loved him.

miss the old days, when lots of hot sex made you happy," Ari complained as I threw a puck at him and smirked.

I didn't miss the old days.

I could barely remember them, actually. I was so lost in this haze of . . . bedazzlement, it was hard to think of before.

Sometimes, I did miss the days when I was capable of rationality . . . but my sanity was a sacrifice that had to be made.

Monroe's altar was the only thing I wanted to worship.

Fuck everything else.

"So, it's good then?" Ari pressed, his smile fading as he stared at me pensively.

I tried to think of how to describe it to my best friend. To make him understand how, in a moment, my whole axis had shifted. How I'd been completely reborn.

"She's everything," I finally said simply.

And he nodded. Almost like he got it.

"You guys looked like you were in your own little world last night. It was fucking weird."

I chuckled, shaking my head as he winked and started wrapping tape around his hockey stick.

My smile faded as I thought for the thousandth time of those three little words she was refusing to say.

I couldn't stop thinking about it.

It tore at my skin, burrowing under the surface, like a sliver I couldn't get out.

I understood she was scared. I was, too.

Falling in love with her had been the scariest thing I'd ever done. Knowing that someone existed on the earth that you would do anything for . . . die for . . . cut yourself open and bleed out for . . . it was a heavy, life-altering feeling.

But I'd jumped over the edge with her. Fallen hard in a way I could never come back from.

I loved her. I loved her so much it hurt. Like she'd torn out a piece of my heart and put it in her chest instead, and now I was dependent on her even to breathe.

She'd wanted to keep us a fucking secret?

That had been one of the craziest things I'd ever heard in my life. Women had *always* wanted me, even as a young kid. They'd follow me around the playground in droves, begging me to be their boyfriend—whatever that meant in first grade.

As I got older, it only grew worse.

I was the perfect gold star alpha hero that women all over the world thirsted for . . . would do anything for. Any girl I'd slept with or gone to an event with went absolutely nuts on social media, wanting to tell every person alive they'd managed to bag me for one night.

And the girl who had finally captured me, fucking body and soul . . . wanted to hide us?

Fuck that.

The door to the locker room swung open and in walked Coach. "Alright, boys," he barked. "It's time to go out there and kick some ass. Don't do stupid shit, remember how to fucking pass, and let's bring home a win."

As Coach finished his speech, the locker room erupted into a loud cheer, with everyone shouting and pounding their sticks on the ground. The energy in the room was electric, and a surge of adrenaline rushed through me as I tightened my skates one more time.

"Let's do this, boys!" I yelled, my voice barely audible over the noise of the others.

The guys around me were all fired up, slapping each other on the back and exchanging fist bumps.

That feeling. It was what every fucking competitor on earth lived for. The feeling you could do anything, your team could do anything . . . the energy was contagious. We were ready to win.

I gazed around the room, taking it all in, reminding myself how lucky I was to be here. I could never forget this. Could never forget the sacrifice that had gotten me here.

My brother's sacrifice.

This was *my* team. The guys I'd gone to battle with countless times before.

"Fuck yeah!" screamed Ari as we headed down the hallway, into the arena.

It was game time.

———

The puck dropped, and it was on. The crowd roared as the players raced down the ice, and I lost myself in the game. The sound of the skates cutting through the ice, the slap of the puck against the boards, it was all music to my ears.

The energy of the crowd was on crack as they cheered on both teams. Thanks to Ari and me, the team had amassed quite the following over the last few years, and we could be assured of having a good turnout of our fans at every arena in the country.

We were getting close to scoring, and I could feel the tension building. Suddenly, the puck was flying towards me, and I saw my opening.

I deftly maneuvered around the defender, and with one swift move, I flicked the puck towards the goal. The goalie never had a chance as the puck sailed past him and into the net.

"Better luck next time, boys," I crowed as I skated past Boston's goalie—a douchebag if there ever was one.

And then I got a brilliant plan. Before I could get tackled by my teammates, I skated right up to the glass in front of Monroe's seat, just a few rows up, and I stared right at her. She'd been screaming and cheering for me along with most of the arena—even Boston fans loved me—but she quieted right down as I stood in front of her. Monroe eyed me warily, and it only made my grin wider about what I was about to do. I pointed right at her . . . and then I made a fucking heart sign with my hands as I stared. The crowd went fucking wild, people starting to point at her.

Monroe wasn't going to play along, though. She shook her beautiful fucking head and stared off . . . like I'd been throwing up a heart to someone else.

Alright, dream girl. It was on.

I obviously would have to make it clearer.

The second goal I scored was even better. Ari had just slammed an opposing player into the boards, jarring the puck loose. I had already been charging towards the goal, and as soon as I saw the puck come free, I made a quick pivot, snatched it up, and took off with a burst of speed.

I was skating so fast that Boston's defenders couldn't keep up with me. I faked left and then right, and then deked the goalie so convincingly that the prick was left sprawling on the ice. The puck sailed into the net with a satisfying thunk, and the crowd went wild.

I went right to the same spot in the glass, catching Monroe's eye. Once again, I pointed at her and made a heart sign with my hands. The crowd erupted into even louder cheers. Monroe looked away again, a dark blush creeping up her cheeks, but she was grinning that time . . . and she didn't shake her head.

Progress.

"Get it, Linc!" Ari roared as he tackled me against the glass, joined by Peters, Jones, and Fredericks.

The adrenaline coursing through me was making my head spin. What a fucking game.

I scored two more goals, and every time, I repeated my actions.

After the fourth goal, when I immediately skated up to the glass and made the heart sign, she didn't look away. Instead, she finally met my gaze and held it for a long moment, before smiling and glancing down at her lap.

The crowd's roar almost burst my fucking eardrums. There was definitely no doubt in anyone's mind at that point that I was talking to her.

As the final buzzer sounded and the game ended—with a Knights win, of course—I skated over to the bench, a heady sense of satisfaction floating through me that I hadn't felt on the ice in a long time.

I knew I'd played my heart out tonight, both on *and* off the ice.

And later, as I headed towards the postgame press conference, I couldn't help but feel a little smug about the next part of my plan.

When I arrived at the podium, I walked in front of it first. And then I slowly did a turn, showcasing the custom jersey my assistant had wrangled up for me.

I could see the confusion on the reporters' faces as they noticed the name on the back of the jersey. It was Monroe's last name. There were murmurs and whispers, and then the questions started to fly in.

But it took me a minute to answer them.

Because the most fucking gorgeous girl in the world was

standing in the back of the room, a satisfying, awestruck look all over her pretty face as she stared at me. Her awe morphed into a brilliant smile, and for a second, I was afraid my heart had actually stopped beating.

We just stood there, smiling at each other like fucking clowns, cameras flashing around us.

And I wondered if I'd finally succeeded in chipping past that last wall Monroe had been guarding her heart with.

# CHAPTER 32

## MONROE

**D**allas was buzzing with excitement as the Knights, led by Lincoln, won the first round of playoffs in a "stunning four games series" as the *Fort Worth Star-Telegram* described it.

And it *had* been stunning.

I'd never had a thing for sports before meeting Lincoln.

But, oh, did I have a thing for them now. Or, at least for hockey . . .

The streets around the arena were filled with fans after the games, chanting and cheering as they celebrated the team's victory. They even came to the airport to wait for the team and celebrate after game three in Chicago.

The next round was going to be difficult, but the whole city seemed to know the Stanley Cup was as good as ours.

The fans were absolutely rabid for Lincoln. Everywhere he went, there were screams of adoration and chants of his name. They crowded around him, waving signs and asking for autographs, even when he was trying to get from the locker room to the parking lot. It was like being in the presence of a rock star.

He handled it all with the same ease he seemed to handle

everything else, and through it all, he put me first. It became clearer and clearer every day that Lincoln Daniels would do anything for me.

I knew what people thought now that Lincoln was taken, and that I was the one who'd done the taking. They wondered how someone so unextraordinary . . . so average . . . managed to snag someone as brilliant and dazzling as him. I was the dim street-lamp, and he was the stadium lights.

And I was perfectly okay with that.

There were even news stories over the last week that had dug into my background, and were now referring to me as "the daughter of a drugged out prostitute."

But they didn't have quite the effect on me that I'd worried they would.

It was like problems seemed to disappear around Lincoln, like they stopped existing at all. Any time I felt anxious, he'd make love to me for hours, until I'd forgotten what I was stressed about in the first place.

With Lincoln by my side, I'd suddenly found myself in the spotlight, too. People started recognizing me when we were out and about, and some even asked for *my* autograph. It was . . . weird.

And I still hadn't been able to find a job.

I'd been applying for one every single day, sending out countless applications, but not a single response came back my way. I'd even applied to some fast-food places, places I knew from talking to others that hired *everybody* who applied.

But I hadn't gotten a single call.

It was frustrating and unnerving, but I refused to let it bring me down. For the first time in my life, I had some free time, and I was determined to make the most of it.

And Lincoln was always willing to use any of those moments I didn't fill . . .

My phone buzzed, and I finished typing my thoughts before I

glanced at it. This was my last paper for finals and then I would be free for a few weeks until summer semester.

> Unknown: Hey. It's Ari Lancaster. I stole your number from Lincoln's phone.

I eyed the text warily.

> Hi?

> Unknown: How is Lincoln doing?

I frowned, confused, because they'd just seen each other at practice last night.

> He's out for a run . . . as far as I know, he's okay. Why?

> Unknown: It's his brother's birthday today. I just wanted to make sure he was alright.

My phone slipped from my hand and clattered to the floor as my mind raced, wondering if he'd been off this morning. Had he seemed more needy than usual? He'd kept me in our bed for hours as he worshiped my body. There were marks all over my skin from his mouth and his hands.

And he *had* been quieter than he normally was.

He hadn't called me "good girl" once.

I jumped up from the couch and paced, wondering what I should do . . . what I could possibly say. Would it be like his brother's deathly? Was he even out running? Or was he at the cemetery torturing himself?

I was about to go out and try to find him when I heard the elevator doors ding. I ran out into the hallway, almost forgetting everything with the sight of him standing in the entrance, shirtless, his muscles glistening with sweat, his tank top tucked into the back of his basketball shorts.

I bet there were women passed out all over the streets from catching sight of him this morning.

He was beautiful. The most beautiful thing I'd ever seen. His hair had gotten longer since we met, something to do with a superstition he had that you couldn't cut your hair during a winning streak—and it had been awhile since they lost.

The longer hair looked good on him. Perfect, really. If there ever was male perfection, it was Lincoln Daniels.

He smirked at me, clearly reading my dirty thoughts, as those golden eyes of his lazily drifted down my body.

After a second, though, his grin fell, and a blank, distant expression took over his features.

"Hi," I murmured sadly.

He flinched at my tone, staring down at the ground for a long moment before finally glancing at me. "Who told you?" he asked despondently, eyeing me warily as I came up and wrapped myself around him, ignoring the sweat peppering his skin.

"Ari texted me."

He snorted out a humorous laugh. "Of course, he did. How did that fucker even get your phone number?"

I cracked a grin. "He stole it from your phone, apparently."

He shook his head, cursing Ari out under his breath.

"How—are you feeling?" I asked tentatively, immediately cursing myself for the stupid question.

"Better than I usually do," he admitted, biting down on his plush lower lip. "Which only makes me feel fucking guiltier."

I hesitated for a moment. "Can you tell me more about him? Some happy memories?"

He cocked his head, staring at me pensively, before he grabbed my hand and led me back into the living room. Lincoln flopped onto the couch, pulling me onto his lap, his favorite place for me.

"Okay," he said, taking a deep breath. He huffed. "There are so many to choose from." He thought for a minute. "There was this one time when we decided to go camping, and my brother and I decided to catch a fish for dinner. The problem was . . . neither of us knew anything about fishing or camping. We were the sons of a billionaire who hated the outdoors. We spent the entire day out there by the lake, but we didn't catch a single thing. We were about to give up when Tyler decided to try one last time. He cast his line out, but it got caught on something, and when he tugged on the line, he ended up falling in the water. And of course, because my brother was golden-touched, a huge fish ended up swimming past right then, and he managed to catch it by smacking it with a rock. I've never seen anything like it." He snickered. "We got back to our attempt at a makeshift campsite though . . . and remembered neither of us knew how to make a fire. So eventually, we just ended up ordering pizza like the spoiled rich kids that we were."

I giggled and a ghost of a grin slid across his face.

I smiled, feeling the warmth of Lincoln's memory. "I love that," I said.

"Me, too," Lincoln replied. "Tyler had a way of making even the smallest moments feel fucking fun. He had this ridiculous laugh that would light up the room, and he always knew how to make people feel special."

"You're like that too," I murmured, "Except I'd call your laugh sexy, not ridiculous."

Lincoln scrunched up his face like he didn't believe it.

After a second, though, he chuckled softly. "There was this other time, when some kids had been jerks to me at school. And Tyler took me to this county fair that was going on nearby. He took me on every ride, and we both stuffed ourselves with all the fried food they had. And then I threw up all over Tyler's car at the end of the night . . . And he just laughed. He wasn't mad at all; he just was glad I felt better."

A tear slipped down his cheek.

I smiled at the memory, feeling a sense of longing for something I'd never experienced. "It sounds like he loved you a lot," I said softly.

"He did. He was probably the only person who did growing up," Lincoln murmured, his voice filled with emotion. He turned to look at me. "I miss him so fucking much."

I laid my head on his shoulder, crying for him because life was so fucking unfair sometimes.

"As you can probably guess, I don't have a lot of great memories of my mom," I whispered a little while later.

Lincoln's entire body flinched, because my mother was someone I *never* talked about.

But I felt like telling him this; he deserved that at least, when he was so free with his own pain.

"But the grief still comes in waves sometimes, you know? And anger, too. Because even though she couldn't be who I wanted . . . who I needed . . . she was still my mom. And maybe she did the best she could, and I just need to accept that— anyways—what I'm trying to say—is that sometimes when it hurts, when it hurts so bad I feel like I can't breathe, I send her light."

"You send her . . . light?" Lincoln asked, clearly confused.

I nodded against his neck. "I think of the happiest things I can, and I picture sending them to her, wherever she is. Every time it hurts, I send her light. I tell her that I hope she's happy, that I love her . . . and, that I forgive her. And then I release whatever emotion I'm feeling at that moment, and I send it her way."

I gazed up at him and saw he was staring at the ceiling thoughtfully.

"I think, maybe, you should send Tyler light. You should talk to him. Tell him you hope he's happy, that you love him, and then . . . you should *forgive* yourself."

His silence was deafening. Watching his face was like watching a storm gathering on the horizon. There were so many emotions flicking across his features.

"I don't think I know how to do that," he finally whispered.

"I think you do. I think that you just won't let yourself do it." I rushed on, even though I was terrified I was going too far.

"What if the best way for you to honor Tyler's memory is to live . . . for him? And I mean to truly live—to strip off the pain that makes it so you can barely say his name. What if we talk about Tyler all the time? What if we honor his memory by making it happy—like he was?"

There's my own lessons in these words, and I'm unpacking them at the same time as I'm unpacking everything else.

And it's a little overwhelming, to be honest.

"Fuck," he finally murmured, and then his lips crashed against mine and he was giving me more passion in that single kiss than I think I'd experienced across my entire life.

"Thank you," he growled when we finally came up for air. His eyes were starstruck as he stared down at me.

A girl could fall in love in an instant being looked at like that.

"I spend so much fucking time thinking about how much I miss him, I forget to *remember* him. It's been forever since I've thought of some of those memories. It's been forever since Tyler was anything but a knife in my gut, a memory that made me want to die."

"Did I make it better, or worse?" I asked.

"Better. Always better, dream girl. You've changed my whole life. I love you so fucking much," he breathed, his lips slamming against mine once again, his tongue sliding inside my mouth. I could feel him everywhere. And if there was one moment for me to tell him I loved him, to tell him I'd do anything for him.

It was that moment.

But I didn't.

Not because I was terrified of it anymore.

But because Lincoln didn't let me talk that morning, for a long, long time.

# CHAPTER 33

## MONROE

E vidently, a nonnegotiable in Lincoln's family was that on Tyler's birthday, they all ate dinner together. While I would think that was a sweet way to remember him in most families, I was sure it was something akin to torture in theirs, after everything Lincoln had told me about his parents.

"You're not going with me," Lincoln said calmly as he buttoned his white dress shirt in front of the mirror, refusing to even look at me.

"Yes, I am."

"I'm not putting you through that. I'm not an idiot. I'm not going to take the most beautiful thing in my life and put it in the same room as . . . them."

"You would do it for me if the situation was reversed—wouldn't you?" I snapped, my hands on my hips. I was already dressed. I'd thrown on a dress the moment he'd told me what his plans were, determined to go with him.

He'd made so much progress this morning. He'd actually smiled at points today.

I just knew his parents were going to destroy that.

Lincoln finished getting dressed, not speaking another word

to me until he was done, breaking my heart because he looked so fucking amazing in his fitted suit.

He finally turned and stalked towards me, until I was backed up against the wall. His hand went around my neck as his other hand threaded through my hair.

"You will listen to everything I fucking say when we're there. And when I tell you it's time to leave, we're leaving."

I would nod, but I couldn't move. I'd never seen him like that, and my heart skipped, a mix of terror and happiness buzzing through me. The terror because I was about to go into the lion's den, and happiness . . . because he was letting me take care of him just like he always took care of me.

"I fucking love you," he growled, kissing me hard as the hand in my hair grabbed one of mine, thrusting it under my dress until I was pressing against my core. His fingers pushed two of my fingers into my sex, thrusting inside me and somehow hitting that perfect spot just right.

He groaned as I came instantly, turned on by his aggression.

I was wide-eyed and feeling a mess as he pulled my fingers out and brought them to his mouth, slowly sucking them clean. His lips met mine again, and I could taste myself on his tongue.

Wow . . . that was . . . hot.

"That should keep me sane through dinner," he muttered. I just blinked.

Because what did you do after something like that?

---

My heart pounded like a caged bird as we approached the looming mansion of Lincoln's parents. The sprawling gardens and ornate fountains were like a grand fortress, dwarfing me like the mere speck of dust everyone in this household would think I was.

The door creaked open, and a stern, imposing woman

dressed in a dark suit appeared. "Mr. Daniels," she murmured stiffly, not even bothering to acknowledge me, like I was a ghost drifting beside Lincoln's side.

Was this Lincoln's mother? No—she'd called him "Mr. Daniels." That would just be fucking weird.

"Ms. Talbot, the house manager," Lincoln muttered, not even bothering to greet her with anything else but a head nod.

I shot him a look because—a house manager—I didn't even know what that was.

We were led into a formal dining room where a table, longer than my whole old studio apartment, was laid out with crystal glasses and fine china. It was clear this was not the kind of dinner where you put your elbows on the table.

The dress I'd thought made me feel so pretty an hour ago, suddenly felt like it was made of sackcloth.

I took in the sight of Lincoln's parents, both impeccably dressed. Lincoln's father was wearing a black suit, perfectly tailored to his frame. His hair was styled in a slicked-back fashion that oozed confidence, but also reminded me of how I'd imagine the devil would look right before he ended someone. Meanwhile, his mother was stunning in a dark violet cocktail dress that seemed far too fancy for a dinner in her home. Her hair was intricately styled in an updo that looked like it had taken hours to perfect. They both looked like they belonged on the cover of a high-end fashion magazine.

The hate I felt for them could not be adequately described. I had the urge to throw myself over Lincoln, shield him from their horribleness.

Because they may have been beautiful looking—similar to their son—but you could literally feel their ugliness—like it was coating your skin.

"Lincoln," his dad said coldly, his gaze licking over me from top to bottom, a tiny smirk peeking out from his lips that made my blood freeze.

"Father," Lincoln replied nonchalantly, like we hadn't just stepped into hell. He pulled out my chair for me and waited for me to sit before pushing me in.

Despite the fact they weren't speaking to me, their cold eyes were all over me as I sat there, judging my every breath.

"Wine," his mother finally announced, holding up her glass. I glanced around the room because there was no one in here. Was she expecting someone to just materialize from the wall?

Evidently, people did do that here, because a second later, a man dressed in a sharp gray suit practically materialized from a door I hadn't even noticed, hurrying to fill up her wine glass.

"Lincoln, darling, when are you going to cut that hair of yours?" she asked, her voice dripping with condescension, staring across the table at him like he was a bug she wanted to smash.

I wasn't sure at that moment *who* actually had the worst childhood, me or him. My mother had been disinterested in me, she'd forgotten me 99 percent of the time, but she'd never looked at me with so much distaste as I was seeing right now, like she was regretting the day I was born.

"When you stop drinking, mother dearest," Lincoln drawled.

Lincoln's mother made an affronted gasp, before throwing back the very wine he'd just made fun of.

Lincoln's father seemed bored of it all. He was lounged back in his high back chair, toying with the dark amber liquid in the tumbler in front of him. "That's enough, Shannon," he said in a silky, dangerous voice that had Lincoln's mother shutting up immediately.

I was sitting up straight as well, and I could see how he'd be a success in the boardroom, even having never been in one myself. There was something commanding in his voice, something dangerous that made you terrified to disappoint him.

I shot a quick glance at Lincoln, but he didn't seem to be affected by it at all, though.

"Tonight's a night for celebration after all," continued his father, his gaze flicking briefly to one of the many empty chairs at the table.

"Haven't called it a celebration for a while, Father. Have you turned over a new leaf?" Lincoln asked lightly, playing with the knife at his place setting.

His father chuckled darkly, not seeming to mind the sarcasm in his son's tone in the slightest.

"I'm talking about the fact that I've set up a meeting with the board, to announce the start of your work with the company, the day after you finish that silly little game."

My gaze bounced between Lincoln and his father, not understanding what he was talking about. That silly little game? I couldn't imagine someone would think Lincoln's career as the most talked about hockey player in the NHL would be called "silly" or even "a little game," but I guess there was a first time for everything. I wondered what it would be like to be that blind. To see a star shining right in front of you, and to completely ignore it.

It was beyond my comprehension.

"Monroe and I will actually be in the Bahamas celebrating our Stanley Cup win. So I'm afraid we won't be able to make it," Lincoln said coldly.

Oh! He hadn't mentioned anything about the Bahamas before. I tried to think about my school schedule, even knowing I would follow Lincoln anywhere.

Lincoln's gaze flicked to mine. "Surprise," he said in a deadpan voice.

Lincoln's mother, Shannon, suddenly snorted. "Lincoln, you've got to be kidding me. She's just a child." There was a slightly demented sounding giggle in her voice as she said the word "child."

I stiffened in my chair. I didn't like being called a child—or talked about like I wasn't in the room.

"Her name's Monroe, Mother," Lincoln growled, the first sign of aggression in his voice at his mother's slight insult toward me.

"Monroe," she snorted, her gaze flicking across my dress like someone had shoved shit in her face. "A fitting name."

"What does that mean?" snapped Lincoln.

"That's a lovely dress, Mrs. Daniels," I blurted out, trying to avoid a fight when we were only five minutes in.

The three of them stared at me like I'd lost my mind.

"And what is that delicious smell? I bet you were cooking for hours today. That was so kind."

Lincoln's whole body was shaking as his laughter broke free.

Shannon looked shocked. Her eyes widened as she glanced at Lincoln, then back to me. "Well—"

"My wife hasn't cooked a day in her life," drawled Lincoln's father. Anstad. That was his name. I needed to use that in my head before he took on the life of Voldemort and I started referring to him as "He Who Must Not Be Named."

Anstad's comment effectively shut off any commentary on my insane behavior, but luckily, people—staff—started bringing in plates of food then, setting them down in front of us in something that resembled an orchestrated dance.

I had absolutely no appetite. I noticed Anstad was the only one who seemed to have one, actually. Lincoln was moving his food around on his plate, and Shannon was just . . . drinking.

I think she'd gone through an entire bottle of wine already.

Besides the terrible atmosphere, I was a little afraid they'd poisoned my stuffed chicken—because, honestly, I wouldn't put it past them.

"I wonder what Tyler would have been like today. Where he would have led the company," Anstad suddenly mused. "If he hadn't drowned at your hockey exhibition."

I heard Lincoln's sudden intake of breath. Glancing at him, it was obvious that one had hurt. His fists were clenched under the table and there was a tic in his cheek.

"Let's be honest . . . he would probably have been miserable trying to please you at the expense of everything he wanted in life," responded Lincoln, in an almost teasing voice. Anstad's fork clattered on the plate. I was certain he would lunge at Lincoln . . . or at least storm out of the room, but after a second, he picked up his fork and resumed eating, like nothing had even happened.

This was so unhealthy. Was it too soon to leave?

"Did he tell you, little girl . . . Did he tell you how he killed his brother?" Shannon spat out, a sob in her voice.

Alright, that was it.

I couldn't take it anymore.

I sprung to my feet, my hands shaking with fury, my heart flickering in my chest so fast, I was afraid I would pass out. "How dare you. I've never been more disgusted with two people in my life, and if you truly understood where I came from, you would understand that is the worst insult I could ever give you. You don't even care that you actually lost two sons that day," I spit through gritted teeth. "The fact that you can't treat Lincoln like he's at least a human being . . . let alone like he's your son." I shook my head, adrenaline sparking through my veins to the point I was shaking. "Your son is the best person I've ever known. He is everything. And you two *fuckwads* don't even deserve to breathe in the same space as him."

There was a short silence . . . but then his father and mother had the nerve to laugh, like I'd just told a fucking joke. I grabbed my wine, prepared to throw it all over the two of them. But Lincoln caught my hand before I could do it.

"Come on, dream girl. Let's get out of here," Lincoln murmured, amusement laced through his voice. He threaded his fingers through mine before standing up.

"I say this with absolutely no respect," Lincoln commented to his parents. "But fuck off."

He dragged me away then, and their laughter followed us out of the room.

"If she only knew . . . " I thought I heard Anstad cackle, but I paid him no mind.

I stepped outside the mansion, feeling the muggy night air on my skin, trying to calm down my racing heart. I was so fucking relieved to be out of that house. I'd thought I could anticipate what it would be like, but that went so far beyond anything I could have dreamed up . . .

I glanced at him, expecting to see him angry . . . or devastated about what just transpired, but instead, he was staring at me like he couldn't help himself, like I was the answer to every hope and dream he'd ever had.

"You're going to be the end of me, dream girl. You're so fucking . . . everything," he murmured, his voice thick with emotion.

We used that word a lot. That we were *everything*. And it seemed so fitting. It seemed the only word to use when explaining the fact that your soulmate was a living breathing being that set your world on fire just by looking at them.

My heart swelled, and there was just so much love there . . . for a second, I wasn't sure I could take it. It felt like too much.

"You are, too," I whispered, knowing I'd follow him anywhere.

We walked down the long sidewalk, the moon casting an ethereal glow over the trees and bushes. It was easy to imagine we were in the pages of a dark fairy tale, escaping the clutches of the evil king and queen.

"They're so awful," I said after a moment, my voice tinged with a deep sadness that settled over me like a cloak.

Lincoln's grip on my hand tightened. But he just snorted. "I know. Beyond. But for the first time . . . I actually don't fucking care."

I gave him a shy smile, realizing I'd just called his parents . . . fuckwads.

Who even was I?

"A badass," Lincoln murmured, and I realized I'd spoken that thought out loud.

We drove away from that house of horrors, and I made a promise for both of us.

That would be the last time either of us set foot in that mansion again.

# CHAPTER 34

## LINCOLN

**DALLAS KNIGHTS**

First game of the second round, and it was going fucking awful. New York hadn't been a particularly hard opponent during the regular season, but tonight they were playing like their balls were on fire.

I'd blinked and we were down by four goals. Bender, our goalie, was having the literal worst game of his life.

We were trying to rally when Ari was checked hard, slamming into the boards so forcefully, I was shocked he wasn't knocked out. As he fell to the ice, my blood boiled. I rushed over to Andrews, one of New York's douchebag forwards, and our sticks clattered against each other, the sound echoing through the arena. I threw my first punch and it connected with his jaw, sending him stumbling backwards. He recovered quickly, landing a hit to my stomach, knocking the wind out of me.

I gritted my teeth and charged back at him, as more players pushed into the fight. Someone hit me from behind and I stumbled forward. The crowd was a powder keg, their cheers a roar around us. Their energy pulsed through me.

Suddenly, the refs intervened, pulling us apart and dragging us to the penalty box. As I sat there catching my breath, I glanced at Ari who'd managed to somehow *not* get a penalty in the ruckus. He was grinning from ear to ear, like he'd just been to Disneyland instead of given a black eye. He gave me a head nod, because that was fucking fun, and then play started again.

After the fight, the team was fucking fired up. I was out of the penalty box in two minutes—the "superstar" special treatment I guess—and then we went to work, slowly but surely, starting to chip away at New York's lead. The crowd was going berserk with every goal, giving us new life with every roar.

As the clock wound down in the third period, we tied the game up, 4—4.

And then it was overtime.

The minutes dragged on, with neither team giving an inch. At least Bender had figured out how to stop a fucking puck. He was playing like a new man.

Finally, in the last minute of overtime, I got a breakaway. I skated towards the net, New York's goalie coming out to challenge me. It was a terrible mistake on his part, because I lived for that shit. I feinted left, flicked my wrist, and sent the puck . . . soaring into the net.

The next few minutes were brief flashes of ecstasy. My teammates rushed onto the ice in a flurry of screams and shouts. I felt hands on my back, pushing me forward as the weight of everyone piled on top of me in celebration. The sound of sticks hitting the ice and skates clattering together filled the air as we all jumped up and down in elation.

If I had known the end was coming, I would have held onto that moment for just a little longer. Taken a picture of it in my head to take with me . . .

Before everything changed.

---

*Monroe*

I was humming to myself, tucking the sheets under the mattress, when my phone beeped. I reached over and saw a message from an unknown number.

> Unknown: You're going to want to see this.

I frowned . . . and a second later, a video popped up on my screen. At first, I couldn't make out what was happening, the video was grainy and hard to see. But as it played on, my blood iced over.

"What do you want, fancy pants?" my landlord Jared growled . . . at Lincoln.

"I want to talk about Monroe," he said calmly.

Jared's grin turned into a smirk. "What do you want with my sweet little tenant, huh?"

"I need you to evict Monroe out of her apartment. And I need you to do it tonight." Lincoln's voice was cold . . . and matter of fact.

Jared chuckled. "Now, why would I do that? Monroe's a good tenant. Always pays her rent on time. And she's . . . very accommodating."

I grimaced. He was such an asshole. I had certainly never been "accommodating" to him in any way.

Not that it mattered. What mattered was that Lincoln . . .

"I don't give a shit about that. I just need her out of here."

Jared shrugged and leaned back against the door frame. "Sorry, kid. Can't help you. I happen to like having her around."

Lincoln lunged forward, scaring Jared to death. "Listen, you little shit. You're going to do what I say, or I'll make sure you're very sorry. Got it?"

"O-okay, okay. J-just calm down, all right? I'll do it. Don't hurt me."

Lincoln pulled out a checkbook and wrote something. "Good. You don't deserve it, but I'm going to make it worth your while." He handed my landlord the check, and although I couldn't see the amount, I assumed it had been good, since I'd never seen Jared look that . . . ecstatic.

The video cut off and I fell to the bed, a mess of disbelief.

Another video popped up. My hands shook so hard I had to restart it twice to even watch it.

Lincoln was knocking on a door, and a second later, Dr. Kevin answered.

"Lincoln Daniels, to what do I owe the pleasure?" he asked sarcastically.

Lincoln punched him in the face, and Dr. Kevin fell backwards into what I assumed was his house.

"I just wanted to have a friendly conversation," he said, smiling down at Dr. Kevin with a smile I'd never seen before, a smile that made my skin crawl.

"Fuck you," Dr. Kevin spat, blood all over his face like a gruesome canvas.

"I want to talk about how tomorrow is going to go."

"If you're worried about me stealing your girl, that's your problem. Anyone would want a piece of that."

Lincoln kicked him in the chest, and even from how far away the camera was, I could hear something snap inside Dr. Kevin's body.

I flinched as the video showed him screaming in pain.

Lincoln held up his phone.

"Let's see what I have here," he said, as he held up his phone, its screen displaying an image that was obscured from view. However, the effect it had on Dr. Kevin was immediate and unmistakable—a look of pure terror etched across his face.

"How did you get that?" he snarled.

"Well, it doesn't really matter *how* I got it, right? It only matters that I have it. And if you don't do exactly as I say, I'll send it to your partner, and your wife." Lincoln patted his cheek condescendingly. "I don't think either of them would be too happy about this."

"What do you want?" Dr. Kevin asked.

"You're going to fire Monroe. Tomorrow," Lincoln said silkily.

I watched in stunned horror as he demanded Dr. Kevin fire me, and accuse me of being a thief.

Another video, this time of Lincoln on the phone, casually strolling through the penthouse. You could see me through the entryway, sitting on the couch, my head nodding up and down as I listened to some music with the fancy headphones he'd given me two weeks ago.

"Don't give Monroe any more jobs. She's done working," Lincoln murmured.

I heard Clarice's voice through the phone. "Oh, I love this for her . . . "

And then, there was a video of him on a phone call with someone, giving him a list of all the places I'd applied to and instructing him to call everyone and make sure they knew not to hire me.

The videos stopped.

One last text came in.

> Unknown: You're welcome.

In my nineteen years on earth, I'd been through a lot. I'd been forgotten, abused, and unloved.

But I'd never been betrayed.

I'd never been destroyed.

I was bleeding from the inside out. The pain was a crescendo that built and built until it felt like my skin was literally going to explode from being unable to hold it in.

Those butterflies inside me, the ones he'd grown and

nurtured and said he'd fucking do anything for . . . they turned into dust.

There was a knife in my heart, twisting and turning with each second.

There were tears streaming down my face.

But it was like they belonged to someone else.

It was like the person sitting here, broken and shattered, was not me. My brain was having trouble comprehending how someone who'd seemed so perfectly golden, a hero of a story I never could have dreamed . . .

Had actually been the villain all along.

The worst part of the story . . . the one that would no doubt keep me up at night for the rest of my life . . .

Was the ease of his lies.

The way he'd held me after manipulating my life, like he was a puppet master holding my strings.

He'd held me in his arms. He'd licked away my tears. He . . .

He was a monster.

That was all there was to it.

A monster behind a beautiful mask.

And I'd never get over his damage.

Mama had been right all those years ago.

And I was a fool who hadn't listened.

You don't hear the advice of a dying woman and say it means nothing.

It took me a minute to think about the next step. Because he'd taken everything from me.

There was that word again. *Everything.*

I just didn't know when we'd started saying it, what it really meant.

That he was going to take *everything* from me. Make me depend on him for *everything*.

And then destroy *everything* about me.

I knew what I had to do.

I had to leave.

It was a truth burned into my bones.

But I also knew the Lincoln I thought I'd known, the one who I'd thought had loved me like no one else ever had . . . or could . . .

He was a psychopath.

He was also out for a run at that moment, the only silver lining on a cloud so black you'd never be able to get through it.

I could gather some things in a bag, get away before he came back.

Yes, that's what I'd do.

I quickly grabbed a backpack and started throwing some clothes and essentials into it.

My breath came out in harsh gasps the whole time, because my body was having trouble functioning.

The demise of my love story, my happily ever after, had been so sudden, so cruel, my body was having trouble taking it.

I grabbed my backpack and headed out of the room and down the hallway towards the elevators.

"Hey sweetheart, what's the hurry?" Lincoln's voice shot out from the living room. I froze, my heart pounding in my chest, so loud I was sure there was no way he wouldn't hear it.

And know what I was about to do.

I squeezed my eyes closed, and then finally turned to face him, pasting a placid smile on my lips, like his very existence at that moment wasn't fucking destroying me.

"I didn't hear you come home. How was your run?" My voice was perfectly calm, a feat deserving a gold medal, honestly.

He was standing there, shirtless as he always was after a run in the humid heat that had been building every day. A sun-drenched, ripped god. My heart broke again just staring at all that beauty.

And knowing it was lost to me forever.

"It was fine. But where are you going?" His gold eyes were searing my skin as he stared at me in that magical way of his, the one that had always seemed like love.

But I now knew it was madness.

"I have to go to the school to talk about credits for the upcoming semester."

"I'll drive you," he said, pulling his shirt from his pants and sliding it over his head.

Blind panic surged through me. No. I had to get away now. I couldn't wait until his game tomorrow. I'd never be able to stay here, to sleep in his arms . . . to pretend.

"Uh, no, that's okay. I don't know how long it's going to take, and then I was going to go to the library," I threw out, trying to sound flippant, and hoping desperately that today would be the one day he wouldn't want to spend every second with me.

If only those stupid videos had come in five minutes earlier.

He frowned. "Everything okay?"

"Of course," I grinned, the smile like acid on my lips. I walked over and pressed a kiss on his cheek. "I'll see you in a bit."

I turned to leave, feeling his questions following me as I forced myself to walk slowly to the elevator.

And then I heard him chuckle . . .

"Sure you don't want to talk about those videos on your phone?" he called out casually to me.

I froze in place . . . goosebumps gathering on my skin.

"What videos?" I asked, unable to get myself to turn around and face him. I was a terrible actress, perhaps the worst, actually.

His footsteps slowly approached me from behind. One step . . . then another.

I was trying to calculate what chance I had to make it to the elevator and close the doors before he caught me.

The answer was zero, though. Zero percent.

His breath danced over the back of my neck.

"You really think after going to all this effort to make you mine, that I wouldn't be monitoring your phone too?"

I screamed.

But there was no one to hear me.

A second later, I felt a prick in my neck.

And then the world went dark.

# CHAPTER 35

## LINCOLN

**I**'d gone mad, but I couldn't help it.

Monroe was mine, and I'd do anything to keep her.

I watched her sleep like my darkest dream in my bed, knowing she'd be out for hours thanks to the sedative I'd shot her with.

I'd had to do it.

She was going to leave me, and I knew there would be no way to reason with her, not so close to finding everything out.

I would've been able to track her down—the tracker she thought was just a birth control implant took care of that—but even being away from her for that long was something I couldn't allow.

Right and wrong had somehow lost meaning since I'd found her.

I tangled my fingers through her hair, marveling at how smooth it felt, unable to not touch her.

She was going to be pissed off about the cuff around her ankle, but eventually she'd understand. She'd understand why I would do everything to keep us together.

Since the moment I'd seen her picture, I'd wanted to possess her, to keep her locked away where no one else could have her.

And I guess now I finally had.

I'm sick. But she made me this way.

She should have to face the consequences of that, just like I did.

I'd do whatever it took to keep her. Even if that meant locking her in this fucking penthouse for weeks, months, years. I could make her love me again. I knew I could.

I'd run faster than I ever had after my phone notified me that the first video had hit Monroe's phone.

My father had sent it to her. And while I would deal with him . . .

I needed to deal with her first.

I'd sprinted back to the penthouse, checking my phone every couple of seconds to make sure she was still where she was supposed to be.

She was so naive though, to think I would just let her go.

Another reason I had to keep her with me . . . so I could keep her safe.

She moaned in her sleep and I found it was enough to make my cock hard. I wondered what she was dreaming about. Was it me?

It had fucking better be.

Monroe was everything to me. She'd become the reason I woke up every morning. The reason I breathed.

We'd both bleed out before I let her go.

I sighed, trying to calm down, to channel that peace I always got when I thought about forever with her.

I'd wait for her to wake up, and then I'd make her see. See we were meant to be together. That she couldn't leave me.

Not now, not ever.

I'd do whatever it took to keep Monroe by my side. Even if that meant losing myself in the process.

————

*Monroe*

I woke up with a pounding headache and a heavy feeling in my limbs. I stared at the ceiling, trying to figure out why I was in bed.

After a second, I tried to sit up, but my head was spinning and there was bile in my throat like I was about to puke.

What happened to me?

The memories came back to me in waves, until panic was clawing at my chest.

I leaned over to vomit, nothing coming out but acid since I hadn't had a chance to eat breakfast before everything happened that morning. Had it even happened this morning? That prick of pain I'd felt . . . had he drugged me?

My brain couldn't quite comprehend that. Even after all he'd done, after the fact that he'd admitted to bugging my phone . . .

Okay, I'd think about all that later, in the decades of therapy I had ahead of me. Right now . . . I needed to figure out how to get out of here.

I gingerly shifted my legs to get out of the bed, only to feel a sharp pain in my ankle. Glancing down, horror hit me when I saw a cuff around it . . . attached to a chain that was attached to the bedpost.

I yanked at it, but the post didn't even move, and the metal dug into my skin, sending a sharp pain through my body.

The door was thrown open and Lincoln rushed in, his golden gaze almost comically wide with concern. "Hey, don't do that," he murmured, his voice gentle but firm. "You'll hurt yourself."

"You chained me? Really? What the fuck is this?"

"I couldn't let you leave," he said simply. He grabbed my chained ankle and started massaging it.

I kicked at him and scrambled away, pressing myself against the headboard. "Don't. Touch. Me."

Lincoln resembled a kicked puppy. Like he had no idea why I would act like this.

"What did you do to me?" I demanded, tears already streaming down my face.

"I drugged you," he said, his eyes never leaving mine. "To keep you with me. To keep you safe."

My heart was pounding so hard, it felt like it might burst out of my chest. "Why?" I sobbed. "Why would you do this to me?"

"Because I love you," he said, his voice almost a whisper. "More than anything. And I know this is crazy, Monroe. But I can't lose you. I just need to keep you here, until you understand."

His gaze grew determined. "You may be mad now, baby, but I promise you . . . I will make you fall in love with me again."

I felt sick to my stomach. I couldn't even look at him anymore. "You're a monster," I spat as I buried my face in my hands.

I felt the mattress move, and I flinched when I opened my eyes and saw him crawling towards me.

He licked the trail of tears falling down my face and I shivered, and, for some reason, just let him do it.

"Maybe I am a monster, dream girl. But I'm your monster. And that's all that matters."

He stared at me for a long time, and the desperate, lonely girl inside me wanted to fall into his arms, to give him what he wanted.

I was pathetic.

Finally, he shook his head. "I'm prepared to wait as long as it takes," he finally murmured, stroking my face. He leaned close. "Just don't fucking hurt yourself anymore. I don't want to have to sedate you again."

A sob slipped out. "How can you just say that to me? What is wrong with you?"

He shrugged and kissed my lips softly. "I've stopped asking myself that, baby."

Then he left the room.

---

An hour later, he brought in a tray of food. It smelled amazing, Mrs. Bentley's chicken parmesan, my favorite. My stomach growled, finally settled after the sedative, but I turned my face away, refusing to eat when he set the tray down.

Lincoln sat on the edge of the bed, his eyes fixed on me.

"I know you hate me right now," he said, his voice thick with emotion. "But I promise you, Monroe. I will make this right. I will do anything to make you happy."

"You've broken us," I whispered, another stupid tear sliding down my face.

"No, I haven't," he growled, but a few minutes later, he again left the room.

He didn't return until night had fallen, walking into the bathroom and going about his routine like it was just another normal night.

A few minutes later, he appeared in the doorway and leaned against the door frame, wearing nothing but a pair of tight gray briefs. My eyes danced over his taut, golden skin stretched over perfectly defined muscle.

I watched as he grew hard under my gaze.

Ugh, the bastard had broken me. Because I was sitting here, chained to a bed . . . and I was wanting him with every fiber of my being.

"Want to get ready for bed?" he asked innocently. As if the crown of his cock wasn't peeking over the waistband of his pants. As if he didn't know he was torturing me.

"Oh, is that allowed?"

He sighed and rolled his eyes. "I have cameras in here. I

know you've already gone into the bathroom a couple of times. Everything's allowed. You just can't leave our house—"

"Your house," I corrected him stiffly, wanting to make that important distinction for some reason.

"Monroe. Your name is on the title."

"What?" I stared at him, horrified. "I guess I won't ask if you're out of your mind, because you clearly are," I screeched, lifting my leg up and shaking it so the chain rattled.

He shrugged. "It is what it is. I told you that you were my everything, Monroe. My dream. That involves giving you every-thing as well."

"Except for my freedom," I whispered.

"You don't actually want that," he insisted, taking slow steps towards me like he was a panther and I was his prey. "Or at least you don't want *that* kind of freedom."

I glared at him and the asshole smirked. "You were miserable in your old life. You were trapped. And you were refusing to let me help you. You were scared. All I wanted to do was make you happy. To give you everything—"

"Don't say that word," I whispered.

He sighed again, biting down on his bottom lip, his eyes two pools of frustration.

"Get ready for bed, baby," he finally murmured, sliding into bed.

I stared at him, shocked. "You've got to be fucking kidding me. We are *not* sleeping together."

He was looking at me like I was the one being unreasonable.

"I don't intend to spend a single night without you for the rest of my life. And if you go before me, I'll make sure I have a plan in place to go minutes later, too. So I never have to."

He was crazy, obsessed. Out of his fucking mind.

And, oh hell, was there something wrong with me, too. Because a part of me, much bigger than I would ever admit, was desperate for it.

It turned out that a girl could easily get addicted to madness when she'd been alone for almost her entire life.

I didn't say anything to his pronouncement. I just got out of bed. He'd adjusted the chain earlier so that I could easily get to the bathroom. And after washing my face and changing into a nightgown—that I was not going to let him take off—I got into bed with him.

"I hate you," I whispered, my pain bleeding out into the inky darkness that surrounded me as his arms wrapped around my body, holding me close like he always did.

"No, you don't, baby. You just wish you did," he murmured.

And I don't know how, but I fell asleep.

Lost in him.

———

His mouth was on my aching clit, the intense sensations making my body quiver.

"No," I panted, trying to push him away.

But he wasn't having it.

His golden eyes burned with possessiveness as he pulled back, licking his lips. "It's been twenty two hours since my dick has been inside you. I doubt *that's* an option at the moment. So I'm going to bury my face in this sweet cunt instead."

He growled, then gave me another firm lick. "*You* can have breakfast after I'm done," he said with a wink.

He grabbed the back of my thighs, shoving my legs towards my shoulders, and his mouth closed over my pussy again, sucking my clit.

I squirmed, trying to rock my hips, but he held me still, his grip unyielding. He fucked my pussy with his mouth, his moans of hunger filling the room. I released a new flood of arousal, my core tightening viciously.

"Fuck. Baby. You're perfect. So fucking sweet," he groaned, as if he were in pain.

His tongue was hot and wet, flicking and circling my aching clit. It slid down to my opening, probing and licking, taking every last drop of my juices. He rubbed on my clit, my moans reverberating around us. I arched my back and clutched the sheets as the pleasure built up inside me, threatening to spill over at any moment.

I tried not to enjoy it. I really did.

But I couldn't help it.

My eyes closed as my core tightened, sobs ripping from my lips as my orgasm washed over me. Lincoln was ravenous as he devoured me, licking and sucking my pussy like it really was his favorite meal.

And when he'd given me two more orgasms, and left the room with his face soaking wet, I couldn't help but think . . .

I was sick, too.

# CHAPTER 36

## LINCOLN

**DALLAS KNIGHTS**

T hings were going . . . well.

As well as they could go when you were keeping your soulmate trapped in your penthouse apartment.

This was the last game of the Conference Finals, though.

And I could finally feel her softening.

Her body had been an easy sell. She was addicted to what I could do to her, I knew that. And although she hadn't let me fuck her, she was all about our new morning routine.

Which consisted of me with my head between her legs.

I wasn't complaining about that.

It was my favorite place to be.

My dick wasn't happy. But my hand was helping him through it, as was the smell of her pussy all over my tongue.

"Monroe's missing the game tonight, too?" Ari asked, frowning as he glanced behind us at her empty seat as we settled onto our bench. "She hasn't made it to any of the games this series. Are y'all okay?"

"Finals. They're killing her this semester," I tossed out, knowing Ari wouldn't have any idea what her school schedule was and that she'd been done for most of the series. It's not like I could actually tell him that Monroe was currently chained to a bed.

That was probably the worst part of our current situation. For the first time since Tyler had died, I'd had someone in the crowd watching me, someone I loved.

The fact that she wasn't there was like an aching hole in my chest. I'd only scored one goal last game. Without her eyes on me, it just wasn't the same. Even though I'd vowed to never spend a night apart from her, I couldn't figure out how to drag her unwillingly to Detroit without arousing suspicion. So I'd spent the entire night talking her ear off through the cameras while she pretended to ignore me.

Really great relationship building if you asked me.

I'd set up the tv so the games were on. But she'd turned it off every time, refusing to watch a single one.

Tonight, I'd set her up in the living room and rigged the television in there so that she couldn't turn it off. Her eyes would be on me, even if she didn't want them to be.

My girl was a sweetheart. I knew she would end up watching even if she didn't want to.

I'd also locked the elevator, and made sure all the knives and electronics were hidden.

She was a sweetheart, but we also weren't quite there yet.

Trying to get my mind off Monroe and our current issues, I put on my headphones and blasted Kendrick Lamar's "Humble" to get in the right headspace.

Fuck yes.

By the end of the song, my adrenaline was where it should be, pumping loudly through my veins and ready to get out there.

The arena was packed, a sold-out crowd, desperately cheering and roaring as we hit the ice. I could feel their energy fueling me as I skated.

The game started off rough, both teams pushing and shoving to gain control. But I was ready. My mind was clear, my body primed for action. And then it happened—I saw an opening and I took it, slamming the puck into the net.

The crowd erupted into cheers as I held up my hockey stick and skated over to the nearest cameraman, making the heart sign into the camera so Monroe would know it was for her.

"That's how you do it, baby!" Ari shouted as he slapped me on the back before we regrouped for the next play.

We kept fighting, back and forth, but I wasn't done yet. I wasn't going to leave the game with just one goal again.

I took a deep breath and surveyed the ice, my eyes scanning for any opening as I took control of the puck. I maneuvered it around one defender and then another, zigzagging my way towards the goal.

Approaching the net, I saw the goalie tense up, preparing for my shot. Quickly shifting the puck to my left and then back to my right, I faked him out, leaving him sprawling on the ice. I shot the puck towards the net . . . and it bounced off one of the Detroit's forwards' heads and ricocheted into the net.

Well . . . I hadn't expected that.

Pumping my fist in the air in triumph, I grinned as I skated around the ice, taking in the screams of the fans and my team-mates. I ended up in front of the camera, making another heart sign with my hands.

The crowd got even wilder.

I'd just turned to skate to the bench when . . . I was hit from behind. I hit the ice hard, the wind knocked out of me.

Rolling over, I realized there was a naked fucking chick on top of me. She was trying to wrap herself around my body like a fucking anaconda. I tried to push her away, but there was boob and butt everywhere, and I was at a loss what to do.

Security rushed in then, dragging the girl away.

"I love you, Lincoln. I love you. Please marry me," she screamed as they rushed her off the ice.

Ari skated over, barely able to stay up, he was laughing so

hard. "Oh my gosh. I'm getting tape of that. That was the best fucking thing ever. Your face when she hit you!" He bent over his knees, his whole body shaking as he howled.

"How did she even get on the ice?" I asked, pushing to my feet. Fuck. That was crazy. The NHL almost never had streakers. The fact that she'd been able to get out here like that . . .

Impressive and a bit terrifying.

Ari and I skated over to the bench where Coach was freaking out to the officials about what had happened.

"Daniels—get on the bench. You're going to need a minute to get your head right after . . . that," he snapped, not even bothering to suppress his amusement.

I rolled my eyes as guys clamored onto the ice and Ari and I settled onto the bench. I wondered what Monroe had thought of that.

The team pushed hard until the final buzzer sounded . . . and we'd won.

The noise in the arena was deafening as the crowd erupted in cheers and screams. Streamers and confetti rained down on the ice, creating my favorite kind of spectacle. My teammates were jumping and hugging each other, whooping with excitement. I joined in, grinning from ear to ear, feeling the thrill of victory pulsing through my veins.

Ari practically tackled me as we freaked out.

We were going to the Stanley Cup finals.

It was every guy's dream, from the moment he stepped on the ice as a kid, that someday he was going to be here. Before Monroe, dreaming of this moment used to be the only thing that got me through.

One more series.

I tried to savor the moment and soak up the atmosphere. The air in the arena crackled with energy, and I was proud to be a part of this city, this organization. The fans were chanting our team's name, and gratitude for their faithfulness surged through me.

As the celebration continued, I missed Monroe desperately. I wanted her to be here with me, to share this moment.

I had to move things along quicker, get us back to where we were before. Immediately.

Because there was no way I was going to play in the finals without Monroe in those stands.

---

*Monroe*

The elevator dinged as it opened and I pretended to read the book I had in my hands. It was annoying I couldn't even read a romance novel anymore without thinking of him.

Before Lincoln had turned into the psycho of the century, none of the heroes in these books were anything compared to him.

Now I was comparing him to the villains, too . . . and still having the same problem.

I'd always been a sucker for the irredeemable sinners.

And now it appeared . . . I had one of my own.

He materialized in the doorway, his gaze . . . relieved, with that same hungry, awestruck edge he'd had from the beginning, like he couldn't believe I was still there.

"Hey, dream girl," he murmured, leaning against the wall.

I'd been doing my best to ignore him, trying to "ice him out" so to speak. The only time I'd engaged was when he was between my legs and I had no choice but to scream out his name.

But . . . I was weakening. Getting tired of the distance between us.

I hated it.

I couldn't believe this was a thought in my head, but besides the chain around my ankle, he'd been perfect.

He was making me even needier. He had started pulling me into his lap every time he brought me a tray to eat, and spoon feeding me. He'd pull me on his lap to watch TV at night. And he'd just cuddle me . . . constantly. Until I was more addicted to his touch than I'd been before.

I knew this was some kind of executed plan. Every move he made, every sweet word he murmured, it was with an end goal in mind.

Only, I was going back and forth on whether I hated the idea of the end goal so much anymore.

I was having crazy thoughts . . . like asking myself if what he'd done was actually so bad . . .

Because when I really looked at the consequences of what he'd done, I couldn't deny I was better off.

Where had I been before? Barely making ends meet in a tiny apartment that should have been condemned, working two jobs while going to school. Dealing with sexual harassment at work. Starving a lot of nights.

And where was I *after* his actions? Living in an enormous penthouse apartment right out of a dream, a closet full of designer clothes, a full belly of gourmet meals . . . and hotter sex than I ever could have dreamed or comprehended. He hadn't done anything to interfere with school—which was the most important thing to me out of them all—he'd just bought me a new laptop and made sure I didn't have to take the bus home at night anymore after late classes. Without having to worry about money, I could actually take daytime classes next semester if I wanted, and get my degree faster.

And he'd made me feel so freaking loved. For the first time in my life.

*That was what crazy people said,* I chided myself.

He'd lied. He'd hurt people.

He'd manipulated me.

I couldn't trust him.

My breath caught in my throat as his gaze clung to me. He was in his workout clothes, his gray Knights sweatpants hanging low so I could see his V. His hair, damp from the shower he'd taken after the game, was tousled and sticking to his forehead. Knowing him, he would have raced home the second he was able to. The muscles in his arms bulged as he crossed them over his chest.

I was having a visceral reaction just staring at him. Heat was rising up my neck, my heartbeat was quickening.

Ugh. Fuck him for being so fucking hot.

I swallowed hard, feeling a fluttering in my stomach. "Hey," I finally replied after I'd finished eye-fucking him, my voice barely above a whisper.

He pushed himself off the doorway and sauntered over to me, a cocky grin spreading across his face. My heart skipped a beat as he approached, and I was practically drooling as I took him in.

*Get yourself together. You currently have a chain around your ankle.*

"You look amazing," he said, his eyes tracing over my body appreciatively. I stared down at the T-shirt and leggings combo I was wearing—the same outfit I'd had on when he left for the game this afternoon. Since I could only change when he was around to take off my cuff.

Unable to stop myself, I blushed, warmth blooming in my chest. "Thanks."

I hated that he was so sweet.

Lincoln leaned in closer, his lips hovering just inches from mine. "Did you watch the game?" he asked hopefully.

This was where I needed to lie to him. To tell him of course I hadn't watched. That I hoped he'd lost. And fuck him.

"Yeah, I did," I found myself saying instead, watching a beautiful smile spread across his already too handsome face. "Congratulations."

I'd screamed and cheered after his two goals . . . and the accompanying heart signs he'd made just for me.

Because obviously, Stockholm Syndrome had sunk in much faster than I'd thought.

I'd also been insanely jealous when that naked chick had appeared out of nowhere and tackled him.

His body was mine.

I was never, ever going to admit that, of course.

He was still staring at me, and warning signs were blaring in my head. I wanted to reach up and run my fingers through his damp hair, feeling the soft strands against my skin.

I dragged my gaze away and pretended to read my book. Before I did something crazy like that.

He plucked it out of my hands and threw it across the room.

"Hey!" I cried out, my mouth snapping closed as he took a small key from his pocket and unlocked the cuff around my ankle.

He scooped me into his arms and strode out of the room, down the hallway, and into his bedroom.

"This is done," he said, throwing me onto the bed.

"I get it. You're mad. You're furious. You don't trust me. But I don't fucking care. Because I know you're also crazy about me. Not as crazy as I am about you. But I know you. I know that if I were to tell you you're free, you wouldn't go anywhere."

"Are you freeing me?" I asked, confused.

"Fuck no," he snapped, sounding affronted, like I'd offended him.

"Then what are you saying?" My voice was petulant . . . bratty.

"I'm saying that we're moving on. We're going to proceed with our relationship with you knowing that I'll do anything to keep you. Anything to make you happy. To make you love me. And I'm going to keep doing all of those things."

"So it's never going to matter what I want? You're just going to do whatever *you* think is best?"

"Probably!" he suddenly yelled. The first time he'd ever

raised his voice at me. "Or at least until you figure out that this thing between us defies all logic. That it isn't going to follow any rules that the rest of the world . . . or your fucking mom has set."

"You don't know anything about my mother."

He cocked his head. "I know she ripped your heart out, just like losing my brother took mine. I know you hear her voice in your head, that your past haunts you. I know she's made you terrified to take what I'm begging to give you!"

"This isn't what love is supposed to be like," I cried out, squeezing my eyes shut as my tears threatened to drown me.

He grabbed my chin and forced me to meet his eyes. "Fuck love, Monroe. Love is nothing. You can feel love for anyone. What I feel for you is pain. Knowing that a part of my fucking soul is living outside of my body and now that I've found it, I'll die if I ever lose it. That's what we have. Love is a shadowed imitation for people unlucky enough to never find their soulmates. What we have is everything."

His words did something to me, rewired something in my brain, like they'd given me permission to accept the crazy, accept the darkness, accept that this went against what society—and my mother—had warned me about.

Accept that I couldn't live without it.

Lincoln kissed me hard. Desperately. Like that moment was the sum total of our existence. Lips tangling, our moans filling the air, I allowed myself to actually touch him for the first time in a week, to run my hands all over that beautiful body. He shuddered and whimpered against my fingertips like my touch gave him pain.

I moaned when he abruptly pulled away. Like he was possessed, he ripped off my clothes before yanking off his sweats and briefs and tossing them to the side.

His fingers ran over my throat, rubbing against my pulse for a moment before he gently pushed me to my back. His grip released and he grabbed my legs, spreading me wide and shoving his thighs between mine, settling into the space. He lined up his cock, rubbing it through my folds before he forced it inside a few inches.

"Fuck yes," he growled hoarsely. "I've been desperate for this, baby. Desperate for you to take my cock. Let me fucking in." His back arched, his chin tilting up to the ceiling, his straining muscles displayed like a feast before me. His abs flexed with each thrust, arms bulging as he pushed my thighs wide.

I *instantly* orgasmed, unable to stop myself in the face of the highly erotic image in front of me. It was *me* that did this to him. *Me* that made him crazy. So turned on he couldn't think.

"Lincoln," I moaned, trying to take all of his brutally thick dick. My body resisted at first—he was so big that a week without him was a long time—and I whimpered in protest. He grabbed my hips, yanking me closer and locking eyes with me as he drove his thick shaft deeper into my throbbing pussy.

"Almost in, baby. You can take it." His voice was both commanding and needy as he thrust himself inside me, filling me and stretching me to my limits. "You're such a good girl," he praised me in a lust-drunk, gravelly voice as his fingers dug into my flesh, holding me in place. There was a sharp pain that morphed into a throbbing, spreading sensation that gradually transformed into ecstasy.

I moaned, my body instinctively responding to his skilled touch.

His thrusts were aggressive, his cock battering in and out of me, pounding into me fiercely, like he was desperate for me to feel where he'd been for the next week.

I loved it, though. Loved the sound of his grunts filling the air as he fucked my swollen sex. The sensation was almost too much to bear, an intense and all-consuming pleasure that reverberated throughout my body. His powerful thrusts hit my cervix, driving me closer to the edge.

He held himself there, deep inside me, as he groaned, "Fuuuck."

My core tightened, and then I was pulsing around his thick cock. I was awash with a scorching rush of pleasure, my heart hammering in my chest, my breaths coming in erratic gasps.

He groaned. "Fuck, yes. Choke my cock. You're so perfect."

"Lincoln, I need—" I whimpered, my hips rocking against him.

"What do you need, sweetheart? Do you need me to fuck you? Take care of that pretty pussy?" he growled.

"Yes! Yes . . . please," I begged. He kissed me hard before he pulled out and slammed back in once more.

Suddenly, he came to a complete stop. He stared down at me, his eyes wild . . . and determined.

"Well, I need something from you first, baby," he murmured as he slid his cock out achingly slow . . . his shaft glistening from my wetness.

"Anything," I breathed. He held my hips down with one hand so I couldn't move an inch . . . and I was immediately hit by deja vu of what he'd done before.

He hadn't gotten what he wanted then.

But I was positive he was going to get it now.

"Yes, I can see it in your face. You know what I need. What I have to have. What I'm desperate for. Just say it, sweetheart," he begged, moving back in so slowly I was choking back a frustrated scream.

His teeth were clenched, his muscles flexing as he worked to control himself. He was torturing himself just as much as he was torturing me.

I wanted it, too. I couldn't deny it any longer, and honestly, I was tired of fighting it. I might as well give him what he wanted.

"Tell me. Give me what's mine," he growled as my pussy sucked on his length.

"I love you," I whispered, hot tears flooding my eyes.

He groaned and came, hot spurts of cum filling me completely.

I knew from experience that Lincoln had crazy control. Which meant he'd come undone just from my words.

A heady warmth floated through my chest.

"You're so proud of what you just did to me, aren't you, sweet girl?" he smirked as he pounded inside me, somehow still perfectly hard despite just coming.

"Lincoln," I cried, my body on the verge of my own devastating orgasm.

"Yeah, my baby. You belong to me, don't you? Never going to fucking leave me. You're going to let me take care of you. Let me give you everything. Aren't you?" he demanded.

"Yes," I cried as he hammered into me.

"And you love me. Only me." His voice was rough and insistent, emphasized by a deep thrust that hit that perfect spot. "Say it."

Breathless, I gasped, "Only you, Lincoln. I love you. Please . . . "

His hips fucked into me unrelentingly, pushing me closer to the edge. My core was swelling around his cock, sucking and pulling with each movement.

"I'm the only one who knows what you need, Monroe. The only one who can give you this," he growled, angling his hips and driving into me with long, deep strokes that left me gasping for air.

He fucked me fast and hard, driving me into a spinning, starstruck orgasm that had me convulsing from head to toe. He groaned, "Sweetest pussy ever, baby. Giving me what I want. Tell me how much you love it."

My hips bucked uncontrollably as I clenched around his cock, my entire body shaking with pleasure.

"I love you. I love you so much, Lincoln," I whimpered through the pleasure.

"I love you so fucking much. I need you. I can't survive without you."

And that was the truth right there. The truth for both of us. We'd gone so far down this crazy ride, that there was no coming back.

We'd either be blissfully, completely happy with an ever after that overshadowed every love story that had ever been told.

Or we would destroy each other.

And I was more than happy to take that risk.

There was no other option for me.

He lifted my hips, hitting a new spot inside me, and I was on the edge once again. He reached down between us and worked my clit, pushing into me with a short staccato rhythm that had me screaming.

Lincoln lifted me higher, and his hand slid farther down, fingers pressing lightly against my rosebud while he hammered in and out of me. "Come on, dream girl. Give me one more. Take me to heaven."

My entire body shook as a violent orgasm ripped through me, and I clenched down on his throbbing cock.

"Fuck, fuck, fuck," he growled, throwing his head back as he pulsed inside me . . . again. I was so incredibly wet, our combined fluid dripping down my ass cheeks and onto the bed.

He pulled out, his hands reaching between my legs, his fingers methodically pushing his cum back inside me. As he caught his breath, he murmured, "I love you so fucking much," his lips brushing against my pulse.

I was thoroughly fucked.

And I was also . . . thoroughly at peace.

Yes, Lincoln Daniels could ruin me.

But what a ride it would be.

# CHAPTER 37
## LINCOLN

**T**his was it. It felt a bit like my life was counting down as the game clock showed one minute left . . . the last seconds of the most important game of my life ticking down mercilessly.

It was game 7 of the finals.

And we were about to lose to fucking Nashville.

We were tied, but the momentum was on their side. Every shot we took was blocked, like they had been for the entire game. Bender was slowly bleeding out from all the shots he was having to stop.

The pressure I felt was like nothing I'd experienced before. The weight of the entire season rested on my shoulders like a boulder, threatening to crush me at any second. I could see it in my teammates' eyes . . . they thought we were done.

I *lived* for this shit, and even I was doubting.

Needing some fucking motivation . . . some hope, I turned my gaze to a few rows behind our bench, where Monroe's seat was. The crowd was roaring around me, and every second felt like an eternity. Finally, I saw her, and my eyes locked onto her perfect face.

Her eyes were fierce, and she was standing along with the rest of the crowd, her posture determined, like she could *will* us to win. She saw me looking and she lifted up her hands, making the fucking heart sign that I'd done every time I scored.

It was the first time she'd done it back, even though I made her tell me she loved me at least fifty times a day, being the needy bastard that I was.

My heart swelled in my chest. It was like a bolt of lightning went through me, igniting a fire in my gut.

Suddenly, the game didn't seem unwinnable.

I could do anything, *be* anything . . . for her.

She deserved a winner.

So she was going to get one.

I turned my attention back to the ice, feeling renewed.

A few seconds later, Ari sent the puck flying towards me, giving me one last chance. My heart was pounding in my chest, my palms slick with sweat as I skated towards the net. The seconds felt like an eternity as I took the shot, the sound of my stick hitting the puck echoing through the arena.

I held my breath as the puck flew towards the net, willing it to go in. And then, as if in slow motion, it hit the back of the net with a resounding thud. The buzzer sounded a half a second later, and the crowd erupted in a deafening roar.

I fell to my knees in disbelief as my teammates tackled me, and we all erupted in a frenzy of screams and fist pumps.

Emotion clogged my throat and I blinked away tears, because fuck, I hadn't even come close to imagining what this would feel like.

To win the fucking Stanley Cup.

"Lincoln. Holy fuck!" yelled Ari, pushing Peters off to tackle me himself. "We fucking did it. Fuck, fuck, fuck."

I wrapped an arm around his neck, squeezing him. "Yeah, bud. We fucking did it."

After a second, he pulled away, his own eyes glistening in a rare show of emotion from my best friend.

But if you didn't cry a little when you won the championship . . . there probably wasn't much you were ever going to cry about.

"Look at us," crowed Ari as confetti showered us from the rafters.

"Who would have thought?"

"Not me," he cackled, channeling his best Paul Rudd impression, because that man was comedy gold.

Okay, everyone needed to fuck off now. I needed to get to Monroe.

I pushed my teammates out of the way as I skated towards the boards, and I saw Monroe jumping up and down, screaming and cheering, tears running down her face.

One of the security guards let her into the bench area, and a second later, she launched herself into my arms, her legs wrapping around me, my hands on her ass . . . and it officially became the best moment of my life.

Our faces were pressed together as I spun around.

Everything disappeared, but me and my perfect dream girl.

"I'm so happy for you," she whispered through her tears.

I brushed a kiss against her lips.

"Tell me you love me," I ordered, and she grinned before scrunching up her nose.

"I love you."

I smacked another kiss on her lips, needing to fuck her the first chance I got, and then I lifted her up. The crowd screamed around us as I skated around the arena with Monroe on my shoulders. She had a death grip on my hair as I skated in a few tight circles . . . just for shit and giggles. Her thighs squeezed around my neck a few times, and I decided it would be a beautiful way to die.

The crowd loved it, their screams wild and delirious at the sight of us.

Who could blame them? My girl was fucking *everything*.

As we circled around the ice, I caught glimpses of my teammates who were all cheering and shouting, their faces red and contorted with joy.

Monroe finally let go of my hair, probably remembering I'd rather die than ever see her get hurt, and she waved and laughed at the crowd. Her arms stretched out wide, taking in the moment.

I hoped I remembered what it felt like to be this happy forever.

And I hoped that somewhere, wherever he was . . . Tyler was happy right then, too.

For the first time, I sent him some light.

And for the first time, I swore he sent some back.

We came to a stop at center ice, and I lifted Monroe down from my shoulders, pulling her into a tight embrace. The noise of the crowd was still ringing in my ears, and I felt like I could stay in this moment forever. I buried my face in her hair, taking in her sweet scent and feeling her warmth against my skin.

"I can't wait to fuck you," I whispered in her ear.

Her eyes went wide before she coughed out a laugh.

"Me, neither."

I winked at her right before Ari decided to bless us with his presence. I let him hug her for one second before pulling him off.

"No touching," I growled, and he threw his head back and cackled like the asshole he was.

Monroe just cuddled against me, because what could she do?

She was stuck with me.

Champagne poured down on us moments later, and for the rest of the fucking night, it was all about the afterglow.

———

She was riding my cock like a fucking pro on the visitor's bench —a final "fuck you" to Nashville—in nothing but my jersey, her breasts bouncing as she slid up and down my cock.

I groaned. "Fuck. Use me, dream girl. Fuck yourself on my big cock," I urged her on, my hands fisting at my sides as I strained against the wood. Her movements were perfect, her tightness surrounding me completely as she rode me harder and harder.

Her hands pressed against my chest as she leaned forward, her hips grinding into me with wild abandon. "How is your cock so perfect?" she muttered, her clit rubbing against my base and driving me wild.

"Fuck. Fuck. Fuck," I gasped, my hands sliding up to push the jersey up so I could cup her incredible breasts. I pinched and worked her nipples under my thumbs, and it only made me harder.

"I love these . . . Look at these perfect fucking tits," I murmured, my hips pumping up into her in perfect sync with her movements. I could smell her sweet pussy and it was driving me mad with need. I sat up enough to take her right nipple into my mouth, my fingers working the other into a painfully hard point.

Her whimper of pleasure was music to my ears, spurring me on as I kissed and licked my way across to her other breast. "Yeah. Just like that. Get what you need, baby," I growled against her skin, my fingers pinching and tugging her wet nipple as I suckled on the other.

She panted and moaned as her orgasm approached, her hand sliding through my hair and holding me to her. Just a little bit more . . . I hollowed my cheeks and sucked her nipple hard, driving her over the edge.

Her body convulsed around me, her hips jerking wildly as she pulsed and tightened around my length. It was too much to handle, and my own release crashed through me like a tidal wave.

"Congratulations, baby," she murmured, her gaze half lidded and lust-drunk.

"We're not done celebrating yet, sweetheart," I said through gritted teeth as I started bouncing her on my dick once more.

# CHAPTER 38
## LINCOLN

I walked into the lobby of Daniels International, whistling the newest Sound of Us single as I strode past the front desk. The attendant's eyes widened as she looked up from her computer screen and saw me. She quickly regained her composure and put on a polite smile, but it was clear she wasn't sure what to do.

I could see her eyes darting nervously around the room, searching for someone to help her. I decided to put her out of her misery.

"Is my father in?" I asked, knowing she knew exactly who I was.

She hesitated for a moment, then nodded, "Yes, he's in his office, sir."

I gave her a small nod of acknowledgement and turned towards the elevator. As I pressed the button, I could feel her eyes following me.

I stepped into the elevator as soon as the doors opened and hit the button for the top floor. As the elevator ascended, I grinned. Today had been a long time coming, and I was ready.

I checked the penthouse cameras on the way up, making sure

that Monroe was still watching a movie. There was a wide smile on her face as she lounged on the couch in one of my T-shirts, watching *Wedding Crashers*. I took a screenshot so I could make it my new background on my phone.

She was so fucking gorgeous.

When the doors finally opened on the top floor, I strode confidently out of the elevator and toward my father's office. As I approached the door, I could hear voices coming from inside. Without bothering to knock, I pushed the door open and strode into the room.

"Lincoln, what the hell are you doing here? I'm in the middle of a meeting," he snapped.

"Hey, Bart," I shot out to my father's mousy looking Chief Technology Officer, Bartholomew Taylors. There was sweat beaded on his forehead and his cheeks were red. Obviously, he'd been getting his ass reamed in here. "You can leave now."

"Lincoln, what the f—"

"I have something you're really going to want to see," I replied calmly, knowing that it would only rile him up more. "You could say it's life changing."

My father rolled his eyes and muttered something under his breath, but gestured for Bart to leave the room.

Bart practically ran out, and I wrinkled my nose in disgust at his cowardice.

As soon as the door swung closed, it was on.

"You want to tell me what the fuck you thought was so important that you barged into my meeting?"

"I wanted to tell you a story," I said lightly and he growled, his gaze narrowing as he studied my face, finally getting the picture. This wasn't business as usual. He glanced at his watch. "Well—get on with it. You have five minutes."

"Thanks for the generosity," I drawled, drawing another snarl from my father.

I settled down casually onto his couch, crossing my legs as if

I really was about to watch a movie or do something else not related to destroying someone.

"As you know, Tyler and I were very close," I began.

"To his detriment," my father inserted.

I ignored him. For once, his snide remarks didn't hold any heat.

"Tyler wanted to make sure that I would always be taken care of, in light of our . . . difficult relationship," I said, a hint of smugness in my voice. "He had a will in place at the time of his death that gave me all of his shares in the company if he passed."

My father's eyes briefly widened in shock, but he quickly shuttered his emotions so that only his usual blank malice was present.

My father scoffed. "Alright? Are you here to brag about owning 30 percent of the shares for the company? That's not going to get you anywhere."

I nodded. "You're right. Thirty percent wouldn't get me very far. But all the shares I've purchased since, with all the money I've earned from my 'little hobby,' *will* get me far."

I picked up my phone and sent him the document my accountant had pulled together after I'd purchased the last shares I needed this morning.

"You can check your email," I smiled.

I sat calmly as his phone dinged with the notification he'd gotten my message. I watched as his face contorted with confusion, then realization, then sheer panic.

"What is this?" my father demanded, waving his phone wildly in the air. It was the most undone I'd ever seen him. "What have you done?"

I pretended to peruse the email on my phone, a small smirk playing at the corner of my lips. Finally, after enough of a dramatic pause, I looked up at him. "As you can see, I now own 51 percent of the company . . . enough to get me wherever I want."

My father's face flushed crimson, the veins on his forehead bulging as he glared at me with fiery eyes. His fists clenched at his sides, and I could see the muscles in his jaw tensing as he struggled to maintain control. It was a shame my father had sent a proxy to board meetings over the last year, and that I'd been *paying* that proxy to leave out certain details in his reports.

"You are out of your fucking mind!" he spat, standing up and pacing back and forth behind his desk. "You have no idea what you're doing. You're going to ruin everything!"

I leaned back against the cushion, folding my arms across my chest. "Oh, I *am* going to ruin everything," I said, my voice calm and measured. "I'm going to sell off this company piece by piece until there's nothing left. I'm going to ruin what you've spent your entire life building."

"You're out of your mind if you think I would allow this to happen!"

I had imagined how good all of this would feel, but honestly . . . this moment might be right up there with winning the Cup. The shock on his face was just . . . delicious.

I pulled out my phone and tapped a few buttons. "You haven't exactly been discreet with all your shit, Father. A long time ago, I started collecting videos . . . just for a rainy day."

"What are you talking about?" he growled, but his face had paled to that of a corpse.

He knew exactly what I was talking about.

I pressed a button on my phone and sent him one of the videos I had. He pressed play, and after watching it for a few seconds . . . he collapsed in his chair, the very image of defeat.

"Videos of you bribing officials, soliciting prostitutes, doing drugs . . . you've been very, very naughty. And I have video of it all."

I'd never seen fear in his eyes, but I saw it now.

And it might have been wrong, but the little boy I'd been, the one he'd terrified and abused . . .

He felt much better.

"What do you want?" my father finally asked, his voice trembling.

"I want you to move your office to New York and pretend that I don't exist anymore," I said coldly. "And if you happen to get a wild hair about doing something to get rid of me, just know that I have things set up so that those videos will be released to various outlets and organizations if anything happens to me or Monroe. I also have a clause set up that all my shares will be sold to Kingston Venture if anything happens." I dropped my smirk and stared at him, letting the darkness out so he'd know just how serious I was. "Meaning, Father, that if you do anything to me . . . I'll destroy everything."

My father sat there, speechless, and I basked in my victory, a heady thrill running through my veins. I'd been caught up in all my guilt over Tyler, all the bullshit . . . and Monroe had finally set me free.

"So, what's it going to be?" I asked, smiling broadly.

My father glared at me, but I could see the defeat in his eyes. He picked up his office phone and pressed an extension. "Arrange for everything to be transferred to the New York office. Immediately. I'll be flying out tomorrow."

He didn't answer the questions being thrown at him. He just hung up, all the fire out of his gaze.

"I'm your father," he finally said, as if that were of any consequence.

I stood up slowly, towering over him. "And you forgot that before I was even born. You should have known I was going to make you pay for what you did with Monroe."

His eyes widened as realization sunk in. He'd had no idea through our entire conversation that this was related to what he'd done with her.

Fucking idiot.

"I better not see you ever again," I threw over my shoulder as I ambled out of the office, resuming my earlier whistling.

He would think of me for the rest of his life.

But I vowed I'd never think of him again.

———

*Monroe*

I was sitting on a bench in the park with Bill, the same bench where he'd watched over me that night long ago, enjoying the sandwiches I'd brought for us. The sun was high in the sky, casting a golden glow over everything in sight. The heat was palpable, but it wasn't oppressive. It was one of those rare days in Dallas where the air wasn't thick with 100 percent humidity. Instead, there was a gentle breeze that carried the scent of blooming flowers and fresh cut grass—the kind of day that begged to be enjoyed outside.

"Hmm, have I told you the one about Yorkshire?" he asked, his voice thick with his characteristic accent. He took a big bite of his sandwich, his eyes far off, already lost in the story.

"I don't think you have," I answered fondly. It was nice to spend some time with him. He didn't feel as comfortable in the ritzy part of town as he had by my old apartment, and he still refused to take any help from Lincoln or me.

The park was our middle ground at the moment, but I was determined that would change.

"Ah, okay, let me tell you about the time I was a wee lad and got lost in the moors of Yorkshire. I was only six years old, and I had wandered away from my family during a picnic. I wandered and wandered until I found myself all alone, surrounded by fog and heather as far as the eye could see. I was getting quite frightened, I can tell you . . . and then I heard a sound. It was like a distant whistle, and I knew I had to follow it. So off I went, trudging through the heather, tripping and stumbling over rocks and brambles. Finally, after what felt like hours, I stumbled upon a—Little duck, are you happy?"

I'd been lost in the story, but I was also used to him changing topics quite suddenly when it suited him. He'd asked me that question before, and in the past . . . I'd also had to hesitate.

Today, I didn't need to think at all.

"Yes. Crazy happy, Bill."

"I love that, my dear," he said with a smile, placing a hand over his heart.

I was just about to ask him to continue his story, when my phone chimed with a text.

> Lincoln: Give me a second chance, babe . . . and I'll blow your mind.

I stared at the text for a moment, confused . . . but intrigued. I tried to think if there was anything special or different about the day . . . but as far as I knew, there wasn't. I decided to play along:

> Not in a million years could you blow my mind.

Those first texts were engraved in my memory. This would be an easy game.

> Lincoln: We both know that's not true.

Bill made a sound, but before I'd even turned my head to see what had caught his attention, I knew.

It was Lincoln.

I could feel him now, like an electric hum in my veins.

Taking a deep, relieved breath—because no matter who I was with, I always missed him—I turned and saw him standing a few feet away.

For the millionth time, I got starstruck by his beauty. He was the most captivating man I'd ever seen. There was a raw, potent energy about him that wrapped around me every time he was near. Alpha-male perfection I would do anything for.

My heart was skipping a few beats as he walked forward, and I could see he was holding a single black rose. He was dressed far fancier than the park called for, with a fitted black shirt that clung to his chiseled chest, and jeans that had to have been made just for him. His hair was perfectly styled, and the sun-kissed strands shone like gold in the bright Dallas sun. His piercing gaze was unnervingly focused on me, just how I liked it.

Once I'd stepped over the edge and accepted that our obsession for each other was a living, breathing, growing thing . . . it had been easy to let go and accept everything that came with that. Including the fact that he was always watching me, always seeing every little piece of me, even the things I wanted to hide.

"Hi, dream girl," he murmured, his voice low and sultry as he handed me the rose. I fingered the petals, admiring them for a moment before I met his gaze, nervous butterflies in my stomach for some reason.

What was going on?

Then, I watched as my world once again reformed and took on a new shape . . .

And he got down on one knee.

I was shaking, the air seeming to glimmer around me, a hazy wonderland where all your dreams actually came true, appearing right in front of my eyes.

"You're not supposed to cry yet," he teased, tracking the tears falling down my cheeks. "I haven't even gotten to the good part yet."

"I can't help it," I sobbed.

"Monroe . . . sweetheart," he began, his voice warm and gravelly. "From the moment I saw you, it was like a bolt of lightning hit me, like all the stars had rearranged themselves and taken every single wish anyone had ever thrown at them . . . and combined them all to give me my perfect dream. The one girl made just for me." His breath shuddered and I leaned down to brush a kiss against his lips.

"To me, you're everything," he continued, and I laughed, because there was that word again.

"I didn't know how lost and lonely I was until I met you . . . and now that I have you . . . you are my home."

There was a deep, pulsing ache in my chest, because it hurt, how much I loved him. As he continued to talk about fate, of destiny, of the inexplicable pull that had brought us together . . . I thought about what life would have been like if I hadn't answered that text that night. If I'd just ignored it, and gone about my day.

It hadn't even been that long ago, but already it was hard to picture the girl I'd been. Scared and exhausted and alone. The phrase "changed my life" couldn't even begin to adequately describe what he'd done for me. His presence in my life was my best gift, my brightest star . . .

"I'm going to spend every day making you the happiest you've ever been, baby," he whispered.

And then, he said those words that changed everything: "Marry me."

I laughed, a sound that bubbled up from deep inside me like champagne. "Are you asking me or telling me I'm going to be your wife?"

His response was immediate, his eyes blazing with a fierce wild-eyed determination, "Definitely telling. I think I've told you before, dream girl. I'm never going to leave anything to chance when it comes to you."

My laugh was a half sob as I brought my shaking hands to my mouth . . . and he pulled out a ring with a diamond that could have been as big as my fist. He gently pulled my left hand away from my mouth and slowly slid the ring on my finger, before bringing it to his lips.

We hovered in that space between magic and starlight for a few mesmerizing minutes . . . and then I jumped into his arms and peppered his face with a thousand kisses. I was faintly aware of Bill whooping and cheering from nearby.

"What would you have done if I hadn't said yes?" I finally murmured in between breathless kisses.

Lincoln took my hand and dragged it to his pocket, where I felt the distinctive shape of handcuffs. A shocked laugh escaped me and he smirked, not ashamed at all that he was certifiably insane.

"Okay, crazy," I murmured, and he just winked, not ashamed at all.

"You ready to marry me tomorrow, Monroe?"

"Tomorrow?" I gasped. "What's the rush?"

"I've been ready for you to be Monroe Destiny Daniels from that very first day. I *need* to own you. I'm desperate for it."

I didn't argue, because . . . he was right. If you got the chance to experience the kind of love that breaks you and heals you all at once . . .

The answer should always be yes.

———

We didn't get married the next day.

We got married that night.

Lincoln called in a favor and somehow, I found myself standing with him in a simple white dress, in a Dallas court-house, in front of a judge and his cute wife, vowing my life to Lincoln forever.

Lincoln had made sure the vows didn't say until death do us part.

And it felt right.

Because we both knew that Lincoln wouldn't let a little thing like death keep us from each other.

"We're just starting the good part," he promised.

And I said, "I know."

And then he took a selfie of us and sent it to his publicist with strict orders for her to "tell the whole world."

And that felt perfectly right.

———

### Monroe

Sometimes it felt like too much, this love of ours, like the emotions we had would engulf us and ruin us. *This couldn't last forever*, my demons whispered. He'll leave.

Lincoln seemed to always know when the darkness crept in. He held me close and worshiped my body for hours every time, whispering how much he loved me, that I was his soul. That he'd never let me go.

His obsessiveness was a living, breathing thing that I was addicted to, that I craved with the very marrow in my bones.

Everything about our relationship was unhealthy, the kind of codependence that therapists the world over warned their clients against with every breath in their body.

And I would never let it go.

He gave me everything.

His attention, his love, his body . . . his very breath. And I gave him everything of me in return.

"You're mine," he whispered, his forehead scrunched in concentration as he moved in and out of me.

And I believed him.

If you would have told that ten-year-old girl, bending over the cold body of a mother that never put her first, that someday she'd become someone's whole world, she never would have believed it.

But I had no choice *but* to believe it now, because he breathed it into my very soul.

"I love you," I murmured as he licked a tear from my cheek, desperate to own every part of me, even my tears.

"Tell me again," he ordered, his gaze never leaving me. The intensity between us grew every day, like ivy across stone.

I think he would kill us both if I ever tried to leave.

And that thought brought a sadistic, sick comfort to me.

I would gladly take everything this man would ever give me.

And it was all because of a simple text . . . to the wrong pucking number.

# EPILOGUE

## MONROE

I could feel him watching me. He always was.

I pretended not to notice him as I walked across SMU's campus, the college I'd mysteriously got accepted to not long after marrying Lincoln.

The college where I was *officially* majoring in English.

I was famous here because of him, but Lincoln was always happy to make sure that everyone knew just how off-limits I was, for anyone thinking they'd make a move.

It still blew me away how jealous he got—not because I thought it was annoying, but because, how could I even be able to see any other man when *he* existed.

I was walking down a hallway when, all of a sudden, I was pulled into an empty classroom.

"You're playing with me," he growled as he pushed me against the wall, his voice a rough whisper that sent shivers down my spine. His fingers skimmed along the bottom of my skirt, and I struggled to stay composed, my thighs clenching together in a futile attempt to contain the arousal rapidly building between my legs.

There was a crowd walking by the classroom right then; I could hear the din of their voices. Anyone could walk in.

I was sure it would be quite the shock to find Lincoln Daniels, NHL superstar, fucking his wife against the wall.

But that only made the moment all the more thrilling.

Lincoln's hand pushed my skirt up, brushing up my inner thighs teasingly before he slipped under my drenched thong. I gasped as he entered me with a single finger.

"You're so wet for me. You're such a good girl," he muttered, those words sending waves of desire coursing through my body. I moaned in frustration when he wouldn't give me more, my need for him growing with every passing moment.

Suddenly, he withdrew his hand, and I whined in protest, my eyes glued to his face as he leaned in close.

"Do you want to come for me, sweetheart?" he murmured, his lips brushing against my pulse. "Because I'm dying to taste that sweet pussy."

Without a second thought, he sank to his knees. I watched with heavy lidded eyes as he tore away my panties, his eyes locked on mine, and then his mouth was on me, his tongue darting out to lick and suck at my clit with skilled precision.

The sounds that spilled from him were primal and raw, and I was dripping. My leg hitched up onto his shoulder as I thrust my hips forward, fucking his face, desperate for more of him. He hungrily licked through my folds, everywhere, obscene and worshipful all at once.

My orgasm was building, the tension coiling tighter and tighter until I thought I would burst.

And then it hit me, brutal and furious, sending me spiraling into a frenzy of pleasure that left me gasping and trembling against the wall. Lincoln's mouth stayed on me, his fingers slipping inside and curling upwards to stroke that perfect spot deep inside. I cried out in ecstasy as he brought me to the brink again and again, my body shaking and quivering under his expert touch.

Finally, when I was about to collapse, he stood and spun me around, pushing me forward so that my hands were on the wall and my ass was exposed to him.

"Please," I whimpered, desperate for him as I always was.

He growled in response, his eyes smoldering with a possessive heat that set my body ablaze.

"Spread your legs," he commanded, and I obeyed without question, watching him over my shoulder, dying over his beauty.

He pulled his sweatpants down and I licked my lips as he jerked his hand up and down his hard, perfect dick before rubbing it through my folds, torturing me with every slow pass. He bit down on his plush lower lip as he grabbed and squeezed my ass.

And then he pushed inside, pounding into me with a fierce intensity that left me breathless and begging for more. I could feel him everywhere, his hands on my hips, his chest pressed against my back, his teeth nipping at my skin as he claimed me over and over. It was wild and raw and untamed, a perfect expression of our obsession for each other.

His hand covered my mouth as I came, muffling my scream even as his groan filled the room.

We finally collapsed against the wall in a sweaty, panting heap. My golden god immediately slipped a hand between my legs, and pushed his cum inside me insistently, his fingers massaging me gently as he licked drops of sweat off my neck.

"Tell me you love me, dream girl," he demanded.

And I did.

Of course.

Although, I loved it when he *made* me tell him, too.

# EPILOGUE NO. 2
## LINCOLN

**M**y phone rang at midnight, right when I was about to wrap myself around Monroe. I glanced at it and saw that it was Ari.

"I need to answer it. He knows better than to call me this late nowadays, so he probably needs something," I told Monroe. She nodded sleepily, her eyes heavy-lidded and satisfied from the three orgasms I'd just given her.

"Everything okay?" I asked without saying hello.

There was a long pause.

"No," Ari finally said, his voice sounding choked and funny.

"What's going on?"

"Can you meet me at that bar on 7th?" he asked gruffly.

"Yeah, of course. I'll see you in fifteen minutes."

"Thanks," he murmured before hanging up.

I was still for a minute, feeling uneasy. It was Tuesday night at midnight. Not our usual night for a bar crawl, even before I'd met Monroe.

"I've got to go meet up with Ari for a little bit, he doesn't sound good," I whispered to Monroe, softly stroking her hair and breathing through the ever-present lust I felt whenever I was around her—so fucking *always* nowadays.

I drove over to the bar he'd picked, one we'd go to from time to time when we wanted a quiet place to drink. I was relieved when I walked in to see that it was even slower than usual tonight. The place was dimly lit, the soft glow of neon lights casting a red and blue haze across the room. The air was thick with the scent of alcohol, a mixture of stale and fresh. The wooden bar top was well-worn and marked with rings from countless glasses and bottles. Behind the bar, shelves lined with bottles of all shapes and sizes reached up to the ceiling. The music was loud and upbeat, the bass vibrating through the floor. The place had a gritty, chill atmosphere that we'd always liked.

I spotted Ari right away. There were four beer bottles in front of him. He'd been busy.

Striding over to where he was seated, I noted he looked like shit. His usually bright and lively demeanor seemed to have been sucked out of him, replaced by an expression of exhaustion and anxiety etched into every line of his face. His eyes were sunken and dull, with dark circles underneath as though he hadn't slept in days. His shoulders sagged with weariness as he sat at the table.

What the fuck was going on?

I'd just lifted with him a few days ago—or was that last week? A slash of guilt hit me . . . I'd been a bit preoccupied lately with Monroe.

"Hey, Lancaster, why'd you start the party without me?" I joked as I slid into the seat across from him.

His lips barely twitched . . . and I got even more worried.

His phone was lying on the table, a vaguely familiar-looking woman on the screen. Had Monroe pointed out her picture on a billboard recently?

I glanced at Ari expectantly and he met my gaze, reluctantly it seemed.

"I just wanted to tell you before the news breaks tomorrow, Linc."

"Tell me what?" I asked, confused and anxious for what he was about to say.

"I've asked to be traded to L.A."

# BONUS SCENE

Want more Lincoln and Monroe? Come hang out in C.R.'s Fated Realm to get access to an exclusive bonus scene!

Get it here: https://www.facebook.com/groups/C.R.FatedRealm

# Mrs. Bentley's
# Chorizo Breakfast Burritos
## SERVINGS: 4

## INGREDIENTS

### FOR THE AVOCADO-TOMATO SALSA

- 1 LARGE AVOCADO, PEELED, PITTED, AND DICED
- ½ CUP DICED SEEDED TOMATOES, FROM 1 TO 2 TOMATOES
- 1 SMALL SHALLOT, MINCED (ABOUT 2 TABLESPOONS)
- 1 CLOVE GARLIC, MINCED
- 1 JALAPEÑO PEPPER, SEEDED AND MINCED
- 1 TABLESPOON FRESH LIME JUICE, FROM 1 LIME
- ½ TEASPOON SALT
- ¼ TEASPOON GROUND CUMIN
- ¼ CUP FRESH CHOPPED CILANTRO

### FOR THE BURRITOS

- 4 LARGE EGGS
- ¼ TEASPOON SMOKED PAPRIKA
- ¼ TEASPOON SALT
- ½ LB SPICY CHORIZO REMOVED FROM CASINGS
- 1⅓ CUPS (6 OZ) SHREDDED MONTEREY JACK CHEESE
- 4 (10-IN) BURRITO-SIZE FLOUR TORTILLAS
- VEGETABLE OIL

## INSTRUCTIONS

MAKE THE AVOCADO-TOMATO SALSA: PLACE ALL OF THE INGREDIENTS IN A MEDIUM BOWL AND MIX TO COMBINE. SET ASIDE.

IN A MEDIUM BOWL, WHISK THE EGGS WITH THE SMOKED PAPRIKA AND SALT. SET ASIDE.

HEAT A LARGE NONSTICK PAN OVER MEDIUM-HIGH HEAT. ADD THE SAUSAGE AND COOK, STIRRING FREQUENTLY, UNTIL BROWNED, 4 TO 5 MINUTES. USE A SLOTTED SPOON TO TRANSFER THE SAUSAGE FROM THE PAN TO A PLATE, LEAVING THE DRIPPINGS IN THE PAN. REDUCE THE HEAT TO LOW. ADD THE EGGS AND SCRAMBLE UNTIL JUST COOKED THROUGH. TRANSFER THE EGGS TO A PLATE. CLEAN THE PAN (YOU'LL USE IT AGAIN).

ASSEMBLE THE BURRITOS: SPOON ABOUT ¼ CUP OF THE AVOCADO-SALSA ONTO EACH TORTILLA (YOU'LL HAVE A LITTLE LEFTOVER SALSA; THAT'S FOR THE COOK!), FOLLOWED BY A QUARTER OF THE SAUSAGE, A QUARTER OF THE EGGS, AND ⅓ CUP CHEESE. FOLD IN THE SIDES OF THE TORTILLA OVER THE FILLING AND ROLL, TUCKING IN THE EDGES AS YOU GO.

LIGHTLY COAT THE PAN WITH OIL AND SET OVER MEDIUM HEAT. WHEN THE PAN IS HOT, ADD THE BURRITOS, SEAM SIDE DOWN. COOK, COVERED, UNTIL THE BOTTOM OF THE BURRITOS ARE GOLDEN BROWN, ABOUT 3 MINUTES. FLIP THE BURRITOS OVER AND CONTINUE COOKING, COVERED, UNTIL GOLDEN, A FEW MINUTES MORE. SERVE WARM.

# ACKNOWLEDGMENTS

I needed this book.

I needed to run with inspiration when it hit me.

I needed to have fun.

And I did.

Lincoln is my ideal book boyfriend—for future reference. He's the sum total of what I love about the heroes . . . and the villains. I fell in love with writing again thanks to this book.

I hope you fall in love with this book, too.

*A few thank-yous . . .*

To my beta readers, Anna, Crystal, Samantha, Blair, and April. Thank you for stepping in and giving Lincoln and Monroe your love and effort. You guys have been a support system for me for a looooong time. Means the world to me.

To Jasmine, my editor. We've been working together for awhile now, and I'm more grateful for you every day. Thank you.

To Summer. Thanks for loving me even when I use "just," "that," and "beginning to." Love your effort, your insight . . . and you.

To my PA and BFF, Caitlin, the only person who could have me putting Paul Rudd references in my books. Love you.

And to you, the readers who make all my dreams come true. It is a privilege to be able to write these words for you, and I will *never* take you for granted.

# ABOUT C.R. JANE

A Texas girl living in Utah now, C.R. Jane is a, mother, lawyer, and now author. Her stories have been floating around in her head for years, and it has been a relief to finally get them down on paper. Jane is a huge Dallas Cowboys fan and primarily listens to Taylor Swift and hip hop ( . . . don't lie and say you don't, too.)

Her love of reading started when she was three, and it only made sense that she would start to create her own worlds, since she was always getting lost in others'.

Jane like heroines who have to grow in order to become badasses, happy endings, and swoon-worthy, devoted, (and hot) male characters. If this sounds like you, I'm pretty sure we'll be friends.

Visit her C.R.'s Fated Realm Facebook page to get updates, and sign up for her newsletter at **www.crjanebooks.com** to stay updated on new releases, find out random facts about her, and get access to different points of view from her characters.

# Podium

DISCOVER MORE

# STORIES
# UNBOUND

PodiumEntertainment.com